PRAISE FOR CHARLIE N. HOLMBERG

"The quirky characters, period detail, and personal journeys . . . are well wrought."

—*Library Journal*

KEEPER OF ENCHANTED ROOMS

Winner of the 2023 Whitney Award for Speculative Fiction

"Filled with delightful period details and artfully shaded characters, this whimsical, thoughtful look at magic and its price is the perfect read for a cold fall night."

——*Publishers Weekly*

"[R]eaders will be drawn in . . ."

——*Booklist*

"Holmberg . . . has a deft hand portraying internal emotional responses . . . *Keeper of Enchanted Rooms* combines lighthearted entertainment and nail-biting excitement."

——*Historical Novels Review*

"There are twists and turns, some of which are expected, but they all lead to a lovely ending after a suitably thrilling climax. . . . [I]f you enjoy fantasy, suspense, and romance, you will be delighted by *Keeper of Enchanted Rooms*."

——Bookreporter

"This is Charlie at her best——intriguing mystery, creative magic systems, with plenty of romance to keep me turning the pages."

——*Wall Street Journal* bestselling author Jeff Wheeler

THE HANGING CITY

2023 Goodreads Choice Awards Finalist

"Holmberg does a fantastic job of humanizing her nonhuman characters . . . This twisty adventure will have fantasy readers hooked."

——*Publishers Weekly*

"Holmberg's worldbuilding is detailed and dystopian but still possesses the same enchantment as tales told once upon a time. For fans of T. Kingfisher, this sweet story of belonging is a romantic twist on the classic bridge-troll fairy tale."

——*Library Journal*

"A tale of love, belonging, and embracing one's fears, Holmberg leaves readers asking who the real monsters actually are in a tale full of creative world building."

——*Booklist*

"Lyrical and striking."

——Robert Jackson Bennett, author of *Foundryside* and *City of Stairs*

"Rife with forbidden romance, monsters, and unique world building."

——Tricia Levenseller, *New York Times* bestselling author of *Blade of Secrets*

STAR MOTHER

Winner of the 2022 Whitney Award for Speculative Fiction

"In this stunning example of amazing worldbuilding, Holmberg (Spellbreaker) features incredible creatures, a love story, and twists no one could see coming. This beautiful novel will be enjoyed by fantasy and romance readers alike."

—*Library Journal*

THE SPELLBREAKER SERIES

"Those who enjoy gentle romance, cozy mysteries, or Victorian fantasy will love this first half of a duology. The cliff-hanger ending will keep readers breathless waiting for the second half."

—*Library Journal* (starred review)

"Powerful magic, indulgent Victoriana, and a slow-burn romance make this genre-bending romp utterly delightful."

—*Kirkus Reviews*

THE NUMINA SERIES

"[An] enthralling fantasy . . . The story is gripping from the start, with a surprising plot and a lush, beautifully realized setting. Holmberg knows just how to please fantasy fans."

—*Publishers Weekly*

THE PAPER MAGICIAN SERIES

2015 ALA Fantasy Reading Shortlist (The Paper Magician)

"Charlie is a vibrant writer with an excellent voice and great world building. I thoroughly enjoyed *The Paper Magician*."

—Brandon Sanderson, author of *Mistborn* and *The Way of Kings*

"Harry Potter fans will likely enjoy this story for its glimpses of another structured magical world, and fans of Erin Morgenstern's *The Night Circus* will enjoy the whimsical romance element . . . So if you're looking for a story with some unique magic, romantic gestures, and the inherent darkness that accompanies power all steeped in a yet to be fully explored magical world, then this could be your next read."

—Amanda Lowery, *Thinking Out Loud*

THE WILL AND THE WILDS

Winner of the 2020 Whitney Award for Speculative Fiction
Winner of the 2022 Whitney Award for Novel of the Year (Best Adult Fiction)

"Holmberg ably builds her latest fantasy world, and her brisk narrative and the romance at its heart will please fans of her previous magical tales."

—*Booklist*

THE FIFTH DOLL

Winner of the 2017 Whitney Award for Speculative Fiction

"*The Fifth Doll* is told in a charming, folklore-ish voice that's reminiscent of a good old-fashioned tale spun in front of the fireplace on a cold winter night. I particularly enjoyed the contrast of the small-town village atmosphere—full of simple townspeople with simple dreams and worries—set against the complex and eerie backdrop of the village that's not what it seems. The fact that there are motivations and forces shaping the lives of the villagers on a daily basis that they're completely unaware of adds layers and textures to the story and makes it a very interesting read."

—*San Francisco Book Review*

THE HALF-HEARTED QUEEN

ALSO BY CHARLIE N. HOLMBERG

The Whimbrel House Series

Keeper of Enchanted Rooms

Heir of Uncertain Magic

Boy of Chaotic Making

Wizard of Most Wicked Ways

The *Star Mother* Series

Star Mother

Star Father

The *Spellbreaker* Series

Spellbreaker

Spellmaker

The Numina Series

Smoke and Summons

Myths and Mortals

Siege and Sacrifice

The Paper Magician Series

The Paper Magician

The Glass Magician

The Master Magician

The Plastic Magician

The Shattered King Duology

The Shattered King

The Half-Hearted Queen

Other Novels

The Fifth Doll

Magic Bitter, Magic Sweet

Followed by Frost

Veins of Gold

The Will and the Wilds

The Hanging City

Still the Sun

Writing as C. N. Holmberg

You're My IT

Two-Damage My Heart

Nonfiction

Charlie N. Holmberg's Book of Magic

THE HALF-HEARTED QUEEN

CHARLIE N. HOLMBERG

47NORTH

Published by 47North, Seattle

www.apub.com

EU product safety contact:
Amazon Media EU S. à r.l.
38, avenue John F. Kennedy, L-1855 Luxembourg
amazonpublishing-gpsr@amazon.com

ISBN-13: 9781662531194 (hardcover)
ISBN-13: 9781662531187 (paperback)
ISBN-13: 9781662531170 (digital)

Cover design by Logan Matthews
Cover image: © Sybille Sterk / ArcAngel Images; © Else_lalala / Shutterstock

Printed in the United States of America

First edition

In loving memory of Mary Ann Holmberg.

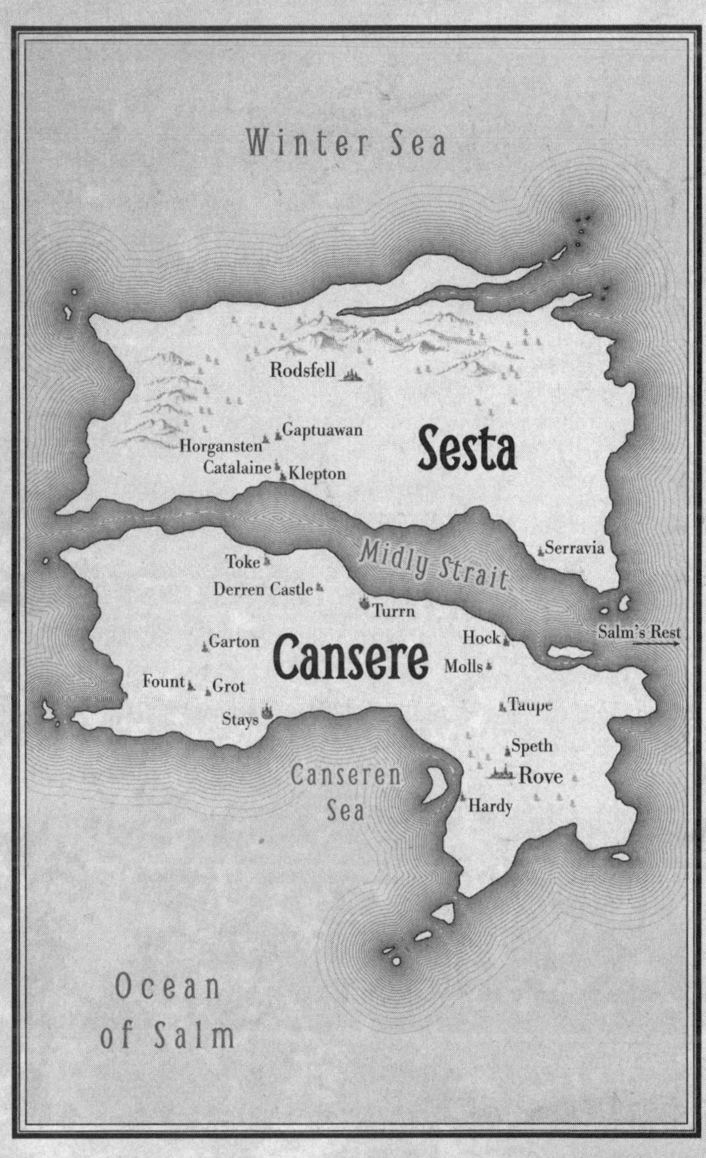
Winter Sea
Rodsfell
Gaptuawan
Horgansten
Sesta
Catalaine
Klepton
Midly Strait
Serravia
Toke
Derren Castle
Turrn
Salm's Rest
Garton
Cansere
Hock
Molls
Fount
Grot
Stays
Taupe
Speth
Canseren
Sea
Rove
Hardy
Ocean
of Salm

AUTHOR'S NOTE

This book contains themes of and references to physical, emotional, and sexual abuse; PTSD; and war and violence. It may not be suitable for all readers.

Chapter 1

I never told Renn I loved him.

The fact haunted me as I sat in the hold of a Sestan ship, rocking back and forth on cold ocean waves as I sailed north into our enemy's heartland. It sat heavy in my gut as I waited for Adoel Nicosia, king of Sesta, to lose his patience with me and slice my throat. Though I supposed throwing me overboard would save him the mess. I'd tried to throw myself overboard already. I had so little opportunity to act, as Nicosia, who had *read my mind* to discover I was Rove Castle's healer, had also *used a soulbinding* on me. He wielded two separate forms of craftlock—something that shouldn't have been possible. And yet the magic had such a hold on me I couldn't move more than six feet away from him at any given moment, no matter how I pushed. Weight and momentum had no effect on one's soul.

Earlier in the voyage he'd tried to shift my soulbinding. The moment it unclamped, I'd rushed the starboard side of the ship, but three separate Sestan dragons—soldiers—trounced me.

I was far more afraid of them than I was of the sea.

Now I sat in the hold of the massive ship, the wood planks beneath me hard and unpolished, splinters constantly catching my dress and my skin. The scent of a thousand bodies over endless years of sailing clung to every facet of the woodgrain, along with the sharp aroma of urine from soldiers who couldn't be bothered to climb up the ladder to the main deck and relieve themselves in the ocean. Fish, oil, and sweat mixed with my own fear, broken up by the faintest whiff of the sea when it came through the grating in the ceiling—the only exit from this hell.

The grating had lifted, now, letting in ocean breeze and a thick beam of sunlight, better highlighting the half-filled cargo hold, the ropes hanging on the walls, two spare cannons, and now, three monsters staring at me.

Don't let them see your fear, I reminded myself. Though surely the dog could smell it.

The mastiff growled as I met its eyes. It was a burly, overmuscled creature with an underbite and pigeoned feet, incredibly well trained. Again, no matter how hard I pulled on the binding, the dog didn't budge. If the anchor in the magic came down to the weight of *souls*, mine was apparently lacking.

The second beast was a Sestan dragon, also overly muscled and with an underbite. He couldn't care less about me. He lingered by the ladder in sunlight I hadn't touched for days, hand on the hilt of a dagger in case I proved feral. Much longer in this hold, and I would be.

But the worst of them crouched right in front of me. Eyes cold as ice, chin sharp and spotted with black facial hair matching that slicked back on his head. Fur lined King Adoel Nicosia's cloak and the tops of his boots, because the farther north we sailed, the colder it became.

Give me Rove's dungeon. Give me the end of Prince Adrinn's knife, or Queen Winvrin's ire. Give me a hard winter and dead beehives. Anything but him.

If the gods heard my pleas for help, they did not answer.

"You've had a little time to think." The king's Sestan accent curled sweet as honeycomb, the tassels of his violet cincture brushing the floor. "Would you like to talk?"

I had plenty of things I'd like to tell the king, but I kept them to myself. The one gift Queen Winvrin had bestowed upon me was a better ability to stay silent.

I stared at the mastiff, preferring its gaze. The king couldn't read my mind further, as I'd built a wall in my lumis, around the entirety of it, back in Speth. I'd built it of ethereal basalt, dark and thick. I was no mindreader, but the mind was part of the body, and the body was the lumis. I'd taken a shot in the dark, and so far, it seemed to be paying off, blocking him from reading my past, my present, and my secrets. King Nicosia had seen the wall, because in addition to using soulbinding and mindreading, he was, somehow, also a healer.

"I don't think he'll hurt you," Ursa, my dead sister, murmured from within the same space. *"He needs you too much."*

I tried to dowse on myself, to further strengthen that wall in my lumis as I had done again and again during the long hours of this endless journey, but the king's hand whipped out and grabbed my chin, forcing me to stay present, to look at him.

I'd rather touch a snake.

"None of that." The honey slipped from his voice. "Are you truly so loyal to the dead? I am your king now, Nym Tallowax. Your loyalty belongs to me."

I inhaled sharply through my nose as a sudden pain rang out from my upper arm, like something had struck me. Set my jaw. Another phantom pain? King Nicosia had made no move against me, nor had his guards or his dog. I feared I knew its source, but I couldn't think of that now. Even with the wall, I feared dwelling on anything that would give this bastard what he wanted. He'd been hounding me for answers for seven days.

Eight days since I healed Renn. Since I gave him half my heart and rebuilt his lumis into something even I, so familiar with it, could never have imagined. Seven days since Renn burned with light, since Sten called him gods-touched. Seven days since I met King Nicosia. Since he learned who I was and abducted me. Six since I'd been dragged onto this ship.

How much longer until the King of Dragons lost interest and killed me? Would he do it quickly, or slowly? Despite the chill, a new bead of sweat ran down the dip of my spine.

Adoel Nicosia frowned. "You try my patience—"

"Where is Princess Eden?" My voice crackled as it passed my lips, I'd used it so little. Even communicating with Ursa, I never spoke above a whisper.

His expression didn't change. "Whatever do you mean?"

I glared at him before moving my vision, again, to the mastiff. It looked at me like I was dinner. I'd never seen such hatred in an animal before. I dug deep, past the fear and anguish, to anger. It was so much easier to be angry. "If you want me to cooperate, *Your Majesty*, then perhaps you should do the same."

Perhaps Queen Winvrin hadn't schooled me as well as I thought. And now her head rotted on a pike at Rove Castle.

But I knew Princess Eden had embarked on this same ship. I'd glimpsed her on the deck, before they dragged me into the hold. Kari, a brothel owner in Rove, had told me she'd been captured. I feared for her, for what they might do to her, and yet I found myself relieved she was alive.

Renn, too, lived. I . . . felt him. Even now, I felt him. I felt him between the hard beats of my weak heart and in the pain still radiating from my arm. And that was something King Nicosia could never, *ever* know.

He sighed. "She is well, of course. She is a guest on this ship."

I snorted. I couldn't help it.

"Be careful, Nym," Ursa warned.

But Nicosia pressed. "And what is the dear princess to you?"

I shook my head. "She is my queen, now. I live to serve her."

He chuckled. "For someone who lived in the castle, you misunderstand your own laws."

Oh, I knew them. Princess Eden could only become queen if she married, and even then, only if she wanted the title. Which made Renn king. He became king of the whole of Cansere the night Sestan dragons murdered his father, mother, and brother.

The Sestan king regarded me with curiosity, never taking his foul hand from my face. Waited a beat before saying, "Sesta is a refuge for people like you. For people like *us*. I'll take off your chains and set you free; all I ask is to know how you did it. I know about the draft for doctors and healers by your late queen. She even sent requests into Sesta. But no one could heal her decrepit son. Until you. I want to understand you, Nym. Do you not see how your knowledge could benefit mankind as a whole? Sestan and Canseren both?"

I bit my tongue. *Some freedom I have, bound in the bottom of this ship.* But even if I were treated as nobility on this ship, I would say nothing. Not after the brief exchange we'd had in Speth. If I understood anything, it was that King Nicosia could not be trusted.

My stomach rumbled. I hadn't eaten in three days.

Nicosia didn't move, but I could taste his magic in the back of my throat. He was trying to read me, trying to pierce my mind and hear me like he could others. I'd learned the difference with him, between mindreading and dowsing. When he listened to my thoughts, his face grew tight, his brow furrowed in concentration, his green eyes sharp. When he dowsed, his face went slack, his eyes unfocused. He dug into my mind, and then switched to my lumis, trying to get past my wall.

I still couldn't wrap my mind around it. All three forms of craftlock. Such a thing should have been impossible.

Yet I'd been waiting for this moment. Prepared for it. All craftlock required touch to work, and I'd realized touch worked two ways. This time, without lifting my hands, I let my vision unfocus and dowsed into his lumis, the ethereal space that represented his physical body.

What I saw shocked me.

A great black wall, just like mine. Something felt oddly familiar about it—not visually, not because it matched mine, but—

My connection broke immediately, sending my consciousness crashing back into the hold of the ship. The king had whipped his hand back, breaking our connection.

"None of that, my dear." He smiled, but his voice cut like a razor. "But thank you kindly for the idea."

He stayed a step ahead of me. He knew I could slip into his lumis as well. Copied my wall. But he'd yet to penetrate mine. He'd yet to see the crenellated puzzle of my lumis, built like merlons on a tower. Hadn't seen the green blocks of my sister, given to me so I might live while she perished. Hadn't beheld the shadowy stains across all of it, from when I had died, only to be pulled back to the living by her.

I supposed if Renn was gods-touched, I was death-touched. What a pair we made.

Most critically, King Nicosia had yet to witness the merlon of my heart half-shaped with translucent blocks, something like frosted glass. Pieces of magic I'd created, tied off, and used to make myself whole. Pieces I had to feed magic into on a regular basis, for they faded a little every day. But the addition of those new pieces of myself was not the only change my lumis had undergone: Fine filaments of gold, the same gold that had burned so brilliantly in Renn's own lumis, threaded through my heart merlon like vines of ivy—slender, lovely, and damning, should King Nicosia ever lay eyes on them.

My arm still ached from the blow I never received. My pulse sped from something, a battle, perhaps, that I didn't fight. For a week, I'd felt things in my heart and my body that I did not and could not experience. They could only be from him: the king who possessed the other half of my heart, literally and figuratively.

I feared what that meant for us. But for now, I still had a chance. *We* still had a chance.

"Why?" I asked, looking into King Nicosia's eyes and finding little there. "Why are you doing this? Why attack Cansere? What do you *want*?"

Our countries had been peaceable for centuries. Dyadic continents separated only by a narrow strait. So similar, yet so very different. No one had expected the unprovoked attack on Rove.

The capital had fallen in a single night.

The corner of King Nicosia's mouth ticked upward. "Perhaps, my dear Nym, if you share with me, I'll share with you."

Lie. I knew it for a lie. Everything he said was lies.

The manner in which the Sestan king prodded at me, pleaded, threatened . . . the man seemed obsessed with Cansere's king. Most wouldn't even recognize Renn Reshua Noblewight because he'd spent most of his life as an invalid indoors, chained to a bed in much the same way I was chained to this gods-forsaken mastiff.

So you're the one who undid all my hard work, King Nicosia had said to me behind the thicket in Speth, my dress damp with snow.

I had theories, but they seemed so far-fetched, so impossible . . .

I swallowed my retorts, my questions, my curses. I refused to speak. I had a habit of letting my tongue get me in trouble, and I could not risk that here. Not with Renn in the balance. Even Ursa remained silent.

King Nicosia gave me a tight-lipped smile and stood. "Your choices, Nym. All consequences come from *your* choices." He brushed off his slacks. "I'll feed you when you're willing to trade for it."

And he left me alone in the bottom of his ship.

King Nicosia proved a man of his word.

I did not receive even water for the rest of the day, nor the next, though that night Rolys, god of the skies, opened the sky to rain and sleet, much of which fell through the grated door and into the hold. The mastiff growled at me when I pulled on our soulbinding, which did not allow me to get more than six feet from it, to lap water off the floor, but the beast did not attack me. Well trained, that one.

I'd rather starve in this hold than spend another minute with Adoel Nicosia, so I supposed it worked out for the better.

The next day I began to feel delirious with thirst, and my stomach had cramped into a hard lead ball within me. I slept a lot, hiding away from the ache of physical need, though upon one waking—somewhere midmorning, I presumed—I felt a distant fullness in my stomach. I'd ingested nothing—I was starving. I'd lost weight and continued to do so, my ribs more defined when I felt them through my dress. And yet for a few hours, I felt a distant fullness that was not my own, which only lent to my building theory about my split heart.

I never told Renn I loved him. Three times he'd confessed to me, and I'd failed to reciprocate.

What if I never got the chance?

I spent much of my time—how much, I wasn't sure—in a state of half-consciousness, lost in the realm between wakefulness and sleep, often dipping into the latter. When I woke again, evening light poured through the open hatch. I jolted to alertness, surrounded by water, thinking at first that I'd been thrown overboard or that I was hallucinating. But there were puddles of water all around me. I pressed my palms to the ship's wooden floor and drank, only to spit it out again. Seawater.

"Don't let him kill you," Ursa pleaded silently, hidden behind the basalt wall of my lumis. *"It isn't worth it."*

Isn't it? I wondered, but Ursa could not read my thoughts, even if I wanted her to.

I felt Renn, still: guilt that belonged neither to me nor Ursa winding up through me like poisoned thorns—

I finally recognized the hold and noticed King Nicosia standing over me, looking tired, the way a parent looks tired at the end of a long day in a house full of children. He had one hand propped on his hip. One of his soldiers came forward with a waterskin and handed it to me. I snatched it from him before he could change his mind, drinking greedily, water running down my chin and joining my half-soaked dress. My stomach cramped, forcing me to pause, but I held on to that bladder with both hands, nails digging in, protecting it like a mangy cur.

"I'm happy to feed you, as well. The best of foods," King Nicosia offered. "I realize I've been unfair to you. Here I want your cooperation, your trust, and I treat you like an animal." He gestured weakly to the mastiff. "Perhaps we could talk over dinner."

I said nothing, but the king retreated, snapping his fingers as he did, and the mastiff took off after him. My leash stretched to its limits within a few steps, forcing me to rise and follow. I stumbled on my feet, clutching the waterskin, and blearily climbed up the slanted ladder after the dog. The evening light seemed overbright to my eyes, and I winced, shielding them as I peered out to the ocean. Was that land out in the distance? A glacier? I'd only heard of them, never seen—

Princess Eden.

I stumbled as I spied her near the port side, hands on the railing, wearing a scarlet dress cut in Sestan fashion, her cloak billowing in the wind, her long bronze hair tangling over it. No ropes, no chains, but someone had fastened a heavy iron collar around her neck like she was an ox to be hitched. If she tried to jump, that collar would sink her to the bottom of Salm's restless sea.

Her pale face, sunburned, turned toward me. Eden's eyes widened in recognition, lips parted, but that damn mastiff dragged me after its owner, who stepped inside one of the two ship's cabins. I prayed the other one belonged to Princess Eden. At least it looked like she was eating.

The door slammed shut behind me, stealing my view of her and making me aware of my own shivering. The winter chill clung to my wet dress, and by the time Nicosia secured me in the cabin, my teeth were chattering.

Not all the shaking came from the cold.

"Sorry about that." He tilted his head toward my clothes and moved to a small cupboard above his bed and pulled out a slim dress. Handed it to me. "We couldn't get you to wake by normal means."

So the water hadn't come from sea waves, but from a bucket. "Then perhaps you should have had a change of heart before dehydration nearly killed me," I spat, my voice coarse, embracing my shield of anger. I could heal away the edges of thirst, but no amount of magic could create water in my blood or food in my stomach.

He grinned. "So she does speak."

I took the dress, eager to be warm. I hadn't been warm in ten days. However, the king did not leave the room.

"Are you modest, then?" He sounded genuinely curious. "I know the Noblewights like to have their way with their servants. I wasn't sure if you were among the . . . favored."

I wanted to growl like the mastiff heeling at my ankles, but resisted. He was not entirely wrong. Prince Adrinn had . . . partaken . . . of many women at the castle, and I imagined elsewhere, too. And now his head, too, rotted on a spike in Rove.

Take care of my brother. His final words to me.

I felt the distance between Renn and I so acutely I shuddered.

The Sestan king turned around. "Quickly, if you would."

I did not trust him. I trusted myself alone with very few men, especially if I were to undress. But I would be miserable remaining in my soaked clothes, even if I dowsed to keep illness at bay, so turning my back, I stripped as swiftly as possible, glaring at the cabin door, daring a soldier or crewman to come through. I even had to strip off my shift, making me feel doubly exposed. The dress fit snugly, even with my weight loss, but the rich fabric had some give to it. I could not fasten the dress myself, but I refused to ask for help, so I did as many buttons as I could, bending my wrists and shoulders at odd angles, hiding those I couldn't reach with tangled hair that, unkempt as it was, reached a hand's length past my waist.

I paused, staring down at the dress. Simple, modest, and white, its hem hit my big toe, too long for my frame. Canseren style. I knew this dress. It took me only a moment to place it.

Eden. Princess Eden had worn this before. It was cut to her measurements.

I shivered, considering what situation Renn's sister had found herself in to have to discard this dress. She'd seemed hale enough on the deck, but I knew personally that looks could deceive. I hadn't heard her scream, or any foul language regarding her person on the tongues of sailors. I hoped for the best. I might lose my mind if I didn't.

The king turned around before I gave him any indication of my state of dress, and he grinned at me in a way that made me feel covered in oil. "I thought that might suit you."

I did not ask why he had the princess's gown. A casual servant in the castle likely would not have noticed it. And I could not let him think I was close to the royal family . . . or what was left of it.

Relief, and I daresay a bit of elation, sparked in my chest. Something muted, like I was reading a story, but not truly feeling the sensations for myself. I pressed my hand to my breastbone, then drank more from the water bladder to hide the sudden shift in emotion.

What, Renn? I wondered. Had he discovered a strategy against Sesta? Had he recruited new soldiers, or obtained useful information? I couldn't know where he'd ended up after my capture, but the sensations I received made it feel like he was fighting back, or at least trying to.

He felt like the other end of a dream. I'd never wake up without him.

A knock came at the door. I stepped aside—even a king's cabin on a ship was small—and a crewman came in carrying a wooden tray with strange foods on it. Sestan foods, with sauces and fried patties and a strange fluffy grain. He set it down on the small table in the room, bowed, and left.

"Sit." King Nicosia gestured to the chair nearest me. "I'm not going to poison you."

Of course he wouldn't, unless he wanted his precious information to die with me. So I sat and started eating without invitation. The king watched me for a full minute before taking a seat and serving himself in a more dignified manner. I didn't care. I was not here to impress him, nor to help him.

"Why are you so mistrusting of me, Miss Tallowax?" he asked, that honeycomb sweetness returning.

I'd had plenty of time to ruminate on the best way to answer his questions, and I'd practiced with Ursa as well. I could not be silent forever. That might indict me more than words would. "Because you burned down my home and captured me against my will. What kind of a question is that?"

I easily could have been born and raised in Rove, for all he knew. Though with the draft, he could figure I'd come from afar.

He nodded. "I do apologize. My army got a little . . . out of hand. The general has been disciplined."

Liar, I thought, and ate bland grain and tart sauce.

"And you lived in the castle?"

I bided my time before answering, glad to have the excuse of chewing food to mull over my responses. "I served there."

"Served Prince Renn."

"I served anyone who needed healing." I took a long drink from the bladder, swallowing its last drops. The king offered me wine, but I did not accept it. The last thing I wanted was inebriation. Not when I had so much to protect. "The Noblewights, the servants, the livestock."

"And what's so special about you, hm?" he asked. "Why you over the many others who'd come for the same position?"

I shrugged. "I guess I'm fast. I'd be happy to demonstrate."

Demonstrating would mean hurting him first, but I need not explain that. The way the king's lip turned up, he understood my meaning.

"You are not a very . . . demure servant, are you?"

I set down my fork. "Why should I be?" I asked around a mouthful of meat. I swallowed, letting genuine frustration leak into my voice. "I was hired against my will and forced to take unpaid work for nobility who didn't give a pig's backside about me, my family, or my people.

Nobility who would have killed me for the craft had their precious baby not fallen ill."

He reached across the table to touch my hand. Outwardly, it would seem a sign of comfort, but I knew what he wanted. Knew that focus in his eyes. He was trying to read me again, dive into my thoughts. But my basalt wall held firm.

He released me a moment later. "Why won't you let me understand you? Truly understand you. Surely you do not despise the craft of mindreading, when you yourself have experienced so much prejudice against your own."

I glowered at him. "My thoughts and memories are mine. I do not wish to share them with anyone."

"Not even your family? Your husband?"

I frowned. "No." All the better if he thought me married. The half-heart connection aside, if King Nicosia understood how Renn and I felt about each other, he could still use me against him.

My own guilt twisted in my gut. Renn had already lost so much. If I'd grasped the chill of death clinging to the castle, if I'd been able to save Adrinn in time . . . how might these events have transpired differently?

King Nicosia leaned back then, folding his arms, studying me. I glanced at the mastiff, wondering if I could possibly grab the beast by the collar and haul it overboard with me. Would the dog sink and drown me with him, or would he swim and keep us afloat? I could swim decently, but not for long. Not in the icy waves of Salm's Rest.

As the king watched me, his smile slowly faded. "Well. I'm sure we'll have plenty of time to get to know each other better." He slid the wine toward me. "Tell me about yourself."

Full, I pushed back from the table as much as the small cabin would allow me. "You first. Please."

He chuckled. "Such heartless disrespect for chivalry you have, Miss Tallowax. It surprises me, the way women are treated in Cansere. I wouldn't think you'd have the opportunity to develop it as you have."

My stomach churned, trying to remember what to do with the food I'd given it. I dowsed to soothe it, only to have the king's toe hook around a leg of my chair and jerk me forward. "None of that."

"I feel sick," I shot back. "I was deprived for five days and just gorged. Of course I feel sick."

"Then I suggest you drink something. *Slowly* this time."

I met his eyes, staring, waiting for my stomach to settle. Did not touch the wine. Sighing, he handed me a new waterskin. I sipped at it contents, then pulled it away and sniffed.

"You're rather smart," he offered.

"You son of a whore." My tongue started to thicken in my mouth. He'd put something in the water.

He shrugged. "You'll be easier cargo this way. Don't take it personally."

I absolutely did, even as my body went slack in the chair and teetered over.

I couldn't do this. I couldn't slip away and let him beat down my carefully placed wall.

The moment I hit the floor, I dowsed, my lumis tipping and shifting as I tried to focus on where the drug made the stones of my crenellated wall slick. Tried to clear as much as I could before—

"Wake up, Nym," Ursa whispered. *"It's been too long. He's going to try to fight his way in."*

I blearily opened my eyes. I lay in the hold again, soulbound to the mastiff. I could feel the tether linked somewhere behind my breastbone. My heart beat weakly, sickly. I hadn't been able to refuel the magic holding it together.

"Be quiet," she urged.

My body weighed a thousand pounds. Closing my eyes, I tried to keep my breathing even and slipped into my lumis. It shimmered before my eyes, the way a hot road shimmers with summer heat. I fed the pieces of my heart first, steadying it. Then, leaning against the basalt wall, I pulled magic into me, demanding extra through Ursa, and bade the wall grow thicker, harder. Imagined it forming a sphere beneath the floor, guarding my lumis from all sides, even the unseen. As much as I could before he drugged me again. I had to stay ahead of him.

King Nicosia may have had all three forms of craftlock, but I had a second healer within me. I prayed to Alm, god over healing, that it would be enough.

A flicker of worry, deep in my chest. Like the scent of an oncoming storm.

Renn, I thought, and pushed myself harder, channeling as much magic as I could.

I heard approaching footsteps as my consciousness slipped again.

You will not have him, I promised, and sank into the black.

Chapter 2

The drug knocked me out for hours at a time; when I managed to dowse away some of its oily touch, I'd wake a little sooner, pretend to be asleep, and rebuild what Nicosia had torn down. I found it curious, how my lumis would accept this massive basalt wall, while my previous experiment—mimicking existing pieces of myself with magic—fizzled into nothing. I thought, perhaps, that this wall wasn't trying to replace part of my lumis, only protect it, as a bandage protected a wound. Or my body or my magic recognized the wall was a *need*, and therefore allowed it. If I ever got out of this hell, I could study it further. I didn't have the strength now to do anything more than survive.

Nicosia permitted the drugs to wear off the last day on the ship, allowing me to take in the sight of Sesta across Salm's Rest and glimpse Princess Eden before a soldier forced more of the noxious stuff down my throat. One could sail from Cansere to Sesta across the Midly Strait in a day, but Nicosia had sailed up the east coast instead, in the ocean separating Sesta from Antsan—I assume to make easier escape from Cansere, but perhaps sailing made for easier traveling to the Sestan capital, Rodsfell, even in the winter. I didn't wake again until I reached Rodsfell. I dowsed away numerous bruises and sores on my body from riding in a wagon, but other than being manhandled like a sack of potatoes and forced away from maintaining my heart, I didn't seem to have been otherwise harmed.

Princess Eden had been placed in the armored carriage ahead of me, where King Nicosia rode. What value did he place on her life compared to my own? Yet I determined he likely didn't want us together, period. He was a smart, conniving man—he didn't want us planning anything, or worse, offering comfort to one another.

A passing dragon was obliging enough to give me the date. Two and a half weeks had passed since Adoel Nicosia took me from Speth. But Renn lived. I knew he lived; I could feel it. Half my heart nestled in his lumis, and his lumis branched across the fourteen hundred miles now separating us. I felt him as though he was part of me, similar to the way Ursa was part of me, but no matter how I tried to speak to him or send my thoughts through that golden line, I could not communicate with him. If he ever heard me, he did not reply—at least, not in a way I could hear.

Surely that sensation of fullness I'd felt on the ship had been in response to the depth of my hunger. I wondered if Renn had sorted out the connection as well, and if he'd eaten extra in hopes of comforting me. While the thought brought me peace, it also renewed a constant ache in my chest, the one I felt when not terrified of my future and the men around me, when not occupied scheming my escape or otherwise asleep. It was a dull ache, but now it spiked, like a cleaver coming down through the center of my heart. I wanted only to see him again, to touch him, to tell him I love him. I took deep breaths and blinked rapidly, steeling myself for what was to come, for surely this was only the beginning of this unknown journey. I feared it would be a long one.

Rodsfell was a contrast to Rove. It was large, yes, but the city buildings and houses seemed to squat, nestled close to the ground to better weather the cold. Great blankets of snow lined everything—eaves and roofs, tree branches and garden walls. Dark pebbles dotted the cobbled roads to provide better traction for wagons and carriages. Blue mountains and rows of dark pine forests looked painted onto the northern horizon, and thick winter clouds clogged the sky, making the whole sight gray and sad.

King Nicosia did not live in a castle, as the Noblewights had, but in a palace. It was larger than Rove Castle, long and spired, its windows glinting even in the muted sunlight. From a distance it seemed to be carved from ice itself, but as we neared, I realized it must have been white granite, perhaps marble. Closer, I saw flourishes of silver on its face, a true boast of wealth in stark contrast to the rest of Rodsfell. Three rows of high fences separated the palace from the rest of the city. The first was made of thick, blocky stone. The second of tall spikes of wrought iron. The third also iron, but twisted into a semblance of elegance, its large gates painted in silver and boasting the likeness of a dragon.

After passing through the fences, the wagon stopped. King Nicosia approached one of the soldiers, simply touching him on the wrist for a moment before walking away. Speaking to him mind-to-mind. The soldier, with two silver stripes on his collar to denote his rank, cut through my bonds, then helped me to the ground. My flimsy slippers instantly sank into the snow; the king's men had absconded with my cloak and boots. Perhaps these shoes had been Princess Eden's as well.

The touch of darkness, colder than the snow, snaked between my shoulders. I glanced up at the soldier. He looked hale enough. I could have checked, but found no kindness within me.

"You're going to die soon," I whispered.

He glanced at me with a raised eyebrow, but didn't speak.

I stood there, shivering, for about five minutes until the king returned.

"I will escort you personally, Miss Tallowax," he offered, his most charming grin plastered onto his face. He grasped my upper arm to guide me forward, and I instinctively shifted away, though I knew I would fare better if I at least put on an act of warming up to him. Still, I did not like men touching me, not since Ford, and I corrected myself too late.

The king seemed unperturbed and walked toward the palace, slowing his step to match mine. I spied Eden being escorted by no fewer than five soldiers, but they took her around the side of the palace. She went without fuss, silent, head bowed.

"Rodsfell Palace is nearly seven hundred years old," King Nicosia explained as we approached, guards opening the heavy double doors for us. "It's been added to over the centuries, remodeled, but its bones are old. This entry hall is the original, the marble quarried in our Songrift Mountains to the north. I'm sure you saw them as you came in."

I didn't reply, but since he had invited me to look around, I did so. Thoroughly. The better I knew the layout of the place, the easier it would be to escape. King Nicosia either had a lot of confidence in his security, or he truly believed he was going to sway me to cooperate with him.

He led me through the Great Hall, gesturing toward a ballroom, a throne hall, and a gallery before leading me up narrow stairs, pointing out more halls and drawing rooms. Up the stairs again, now focusing less on rooms and more on décor—the bust of Emperor Frensige, a painting he'd had commissioned of the sunset over Salm's Rest, imported rugs from Antsan, our neighbor to the east. I tried to memorize passageways and rooms, noting which doors were left open and which were shut, but as we ascended yet another set of stairs, something remarkable caught my eye, and I couldn't help but ask about it.

"Who is she?"

Across the stairwell, in an east-facing wall, were three large stained-glass windows, easily ten feet tall if not more, but my eyes were immediately drawn to the first. It lit up like a gem with the cloud-choked sun, and upon it curled the body of a woman, as though she were leaning forward, her face large in proportion to her body. Her eyes were silver and seemed to look straight at me, and her black hair swirled around her, ribbonlike. White lilies occupied the corners of the window.

King Nicosia smiled. Genuinely, I thought. "That is the goddess Zia, of course."

His answer gave me pause. I knew Sesta worshipped the same gods as Cansere. Six of them, each a child of the last. But only one of those gods was a woman: Zia, the youngest, to which most assigned anything not already given to other gods. Usually feminine things, such as fertility. I'd seen representations of her before—there was one in the all-gods shrine in Rove Castle—but never such an artistic rendering of her, and *never* without the other gods present. To see such singular focus on the goddess in this place . . . it confused me.

King Nicosia wore the violet cincture of Zia as well, looped around his waist. He was the only man I'd ever seen sport it.

"Do you like it?"

"Yes," I admitted, because I wanted the king to like me to better my circumstances, but I found my answer to be true. Yes, it was stunning. Yes, something about seeing the glorification of a deity of my own sex affected me.

"That is Antaniat Felide, the gods-touched from the stories." He pointed to the third window, as if I should know the Sestan story he referred to. I did not. The window depicted a dark man with topaz eyes, one hand reaching heavenward. "And, of course, you recognize the other."

The center window, placed higher than the other two, depicted a pale man with dark hair and green eyes, staring forward, grim, as though judging all who passed. It bore a likeness to Nicosia. That it was placed higher than both a goddess and a gods-touched legend did not surprise me.

We continued up the stairs, and at the top, I asked, "Why not Hem? He is the god of kings."

"Hem is the greatest grandfather and, of course, revered," King Nicosia answered, leading me down a long corridor. "But I have always felt closest to Zia."

I did not know what to do with such an answer.

We took another, darker, shorter set of stairs up, then stepped into a large domed conservatory at the back of the palace. It had a view of the north side of the city, faraway mountains, and pine forests. Quite the view—two-thirds of its walls were made of glass, making me truly marvel for the second time. Perhaps more prominent, however, was the enormous tree rising from its floor, the tiles cut into an uneven polygon around its trunk, forming a narrow aperture, its thick boughs reaching up, and in many places *through* the ceiling. The girth of its trunk spoke of its age. Surely the tree was as old as the palace itself, if not older. It would take four of me to wrap my arms around it.

"This is the Egroran." He gently touched my neck, and I felt the moment his magic took hold of me, soulbinding me to it. I pulled away, unable to hide my scowl, but the king did not look at me but at the tree, one hand splayed to its rough bark. "This tree was planted upon the founding of our nation, or so the lore says. Though this country has changed names, shifted from kingdom to empire and back again, and traded ruling families, the tree still stands, and so do we."

"Is that why you attack Cansere?" I asked. "To restore your old empire?"

He chuckled. "It is not an empire of land I seek, Miss Tallowax, but that is a tale for another day. I'll have some things brought up for you; this will be your space, for now."

"My prison," I corrected.

"You should be able to walk the whole of the room," he offered, as though the lengthening of my leash should please me. At least I didn't have an ugly dog glaring at me. "Enjoy the view. We will talk again soon. Alas, I'm a very busy man, and I've been away some time. Until we meet again."

He nodded at me, still smiling, and left the room. I heard the subtle *click* of its door and waited for a lock, but none came. This conservatory hadn't been built to be a prison. Alone, I tested the soulbinding, and yes, I was able to touch the walls of the room but pulled up a few feet short of the door. A lock, bars, chains, none of it mattered so long as the king's magic held me here. Still, I circled the conservatory, searching for . . . I didn't know what. There were no other doors, no exits or entrances, no decoration. The beauty came from the tree and the great window alone.

I pressed my hand against the glass, fog climbing up from the warmth of my fingers, and looked out to the horizon beyond the mountains. The opposite direction of my home. I missed it dearly. I missed my family, though they would see themselves through the winter in one piece. Renn had made sure of it.

"Is it selfish of me," I whispered, "to miss *him* more than the rest of it?" I'd only just found him, just touched him, just thought I might have him, before King Nicosia tore us apart. Finally allowed myself to give in to my feelings, only to have them shattered all over again, though I supposed the manner of breaking was different, this time. Politics instead of betrayal.

"No," Ursa offered, soft and reassuring. *"Lissel and the children have each other. Brien has the army. You have . . ."*

She didn't finish the sentence, but I knew what she'd intended. *You have nothing.* A tear came to my cheek.

"I have you, Ursa," I whispered.

"And I will be here for you, always," she promised. *"But I am not all here, Nym. I can't be. But he can. Somehow, you'll find a way. Love always triumphs."*

It did not—I knew from repeat experience that love was never enough—but Ursa sounded so hopeful and resolute, it felt wrong to debate her.

I heard a soft cry, so soft I barely perceived it. I thought, at first, it was Ursa who wept, but I couldn't recall a single time she'd done so since merging with me. Holding my breath, I listened. Nothing, and then a sniff.

It came from the tree.

Hesitant, I slipped off my shoes and toed to the tree, trying to remain quiet. Pressed my hand to its bark as Nicosia had. Heard another sniff.

My eyes were drawn down to the tiles of the floor, cut to hug the trunk, but the shape made small gaps around it. On my hands and knees, I pressed my face to the largest, about an inch wide, and peered downward.

The room below was white, perhaps another conservatory. I spied a woman sitting against the tree, trying very hard to weep gently.

I recognized the color of her dress. "Princess?" I whispered. She did not hear me, so I risked speaking louder. "Princess?"

She stiffened, looked around, then up. Her blue gaze met mine, widened. Then she drew a hand across her neck. Death? Cutting—

She wasn't alone.

I held my breath again, hoping I hadn't been heard. I waited for a soldier to walk over, to discover me, but none did. I waited a long time for the princess to say something, but it seemed she could not.

Eventually, I withdrew from the aperture, cold and lightheaded. Returned to the massive window and stared out into the mountainous forest, so far from home.

My chest hurt. I receded into myself, picturing Renn's face just before he kissed me, the pure adoration in his eyes, free of judgment and condescension. Eyes that saw the way Ursa's had—a beautiful, fair world where good won and evil lost, where if two people wanted a happy ending badly enough, they could seize it from the stars themselves.

Pressing my forehead to the glass, I wept, muffling myself with my arm, not wishing to draw the attention of anyone with ears to hear me.

I found another spot in the conservatory where the binding pulled tight—the southwest corner, just past where the window ended.

The tether pulled me up short. When I held my arms out in front of me, my palms hovered about four inches from the wall.

Here, I tested the magic. There was no guard to strike me nor mastiff to bark at me, just me and the tree. So I reached my hands forward and strained.

It felt strange. It wasn't a physical thing holding me back, not like a wall or a rope. My very spirit froze, unmoving, and my body ceded to it. I grunted, I reached, I perspired, but I could not budge myself so much as a hair closer.

I searched my lumis. I'd searched it before, again and again, trying to find a link to my soul the way I could find one to my mind. But craftlock won on this point: The spirit and the body were entirely separate, and I could do nothing to mitigate King Nicosia's spell on me. So I strengthened my walls and my heart, then tried again to reach the wall. I leaned into it, pushed. Jumped, crawled, ran. But every time I froze in the exact same spot, sweat pouring down my back in my struggle, clenching my teeth so hard they neared cracking.

"Even your stubbornness can't change it," Ursa admonished.

I was about to retort when a sudden, keening sadness swept through me, bursting from my heart and flowing into my arms and legs like driven snow. I gasped and collapsed to my knees, holding my breast as though it were a wound I could staunch. *Renn.*

I dared not say his name aloud, despite the semblance of solitude. One mistake could cost everything. If deciphering Renn's lumis was so critical to King Nicosia, then it was critical to everyone, and I was the only thing standing between him and it.

New tears sprang to my eyes, and I didn't understand why. But the grief must have been substantial for me to feel it so strongly here. *What happened, Renn?* Had he learned of Sten's death? Perhaps his guard had been injured in Speth and only just succumbed to his wounds, and I wasn't there to help him. The thought wove my own sorrow through the link.

Lying on the hard floor on my side, I curled my knees to my chest and hugged myself tightly, imagining I was holding him. Tried desperately to send that comfort through those golden threads to his heart. *I'm sorry. I'm here. You are strong, Renn. You'll overcome this. We both will.*

How badly I wanted to believe it.

I crawled to the little pallet the servants had brought to me and lay upon it, breathing through the sadness like one might breathe through child labor. Turning my thin pillow, I held it tightly against my chest, trying to imagine it was the Canseren king in my arms and his heartbeat I listened to.

I had a hunch we both cried ourselves to sleep that night.

"Nym?"

The voice stirred me early in the morning, dawn light drawing across the conservatory's glass. I stared up at the tree-pierced ceiling a long moment before I came to myself. Hope blossomed like new spring flowers as I rolled over to the aperture around the Egroran's trunk, closed one eye, and peered down.

Princess Eden stood below, peering back up at me.

"Are you alone?" She spoke so softly I could barely hear her.

"I am. Are you?"

She nodded. "Only for a moment. We don't have long. The king says he's preparing a room for me."

I wasn't sure what that meant.

"Why are you here?" she asked. "What's happened to—?"

"Renn is alive," I pushed through the crack. "I've seen him myself. He's alive and whole. Truly *whole*."

It was hard to see through such a little crack, in dim light, so far, but I thought relief washed over her. She leaned against the tree. "Thank the gods."

"But Adrinn . . ." My throat started to close. ". . . the others—"

"I know. He told me that much." It was the coldest I'd ever heard her voice. "He said nothing of Renn, so I'd hoped—"

But we had no time for niceties. "Did you see a way to escape? Did he bind you to the tree?"

"A soldier did. I think the king can only bind one soul at a time. I've . . . never been soulbound before."

"On the ship?"

She shook her head. Just the heavy collar, then, which had since been removed from her. But my mind caught on the "one soul at a time." I could not enter two lumie at once; I could only heal one person at a time. It made sense then that a soulbinder could only bind one soul at a time. Surely a mindreader could only read one mind at a time as well. Dan might know.

Thoughts of my brother weighed down my half-heart.

"I think I can get through to him," she murmured.

I choked on a scoff. "To King Nicosia?"

She nodded. "He seems reasonable."

Princess Eden was a mature, levelheaded woman. Privileged, but open-minded and kind—I'd seen as much at her breakfasts with Renn at the castle, and in the way she heeled Prince Adrinn. But such a statement was pure naïveté.

"It's a farce. You must know it's a farce."

"I can play along," she pressed.

I heard a door opening, likely to her room. "Be careful," I rushed. "Don't trust him."

Eden turned away to face the newcomer. I caught a mumbled greeting, saw the elbow of a guard, I think, and then Eden vanished from my sight.

She didn't return.

For two days I stayed in that conservatory. Servants checked on me throughout, bringing me food far better than any prisoner should have—roast chicken, meat pies, fried onions, little cakes. I could just see the floor below through the aperture formed around the tree, but the space was often empty. When a staff member or the like did pass through, they were hardly entertaining. Seeing me bored, a woman in blue-and-black livery brought me a few novels, as well as a canvas and selection of paints. I was not much of an artist, but I made use of them anyway to pass the time, pondering alongside Ursa what exactly the Sestan king thought to gain by this. My menses came—late, likely due to the hunger and stress of traveling here—so she also brought me a girdle and clean cloths to manage it.

Bright and early on the third day, King Nicosia came to me himself, four guards in tow; two of them were women, something I had never witnessed in Cansere, and they had white braids at their wrists. White was for Hem, the god of gods and kings, but he was also the god of justice, which I assumed was the representation here. Still, I rarely saw women don anything but violet for Zia.

The king moved my soulbinding from the Egroran to himself, then escorted me down to a private breakfast chamber. I wondered why he didn't use his magic specifically on Princess Eden, but left her to his men.

I wondered if he saw me as a threat.

Boiled eggs, bacon, crumpets, and jam awaited us in a green, wallpapered room with three symmetrical lancet windows on the far wall. I helped myself, carefully monitoring the king, wishing I could read his mind the way he wished to read mine.

"Where is the princess?"

My concern seemed to amuse him. "She wasn't feeling well today, so she took breakfast in her room."

"In the dungeon?"

"My, my"—he smoothed his napkin on his lap—"what terrible things they've poisoned you with, Nym. Princess Eden Shim Noblewight is a guest here. She stays in a suite."

I studied his face, but he schooled his features better than even Renn.

"I thought"—he buttered a crumpet—"that you might want to understand me better, so I in turn can understand you. Today I will show you my city, and the freedoms you can enjoy here as a Sestan citizen."

I raised my eyebrow. "You wish to make me a citizen?"

"You may make yourself one, if you so desire. Forgive the magic"—he gestured between us—"but until we are on truly peaceful terms, it's necessary, and far less clunky than chains, don't you think?"

Nothing running through my mind would help the present situation, so I focused on my meal.

After we ate, the king had my fur-lined cloak and boots returned to me, and we set out in a little carriage west of the palace, toward the military grounds. There were at least three dozen barracks here and an enormous rookery that housed birds of prey the size of dogs—the same birds that had lifted soulbinders over the walls of Rove Castle. I fought a chill at the sight of them, their beady eyes glaring, their hooked beaks like scythes. A dozen or more training grounds littered the area, along with several buildings for armor and arms. Despite the cold day, many soldiers scuttled about, completing chores, receiving deliveries, or practicing in the frosted fields. We passed several barracks until we reached a narrower field with perhaps twenty people on it performing simple strength training and archery.

"Crafters, like ourselves," King Nicosia explained. "Out in the open, training alongside ordinary men. The only thing separating them is their rank." He directed me to look at the soldiers closest to us. In addition to the silver stitching marking their rank, they had silver shapes—circles, triangles, half circles—beside them.

"You would wear a half circle for healing. Circles for mindreaders, triangles for soulbinders. They are trained in their magic, too, there." He pointed farther west. To which building, I couldn't be sure. "At the school for them."

"Why don't you have a designation?" I asked, looking at his collar. It didn't peek above his coat, but I'd seen it before. Gold bars instead of silver thread, no extra shapes.

He smiled patiently. "I do. I am king. And"—he leaned in conspiratorially—"there is not enough space to distinguish all that I can do."

Seeming pleased with himself, he continued on, clasping his hands behind his back. I kept pace with him, his guards following a few steps behind.

Looking between the buildings, I saw a little boy in uniform. He could not have been older than my brother Heath.

"How old do you start their training?" I asked.

"When they are ready, of course. Usually they're brought in by the age of ten."

"And if they're not?"

His steps slowed. "Not ten?"

I shook my head. "If they're not brought in. If their parents know they're a crafter and don't report them."

He frowned. He didn't like the question. "Then we receive them as we can."

I knew he wanted to paint a pretty picture for me, but I'd heard tales from merchants passing through Fount. A crafter was not killed in Sesta for knowing magic, no, but all users of craftlock were property of the crown. Dan had confessed his craftlock to me during my last trip to Fount; he was a mindreader. Illegal, in Cansere. Were Dan discovered in Sesta, he'd be taken in, conscripted, and . . . I don't know what punishments he'd face for his secrecy. Were I not a crafter myself, and therefore valuable, I'd likely be hanged for harboring him. Perhaps they'd kill Brien instead, to set an example, or make it easy and just aim for Terrence, the baby of the family. Would they test each of my siblings for the craft first? I wondered. But I did not ask. King Nicosia was trying to coerce me to his side, to make me see the freedom I would have under his rule, but this was not true freedom. There was little difference between a crafter losing her life to the noose and losing her life to service. Either way, choice was stripped from her.

"Are they all soldiers?" I pulled my cloak closer.

"Oh, no, not all. We have healers in our hospitals, mindreaders in the police force, soulbinders on the farms." He chuckled. "The sheep can't get very far when they're chained to the dog."

I nodded. "An apt word for it."

The king's smile faltered for a moment. "Let me show you our trade district."

I was grateful for the day's chill as the king walked me through the streets. Very few vendors had anything outside; we had to enter squat buildings, each huddled up to its neighbors, to see the wares, save for those who could afford glass windows, which were few. But keeping my head down, hugging myself, masked the emotions streaming in from Renn: Sorrow, then hope. Sorrow again, a flicker of humor. Farther away, this time. Manageable. But should any show on my face, I would need to explain them, and I worked on possible excuses while pretending to be interested in King Nicosia's tour.

We returned to the palace for an early dinner, where servants served far too much food for two people. The guards and footmen blending into the wallpaper did not eat. I chewed a bite of salted pork slowly, watching the king's expressions.

"I know you wish to ask me something," he offered. "Go ahead."

I swallowed. "Why is it only you?" King Nicosia had to be at least forty-five. "You could have adult children, but you haven't spoken of them. Or lords and ladies in your dominion, but none share this table."

He nodded. "Do not worry yourself."

"I wasn't."

He met my eye. His own glittered with amusement. "I have no need to host my neighbors, not when I already demand their men at the front, and not in this season. And I've chosen not to have any heirs."

He dodged the rest of my questions to the point I stopped asking them and focused on my meal. Afterward, he escorted me out of the breakfast room, but as we entered the Great Hall, we met another contingent of guards, and among them a familiar face.

"Ah, there is my prize!" King Nicosia strolled forward with open arms to greet her.

Princess Eden did not return the sentiment. She seemed unwell, but considering she'd been abducted from her home after most of her family was murdered, of course she did. Her face wore a mask of blankness; even when her eyes landed on me, she hid any recognition. I fought to mirror the expression. Her pale skin glowed all the paler against the deep-blue dress she wore. In Sestan fashion, it had tight sleeves from shoulder to wrist and padding around the hips. No cincture. Nothing to denote her position as princess.

The king took her hand in his and kissed the back of it. "Miss Tallowax, it is a true pleasure to have you in my home during such a joyous time." Pulling her close, King Nicosia ran a knuckle down the side of the princess's face. "Tomorrow, dear Eden is to become my queen."

Chapter 3

"Why are you doing this?" I kept my voice low as the king personally escorted me—his guards in tow—back to the conservatory, the soulbinding he had on me shortened to keep me close. I tried not to let my emotions leak into my voice and did so successfully, though the concern mingling with frustration coming from Renn made it especially difficult. Concern over me, I thought, but I couldn't place his frustration. Couldn't place him, wherever on the lower continent he might be.

As the king opened the door, the light of a single brazier highlighted his smile. "You have much to learn about politics, Miss Tallowax."

I stepped into the room and turned around, looking at him. "Then explain it to me. Surely you could have asked King Grejor for her hand when you barged into Rove last autumn."

He looked at me like I was a child, patient and condescending.

"It's the throne you want, then?" I pressed. I'd been on good behavior today, or so I thought, and the Sestan king had been equally pleasant. Perhaps he'd be willing to throw me a bone. I chose my words carefully. "When I worked in the castle . . . there seemed to be a lot of confusion about the war. So is that the reason? You want the land? The resources?" Though Sesta's climate was colder, Sesta and Cansere shared many of the same resources; there wasn't anything Cansere had that Sesta didn't. Sesta had more precious metals, if anything. "Its . . . crafters, perhaps?"

He chuckled. "What a noble picture you paint. Me coming to save the crafters." He touched his chin, ruminating. "I don't dislike it."

"You said you wanted to get to know me better. Let me get to know you." I tried to sound kind. Interested. Tried to sound more like Ursa—she'd always been the sweeter of the two of us. "I could help you better if I understood your goals."

He seemed to consider that, the brazier's embers glinting off his amused eyes. The way the dim light hit him, with the shadows and his dark clothing, he almost looked like Renn. It painted their noses similarly, their jaws. But the moment the king shifted, the illusion cracked, and a little piece of me did, too.

"I appreciate the sentiment," he said, back to his honeycomb sweetness. "But you needn't worry about it. You'll be taken care of—it's the gods' will."

He patted me on my head before leading me to the Egroran and changing my binding to its trunk. He started away, then paused. "If you're very good, I'll let you attend the wedding." He grinned, and in the light of the brazier, it made him look feral. "It will be a small affair, but I do so want us to be friends."

He departed, leaving me to the shadows.

Gods' will, he'd said.

I mulled over this throughout the night, bearing exhaustion I did not think was entirely mine. A great stained-glass window dedicated to Zia, and a passing comment on the gods' will. A nonreligious man did not make wayward comments about gods; only the devout did that, deities slipping into their tongue often without their realizing it. King Nicosia *had* revealed something to me, then. I just had to determine what exactly it meant, and how I might be able to use it.

Thoughts of religion took me back to Speth, to Sten's basement. The way he'd fallen to his knees at the sight of Renn whole and shimmering with unworldly light, the way he'd called him *gods-touched*, would remain sharp in my memory until my dying days. Gooseflesh rose on my arms when I thought of him muttering the ancient prophecy like a prayer: *When the kingdoms of men falter, the blood of the Allmaster shall rise up, garbed as an angel of fire, and balm its people as rain to the earth.*

Could Renn possibly be the Allmaster from legend? Whatever he was, he was *different*. Not just in light, but in movement, too. I'd watched him catch that arrow with his bare hand. Watched him cut a man in half with a single stroke of the sword. Those abilities were superhuman . . . and yet the more I mulled over it, the more confusing it all became. I had so little to go on. We'd been separated so quickly after his restoration.

Please, I tried to whisper through our heart connection, *please stay safe, Renn.*

I strengthened my heart and lumis wall in the morning before two servants and two guards came to retrieve me; one of the guards was a binder, and he moved my binding from the tree to himself, the leash short. They led me through the palace at a measured pace, allowing me time to look around. I drew the hallways on my palm with my index finger to help me memorize them. I noted things Nicosia had shown me before, like the gallery, and mouthed the names for things that were new, inventing new terms when I did not recognize what I saw—white salon, forgotten bedroom, teal lounging area, very square window. I noted the rugs, though many of them matched, and any art on walls or pedestals, or in alcoves. I counted doorways and stairs, and how many steps I took between each, hoping Ursa could somehow take note, too, or hear what I dared not give voice to. Two minds were better than one.

We were descending a set of winding stairs with a dark wood banister into some sort of reception hall when, while taking note of the oil paintings on the wall, I saw a ghost. A man crossing the room with a familiar pattern of baldness on his head, the red cincture of Alm around his waist. The angle of his shoulders, the pacing of his stride . . .

I would have halted on the stairs had the guard behind me not pushed me forward. He was a specter, he had to be, because I knew for a fact that this man was dead.

He had nearly passed out of my line of sight. Heart racing, desperate to know, I called out to him.

"Whitestone."

My gut sank as he turned around, seeking who had summoned him, showing me his face. My feet and hands went cold.

It was him, without a doubt. Wald Whitestone, the head physician at Rove Castle. The man who had been Renn's doctor all his life, until his dismissal.

The man who had tried to have me killed.

His eyes found mine, and like a ghost, his entire countenance washed white.

I could stare at him, gawk at him, for only a moment; the guard behind me forced me around the stairs and away from the physician who'd earned a death sentence for hiring an assassin to stab me. Who'd nearly stripped Renn of his healer.

How, then, did he walk these halls? *Sestan* halls?

My mind reeled, so much so that I could no longer take in my surroundings, note rooms, nor count steps. I could still feel the assassin's blade beneath my ribs. Renn had sent out men to find the killer and broadcast that the assassin had been captured, with the ruse that a confession was in the making. All of it was strategy to capture the man who'd hired my death. Sure enough, Wald Whitestone had taken the bait and fled, only to be arrested. He'd confessed and been executed. Renn told me he'd been executed.

Renn had no reason to lie to me, so something else was afoot here. Something I did not yet understand.

My retinue brought me to a wide room lit by a single grand chandelier hanging from a black-painted ceiling, illuminating seven marble statues depicting humanesque forms, each with a cincture around its waist: white, yellow, blue, green, red, violet, and gray. The gods, in order—Hem, Salm, Rolys, Evat, Alm, Zia, and another that was not part of the pantheon. Zia and this last one marked in gray were larger than the rest, something many might call blasphemy, for Hem was the god above all, not his forgotten and singular female descendant. As I stared at the last statue, I noted a triangle on the chin and suddenly recognized the likeness.

Adoel Nicosia. The Sestan king had included *himself* in his all-gods shrine, and he stood overlarge beside Zia. No—he had a couple of inches on the goddess.

My muscles felt tight. I had never been strongly religious, but even I gawked at such a display. Did he think himself so great as to be numbered among almighties?

I forced my eyes away, taking in dark wood paneling and blue carpet, elaborate wainscoting. A heavy scent of incense curled through the air. The shrine had been emptied of nearly all its furniture, minus a few chairs along the edges and narrow shelves near the door full of scriptures and other parchments. Only a few people occupied it, mostly guards or soldiers, ranks stitched to their collars in silver. The sight of Eden ahead, standing between Rolys and Evat, pushed my confusion into the corner of my mind; she wore an elegant burgundy gown so thickly stitched with silver it appeared more metallic than red. Against Canseren fashion, her hair had been curled and pinned. Her puffy eyes, red rimmed, spoke of hours of crying. Only minutes after I arrived, kept to the back of the chamber, did a man enter wearing a thick cincture of every color. A priest. He initiated the ceremony.

The wedding. The presence of Whitestone had made me forget entirely. I searched the room once more, checked the door, but the physician did not attend.

A chill wound its way through my veins as the priest recited his binding words, King Nicosia standing there with a smarmy tilt to his countenance, like a man eating bread while starving children on the street watched. Princess Eden did not look at him, but all he did was stare at her, *into* her, and I hugged myself realizing what this would mean, and what he would likely do to her. This was not a marriage arranged by noble parents for the better of a kingdom; this was the sacking of a daughter abducted from her home, her family murdered.

Did she still think she could sway him? By the way defeat cowed her, I thought not.

The priest's words were quick and to the point. He referred to Princess Eden by her full name, but when he gestured to the king, he used the term *Otsozia*. I silently formed the term on my lips, the word completely foreign to me. There was no hand wrapping, no songs, no placing of wedding stones as was custom in weddings . . . Canseren weddings, at least. The administrations finished in less than two minutes. When the priest sealed the union by naming the gods in order, King Nicosia grabbed a fistful of Princess Eden's hair and forced her lips roughly to his. She cradled her mouth when he pulled away, her teeth having cut her lip.

Cold fear curled up my spine, tempting old memories. He was going to hurt her. Now or tonight to unify them by religion and law. He was going to hurt her, and I had a sick feeling he was going to enjoy it.

I dared not reach out to her as she left the room, dared not speak. I could not embrace her even if I wanted to, not with the soulbinding gluing me to my guard. But for the briefest moment our eyes met. Hers glimmered with fear. I hoped mine did not. I prayed she saw something of strength, hope, or, at the least, understanding in that brief connection before the king well and truly broke her.

As she passed and my gaze fell away, it came again to one of the narrow shelves near the door, close enough my skirt brushed its corner.

I didn't really think of it. Had I asked the maid for a set of scriptures, she likely would have given me some. But in that moment, I needed to *do* something, however small. I needed to act. I needed to learn.

So while my guard murmured to his armored friend, I grabbed an old book off the shelf nearest to my hand level. Pretended to cough badly so I could bend over, lift my skirt, and hook the cover under my girdle. Did my best to conceal the shape with penitent hands clasped before me.

If the guard noticed, he didn't care, and I made it back to the conservatory without fanfare.

In the middle of the night, when the brazier light had died and the silvery shine of a half-moon between split clouds illuminated my chamber, I awoke suddenly, sure I heard a woman's scream echoing through the palace. Holding my breath, I listened, but only silence answered.

In the space between sleeping and waking, I felt Renn burn inside me.

It rippled outward from the center of my chest, like a fire-hot stone dropped into a shallow pool. It was pure and precious, fragile and distant, and I pressed both my hands between my breasts, holding it there, savoring the warmth of him.

It was love, unadulterated even by the miles and miles between us. While I couldn't possibly know for sure, in that moment I was certain he had pieced together this connection between us, and this thrum of adoration so early in the morning was very intentional.

I hadn't had the opportunity to explain to him the *how* of healing him. What I'd sacrificed to do so. Our connection must have been confusing to him, without those answers. But I would tell him as soon as I was able, should the gods give me the chance. How desperately I wanted to tell him. To look into the endless azure depths of his eyes, knit my fingers with his, and tell him everything. I wanted so desperately to hear his voice, to hear him murmur against my hair that all would be well, that he loved me, that we would see each other again.

How long would it take for me to forget the cadence of his speech?

I rose, the draft from the glass especially strong that morning. It frosted in triangular crystals along the window panels' edges, though the February clouds had receded and allowed Rolys's white sunlight to shine through, highlighting endless swathes of snow.

Every morning, before I did anything else, I recited the hallways and rooms of the palace, noting any details I could recall, then dowsed on myself. Two of the crystalline pieces of magic holding my heart together had turned watery, and I coaxed them solid again. Smoothed and firmed up their sides. I ran my hands over the three green pieces of my lumis left by Ursa, and wondered again, if I'd only had the knowledge, experience, and practice I had now, if perhaps I could have refortified myself from my injury the way I had with my heart, and Ursa needn't have sacrificed herself for me. Then again, I'd given of my heart freely; it hadn't been damaged. Whether or not that affected the magic, I might never know. Turning from that line of thought, I braided long nets of iron and fortified the wall around my lumis, enough so that, when I finished, I had to go back to sleep.

When I woke, the brazier was lit, this time for heat and not for light, but whichever servant had come in had not brought me a breakfast tray. I didn't change; I had only one shift and two dresses in my possession: the first dress I'd been abducted in. The second was Princess Eden's, given to me on the ship. I wore the first. I combed through my hair and rebraided it while quietly murmuring to Ursa, ever grateful for her stalwart company. We'd talked long and hard about Wald Whitestone, trying to sort out how he existed at all, let alone in Rodsfell. Perhaps he'd found a way to escape or bribed a guard to release him. Perhaps, like us, he had an identical twin, though I found that very unlikely. While there were two sets of twins in my family—Ursa and me, and then Heath and Pren—they were a rare occurrence, with identical even rarer. We combed through the possibilities until they grew absurd, and I knew picking at it would do no good, so I did my best to let it go.

After washing my face, I retrieved my contraband from beneath my thin pallet and turned it over in my hands. The scripture's spine was so worn I feared I'd dropped pages from beneath my skirt on my walk from the shrine to the conservatory. Holding it carefully, I flipped front to back, noting some pages nearly pulled from their binding, others crinkled with water damage. Flipped back to front, past the *Rulings of Alm*, *Wisdom of Priests*, *Marks of Hem*, and *Prophecies*. It wasn't anything in the pages that caught my eye, but the inside of the front cover.

A symbol had been burned into the leather, similar to a cursive *Z*, but with circles on either side of its unfinished tail.

I traced my hand over the marking. Wondered at it. Had this been gifted by someone who used a strange monogram instead of their name?

I heard footsteps just before the conservatory door opened, giving me barely enough time to shove the book beneath my blankets. King Nicosia entered, dressed simply in black save for his violet cincture. I waited for his retinue to follow, but no guard seemed to accompany him.

I should have been relieved, but the king's solitary arrival put me on edge. What was he planning?

In his hands he carried a silver breakfast tray—everything in Sesta was silver—and came over to my pallet, taking a pillow off it to sit upon.

It was meant to be an act of friendship, but I did not want Adoel Nicosia anywhere near my bed. I thought of Princess Eden in hers. Wondered how she'd fared the night. If someone like King Nicosia, who'd attacked innocent Canseren villages without honor or demand, would brutalize his unwilling wife, and whether or not he'd bother to heal her afterward.

He patted the pillow I'd slept on. "Come, Nym. I thought we'd have breakfast together today, privately. I can call you Nym, can I not?"

I didn't answer him. I hesitated only a breath before lowering myself onto the cushion, watching his face the entire time. Were he anyone else, I might have thought him a cheery, harmless man. But the war aside, this was the same man who had taken me against my will, chained me to a mastiff, and starved and drugged me on a ship. King Nicosia seemed to have many faces. This was merely one of them.

He gestured to the plate of food. "Eat, please."

I did. I never knew when or if he'd change his mind about feeding me, so I always ate the food. And if he poisoned me . . . I might be able to clear poison from my lumis in time to survive it. I also might simply pass away and keep all my secrets to myself.

I froze then, a piece of bread halfway to my mouth. *Renn.*

If putting half my heart in him made me feel his emotions and his injuries . . . would I feel his death, too? Would he *die* if I died?

I couldn't know for sure, but the theory only resolidified the fact that I could *never* allow the Sestan king into my lumis, nor my thoughts. If he saw the golden thread, if he pieced together my connection to Renn Noblewight, and if he learned what it meant, he could end this war in a single blow. Kill me, kill the Canseren king. Easy as that.

"Is it not to your liking?"

A shiver coursed through me. "Just thinking." I forced the bread into my mouth and forced myself to chew. It was marbled with a soft, savory cheese—perhaps the best thing I'd had since my abduction. If only I were in the mindset to enjoy it.

I considered questioning him about Whitestone, and yet I felt sure that I should keep anything I learned to myself. There was something here I did not understand, and I could not risk giving Nicosia even more of an upper hand.

"I want you to trust me, Nym." He reached over the tray to touch the back of my hand. In another time and place, I would think him flirting with me, but no, he flashed into my mind, trying to read me again. He pulled his hand away, masking his disappointment. "I want you to let me in."

"My thoughts are my own." I kept my voice level. Picked up a yellow pepper stuffed with thinly sliced pork.

"And yet it only makes me wonder what you're hiding."

I met his gaze. "I am twenty-five years old, Your Majesty. Do you think I've never borne an embarrassment, suffered a heartache, or nurtured a secret? Do you think nothing in my life might be personal or sacred?"

"Ah, but of course." He leaned back. "You don't understand mindreaders. You've probably never met one."

I thought of my brother, Dan.

"I can only see what you show me," he confessed. "Read what you're presently thinking. So if there is a past hurt you keep buried, or an insult you've wished to throw at me, I would only hear it if you actively thought it. You can protect the rest."

I didn't believe him. I reflected back on Dan in Fount, when he'd told me he was aware of my feelings for Renn. I was fairly certain I hadn't been actively thinking of my love for Renn when Dan touched me, but Renn was so often in my thoughts, I couldn't be sure. Dan needed only to brush my skin at one of those moments to hear the secret I myself had not wanted to admit.

I never told him I loved him.

Even my present thoughts were too dangerous.

"Tell me how you did it," King Nicosia pressed. "How you healed the broken prince."

I took my time chewing the pork and pepper. Swallowed. Kept my gaze on the tray. "You're very concerned with him. Did you know him?"

"Only briefly. But stories of him travel."

I shrugged. Thought to throw him a line, however flimsy. "I just *did*. It was luck more than anything. I've always enjoyed puzzles."

Ursa had always enjoyed puzzles.

He hummed deep in his throat. "I don't believe you. The prince was a mess, and Cansere doesn't train its crafters, even its healers. Only drafted them and hoped for the best. No schools, no coalitions, no apprenticeships or meetings. Were you Sestan, Nym, I might believe it was mere luck. But Queen Winvrin drafted healers for twenty years. It's my understanding that only you ever stayed within the castle walls."

I lifted my head. "But no Sestan healers were successful, either, were they?" The queen had sent for doctors and healers, foreign as well as national. I'd met one of them during my stay in Rove.

A shadow passed over the king's face, and at first I thought I'd offended him; his so-called trained crafters having failed to pass Queen

Winvrin's "test." But then another possibility rose to my mind. *Had* Sesta sent any healers to aid the queen's ailing son?

So you're the one who undid all my hard work, he'd told me. The work of keeping Sestan healers from aiding Cansere? Or was it more macabre than that? I dared not ask.

The aggression between Sesta and Cansere was recent; otherwise, we'd coexisted in peace. So either Sesta's training of healers was not what King Nicosia claimed it to be, or he never sent any aid to Cansere at all, not in twenty years of peace. My mind spun trying to find motivation for withholding aid, especially when the desperate queen would surely compensate for the effort. Perhaps there was a feud I didn't know about between the countries' rulers. Perhaps King Nicosia didn't *want* Renn healed . . . but why? Were he the heir, I might think it part of a long-formed plan to overthrow Cansere. But Renn was third in line. Adrinn would have been the target for his disdain, and then Eden, who would take the throne upon marriage. That, and Adoel Nicosia was not a young man. He could have asked for a betrothal to Princess Eden at any time to cement claim to his southern neighbor. Too many holes riddled that line of thought.

I wished I had heard more of his conversation with King Grejor when he'd come for "negotiations" months before. I wish I'd known what they'd said . . . then again, King Nicosia might have been as dodgy with the Noblewights as he was being with me.

Perhaps he did send healers, then, but only bad ones, or people posing as healers who did not know craftlock. By the way he hesitated at my question, I felt I'd touched on something important. One way or another, King Nicosia had not made an effort to heal the sick prince, even though it would form a stronger allyship between Sesta and Cansere.

The question still remained: *Why?*

"I don't think you understand me." He moved past the question as though it'd never been spoken. "This is precisely what fascinates me. You are untrained, unless your parents were healers?"

I shook my head. They hadn't been.

"And no other family, or townsfolk, taught you?"

"No." There was Ursa, but we'd learned our magic alongside one another, and I did not want her name on Adoel Nicosia's lips.

He snapped as though this was some great revelation. "Then there is something special about you. Something *different*, and I want to know what it is. The prince was broken beyond repair, and yet you healed him; I saw him that day, in that little town outside Rove."

"Speth," I supplied, and fought rising anger. *That little town* that he'd ransacked. *That little town* full of innocent people, screaming and running for their lives.

Lord Fell had valued my parents and sister at five silver merits each. What price, if any, would King Nicosia pay for us?

And yet something else about the comment irked me. "*You* are a powerful healer. Did you ever try to heal him yourself?"

His expression tightened ever so slightly. "No, I never had the chance."

I schooled my reaction. Shrugged and picked at the tray. "I just started at the beginning and worked my way up."

If he'd ever seen my lumis, he might believe me. But I couldn't show him, not now. A memory of what it *had* been, before Ursa, perhaps? But one slip and I feared I'd reveal everything I didn't want to. My life in Sesta would fare better with the king believing me an ally, but there were some things I dared not risk.

His mouth turned upward. He picked up the tray, though I hadn't finished, and stood. "There is a place for you here if you wish it, Miss Tallowax. Please consider that offer carefully."

Tray in hand, he strolled out of the conservatory, almost perfectly hiding the tension in his gait. I feared he was not happy with me.

I stared at the door even after he'd shut it. *You slipped again, Your Majesty.*

For he'd contradicted himself. Perhaps he'd realized it, and thus the stiffness of his stride. Either way, he'd given me more information, information I carefully tucked and folded and kept for myself.

He claimed he'd never had the opportunity to heal Renn. In twenty years, he'd never had the chance. And yet earlier in our conversation, he mentioned meeting the Canseren king only briefly. *Only briefly.*

I, too, had met him only briefly upon my first healing of him. It took only a simple touch. Surely if the Sestan king had been in the room with a sick child, he would have tried. The queen would have asked. He certainly could have offered when he arrived unannounced to Rove. That, and Renn had been ill since shortly after his birth; there was very little window for Adoel Nicosia to have met him when he was hale. Something of the king's story did not add up. He was so desperate to see what I was hiding, he'd begun to fail at keeping his own secrets.

I just had to figure out what they were.

Chapter 4

The king didn't deign to see me for a week. Only the two servants assigned to me came, tight-lipped, delivering my meals and taking away my trays. I wasn't sure if King Nicosia's absence was another tactic to get me to speak my secrets, or if his duties kept him away.

I wondered if it had anything to do with Renn. I felt constant spikes of valor from him, of excitement and fear, as though he were in battle, followed by victory, or sadness, or even despair. I tried to reassure him as best I could, but his emotions were so up and down, I was sure they drowned mine out.

One of the days, I spied soldiers moving off the palace grounds, my cheek pressed to the glass wall of the conservatory. The barracks were to the west, not visible from this vantage, but I saw more men in Sestan military uniform than usual, riding on horses, making deliveries, preparing to march. They were mobilizing, which meant something was happening in the south. But was Cansere striking back, or was Sesta pushing in? Had Renn mobilized his forces, or had he been in hiding this entire time, and I'd misread him completely?

All the while I built up the wall in my lumis, stronger and stronger, thicker and thicker. My newest layer was a puzzle, each piece twisting and linked. Ursa's idea. When my efforts exhausted me, I either slept or thumbed through my stolen book of scripture, guided by Ursa, who knew the words far better than I did.

It was in *Marks of Hem* that something finally caught my interest: a lineage of the gods, which is repeated at the beginning of every new section. But in this one, it read *The greatest Hem, to Salm, otso-Hem, to Rolys, otso-Salm, to Evat—*

I sat up straighter and read it aloud to Ursa. "They used this term at the wedding. *Otso.* But it was *otso-Zia.*"

It seemed to be a prefix from an older form of our tongue. I read the paragraph again, as though I might understand something new from it, but the meaning was clear.

Otso. Son of, or descendant of. And the priest had called King Nicosia *otso-Zia.*

Son of Zia?

I thought of the stained-glass image of Nicosia beside the goddess and the gods-touched legend, and again of his likeness included with others in the all-gods shrine.

Air left my lungs. Surely this man didn't count himself *among the gods*, did he?

It is not an empire of land I seek, he'd told me.

I felt Renn's awareness down our link, as though he'd looked over my shoulder and asked what had troubled me.

All of it did. And with this, I no longer had any expectations of what would come next.

I was at the mercy of a madman.

At the end of that week, King Nicosia finally returned as the sun set, casting the sky in dusty shades of rose and mauve. He came alone again, though I thought I glimpsed a guard in the narrow hallway leading to the door. He didn't carry a tray, or a puzzle, or anything else. Just him, a black wardrobe, his violet cincture poking out above a belt with something swinging off its side. He walked straight for me, his face holding a similar focus to mindreading, though he wasn't in my mind, not yet. He had to touch me first to even try.

"I tried using magic, Nym." The cool flatness in his voice had me on my feet before my mind understood the situation. "I tried using magic, I tried being tough, and I tried to be kind. None of it seems to be working. So we're going to try something else." He unsheathed a short truncheon from his belt and gripped it tightly in his bare hand, then smacked it against the open palm of his other.

Cold fear sluiced over me like a January rain. I stepped back from the tree. Memories of Ford rushed up all at once—his fist to the side of my head, his hand against my windpipe. I retreated another step, and another. "Please, don't." It came out barely more than a whisper.

King Nicosia reached the Egroran. He pressed his hand against it, and suddenly I couldn't retreat any farther; he'd shortened my soulbinding, forbidding me from putting more than a few paces between myself and the tree. "If it is so simple, you would not hide it." He stepped away from the trunk and neared me, prowling like a wolf. "No peasant is so loyal. So I'll ask one more time, Nym. How did you heal the Canseren prince?"

I swallowed, but my spit stuck in my throat. I tried to brace myself, because I knew this was going to hurt, and badly. I was a healer, but I couldn't prevent injury, only balm it. Perhaps if I stayed focused, stayed inside my lumis, I could repair it as it cracked—as the pieces of me loosened and fell. Maybe the fixing would distract me from the breaking.

My stomach clenched. *Renn is going to feel it, too.*

I couldn't stop it. I wouldn't stop it. If I told him, he'd sort out the connection. He'd hurt me to hurt him. Right now, he was only hurting me to get answers. If that didn't work . . . maybe he'd move on to another plan. But I couldn't tell him.

Knowing he wouldn't allow me to put him off any longer, I tried to hide the quiver in my voice when I replied, "He's a king, now."

Adoel Nicosia launched at me. I dropped to the floor, knees to my chest, arms over my head, and leapt into my lumis, through the black wall and to the gold-threaded merlon, throwing myself around it to protect it.

"I'm here, Nym!" Ursa cried. *"I'm here. Just focus on me. Focus on me!"*

I wondered if Princess Eden could hear my screams the way I'd heard hers.

They did nothing to stall the Sestan king's hand.

I woke in front of the window. Morning. Of the next day, surely. I'd healed most of the damage, but there was so much, I'd passed out repairing myself. I hissed as I sat up, bones aching from the hard floor, bruises thumping with my pulse. I dowsed on myself and mended the rest of the breaks until the pain ebbed, but memory of it stuck in my mind. I shuddered, and then I cried.

Worry blossomed in my chest.

"I'm sorry," I whispered to Renn, despite knowing he couldn't hear me. "I'm sorry, I'm sorry."

"I can't feel it, Nym. Please stop apologizing."

Ursa misunderstood me, but I didn't mind. Ursa rarely spoke to me in the presence of others, but she had been there through all of it, crying alongside me, murmuring stories in my head. They'd failed to distract me, but the effort comforted me now. Not a bruise or bump marred my skin, so why did I still feel each and every one of them?

"Maybe we can give him what he wants," Ursa offered. *"Or let him think we are. If we figure it out now, if we practice, maybe it will work."*

If Adoel Nicosia had been truthful in only being able to mindread active thoughts, perhaps we had a plan.

I heard footsteps outside the conservatory the following afternoon, hating the whimper that escaped my throat as the door opened. I wanted to be brave. I wanted to be unshakable.

I was not.

The king again, this time with a folded strap of leather in his hand. I fled as far as my leash would allow; he approached as far as the tree. "Tell me what I need to know, Nym."

Tears brimmed on my eyes. "I-I already told you."

"This game again?" he asked, and charged for me.

"STOP!" I screamed, hugging myself. The secondary worry in my chest increased—my spike of fear had surely crossed the strait to Renn. I wished I could shield him from this. I prayed he was somewhere where the beating wouldn't hurt him too badly. Where enemies wouldn't hear him cry out or see him falter and take advantage. "Please, here." I gave Nicosia my hand.

Lowering the strap, a suspicious frown weighing down his face, the king seized my fingers. I focused, burrowing the tiniest hole in my wall, shepherding through a slew of practiced thoughts. I aimed for sympathy. I let him see my long journey to Rove, my indignation over it. The draft letter, the queen's dismissiveness. I skipped ahead and showed my exhaustion every night. The complaint about my smell and the coarse way Queen Winvrin had ordered me washed like a plow horse. I showed him the servant Torr and the plague that killed him, my own body succumbing to it. I showed Prince Adrinn shoving me up against a wall. I showed myself standing in Renn's broken lumis feeling utterly helpless, trying to thread together shards of colored glass.

Then, in hopes of earning his pity, I showed him the death of my parents. Lord Fell handing me a purse of fifteen silver merits, as though that would help me and my seven siblings get by. I showed him Vin breaking off our engagement, leaving me because I'd become too much of a burden. I showed Ford getting caught in his lies and pinning me to my bed while my brothers worked the fields. I even let him see my dead daughter in my arms.

And then I shut the crack entirely, pushing magic into my lumis to close the wall, refortify it, turn it, until the opening was undecipherable from anything else.

I came back to myself. Blinked. "That's all there is." My voice was rushed, breathy. "They got tired of waiting. I sat in that glass pile day after day, treated like a slave, desperately trying to piece it together so I could go home. Please, *please* don't do this."

King Nicosia's green eyes were so dark, not even light from the window reflected in them. "Do you think I'm a fool? You've told me nothing!"

With a bare fist, he punched me low in the gut, hard enough to expel my air. Had I been pregnant, it would have been a killing blow.

"Run, Nym!"

I stumbled two paces before my leash jerked me back. King Nicosia grabbed me by the shoulder and threw me to the floor, my head knocking hard against the tile, my lungs still gasping for lost air. He mounted me and seized my wrists, pinning me down. He was larger than me, heavier. I couldn't fight him. Cold, dark panic surged through me, nearly incapacitating me.

Ursa called out, bringing me to my senses. Nicosia restrained my wrists. Skin to skin.

I dowsed.

My consciousness fled the conservatory and warped me before the black wall of his lumis, built erect and tall, textured and straight. It hid his truth, his death lines, his weaknesses.

Pulling on everything I had and everything Ursa had gifted me, I launched at the wall, sucking sharp magic into my ethereal form and shoving it into the black stone. It flaked under my touch, delicate pieces whipping away like the black were a burnt log and not stone at all. I formed a drill in my mind, pointed and twisting. Pierced through, enough to see—

His lumis was icy, like Kilg's, one of the servants at Rove Castle. Three great sculptures of ice, geometric and massive, came to a central point overhead, like a great tent—

The vision tore from me as reality seized me by the throat and threw me back into the conservatory. I rolled across the tile, a new bruise on my cheek.

"Don't you *dare*." He snatched the leather strap off the floor.

Curling into myself, I reached for Ursa, and she sang to me until King Nicosia grew tired in his administrations and left me to clean up his mess.

Later that night, after I'd healed my hurts, after drowning in the thorns of Renn's guilt and grief, I cried ugly, sobbing cries until not a single tear could be wrenched from my swollen face. Then I lay beneath the Egroran and considered my newest piece of gleaned information.

Adoel Nicosia did not want me in his lumis.

It made sense, of course. Healers could hurt just as they could heal. Nicosia did not know I would see the lines marking how to swiftly kill him, but that didn't matter. If I touched him, I could hurt him, just as he hurt me.

I'd noticed nothing out of the ordinary in his great ice sculptures. Hadn't had a chance to notice or follow his death lines. Unable to touch the windows, I breathed air onto cold tile and drew the sculptures as I remembered them there, trying to find something odd, like the shadow of death, or pieces from another person, pieces made solely of magic, or perhaps a gold thread linking him to another. But there was none of that. *My* lumis had grown to be eccentric. His was not.

"There was something familiar about it," I breathed, barely a whisper. "Like I've been there before."

"It was like Kilg's."

"I felt it before," I murmured, "on the ship. Before I broke through the wall."

"He copied your defenses."

I shook my head, trying to breathe through a distant sense of panic I thought was Renn's, but perhaps it belonged to me. It certainly suited the situation. "No, it was something else. Like I'd been there before."

Yet I knew without a doubt I had never healed Adoel Nicosia.

I dowsed into my lumis, slipping past its walls to stare at the crenellated puzzle of myself. Absently pushed magic into my heart blocks. Ran my hand over the ones tied up in golden string, stopping on one of the green pieces that had come from Ursa, when she'd healed me after the carriage accident.

I deflated as an achy pain rose in my chest—pain that wasn't reflected in my lumis, but seeped from Renn. I absently massaged it, staring at those green blocks. It took me a few seconds before a new thought burst into my mind like the first dawn of summer. I shifted back to reality and sat up.

"I know that feeling," I whispered.

"What?"

"Why it feels familiar. Dowsing on Nicosia is like dowsing on our siblings." I scooted back and leaned against the Egroran. "There's a likeness there." Even though our lumie were wildly different. "That's what I felt inside him."

Ursa took a beat to respond. *"So the king of Sesta is our brother?"*

I snorted, then frowned. "Hardly. There's no possible way we could share even a drop of blood, I'm sure." I drummed my fingers on the floor, trying to think of possibilities, but nothing came to mind. "Anything?"

"No."

I sighed, forming my hands into fists. Considered again the geometric ice sculptures. I felt like I was still there, in a room of ice, the way the draft of the window cascaded over me. I couldn't light the brazier; it had run out of fuel. No one had brought more, and since Nicosia's first beating, I'd only been given a single bowl of thin soup. I opened and closed my hands, then brought them up to my face and repeated the gesture.

"I worry I did something wrong."

"What?"

I steadied myself with a deep breath. "What if it gets worse, Ursa? What if I showed him too much of my magic? What if he senses something off about me?"

"You had to defend yourself."

I drew in a shaky breath. "I . . . I don't think I can do this. I've always thought *I can survive this. It could be worse.* But I . . . I don't think I can if it gets much worse than this."

I thought of my dead baby in my arms, and my heart squeezed. *Please, gods, don't let it get worse than that.*

"He needs you," she reassured me. *"He won't kill you, Nym."*

But the question was, How much longer could I endure living?

I started shaking the next day when Nicosia returned.

"Do you have nothing better to do than hurt an innocent woman?" I asked him. I wanted to shout, but it came out like a kitten's mew. "Do you not have a kingdom to run, a war to win?"

He advanced. Tripped over my pallet and exposed the scriptures lying there. He merely glanced at them, uncaring, and continued forward, a self-proclaimed god.

I backed away. "Does that violet cincture mean *nothing* to you?!"

A twitch of anger at his left eye. He touched the tree and shortened my leash until I slammed up against it.

"You're as stubborn as Alarna," he hissed under his breath. "If you will not tell me, I will take it."

He grabbed me around the throat and dove into my lumis. I followed him there, then staggered with nausea as he began beating at my erected wall, just as I had done to his yesterday. He formed blades and hammers of magic, shucking off layers of braids and knots and basalt. The wall was not *me*, but I had built it, and every blow hurt in a way that felt viscerally wrong. I heard myself screaming far away. Forced myself to agonizing reality before taking the two-way bridge to him again.

I hurt him back.

With Ursa's strength, I slammed into his wall harder than he could hit mine. I sacrificed physical strength for magical power and thrashed at the wall until it cracked. Then, forming magic like water, I poured it into the cracks and let it freeze as ice, hardening and expanding until a huge chunk of the wall collapsed at my feet.

I ran to the far side of his lumis, searching the pillars, memorizing them. Ice, ice, and more ice. The three converged at their highest point, like three priests about to coronate a king. I had to find death lines marking his weakest spots—

Death lines—

Why couldn't I see the king's death lines?

Look harder. I squinted. Conjured magic like light around me to illuminate the sculptures. They were there, barely, but wispy, almost like Renn's had been.

Was the King of Dragons unkillable?

I ran for the closest sculpture. It didn't matter. I had to fight back. I had to *get out of here.*

My knees buckled before I could reach it, sending me to the lumis floor. I tasted blood in my mouth. Heaving, I crawled forward and touched the first sculpture, trying to reach its base—

Nicosia broke contact, sending me reeling back into reality. I touched it for only a moment before surging back into my own lumis, repairing the wall he had failed to break through.

"HOW?" he screamed at me, picking me up by my hair and slamming me into the tree. "How do you break it so quickly? What power is this?!"

I did not answer. I dropped to the floor, knees to my chest, hands protecting my head.

I don't even know what he beat me with, this time.

I never bothered to look.

Chapter 5

In my lumis, I soothed another crack on one of my merlons. It reappeared often—a pain in my spine and neck I couldn't relieve otherwise. Nicosia had pinned me to the Egroran, having shortened the soulbinding until it was no longer than a babe's little finger. I stood against that tree, feet barely able to touch the tile limning the aperture, and could not move from it, even to turn around. My head had to tilt to one side to make space for one of its great boughs.

Renn's distress through the bond had become so steadily constant it had begun to feel like another part of me. As though it had always been there. Like peace was a thing of fairy tales.

I tried not to think about the tree and the pain, which was why I lingered behind the basalt dome with Ursa. I didn't know what I'd do without her consistent, subtle presence. Surely Nicosia would have broken me by now, were I truly alone.

Alone. I looked over at the gold threading around my heart.

"Who do you think she is?" I asked, pushing at my ethereal cuticles. "Alarna?"

It was a Sestan name, one Nicosia had let slip in his frustration. I didn't know if it meant anything, but I ate up any crumb the cruel king gave me.

"Another prisoner, maybe," the green blocks replied. *"Another wife?"*

I shook my head, unsure. It seemed like a dead end.

My eyes slid from Ursa's blocks to the golden, vining tendrils. They glowed with a light all their own, separate from me and my magic.

Gods-touched, Sten had murmured.

I blinked away tears. I couldn't quite remember what Renn had looked like in that basement, after I woke from my craft-induced exhaustion. I kept picturing him in his Noblewight livery, but he'd been wearing something else, hadn't he?

Why couldn't I remember him?

"We've already accomplished so much." Ursa's bodiless voice emanated from the three green pieces of her in my lumis. *"This won't be the end."*

Accomplished so much. Like keeping our family together after such loss. Like mending broken hearts. Like surviving rape. Like healing Renn. Ursa and the bees had inspired me, then. I'd broken down the months of hard work I'd made in his lumis and reshaped it to look like my own, so it might take the donation of my heart, the way mine had taken pieces of my twin sister. Ursa and I had matched perfectly, physically. Renn and I had matched, temporarily, in our lumie.

A cold feeling washed over me so suddenly, I thought for a moment it had come from the conservatory, or from Renn. But no, the horror of it was my own. It crept across my scalp and between each bump of my spine, across to my fingernails and into the soles of my feet.

"Ursa," I whispered. "That's what it is."

"What?"

"Why Nicosia's lumis felt so familiar. Like I'd seen it before. Like he was a sibling."

"What, Nym?"

I swallowed. "It didn't feel like a Tallowax. It felt like Renn's."

I didn't understand it, and Ursa had no insights, either.

When Nicosia returned two days later, I watched him closely. The way he moved, the angles of his face, the darkness in his eyes. Did I see traces of Renn there, or was it only my imagination? And yet *how* would such a thing be possible?

I didn't know. And I didn't have enough information to parse it out. Yet their wispy death lines were similar, too.

"I have lived twice as long as you." Nicosia paced on the other side of the tree like a caged animal. "I have trained harder and longer. I have studied and mastered every element of craftlock. I've had teachers, mentors, libraries, where you have had nothing. So tell me, Nym Tallowax." He stopped a pace in front of me, his gaze narrowing on my face. "Why is it one magical blow from you does more damage in my lumis than two of mine in yours?"

Ursa remained silent, and so did I.

Nicosia's left eye twitched at my stubbornness. But I would not give him Ursa, and I would not give him Renn.

Some small, buried part of me took pleasure in his mounting frustration. The rest of me feared him.

He sighed. "I tire of this, Nym." He reached for my neck, as though he would dowse, then paused, thinking better of it.

Instead, he slipped off his belt. I took some solace in knowing he wouldn't hurt me as Ford had—he couldn't do that without touching me. But he could still hurt me, and he would.

Guilt threaded from the other side of my link with Renn. Guilt, fear, and horror.

I'm so sorry, Renn. If I could spare him from this, I would. If I could take the beatings twice and keep him from the pain, I would, and gladly.

However, the first blow didn't come. Nicosia wrung the long strip of leather in his hands, glaring at me, posture tight. Then he did something perhaps more terrible than striking me.

He smiled.

"I think I know how to get through to you, Nym. It will delight me to do it, but I'll stay my hand if you *tell me*."

I pressed my lips together, hard enough to make my cheeks hurt.

The vein on his forehead pulsed. "Very well."

He left, off to find some other form of torture that might finally break me.

The army was mobilizing.

I could hear it through the walls of the conservatory, the glass. Knew it from Nicosia's absences, though he sent a soldier to carry out my interrogation in his stead, once. Everything seemed too loud and rushed. Surely Cansere had pulled its military to strike, thus inciting this frenzy. Or, perhaps, Nicosia had lost his patience and sought to ransack the entirety of my homeland.

I worried for Brien, my closest living sibling in age. He'd been drafted to the Canseren army the same week I'd been conscripted to Rove Castle. No letters from him, no word, as far as I knew. I had no idea whether my brother even lived, or if he'd been killed in a skirmish before Sesta ever attacked Rove. I might never know. But if he did live, would he be facing these mobilizing dragons?

I would ask Nicosia about the war when he came again. Whether or not he'd answer was another question. He owed me nothing. Then again, he might enjoy gloating.

And yet, on the fortieth day since Nicosia took me from Speth, he rendered me speechless.

This time, he brought Princess Eden with him, flanked by two enormous mastiffs.

I hadn't seen her since her hoax of a wedding. The princess had always been thin. Lithe, like a dancer. But now she looked gaunt, her eyes and cheeks sunken, a shadow of herself. Her hair, pinned up in Sestan fashion, had loosened from its bindings. Like she had fought him. Or he had hurt her, again.

"Your loyalty is most impressive." Nicosia fumed like an overheated kettle. He threw his wife to the floor. The princess's hands were bound, so she was unable to catch herself. I winced as she struck the tile, then remembered myself and schooled my face. "So if I can't extract answers from your flesh, perhaps I can extract them from hers."

I ground my teeth together. This was pointless. Princess Eden knew nothing. She never participated in my dowsing sessions—

Oh.

My limbs lost their strength, and yet somehow I still stood.

If Nicosia could not hurt me physically, he would hurt me emotionally. Use my loyalty to the Canseren crown against me.

"Don't," the princess pleaded. Not to him, but to me. She looked at me, desperate, until Nicosia's boot pressed between her shoulder blades and forced her face to the floor. The dogs watched almost lifelessly. Their masters had trained the very souls out of them.

She knew Renn was alive and whole. Nicosia must have already asked Princess Eden what she knew, which was, of course, nothing. The princess had been taken before I fled Rove. Before I'd given Renn my heart.

That felt like a lifetime ago.

Nicosia pulled out his truncheon. He stayed near the door, where my presently eight-foot leash would not be able to reach. "She can't heal, like you," he gloated. "She won't last long. Will you risk it, Nym?"

Rage reddened my vision.

"I'll make a deal with you," he offered, toying with the truncheon. "You tell me just *one* thing I want to know, and I'll spare her. How you healed Renn Noblewight, or where your power comes from. Your choice. But"—he pointed the truncheon at me, eyes narrowing—"do not lie to me, Nym. I know when you're lying. Tell me it was hard work, or you were born with it, and I'll rip her head off. Do you understand?"

"Are you serious?" I half shouted the words, my voice rough. "Do you have any conscience at all? She is your *wife*. Kill her, and your claim to Cansere is moot!"

The damnable villain smiled.

The air became too warm, too thick. "She's to be the mother of your children. She could be carrying your heir right now—"

He laughed. I hid my hands behind my back so he wouldn't see how tightly I clenched my fists.

"Do you think I *want* an heir, stupid girl?" the king asked through his mirth. "Why do you think none walk these halls, as you yourself so adeptly pointed out?"

The heat of rage gave way to the shock of ice. Surely he hadn't . . . but that would be infanticide. Unless he merely killed their mothers before they could give birth.

Then why does his lumis feel so much like Renn's?

The thought was so immediate I almost mistook it for Ursa.

He readied the truncheon and looked at me, expectantly.

"Don't," Princess Eden sobbed to the marble tile.

I wouldn't. I did not want to watch this kind, innocent woman be hurt, but I knew speaking now would make all this suffering for naught. It would spare Princess Eden for a moment, but doing so would damn Renn. Nicosia would kill all three of us, instead of just the two of us. Or he'd find a way to Ursa, or hurt others, maybe siblings he had, trying to mimic her added strength. Only a fool would think the mad Sestan king would let us walk free after I gave him the secrets he so desperately sought.

So I dropped to my knees as though I were the one about to receive the beating, arms over my head.

In truth, it was to drown out the sounds of the king's brutality.

Were it not for the king's gods-forsaken war, he might have really murdered Princess Eden right in front of me.

As it was, there was some issue with the troops, some missive sent to Rodsfell, for a soldier with four silver lines on his collar came into the room, barely passing the two of us a glance. Whatever the message, it pulled Nicosia's attention entirely. He left with one of the mastiffs, leaving me soulbound to his sacred tree, and Eden bound to the remaining dog.

Eden, like a broken marionette on the floor.

I moved as close to her as the soulbinding would allow. The mastiff growled in turn.

"Your Majesty," I murmured, afraid raising my voice would call back the king. "Reach out to me. I can heal you if you touch me."

Her only movement was the rapid rise and fall of her chest. Her breaths were too short. She had several broken ribs.

"Eden," I said a little louder. "Eden, let me help you." I worried she bled internally, where the skin didn't show it. Even with Nicosia gone, she could still die. *"Eden."*

A soft whimper passed her lips.

"He's gone. He's gone, for now. I need you to reach out to me." I lay on the floor and stretched my arm toward her, leaving about two paces between us. Looking at the mastiff, I said, "Come here and bite me, you ugly monster."

If I could get the dog to move, Eden would move, too.

The mastiff growled.

"Gods dammit, Eden!" I shouted. "Is this really where you want to die? In Rodsfell? By *his* hands? Move!"

"She's too hurt," Ursa started—

But Eden ticked. A quiver of a shoulder. She tried to lift her head, but it dropped again. "B-Broken," she whispered.

"I know, I know. Just a little closer. Stretch your hand to me. Or a foot. I just need to touch you. I'll make it go away."

A sharp intake of breath gave away her tears. "No, you can't."

"Eden."

She shifted, straining toward me. Tried to inch forward with her legs, then gasped and fell limp again.

I clicked my tongue at the dog. "Here, boy. Come here." I made a crude gesture at it. "Fight! Attack! Sic!"

The mastiff glared at me.

A deep, guttural groan emanated from the princess as she dug an elbow into the white tile and pushed herself a little closer, a little closer. Reached out. I stretched, willing the soulbond to extend, but it wasn't enough.

"Again, Eden," I pleaded. "Try again."

She began to cry.

"You're stronger than he knows." I kept my hand out, willing her toward it. "Show him how strong you are."

She tried again, collapsed.

I set my jaw. "If Renn can do it, so can you. Eden, just a little farther!"

Crying out, she dug her elbow in and propelled herself just enough that our fingertips touched.

My consciousness glided into her lumis. It took me a moment to orient myself. Princess Eden's lumis was less visual and more auditory, a symphony of music playing out of harmony. Each part flowed around me like smoke in colors of green and yellow. I'd never dowsed on a lumis like hers before, but when I pulled on the magic, I began to make sense of it. Found the most discordant notes and coaxed them higher and lower until harmony sang again. So many of them—endless abrasions and bruises, bleeds and breaks. Yet even this was not as overwhelming as Renn's had been. This I could manage.

Once I'd corrected the major issues, I followed each individual melody, smoothing it out, adjusting its beat, tuning it with magic, before moving on to the next. I was so focused I didn't know how much time passed. But when I fell back to reality, neither Nicosia nor his lackeys had returned. Eden pushed herself up and began unpinning the nest of her hair.

That familiarity I felt with my siblings, that I'd felt between Nicosia and Renn, hadn't been present in her lumis. Come to think of it, I hadn't sensed anything in Prince Adrinn's, either, and I'd dowsed on him thrice.

"Thank you." Her fingers trembled as she worked.

"I'm so sorry, Eden."

She shook her head, lips straining to keep the sobs at bay. It was one thing to tell me not to give in to Nicosia's demands; it was another to experience the consequences.

We stayed like that for a quarter hour before she spoke.

"Where did he go?" She sounded like a mouse.

She'd been too hurt to notice the messenger. "Called away to war. I don't know how long we have."

She swallowed. Nodded. "Any amount of time is a gift. I . . . I haven't spoken to anyone. He doesn't . . . he doesn't let me speak to anyone but him."

Silence fell between us. The mastiff's dark eyes remained locked on me. Thorny guilt laced with sorrow threaded through me—Renn, somewhere, sad again. Or perhaps sad for me, and what he felt transpiring here.

Throat tight, I said, "While we have the time . . . I'll listen to you, Eden. Anything you want to say. I wish I could do more for you, but he's bound me to this tree." I gestured weakly to it. "But I can listen."

A chuckle, or perhaps a short sob, clicked up her throat. "And what could I possibly say?"

It took me a moment to steel myself, to ensure my words would be even when I spoke. "It gets quieter. That voice inside you that's always screaming, even when you sleep. In time, it gets quieter."

She went very still.

"It feels like it never will," I went on, staring at the wrinkles in my skirt, "but it does. You'll be trapped in those moments for a long time, but the world moves on, and eventually you'll start to move with it. It won't seem like it, at first. You'll be standing in the middle of summer and still feel the cold."

I felt her eyes on me, so I met them. Offered . . . not a smile, but something that might assure her.

"It happened to you, too, didn't it?" she asked.

I dipped my head. "Almost five years ago, now. But he left, after. I wasn't trapped in it, like you are."

She hugged herself. "I . . . can't stand them touching me. Not just Adoel. All of them. The servants, even the kind ones. Their touch feels like lightning."

"And nothing feels real," I supplied. "Everything is a play, and you just recite your lines, do your part. And you keep looking out into the audience, pleading for someone, anyone, to come onstage to protect you, but no one knows, and they wouldn't understand if they did, and the curtain never closes, forcing you to stay beneath the weight of their stares."

Tears fell down her cheeks. Pinching her lips together, she nodded.

"Eden." I lowered my voice so even the dog wouldn't hear me. "We are going to get out of this. Somehow, some way. One of us will find a weakness in him or in this damnable palace, or Renn will build an army and rescue us, or the gods themselves will rage against Sesta for the injustices done here."

She didn't seem to hear me. "He said something strange to me, the first time."

The hairs on my neck stood on end. "Nicosia?"

She swallowed. "He said, *If you ever see your brother again, tell him exactly what I did to you.*"

Rage nearly choked me, but I tamped it down. "Then it *is* personal."

She regarded me, eyes shining.

"Everything comes down to Renn. Nicosia comes in here nearly every damn day and . . . asks . . . me about Renn. How I cured him. He says he's never met him, and yet also has. But why go mad over the baby, and not the eldest? Why Renn, and not Adrinn?"

New tears spilled over Eden's cheeks. "Adrinn is dead."

"I know." I reached for her, but the soulbinding kept me back. But Eden grabbed my hand, our fingers linking for just a moment, before letting go, the mastiff growling the whole while.

"I know, I . . . I was there. I tried to heal him, but it was too late." I swallowed against a sore lump sticking in my throat like a burr. I hadn't liked Prince Adrinn; he'd been a cad more often than not. But Renn and Eden had loved him. He'd died protecting the castle. "He fought to the end. He died nobly."

She drew in a shuddering breath and wiped her eyes on her sleeve. "Thank you," she whispered.

"Eden . . ." I eyed the door. Now was not the right time, but I doubted we'd get another opportunity like this. I had to push forward, however fragile the princess was. "How soon after Queen Winvrin and your father married was Renn born?"

She sniffed. Adjusted her position on the floor. "I was so young, but not long. He was born early, one of the reasons he's been so sick." Hope flickered. "Did you really heal him? Completely?"

I nodded. "I did. At least, I think I did. I don't know . . . Nicosia found me shortly after."

Her expression darkened.

"Renn said he fell ill *after* his birth. Before his first birthday."

She considered a moment. "I think that's right, yes."

I chewed the inside of my cheek, judging my next question. "Eden, I don't mean to pressure you more, but—"

"We've so little time." The large window caught her attention; I wondered if this was her first time here, or if she'd been given a tour, too. "Just ask."

I exhaled slowly. "Are you entirely sure Renn is Grejor's son?"

I surprised her. She startled like I'd pricked her with a needle. "What?"

"I've spent a lot of time in his lumis," I went on. "And I've glimpsed Nicosia's as well. They felt . . . similar to each other. Possibly . . . familial."

Her brow furrowed. "No . . . no, he's a Noblewight."

"Of course." I leaned back. "Of course. I didn't mean to upset you."

She laughed. It sounded cruel. "This is the least upsetting thing I've experienced these past weeks, Miss Tallowax."

"Nym, please."

She simply nodded.

I pushed my luck. As Eden had pointed out, I didn't know when I'd get another chance. I had to learn anything she knew while I could. "Have you seen Whitestone?"

Her delicate brows furrowed. "Wald Whitestone? The physician?"

I nodded.

"I thought you knew . . . he was executed."

I shook my head. "I saw him, here. When they brought me to your . . . wedding. I saw him, and I called out to him. He looked right at me, Eden."

Her features slackened. "I . . . I don't know how. He was executed. Privately, of course, given his station."

Sensing a dead end, I switched to another subject. "Do you know who Alarna is?"

The princess's breath caught. "How do you know that name?"

Her reaction, as though the name were familiar, bolstered me. "Nicosia used it, when . . ." I shuddered. "He let it slip."

Lifting a shaking hand, Eden bit her first knuckle. Considered for a moment. "Adrinn."

"Alarna is Adrinn?"

She shook her head. "No, he . . . he'd been suspicious of our stepmother for some time. Found something that didn't settle well with him—he didn't tell me exactly how. He thought she might have been a spy."

Wait . . . Alarna was *Queen Winvrin*? Or had I heard wrong?

A chill ran through me as I remembered the eldest prince pinning me against my bedroom wall, knife to my throat, accusing me of the very same thing.

"He said she was Sestan." Her voice had dwindled to nearly nothing. "That she'd been born Alarna . . . something. I can't remember the surname. But she had Canseren papers. Perfect Canseren papers, signed by . . ."

She squirmed, obviously uncomfortable with the revelation, but I pressed. "Signed by who?"

She licked her lips. "Signed by my father."

My shoulders slumped. "He knew?"

"I don't *know*." New tears brimmed on her eyelashes. "Gods help me, I don't know. Adrinn could never prove anything, but Hem knew he tried."

I thought of the snippet of argument between the queen and heir I'd overheard in King Grejor's rooms. Thought of the wound Prince Adrinn had asked me to heal in secrecy. Was this what he'd been hiding? Sleuthing after the faithfulness of his stepmother?

But that meant Winvrin and Nicosia knew each other, beyond what would be expected of neighboring monarchs. Nicosia knew her Sestan name. And the queen . . . she'd been so put out, so afraid, when Nicosia arrived unexpectedly at Rove. So afraid that she'd sent Renn down into the tunnel, where the Sestan king couldn't reach him.

Do you not realize what he is?! she'd asked me in a moment of frustration, when Renn had relapsed.

Gods above, she knew. She had to have known. She'd been so desperate to find him a cure—

Gods-touched.

"She was friends with Whitestone," she added, tracing the lines of her knuckles with a fingernail. "Winvrin. Perhaps she was tied to that, too."

I scoffed. "But why? The queen and I certainly had our differences, but if I died, Renn's progress would stop. She wouldn't want me dead. She'd call down Zia's own wrath if the assassination were successful—"

"He thinks she's his mother." A sudden cruelty deepened in Eden's voice, and for a moment I didn't know to whom she referred. "Zia, the goddess. She's everywhere in this gods-forsaken place."

Otso-Zia. But I dared not interrupt her.

"Adoel thinks he has some gods-touched conception. He has a personal shrine to her, a whole window next to one of himself. He has all three crafts, so maybe he is." She scoffed, then shrunk in on herself. "He's mad, Nym. He's absolutely mad."

That . . . was interesting. It explained the dedication to the oft-forgotten goddess. The violet cincture. And I'd seen the window. It was magnificent.

I wanted to ask more about it, what exactly Nicosia had said, or what Eden had overheard, but footsteps were coming toward the door. Heavy armored ones, likely a guard and not the king himself, but still, our time together was about to end. So I squirreled the new information away and rushed, "Eden, where is your room?"

Her focus had turned to the door, fear immobilizing her.

I swung my leg out, nudging her knee with my toe. *"Where is your room?"*

She shivered. "U-Upstairs. To the . . ." She took a beat to think. ". . . left. I mean, the west wing. I can see the sunset. Fifth floor. It's the . . . third. No, fourth door from the stairs."

"I need you to be ready," I whispered. "We are going to get out of this. I don't know how or when, but we will get out. Always be ready. I won't have a way to communicate with you."

She trembled as the door opened, but set her jaw and nodded.

I hoped I would not break my promise.

Chapter 6

That night, in the darkness of a new moon, I jolted upright on my pallet, a cold sweat forming over my body. I'd been thumbing through my stolen scriptures, mulling over my discussion with Eden and the revelations about Queen Winvrin, as I drifted into sleep, catching something on the last tendril of wakefulness.

Adoel Nicosia had all three magics under craftlock.

Adoel Nicosia knew Winvrin by her Sestan name.

Sten had called Renn *gods-touched.*

If Renn *were* related to Adoel Nicosia . . .

I grabbed the old book and moved closer to the window, flipping through the abused pages by the light of the stars until I found the old prophecy: *When the kingdoms of men falter, the blood of the Allmaster shall rise up, garbed as an angel of fire, and balm its people as rain to the earth.*

A man who mastered all facets of craftlock could easily be the Allmaster.

Angel of fire. The words made me think of that dim basement room. The way Renn had glowed.

It had to be him. Everything pointed to him. The scripture spoke of the Allmaster's blood, and Nicosia had eliminated any possible heir he might have. All but one. Because Nicosia knew the scripture, too. Knew his children would be his downfall.

That had to be why the Sestan king was so hell-bent on destroying him. Why Winvrin had been so desperate to keep them apart. Maybe even why King Grejor had taken a Sestan under his wing and forged the papers to paint her Canseren.

Renn was Nicosia's weakness.

And I had healed him.

There was a special kind of madness to boredom.

Even the shock of my revelation could not fuel me forever. As the days gradually grew longer, so did my solitude. I did not miss Nicosia's visits. I'd take eternal isolation over one more day with him. But the Sestan king and his armies had marched south, leaving me alone with Ursa and the Egroran. The palace's staff seemed to be skeletal, but most days they remembered to feed me and take away the pot I relieved myself in. I did not see Eden; she was as much a prisoner as I was.

The palace had gone quiet; I didn't even see staff below through the aperture around the trunk of the Egroran. I spent my days circling the great tree clockwise, then counterclockwise, talking to Ursa as I did, first delineating what circumstantial evidence I had gathered, then anticipating a variety of futures where I might be able to use it, or where I might end up dead. Too many resulted in the latter camp. Eventually our planning became tedious, and I resorted to recalling memories or talking about pointless things, recapping interactions I'd had with friends and strangers, sharing stories from our childhood. Anything to pass the time.

A week passed, and then another. Renn's emotions began to change again. Sleeplessness, anxiety, anticipation, and then surmounting courage mingled with fear. Dread, guilt, aggression, focus. If he were not in a battle, I'd eat my shoe. I shrunk within myself, mulling over the feelings, trying to envision what Renn must be doing, narrating occasionally to Ursa.

I was sitting in the tree, staring up into its few leaves that grew in this chamber, when a sharp pain exploded in my side. Gasping, I nearly fell from its branches. The pain was such I could scarcely breathe, and I gripped a barky knot, trying to right myself. Felt the injury, expecting blood, but there was nothing there. No wound, no blood.

My heart sank into my feet as I gripped my middle and hissed through the agony. *Renn.* Gods, help him. He'd been hurt, badly. A blade, perhaps a spear. The agony radiated in such a way I couldn't be sure.

I dropped from the branch, stumbling on my feet and collapsing to the floor. Ursa called after me, but I had no thought but for the aching heat in my side, and for the man I knew it belonged to.

He is your chosen, isn't he? I asked Hem. *Save him. Please, save him.*

Tears ran down the side of my nose. The pain continued, spreading. "Help him," I whispered, face pressed to the cool tile. "Gods, someone *help him*!"

I should have been there. I should never have left his side. I should have insisted he flee with me from Speth, or I should have joined him in the fray. Then neither of us would be in such stark predicaments.

What a fool I'd been.

Minutes passed, the pain so intense I grew delirious with it.

Was there no other healer? No doctor? "Someone help him!" I screamed. The sound echoed off the domed ceiling.

I slipped into my lumis, searching my merlons for a way to heal him, but of course the wound didn't materialize here. It would be there, wherever he was. In my mind's eye I pictured him lying on a thawing battlefield, staring up at the sky as red soaked his clothes and the grass beneath him. Whispering my name, and how I'd failed him in the end.

I threw myself bodily at the merlon of my heart, feeling it quiver. Pressed the pads of my fingers into his golden light. "Don't die. Please don't die." I was only a projection of myself, an interpretation of magic, but I sobbed, tears raining onto the gray and translucent pieces of the merlon. "Not after all of this, Renn. You've endured so much, endure this, too. You have to. You *have to*."

The pain exploded, momentarily blinding me. I was viscerally aware of my physical self screaming.

"Bear it, Renn," I whispered through tears. "Please, please. Someone help him. Someone save him." I curled around the merlon, pressing my eyes into the golden light until it was all I could see. "Don't leave me here. Don't leave *me*."

I stayed like that, whispering and praying, for hours. Through the rise and fall of torment, through the piercing and tugging of a needle as someone stitched us shut, through the burning of a fever that racked my body—even removing my every article of clothing did nothing to alleviate the heat. I prayed long into the night and into the next day, my sister's voice mingling with mine.

Days later, when our fever finally broke and the injury in our sides became an agonizing but steady pulse, I cried again, grateful that he would survive. I was sure of it, and I sobbed with that certainty.

By the end of this, I would have washed all of Sesta with my tears.

Days later, when the door to the conservatory creaked open, I did not immediately turn toward it. I was rereading *Prophecies*, fruitlessly searching for something that might help my understanding. But as heavy footsteps approached, and I didn't hear the touch of a tray on the cold marble floor, I glanced over, winter cold sending a shock through me.

On the other side of the Egroran, only three paces away, stood Physician Wald Whitestone.

I dropped the book as I rushed to my feet, backing away as far as the soulbinding would allow. This man had tried to kill me before. He had no reason not to try again—

"We do not have much time." He held out empty hands.

I paused, eyeing him. He sounded exhausted. He *looked* exhausted, like he'd aged ten years in . . . How long since his supposed execution in Rove? Over three months, now.

"What do you want?" I asked, keeping my voice down but restraining none of its sharpness. "How are you even alive?"

He touched the tree for support and sat on the cold marble; his knees creaked as he did so. The passive stance took my guard down. He didn't wear his red cincture.

"Winvrin," he answered, affirming Eden's guess. "We had always been close. She never forgave me . . . I suppose now she never will. But she gave me exile over death. For my long years of service."

I gawked at him, at the betrayal of justice, until my mind caught up with my ears.

Wald Whitestone spoke with a Sestan accent.

I neared him until only two paces separated us. "You're Sestan?"

He sighed. "I've little time for chatter, Miss Tallowax. I have come because the past haunts me. I never intended to return to Sesta; my loyalty will forever be to the Noblewights."

I laughed. "To which ones? Half of them are dead. Princess Eden hasn't even laid eyes on you."

He flinched.

Gods, did he speak the truth? Hem make me a mindreader that I might know for sure.

He glanced at the tree and the slits between its trunk and the floor. Peered into them, perhaps to check if anyone might be nearby to overhear his traitorous words. "I'm glad you healed him," he murmured.

I lowered myself to my knees to better study his face. "It was my job. Had your assassin succeeded, he would be dead."

To my surprise, Whitestone chuckled.

Another might have taken offense to the sound, but I did not. I knew Renn was different even before giving him half my heart. A lumis as shattered as his . . . I'd been shocked to see him so alive upon our first meeting. His death lines should have been numerous and stark, but they were few and, oddly, cloudy. *Just like Nicosia's.* As though the gods did not intend for him to die. For either of them to die. At least, not easily.

"For by blood alone shall blood be undone," Whitestone murmured.

"Prophecies," I said.

He raised an eyebrow. "I'm surprised you know it."

I wouldn't have, had I not been given an exorbitant amount of free time and a worn set of scriptures to fill it. I tried not to let the comment rankle me. "Your point?"

"I've little time," he repeated. The roundness of his vowels felt eerie. This wasn't the Whitestone I knew. "Adoel is away, but he does not leave his palace unguarded."

He slouched. He looked a shadow of what he'd once been. Where was the proud, callous, condescending man who'd tried to defame me before the king? Who'd stormed off in anger when I healed the soldier at the portcullis?

Still wary of him, I snapped, "Then speak."

He nodded. "I know you will never leave this place, but the war is not for land—"

"The war is for Renn." If we were going to do this quickly, then there was no point in repeating what we already knew.

His forehead crinkled; perhaps he was surprised I'd pieced together so much. He finally noticed the book. "You've spent some time in *Prophecies*."

"Who is wasting our time now?" I countered.

The physician seemed to age further before my eyes. "He has always hated Renn, Adoel. I wasn't sure why, until I heard the reports of a man lit from within at the front, tearing through soldiers like an axe through trees."

A chill snaked down my spine. *Oh, Renn.*

"I never knew the details of why she came to Cansere, her alliance with King Grejor, but I think I do, now." He let out a shaky breath, and so did I at the subtle confirmations of my inferences. So quiet I could barely hear him, Whitestone said, "It's my fault the prince became so ill. My fault he shattered."

The confession hit me like vertigo; I pressed a palm to the Egroran to stay upright. "Wh-What? *You* broke his lumis?" But that would mean Whitestone was a healer—

The man shook his head. "No. But I let Adoel do it."

Did you know him? I'd asked.

Only briefly, Nicosia had answered.

"Tell me," I demanded. "If you've come this far, tell me." I scanned his face. Thought of Winvrin and of Prince Adrinn. "You were a spy, weren't you?"

He nodded. "He sent me shortly after Grejor's marriage."

"Because of Alarna."

I surprised him with the queen's Sestan name. He did not compliment me on my findings, nor question me. "Yes. I assumed a Canseren name and came to the castle, as she did. She believed it for the same reasons as herself—for sanctuary and protection. I did not understand why, but Adoel was obsessed with the queen and her babe. I . . . I enjoyed my work there. The culture, the people. I did not want to . . . but I feared Adoel. When he told me he wanted access to the castle, I gave it to him. The route of the guards, the layout of the rooms—"

No wonder the Sestan army infiltrated Rove Castle so swiftly. They'd had its blueprints for twenty years.

"—where the baby slept. But his assassins could never get close enough. Too many people, too many fortifications."

Assassins. Gooseflesh pebbled up my arms. In memory I saw the scar over Renn's ribs as his tailor measured him for his birthday celebration. *Assassin,* he'd said.

"Adoel determined to do it himself. Because of the scripture."

I gripped handfuls of my hair in frustration. "Which scripture?"

He gave me a withering look. "For by blood alone shall blood be undone."

The confirmation of Renn's lineage opened chrysalises in my gut. Hearing it on another's tongue made my stomach flutter.

I waited for more. He gave me nothing, so I picked apart the quotation myself.

Renn's death lines . . . Even when he relapsed, his death lines were so cloudy . . .

I met the physician's eyes, ignoring the cold sensation winding down my center. "You think Adoel is the only one who can kill Renn?" *Is Renn the only one who can kill Nicosia?*

The man opened his hands and shrugged. "That is, at least, one way to interpret the scripture. The way he interpreted it, back then." His patronizing countenance slipped back into shame. He waited two breaths before continuing. "I told him everything. His assassins failed, so he came himself. But I . . . I couldn't live with that choice. I alerted one of the guards that they should check on the babe. Adoel . . . He wasn't prepared for a war back then. He couldn't leave any external sign of foul play, so he destroyed Renn from within his lumis. Craftlock was illegal in Cansere—no one would know. But I think . . . I think I warned them in time. He had to flee before he finished. So Renn survived."

"He survived because he's gods-touched," I snapped, reeling. "Anyone else with that much damage would have perished. You didn't save him."

Whitestone's eyes watered; he blinked.

"Did Winvrin know?" I leaned forward, my hands fists in my skirt. "Did Grejor?"

"I didn't tell a soul," he whispered. Cleared his throat. "They never saw Adoel. I'm sure he killed anyone who did. But . . . it was my fault. I tried so hard to heal His Highness—His Majesty, now, yes—but his injuries were magically made. I told Winvrin she should try craftlock. That's why she started the draft."

My skull felt ready to burst with confusion and frustration. "Then why did you try to have me killed?"

He grimaced. Didn't meet my stare. "I'd worked my way up to head physician. It was one of the most prestigious placements at the castle."

"And I hurt your *feelings*?" I asked, too loudly. Surely if anyone lingered in the space beneath this room, they'd hear me through the aperture. "You let that *monster* destroy a prince, a prophesied savior, and you couldn't handle some gods-damned *competition*?"

The physician hardened, showing a glimpse of his old, prideful self. His gaze fell to the gap around the tree's trunk.

I shook my head, ignoring the added confusion dripping through my bond to Renn—he likely wondered where the sudden bundle of emotions on my end was coming from. "Why are you telling me this? It's over. Renn is healed. Winvrin is dead. What could I possibly do for you?"

Whitestone turned away at the mention of the queen. Ran his calloused fingertips over the bark of the tree. Several seconds passed before he spoke. "I was loyal to the Noblewights. I still am. I broke away from Adoel after that incident, and I was too entrenched in the capital for him to come after me. I've been kept on a short leash since my return."

That was hardly an answer, but I waited, clenching my hands tight enough my nails dug into my palms.

Slowly, as if the weight of the Egroran pushed him toward the floor, Whitestone looked at me. "I want your forgiveness."

I reeled back like he'd struck me. "What?"

"She is dead, as you know." Emotion choked his words. "She did not grant me forgiveness when I begged in that cell, and now I cannot beg again until I pass to the other side. You repaired what I broke. You know the truth, now. So I ask . . . forgiveness."

I stared at him, as though I, too, were made of marble. As though I, too, were a tree. I stared and stared, my mind blank and yet overfull, my heart racing, my limbs cold.

I knew what Ursa would have done. She had always been good and tenderhearted, faithful and loving. But though I carried pieces of her with me, I was not Ursa.

"No."

He flinched again.

I rose to my feet. "His illness, his suffering, and *this war* are your doing? Then swim across the gods-damned strait and ask his forgiveness yourself."

He reached toward me. "Please . . ."

"You tried to kill him!" I barked. "You tried to kill *me*! And you've come crawling back to the master you proclaim to hate, for what? To save your own skin?"

He set his jaw. "I was banished."

"Not to Rodsfell, you weren't." I stormed away. The soulbinding tugged, and I twisted on my heel and returned. "You want forgiveness? Take the princess and get her away from here. Break my soulbinding and *let me go*."

The sorry lump of a man merely shook his head. "I can do neither."

A single, sharp laugh tore up my throat. "And yet you led an enemy king through Rove Castle and let him shatter the lumis of an *infant*."

Gripping the tree, Whitestone rose to his feet. He did not meet my eyes. "I should not have come."

"There are many things you should not have done," I snapped. "And it is too late. Twenty years too late, for him."

He walked away.

"If you are truly penitent," I called after him, my constricting throat growing sore, "then *help me*. Help Eden. Get us out of here. I will . . . I will tell Renn your good deeds. I will speak well of you. I will *forgive* you. But please, just help us."

He paused at the door. Turned his head, not quite looking over his shoulder. "You don't understand, Miss Tallowax. I cannot."

Whitestone left. And when I tried to chase after him, the soulbinding brought me to my knees.

The winter seemed longer in Sesta. Snow still fell, chilling the conservatory, but on occasion I spied a daring crocus piercing through the cold soil below. Otherwise, the beauty of the view had long lost its hold on me, the mountains mundane, the forests unremarkable.

Fortunate, then, that I spent so little time looking at it.

Instead, I sat in my lumis, trying to find a way to keep my promise to Eden. It had become clear that I would find no allies here, so any chance of escape fell on my and Eden's shoulders. And, since I could not communicate with her, I could make no assumptions about her own plans. Therefore the possibility of rescue lay solely with Ursa and me.

I'd discovered new things by experimenting with magic before, as seen in Renn's recovery and my half-heart. Surely with my sister's added strength, I could devise a way to overpower Nicosia. To kill him—or at least hurt him—through his lumis swiftly enough that he might not stop me from fleeing. My soulbinding would have to sever if he perished.

I tried pulling in magic in different ways, getting somewhat bizarre in my efforts, but magic was summoned as it always had been; I could only form it into different things, tools to mend and tools to break. I built up some blocks with magic and tested different tools on them, but a giant magicked sword and a giant magicked hammer seemed to have the same effect; one did not damage any faster than the other.

Feeling weak, I went to the crenels and merlons of myself and pushed a little extra magic into my heart, studying the translucent pieces of craftlock keeping it together. Went to one of Ursa's green blocks and studied it, too. Slowly summoned magic into my palms and began shaping it as I had that night in Sten's basement when I'd re-formed Renn. I felt my sister's curious presence around me as I worked. She did not interrupt. However our connection worked, she did not grow bored of waiting, as I did. Then again, in life, she'd been the more patient of our set.

By the end of the day, I'd formed from magic one of the three pieces of lumis Ursa had donated to me, though I had nowhere to put it. Were I not so weary of crying, frustrated tears surely would have come. "If I'd only known this then," I whispered, cradling the translucent piece like a newborn.

"Dwelling on regret does little to bolster the present."

"Thanks, Mother." It was a saying she'd often recited. Thinking of her made me think of Ursa, not as she was now, but as I remembered her, a sixteen-year-old girl full of life. She'd shared my face then, but I supposed she wouldn't anymore. I had aged, and she had not. Even through our connection, she was still an adolescent, never given the opportunity to grow old. How sad, that so many complained of aging when so many more were denied its gift.

I set the piece aside and returned to the present. A servant had come while I was dowsing and left half a loaf of bread and a wrinkled carrot near the door, just out of reach of my current leash. I sighed. I'd have to wait until the next came and ask them to push it a little closer. No dinner tonight.

Day, night, day, night. They blurred together. I paced often, antsy in my solitude when I tired of magic, but to magic I always defaulted, until one day, three months after Nicosia captured me outside Speth, something fundamental clicked in my mind. Something that made my body heavy as lead, my heart dry as chapped leather, my soul flimsy as steam. The effect proved strong enough that I felt Renn's concern through the bond, and Ursa prodded at me until I whispered my thought.

The enthusiastic manner in which Ursa responded crippled me further.

"Absolutely not," I hissed into the darkness, straightening my pallet and thumping my body onto it.

"Surely the pain would be bearable, with enough preparation."

"It's not the prospect of pain that hurts," I snapped back.

"But it might work. Sleep on it."

"No!" The word echoed through the conservatory. I choked on a painful knot in my throat. The space between my lungs burned and twisted. "No, Ursa. No."

"Nym." I could imagine her sitting beside me, taking one of my hands in both of her own, her dark curls falling over one shoulder.

"You've accomplished so much already. You've grown up. Far surpassed me in every way. You don't need me anymore."

Tears blurred my vision. "I will always need you."

"No, you won't, and you don't. You haven't needed me since you found him. *Or haven't you realized?"*

For the hundredth time, I cried myself to sleep, my face pressed into my pillow. And yet, for all the practice this place had given me in sorrow, these tears felt more bitter than all the rest.

They felt like goodbye.

Chapter 7

While all stayed quiet in Rodsfell, war happened elsewhere.

I knew this from Renn—from the surge of his emotions, the ebb and flow of victory and defeat, exhaustion and tumult. I tried to craft a story around all of it, but I had no way of knowing the truth. I could only hope and pray that the good outweighed the bad, and that Renn didn't receive an injury that likewise crippled me.

I was pacing mindlessly around the tree a few days later, stretching my legs and working out nervous energy, when something completely unexpected happened—a release from deep within me. I thought it, at first, Renn, but no other sensations followed it—not joy nor rage nor sadness nor pain.

Then I realized, and I dared not breathe for the want of it.

I moved away from the tree. Farther, farther, until I reached the door.

I *reached* the door.

Shaking, I extended my arm, letting my fingertips brush its smooth wood. Gooseflesh erupted over every inch of my skin, sending shivers into my bones. My heart beat wildly in my chest.

"Nym?" Ursa asked.

"I-It's gone," I whispered, the shock dizzying. "The soulbinding, it's gone."

I heard my sister gasp. *"Is he . . . ?"*

"Dead?" I whispered back. Hem and the gods make it so! Had Adoel Nicosia fallen in battle? Had Renn or one of his soldiers severed his magic definitively? Surely I would feel it from Renn if he took Nicosia's life and ended this horrible war.

It felt like too much to hope. More likely, Nicosia had needed his magic for something else or used it thoughtlessly. If a soulbinder could only bind one soul at a time, then the moment Nicosia soulbound another creature, he would release his hold on me.

Either way, for the first time in two months, I had my autonomy back. I could *leave.*

Sweat broke out all over my body, hot and cold at once.

"Now, Nym. Before someone realizes!"

I turned back toward the great window. Still light out, perhaps late afternoon. It might be safer to wait until nightfall, but what if someone thought to check on me, and I lost my advantage? What if I didn't understand the magic at all, and Nicosia could reignite it again from wherever in the world he was? What if more guards filtered into the palace at night?

What if they didn't?

I couldn't risk it. If the gods had given me an opportunity to run, I had to *run.*

My slick fingers gripped the door handle. It wasn't locked; this place wasn't intended to be a prison. I pressed my ear to the door, but it was hard to hear anything over my own pulse. Carefully I turned the latch. Inched the door open. My heart hammered so hard even my vision shook with it.

I could weep. *We might not need our plan after all,* I thought only, for I dared not make a sound now.

A short hallway led to my door, and from it stemmed marble walkways to either side. I swallowed. Stepped out and snicked the door shut behind me.

A distant voice, male and friendly, came up the hallway, but it drifted away. No guards outside the door. Why would I need guards when my very soul couldn't move?

The name of every god cycled through my thoughts in quick prayer as I toed toward the hallway and peered out. The floor seemed to be shaped as a giant oval, curving out of sight either way. Silver sconces lined the walls, rich carpets the floor, several ferns along the way, old artwork in silver-plated frames. I knew part of this; I knew that I'd been led left for Eden's sham wedding. That the shrine was two floors down. When I'd first been bound to the tree, and when Nicosia had given me his tour, he'd taken me left as well. I had no idea what was to the right. The slapdash map of the palace I'd pieced together in my mind veered left. Perhaps the right hallway came around and joined with the left, and the choice was ultimately moot.

But maybe Eden was to the right. West wing. I just had to hope the layout of this place made sense and led me there.

Upstairs, she'd said. West wing. Fifth floor. I was on the fourth. Would Nicosia keep Eden in *his* bedroom? Or was she kept in a guest room, or somewhere dourer? What if he'd moved her since our brief chat? Had he thrown her in the dungeon? Did the palace *have* a dungeon?

I had to get to Eden.

I steeled myself with a deep breath. Straightened my clothing and combed through my hair. I had only slippers for my feet; they would be quiet enough. Nicosia hadn't paraded me around; I had a good chance most wouldn't recognize me. There was no notable difference, physically, between Canseren and Sestan people. My dress, though old and in need of washing, was refined enough, albeit not in Sestan style. It was Eden's. Still, if I *were* to be spotted, perhaps better I appear as a servant or guest than an escapee.

Light on my feet, I hurried right, my senses hyperaware of every sound, smell, and movement, hindered still by my thumping chest. I peered around the bend and found stairs. *Stairs.* Stairs led down from the left, too, but I couldn't remember these two flights being within sight of one another. And they only led down, not up. Where were the stairs to the fifth floor?

What if Eden had counted wrong? But I had so few options, I had to trust her. Fifth floor, west wing. She could see the sunset. Fourth door from the stairs.

As I neared the stairs, I passed another window. I could break the window and get out that way . . . but the noise would draw attention. The fall might be too great—

Find Eden. I needed to do that first. I'd promised her.

Passing the stairs—indeed, I could not see the other set from their well—I peered around the next corner. There was a single room, perhaps a meeting room? Unlikely to be a bedroom. No further stairs that I could see. Nothing leading *up*. Ursa remained quiet, likely not wishing to break my concentration. Swallowing against a dry throat, I backed up and took the stairs down, my feet moving swiftly, my slippers padding like the feet of a cat.

I heard a voice. Moved to the nearest door and opened it, but it was a closet without space to fit me. The next door was locked. Panicking, I slipped into the next just as footsteps approached. Pulled it shut behind me.

Thank the gods, the room was unoccupied. It appeared to be a salon of some sort, a sitting room filled with furniture, with broad windows on two of four walls. It also had another door. I glanced out the windows while crossing to that door and pushed it open, praying for stairs. Peered outward into a hallway. Two maids conversed twenty feet away. *Move,* I urged them.

They did not.

I'd have to go back the way I came. My fingers, little more than ice on the knob, started to close the door, but just then the maids did start walking away, continuing their talk. They carried either sheets or table linens. It didn't matter.

Could I accost one and steal her uniform? No, not when there were two. And not when they might scream. I was ill practiced at jumping innocent women, nor did I want to, even if they did serve a madman.

I slipped from the salon. Shut the door. *Leave everything as you found it,* I thought. I inched down the hallway. Tested another door. It opened to a bedroom—unoccupied. No sign of luggage or it having been lived in. The next door was the same. The next, a closet, full of linens matching what the maids had been carrying.

I pulled up my memorized map of the palace. The places I'd been. I was on the third floor. If royal bedrooms were on the fifth floor, then perhaps the stairs to them were tucked away, to keep out wanderers?

I continued onward, testing doors. My fourth opened onto an *occupied* room, not for Eden, but an old man I did not recognize. He was in a tub, his back to me. I quickly shut the door, wincing at the soft click it gave, as though the lock was shouting at me.

Footsteps. I dodged into an alcove sporting a lacquered box, nearly knocking it from its pedestal. No voices, just footsteps. They passed. I checked the last door in the hallway—locked. But wouldn't Nicosia lock Eden in her room?

Feeling daring, I rapped the nail of my index finger lightly on the door. No response. Rapped again. Nothing.

I darted into the juncture of hallways, glancing to my right only to see a blue-clad guard heading my way. I'd stepped directly into his line of sight.

It took everything I had not to run, not to freeze. *Walk, walk, walk.* I crossed the juncture, but he was certainly still heading my way. Fear spiked so hard it spawned vertigo. I walked briskly down the remainder of the hall. Heard voices coming up the next. The palace seemed sparsely occupied, but there was no way I'd check everything without being found. Without being questioned or *smelled*—

I searched for a hiding place, panicked. A shorter hallway branched off behind me, unlit and without windows. I jogged to it. Its narrow corridor boasted an array of silvered whatnots, but I saw none of them. I simply walked, getting as much space between me and that guard, that voice, as I could.

The passageway ended at a narrow door. Unlocked. *Please be stairs.* I cracked it—a room. Saw no one within and stepped inside, carefully pushing the door shut behind me—

It felt like being lowered into a half-frozen pond. A shudder started in my feet and radiated up to my crown, making every hair on my body stand on end.

Death. Death painted the walls of this room. Clung to the air and wove between the four simple beds.

I turned to confront it but found no one. Nothing. I swallowed. If this room was not full of the dying, then why did I sense such darkness here?

"Nym?" Ursa asked.

"Death," I whispered, stepping away from the door. The chamber was small, wider than it was long. Four beds, two on either side of the sole entrance. Little more than cots, like beds soldiers might use. Two rounded windows, but they were barred with iron and too high to easily reach. The walls were murals—old, by the cracked state of the paint. City life in Rodsfell, I guessed. Random merchants and townsfolk, livestock and shops, broken up by wood paneling that reached up and across the ceiling. In the center where the panels joined hung a small black chandelier, unlit. No carpeting, no other furniture. I didn't even smell anything off, but death draped over me like a cloak. Why here, and not elsewhere in the palace—

Footsteps. My thoughts screamed. I made a full turn before dodging to the farthest bed on the left. Bruised my knees dropping to the floor. I rolled beneath it. Curled into myself, willing myself to be small, *smaller*—

The door didn't open. I held my breath, listening, then had to gasp for want of air. I stayed there a long moment, cold against the hard floor. Inhaled deeply, trying to still myself—

A mark on the wall, just under this cot. I strained, tilting my head back to see it. I knew that mark. Like an unfinished cursive *Z*, lowercase, with two dots on either side of its tail. Or, in this case, two fingerprints.

It took a beat for me to recall it—the same had been burned inside the cover of my stolen scriptures.

What did it mean?

I reached up to touch it only to recoil at the last second. I knew that ruddy-brown color. This mark had been made with blood. I thought again of my breakfast with Nicosia. How he had no heirs and no queens—

I needed to get out of here.

Climbing out from beneath the bed, I quickly smoothed my hair and dress and crossed back to the door. I had to find a way out before anyone noticed I was missing. Before word of Nicosia, whatever had happened to him, reached the capital. If I couldn't realistically find Eden, I'd have to leave her behind. I could do more for her free than I could trapped. I hated the thought, but I had to work with what I'd been given.

I cautiously turned the handle of the door. Creaked it open.

Fear like a steel beam shot up through my center when I saw a man on the other side of it, wearing Sestan blue. Followed by cool recognition. Whitestone. Why was Whitestone outside this door?

Desperation muted everything else. I grabbed him by the collar and yanked with all my might, pulling him into the room. He stumbled. I kicked the door shut behind me. Acted before he could speak—clutched his bald pate and dowsed, entering a lumis of mismatched drawers in a great eccentric dresser. I had never dowsed on Whitestone before, but I was an experienced enough healer to read it.

Ignoring the death lines, I went straight for a heavy, salmon-colored drawer and shattered it.

In the present, Whitestone howled as his left shin broke. He dropped to the floor, and I dropped with him, clamping both hands over his mouth.

"Make another noise and I'll stop your heart," I hissed.

He squeezed his eyes shut, tears leaking from their corners. His breath came rapidly, uneven. He clenched his teeth. Only a whimper escaped. In another time and place, I would have been completely revolted by my actions. I'm sure Ursa was. But I would *not* let them chain me up again. I had to escape this hellhole by any means necessary.

I grabbed his collar. "Where are they keeping Eden? Where is she?"

He trembled. Took a few labored breaths. "Sh-She's in the west wing, the . . . suites."

"On the fifth floor?"

He swallowed. Hesitated, but I thought it more due to the pain than anything else. Nodded. Lifted a shaky finger and pointed. "That way. I don't know the room, b-but it's always guarded. There will be . . . be a guard outside the door."

"That way to the stairs?" He was pointing southwest, unless I'd gotten turned around. "Where are the stairs to the fifth floor?"

"Yes, to the stairs." He wheezed. "By the . . . arch . . ."

I sucked this information into my mind, painting a picture there. "If I heal you, can you take me there?"

But he shook his head. "I h-have no . . . jurisdiction . . . with the guards."

"You're a doctor. Tell them she needs medical attention."

He half smiled, like it was a joke. "They w-won't believe me. Oh gods." He winced. "Make it stop, make it *stop*—"

I wished I were unaffected by his suffering, but I was not. Dowsing, I repaired half of the drawer. Not enough to heal him, but it would abate some of the pain.

He looked ready to pass out when I returned to the present a second later. "What is this room?"

"I . . ." He glanced around, barely moving his head. "It was, once, a nursery."

"Nicosia has no children." None that were raised here, anyway.

Whitestone managed a nod. Saliva streaked between his lips when he spoke. "No . . . no, he killed them here."

For a moment, my rapid heart froze. "Killed who?"

"A-Anyone," he whispered.

Not just heirs. No baby made that symbol beneath the bed.

He grabbed my wrists. I scowled. "Let me go or you will never walk again."

He released me.

"Can you get me out of here?"

The oaf shook his head. "You assume I have liberties, Miss Tallowax. Have you forgotten already what I told you? I am watched, always. I was a traitor to these people, however gently. Most likely, I was watched coming into this very room."

Chills coursed down my back. I shoved Whitestone away and hurried to the door. Pulled it open—

Someone *pushed* it from behind. The wood collided with my forehead. A blue-clad guard, tall and wide, stepped in. As my heart surged into my mouth, I knew there was no use trying to fool him. If he'd come for Whitestone, he'd divert for me, for he knew who I was. This man had stood guard while Nicosia interrogated me in the hold of that ship. This man had been one of my guards at the wedding.

He seized me by the hair and dragged me out of the room. Another guard was coming down the hallway.

"Don't let her touch your skin." My captor pulled strands from my scalp. "His Majesty must have switched the bond."

The second soldier seized me by the forearms. He wore gloves.

"Please, *please*," I urged as they wrenched me from that dark hall. "Please let me go. I'm begging you—"

The second guard called, "Get us a binder!" I didn't see to whom. My hair was jerked in such a way I couldn't turn my head.

But I watched. I watched the floor pass under my feet. I watched the windows and décor, adding them to the map in my mind, even as my very being unraveled within me at my failure. *Not back to the tree, not back to the tree.*

"It's not the end, Nym!" Ursa tried to reassure me. *"You still have me. We still have a plan."*

A plan I didn't want.

By the time the guards dragged me to my conservatory, I was sobbing, Renn a distant orb of worry and guilt in my chest.

I'd been gifted a chance, and lost it just as quickly.

Chapter 8

I began to change myself the next day.

It hurt, shifting my lumis from what the gods intended it to be. Hurt in a way not quite physical. Deep and raw and wrong, similar to how I felt when that assassin had sunk his blade into my diaphragm—the sensation of otherness that twisted with the shock and pain. I realized how agonizing it must have been for Renn when I'd remade him, especially since I'd done it so quickly, hindered only by my own mortal shortcomings. I whispered late apologies he might never hear as I worked at a careful, measured pace, taking breaks often to reorient myself, or to meditate and remember. I *had* to remember what I'd seen, or this would never work. A little here, a little there, until I scarcely recognized myself, and hardly felt myself, either. A deep sickness took root in my core, in my bones and my blood, but I could not look back, not now. I had to be ready. Always ready. I would not lose another opportunity.

Eight weeks after nearly murdering his wife in front of me, Adoel Nicosia returned to Rodsfell.

I had fair warning; the servants in the palace hustled, their footsteps carrying through the halls and the tree aperture. Activity increased outside, first by the common people, then by returning soldiers. It would be only a matter of time before Nicosia came for me, and my body ached with memories of his cruelty.

The sound of the king's voice jarred my ears the day he returned to the palace; I heard it through the aperture in the room below. Crept to the crevice to listen, holding my hair back for fear it might slip past the tile and give me away.

"—yet, Your Majesty," said an unfamiliar male voice.

A *smack* of skin on skin. "How is that even *possible*? You insolent fool! Why are you here if he's alive?"

"R-Resources, Your Majesty. We were too low."

Another *smack*.

"I ought to unwind you," Nicosia seethed, and the term sent a shock through my skeleton. *Unwind?*

An image of Nicosia clawing at a beautiful, multicolored chandelier rose to my mind. I imagined this man's lumis like a great tapestry, and the king's cruel, ethereal hands tearing away at its threads—

A pause. "He's too powerful—"

"This is your *only* purpose, do you not understand?" Footsteps, and the king's voice grew distant. "Not looting, not land. Stop ravaging the women and *kill their king*!"

I clenched my teeth, pulse thrumming too quickly, lungs desperate for air.

The other man said something, but he'd moved too far from the aperture for me to hear.

Retreating from the tree, I pressed my hands to my heart. "Run, Renn," I whispered. "Don't let them have you. Please, please don't let them win."

Just then, my soulbinding released. I took a deep breath of air, as if I could fill the space where it had been, but I had no confidence in another shot at freedom.

Moments later, the door to the conservatory burst open, slamming into the wall behind it. I soared to my feet, dizzy from the motion and ill with my magic, grabbing a branch of the Egroran to steady myself. The room spun, yet Adoel Nicosia seemed unmovable, as though even my vertigo could not touch him. He was travel worn, his hair disheveled either by weather or a helmet, but his green eyes were sharp, his mouth tight. He still wore his military uniform with the gold bars on the collar, a belted sword, mud-caked boots.

"A disease, the lot of you," he snapped, marching into the room without shutting the door. A mastiff whined from the corridor, but the dog did not enter.

I tried not to shrink from him as he neared, but did not altogether succeed. Yet the king did not strike me but pulled off a glove and snatched my hand only long enough to rebind me to the tree. Then he marched toward the large window, peering out onto the back of his kingdom.

"Do you know how disease works, Nym?" He tugged his glove back into place. "It's imperceptible, at first. The finest grains of miasma, no different from the air and the water. It falls somewhere seemingly harmless: a horse trough, a child's hands, a rising loaf of bread. And yet from there it grows, and as it grows it spreads, choking one life and then another, weaving into families and communities like the branches of a tree." He turned toward the Egroran, pleased with his metaphor. "Humans are much the same. Born sniveling and whining, seemingly harmless, but they grow, and they reproduce, and they spread their mortality from one community to the next, one fiefdom to the next, one *kingdom* to the next." His hand formed a fist, the leather across his knuckles creaking. "Those who overcome it become gods."

That was no doctrine I'd ever heard.

"And I . . ." He opened his hand and looked up, as though a dove were meant to fly from his palm. ". . . have almost overcome it."

I swallowed. *Eden was right. He* is *mad.*

"Yet a few pesky mortals still stand in my way."

He marched over to me. I knew running was futile, but I tried anyway, until he shortened my leash with the Egroran. I thumped up against the tree. Grabbing me by the neck, he shoved my back against the tree's trunk and drew his sword.

I barely had time to gasp before he ran me through with the blade, burying its end into the trunk.

Air stopped. Thought stopped. The wrongness of it flooded me. My legs wanted to quit, and yet even as they tried, pain shocked my middle over and over again as the sword held me up. The pain echoed back and forth—Renn's response. He felt the sword embedded in himself, too.

I dowsed on myself and hastily began picking up fallen puzzle pieces, reorganizing the new formations they'd broken from. I'd only just started when the basalt wall around me boomed as thunder. Quivered as though pelted by the storm god Rolys himself.

I realized his plan, even as I fought to save myself: distract me with my wounds while he ripped my wall apart.

I rebuilt myself, fused the blocks into place, but even as I did, more toppled over. The sword was still embedded above my navel, and I could only heal *around* it. I cursed, prepared myself, and returned to reality.

I couldn't breathe.

Nicosia's face had gone blank with dowsing, his hands around my neck. I tried to grab the sword hilt, but it was too far, and my efforts sent blood pouring down my dress, forcing me to return to my lumis and rebuild myself. Back in reality, I gripped the blade with my bare hands, but my grip was weak, my angle wrong.

Curses swirled through me as I returned to my lumis, Ursa shouting something I couldn't hear over the thundering of the wall. I rebuilt myself, tied magical ropes around the pieces, and used the connection of Nicosia's hands to enter *his* lumis.

I lifted my hands and pulled on Ursa and threw my strength into Nicosia's wall, encouraged by the way it rumbled and cracked as though made from obsidian instead of basalt. Then I changed my tactic, pulling magic from the wall itself instead of shoving new magic into it. The black rippled like molten iron, and I parted it, absorbing the sight of Nicosia's icy sentries, their shape and color—

Returning to reality felt like toppling from a roof. Nicosia had whipped his hands from me, seeing my ploy.

I rushed into my lumis, re-pieced the puzzle—

Shot back into reality as my knees hit the tile of the conservatory. The bloody sword dropped next to me with an earsplitting clamor.

Back in my lumis, I fixed the pieces one piece at a time, staunching the blood—

In the conservatory, Nicosia tugged on his gloves once more, seized me by my hair, and hauled me to my feet, his stale breath filling my senses.

"My time away was good for me." He spat on my cheek. "I've begun to see how useless you really are. You are *nothing*. You have *nothing*. I was a fool to think keeping you would be any benefit to me."

Renn's panic added to my own. I desperately tried to push it away. I had to focus. I had to play this just right—

Nicosia threw me, sending me chest- and elbows-first into the floor. Almost immediately he seized my hair again and hauled me up.

"If the gods gave you no craftlock to teach me, what is the point of your existence?" He shook me, and I cried out as hairs pulled from my scalp, my not-quite-healed wound tearing, that old ache in my side—Renn's side—throbbing. Mouth right against my ear, he screamed, *"Tell me what I want to know!"*

His voice rang inside my skull, deafening. A high-pitched whine immediately replaced it. "One last chance, Nym." He severed my soulbinding and rushed me from the room, fingers tight on my hair, his glove barring me from dowsing on him. I could barely keep up with his stride, and he held my head at an angle that made it nearly impossible for me to see where we were going. I tripped often, each stumble yanking on my scalp, splitting my middle a little more, but I could heal it later, *later*. I had to focus. I had to remember our steps, spot the stairs, see the portraits.

Right. We'd gone to the right and down the stairs. I knew where the closets were, the sitting room, the narrow hallway to that awful, death-choked space—

"I am merciful. You can still have it all." He dragged me down another narrow set of stairs I'd never seen before, my shoulder colliding with the marble wall. Down two floors. "Citizenship, purpose, training. A new home under the greatest of kings. One more chance, but I'll let you think about it in a more conducive environment."

The corridor narrowed, twisted, darkened. Marble turned to stone. Narrower stairs that barely accommodated two bodies together. The air chilled. Though I'd never been here before, I knew exactly where we were going. It had the same air, the same mildewy scent, as the one in Rove.

The dungeon.

The king beat open a heavy door, garnering the attention of a thick, bald man with an eyepatch. The scents of urine, shite, and blood clotted in the back of my throat; moans and screams flowed from the cells below. A whip cracked through them.

Death brushed up against my legs like a hungry cat.

Fear filled my head to bursting.

"Find space for her," Nicosia barked.

"Nym, you have always been the strongest of us," Ursa whispered.

Tears leaked from my eyes as I tripped down uneven steps, led by my hair. A woman started screaming, a man panted—

"You have led us so far. Brien, Lissel, Dan, Colt, Pren, Heath, Terrence . . . They all survived because you are strong. Not because you had me."

"Ursa," I cried. Inwardly, I began tearing a hole in my basalt wall.

"Here'll do." The bald man's keys jingled as he took them off his belt.

"Focus, Nym. It's now or naught."

Tears dripped from my chin. "I love you, Ursa."

"I love you, too, always. No matter what worlds separate us."

Metal hinges creaked as the door swung open. Nicosia dragged me forward.

"We'll see each other again soon, my dear, beloved sister."

A promise. The last thing Ursa would ever give me.

Nicosia took one step; I took two. Twisted in his grip, ripping hair, and grabbed his face, sinking my nails into the skin.

I dowsed.

If he dowsed back, he'd see what I'd done. How I'd recrafted my lumis into three glassy, geometric figures, overly tall, connecting at their highest points like ribbed vaults. Matching his exactly.

Like for like. As though we were *sisters*.

As I'd once done for Renn.

In my own lumis, I shoved the three new, magic-formed pieces of myself into the sculptures, replacing the green ones Ursa had gifted me nine years ago.

Drawing in all the magic I could hold, I drove Ursa through our connection and into *him*.

I blinked into the present as I fell to the dungeon floor, palms striking wet stone.

Nicosia screamed.

He screamed and backpedaled, clawing at his face, thrashing as though possessed. The warden rushed for him, confused, dropping his keys.

I seized them and bolted from the cell, slamming and locking the door behind me.

Then I ran.

Nicosia's screams merged with the cries of the other prisoners, giving me a head start I hadn't planned on, but one I couldn't waste. I ran through the narrow, filthy corridor, toward the torchlit stairs to freedom. Another prisoner called out to me, but I couldn't afford mercy for him. I didn't even know if I could afford mercy for Eden, but I had to try.

I had promised.

Floor above the conservatory. West wing. Fourth door.

I shut the dungeon door behind me and ran until the stone shifted back to marble, then quickly wiped my eyes, combed through my hair, adjusted my dress. Lifted my head to try my earlier guise once more, to fit in as a normal palace denizen—

My torso was covered in blood, dress torn from Nicosia's sword.

With trembling hands I split my hair into two sections, trying to hide my back with half the mangled curls, my front with the other. Curled my arm around my middle to mask the rest. It was the best I could do; I had to get *out.* I hadn't fully healed; my movements smarted, but at least the skin was sealed.

Painting of the black stallion. Around the corner—*stairs.*

I rushed up them, slowing only minutely as I caught sight of a maid. She glanced at me, confused, but did not follow me; I was an unknown woman with a purpose, wearing Eden's old dress. Old, bloody, and in Canseren style, but noble all the same.

I got lost then, trying to remember what I'd seen on my earlier tour. Went right, then down one corridor—no stairs. Retraced my steps, spied a familiar urn, and continued on.

"Hey!" a footman called after me. "What are you doing?"

I passed a corridor with an arch at the end of it—hadn't Whitestone said something about an arch? I diverted down the path. Stairs started right under the arch. Up the stairs, two at a time. Two floors. I counted doors—

The fourth had a guard stationed outside of it.

I ran to him.

He stiffened, tightening his grip on his spear. He wore fingerless gloves. "There are no visit—"

I pressed my hand over his and leapt into his lumis: a spindly forest full of trees.

I followed the first death line to a sapling and railed upon it. Leaves and bark went flying, but I did not want to kill him.

In the present, the guard paled and crumpled.

The door was locked. I fumbled with the woozy man's armor until I found his keys and nearly sliced open my fingers wrenching them free. He had five keys on the ring; the second unlocked the door.

My mind barely recognized the room within, its grandeur and drapings, the large window and larger bed, the painted ceiling. Eden, more gaunt than ever, had risen at the commotion. She went wide eyed at my face, then at my bloody torso.

I shut the door behind me. No one was looking for me, yet. *Zia help me. Turn their eyes away!*

After throwing both sets of keys into a chamber pot, I rushed to her bed and pulled a folded blanket off its foot. "I need you to trust me."

Eden dropped to her knees and reached under her bed, retrieving a satchel stuffed to the brim. She already wore shoes. I smiled. I'd told her to be ready, and she was.

This, unfortunately, was the easy part.

I rushed to the window, unlatched it. Cool April air and early-evening light greeted me. There was a small balcony, large enough for someone to take one step out of the room and go no farther.

I wrapped the blanket around my head to protect it.

"Nym, what are you—?" the princess began.

I grabbed her wrist, pulled her against me, and jumped.

Chapter 9

I didn't remember hitting.

The moment the balcony gave way, my arms wrapped tightly around Eden, I went into my lumis, ready for the breaking. It would be harder to fix, with my patterns still skewed to match Nicosia's, but I didn't have time to reorient them. I'd simply have to do my best.

I made sure I hit first.

So much of me shattered.

It was a five-story jump, but I didn't land on my feet. Pain erupted in all of me, and I winced not only for the ache, but for the knowledge that, whatever Renn was doing, he, too, would feel as though he'd hit stone.

I took care of the most vital parts first—head and neck, internal organs, trunk—terrified at how long it took me. Whether the injuries themselves slowed me, or the lack of Ursa—

Ursa.

—I wasn't sure. I hissed through my teeth as I worked, pain from a broken bone shooting arrows up my leg. Some of the icy sculptures I had to re-form into merlons to get it done, including the one holding my heart. I reinforced the magic blocks there and elsewhere in my body, noting the absence of green but unable to think about it. Not now. Not while she bought me this time.

Coming to reality, I opened my eyes and immediately dowsed on the princess, groaning in my arms. Groaning was good—she was alive. I'd softened the landing, yes, but the awkward angle had snapped something in her back; I found the discordant harmony of that and righted it again. Headache, bruises, a badly broken ankle. I worked swiftly, not perfectly. Perfection could come later.

"Get up," I urged, shoving her off me. I pulled the blanket off my head and—

Gods, more blood. My dress was half white, half red, the white fabric showing all of it. Eden's gown was dark; if she'd bled, the color masked it.

Eden blinked, looking over herself as though she couldn't believe she was hale. Glanced up the way we'd come and paled.

I fixed a few of her pins. "We don't have long—"

She grabbed my arm and hauled me toward the palace wall. We were in a garden budding with spring; she dodged behind a statue, pulling me close. Pointed to the wall; I couldn't tell what she indicated at first, until I saw a dip in the stone. She tugged me in that direction.

I didn't know what it was, but I imagined, locked in that room, Eden had studied this garden day in and day out. Planned her escape much as I had.

I searched for guards. Held my breath. Bolted to the dip with Eden in tow. As I neared, I realized it was a narrow opening to a set of narrow stairs. We hurried down, the air growing exponentially colder as we did.

An ice cellar. This was an ice cellar. We must have been near the kitchens.

Eden trembled but managed to open her bag. "No time to change," she rushed, yanking out a coat. "Put this on."

I did. New blood spotted my dress and would soon crust in my hair, but with this, it wasn't perceptible.

"We have to move," I whispered, again combing through my hair. "Carefully, measured. Act regal, not lost—"

Quick, booted footsteps on the stairs. Eden's skin flashed as pale as marble.

I pulled her behind me as a guard appeared. Of course, it was too much to ask to have no witnesses to two women falling out of a window—

"You there!" He tried to draw his sword, but the stairwell proved too narrow. "What are you—"

I launched at him. Grabbed his hand. He flung me into the wall, but I managed to hold on, dowse into a place of floating goblets. I shattered several. The way the broken shards fell, I couldn't help but think of Renn.

Stumbling back, I watched the guard topple into Eden, who shoved him away like a spider. He hit the stairs and slid, stopping before the first block of ice.

I swallowed against a dry mouth. Shook inside and out. This wasn't how my magic was supposed to be used. I wanted it, I *needed* it, but this wasn't how healers were meant to work.

I was beginning to understand why craftlock had been banned. Why so many feared us.

We recovered quickly. We had to.

"Where are we going?" Eden whispered. Her blue eyes glinted hard as granite.

I shook my head. I truly didn't know. As *away* as we could get. Somewhere we could hide.

We'd landed on the west side of the palace in an inch of crusty snow, and I winced to think of blood smeared against the white. We had to move swiftly. I crept to the opening of the ice cellar and peeked out, waiting for someone to pass before motioning to Eden to follow. We hurried across the garden and headed toward the barracks to avoid the guards and the three rows of gates at the front of the palace. The barracks were no safer, though; tired soldiers moved in and out of them. I recalled the way Nicosia had brought me before, on our tour, like it wasn't unusual at all for nonsoldiers to pass through. Still, when I saw a footpath leading behind the barracks, I took it, hooking Eden's arm through my own to keep her close. Pasted on a smile. Just two women on a stroll, nothing more, nothing less.

No alarm had sounded, not yet. How much damage could Ursa do before the afterlife pulled her into it? Before Nicosia overpowered her? How long would he and the warden have to scream over the other prisoners before someone found them?

A soldier sharpening a pile of blades looked up at us as we neared, his brow skewed. Before I could think, Eden said "Good day" to him with a flawless Sestan accent.

He nodded, then continued with his work.

I had a feeling Eden had been as isolated as I'd been. Nicosia didn't want a queen, he wanted a personal war prize.

I held my breath, nausea roiling in my stomach. I couldn't tell if it came from nerves, from my misshapen lumis, or perhaps from Renn. Maybe all three.

The cool evening air made me shiver; I clenched my teeth together to mask it.

We'd nearly passed the last of the barracks when a woman called out to us. "Whoa there!"

I ignored her, tugging Eden along. We hadn't heard anything. We weren't suspicious—

She jogged to catch up to us. Stepped in front of us to block the path. "Where are . . . ?" She paused, looking at Eden. "Mistress, does His Majesty know you're out here?"

Not isolated enough, it seemed. I noted the soldier did not refer to Eden as *Your Majesty*.

But Eden smiled. "I'm touring the grounds with my maid." Her natural Canseren accent swept into place.

The soldier hesitated. I noted her collar—one silver mark and a half circle. *Healer.*

She frowned. "It's getting late—"

"Would you like to accompany us?" Eden asked.

I tried not to wince.

The woman hesitated. I looked her over—with her gloves, I'd have to go for her face or the strip of neck above her collar to hurt her. But she'd heal quickly, report us—

Try, Ursa's voice said to me. Or, rather, the memory of her voice.

My air left me in a wave of grief like I'd been socked in the stomach. It took a monumental effort to suck it back in again.

The healer frowned. "I have orders, Mistress. But I can retrieve someone else—"

"That won't be necessary." The slightest quiver etched Eden's voice. She tried to step around the soldier, but the healer sidestepped to block her. Eden clucked her tongue, but I could feel her mask crumbling. "Really, do you have nothing else to do but accost me? I shall bring it up to His Majesty. What's your name?"

Something about that was wrong, judging by the way the healer's brow lowered. "I don't think—"

"We're just crafters," I pleaded. "We've been taken from our families and enslaved here. Please." I did not need to fake the tears that came to my eyes. "Please, we just want to go home."

Eden squeezed my arm enough to hurt.

The soldier stiffened, eyes shooting between the two of us. We stood there, at an impasse, for nearly a full minute, until she mumbled something under her breath, followed by "Come with me, *quickly.*"

I dared not feed the hope sparking in my chest as the soldier led us past the barracks, farther north. I wanted to go south, but so long as it was not closer to the palace, I would not complain. She crossed over paths and walkways, through copses of trees and a garden, until we got to a man-made stream.

"This will flow southwest," she whispered, pointing, "and merge with the canals, the sewers. He will send dogs. Stay in the water, no matter how cold it gets, for at least a mile. Do you understand?"

Eden's hands rushed to her mouth to stifle a sob.

"Yes, yes, *thank you.*" I grasped her gloved hands. "I'll tell no one you helped us." And pray that no mindreader dug into her thoughts.

The shrill sound of a whistle cut through the air. I didn't know if it was a summons to the soldiers, or part of an alert that the Canseren prisoners were missing. I didn't stay to find out.

Grabbing Eden's hand, I dropped into the stream, the cold water hitting just below my knees. I could bear the cold and heal the hypothermia for both of us. We could make it.

The soldier didn't offer us a farewell or well-wishes. She jogged back the way we'd come, glancing once over her shoulder. I wasn't sure if the stricken look on her face was regret for helping us, or regret that she didn't accompany us.

I ran through the water, not letting go of Eden's hand until long after dark.

We rested only a quarter hour, long enough for me to heal us. Again, my efforts felt sluggish, like our lumie were filled with honey, even after reorienting my merlons. Not the trauma of injury, then; simply that, without my sister, the healing didn't flow as readily. There was less than before. I was *less* than before, and I kept my back to Eden under the guise of healing myself longer than necessary, trying to come to terms with it. Trying not to sob as I shivered.

Had the magic been like this, before Ursa's death? I couldn't recall.

The night felt so endless. So empty. So dark.

But I had no time to mourn. We were too close to Rodsfell, and Eden was desperate to put as much distance between us and Nicosia as possible. "I'll drown myself before I go back," she promised.

I'd done little running since healing Renn, and it seemed there were drawbacks to my half-heart status I hadn't realized. Its beat quickened too rapidly during exercise, tiring me. I fused more magic into it, but now was not the time to experiment with my craft-supplemented handicap. My sentiment was the same as Eden's. Run, or die.

Running kept me from thinking about what I'd lost in that dungeon.

The dark night surrounded us like tar, but the water provided a path. A slick one, and we slipped on several occasions. I returned Eden's coat, and she gave me a second dress to pull over my ruined one, both for warmth and to hide the blood. The water on our clothes turned to frost, and repeatedly we had to walk, Eden guiding me, while I staved off hypothermia. Had I been any other crafter, we'd be near death now. I wondered if the soldier who'd helped us knew I was a healer, or if she merely understood we were desperate.

By morning the stream widened and began to turn southward. Rove was southeast, but for now the most crucial thing was to distance ourselves from the capital. Surely people had noticed the absence of their king. Surely someone had thought to look in the dungeons for him. Surely he would come for us with the wrath of the gods, for he believed himself one of them.

I prayed he would think we headed straight south or took a main road. I prayed his dogs would not follow this stream.

We could not stay here forever.

Hunger gnawed on my stomach by the end of the second day, and we finally stepped out of the water to head south. Eden had been able to save very little from her food trays that wouldn't go bad too quickly. There was nothing here—no roads, no towns, only a smattering of pine forests and endless miles of winter-starved grassland. I wore my blanket tight around my shoulders, and again we traveled past dark, until both Eden and I stumbled from sheer exhaustion.

"Just for a little while." I knelt in a bed of dry needles beneath a pine. "We'll sleep just a little while, then keep going."

We huddled together for warmth, the large blanket cocooning us. I dowsed on us, healing blisters and bruises, and noticed the gold threading on one of my merlons had . . . grown. The way a creeping plant coils around a tree. It was subtle; had I not spent so much time in my lumis these past few months, I might not have noticed. But it was there, climbing upward, as though helping to hold my half-heart together. As though helping to make up for the missing blocks of green.

I cried silently into my hair. *Thank you, Renn.*

The cold was its own sort of blessing; because it made it difficult to catch restful sleep, it was easy to get up after a few hours and continue onward. It was only near dawn that I thought of the risk of running into wild animals; there were bears in Sesta, or so I'd heard. I'd been so fearful of humans, I'd never considered the chance of another creature harming us.

We saw deer as we collected pine nuts. Had we escaped even a month earlier, foraging would have been near impossible, but even the cold Sestan spring brought up wild leeks, dandelions, and chickweed. We picked much of it, carrying it in our pockets and bodices, eating constantly. The plants were not enough to fully fuel us, not with the desperate pace we kept, but it was something, and we were willing to take anything.

Our fourth day on the run, we found a little village—half a village, really, with only three homes widely spaced apart.

"Hem help us," Eden sighed, heading straight for a farmhouse.

I seized her arm. "No, Eden. We're still too close to Rodsfell. They might have sent out men looking for us, or orders to return us. We can't talk to anyone. Not yet."

Eden shook her head. "We're two starving women. Surely they will be kind."

But I would not risk it, and ultimately, Eden dared not try without me. So we circled the village until dark. I harvested too-young asparagus, and Eden stole a rough homespun dress and some men's clothing from a line. We ran until we couldn't anymore, ate, and fell asleep.

In the morning we changed into the stolen clothing, me into the homespun dress, and hid the old clothes in a burrow at the foot of a tree.

It took three more rainy days to find another village, slightly larger than the first. I still dared not go in, but I snatched a few eggs from a henhouse, drinking one myself and saving two for Eden. We rendezvoused behind a decrepit barn. Somehow, she'd shorn her hair to her nape.

It made her look like Adrinn.

We'd discussed disguises, but not precisely how we'd pull them off. Still, while I mourned her hair, the next day she seemed happier, despite the cold and the weariness and the hunger. As though she had truly become the character she'd envisioned for herself.

"We're just a lost couple, newly married," she offered with a sincere smile. "A man and a woman. No one can hurt us, now."

I didn't know how much time Eden had spent outside a castle, but while I did not share her sentiment, I did not negate it, either. In the end, it didn't matter. Nicosia had already hurt me in one of the worst ways possible.

He'd taken my sister.

The hunger grew to a point where we could no longer soothe its edges with magic and vegetables—especially Eden, who had less fat on her body than I did, less to sustain her through the long, though warming, days. I felt it was my fault. Not because I had spurred our escape; I would have done so in the dead of winter if necessary. But had I Ursa's strength, perhaps I could stave off our pains a little longer. Had I Ursa, I might not notice the yawning stretch of land around us, or the emptiness in my own mind.

How could I feel so alone with Eden constantly at my side?

Even tethered to the Egroran, I'd never felt *so alone.*

A pulse of warmth, of concern, threaded through my link to Renn. I latched on to it with the talons of a hawk, desperate for its company. For its assurance. For its hope.

When we found a dirt road heading southeast, we took it.

We avoided line of sight by citizens where we could, but in wide-open stretches between woodlands there was little to do, lest we lose the road. Fortunately, we passed very few on the way, all folk who weren't overly concerned with us. I caught two older men speaking of the war as they drove a heavy wagon north.

"Might as well give up. The king always gets what he wants," said the first.

The second shook his head. "But an angel of fire? The verses say—"

"Propaganda," called the first. "You know I don't believe in any—"

They then left my hearing, and I feared their notice too much to follow and catch the end of the conversation.

Be careful, Renn.

When we found another tiny village, I agreed to try to talk to someone. We would not survive the trip on our own, not this ill-prepared.

I practiced my Sestan accent with Eden, since Eden could not believably drop her voice to pull off the masculine character she'd adopted. Next was to choose the house. I had no idea how many men would be in the village, since Nicosia might have drafted them. But I didn't want to stay with a man. At least, not a lone one. An elderly couple would do, or perhaps a new mother who needed help with her children. Someone as desperate as we were.

We skirted the houses in the twilight, me taking the lead. That one had too many clothes hanging on the line, which meant it was crowded, and those living there would struggle to find room for newcomers. This one was completely dark; waking someone for shelter would not garner hospitality. I approached one farther out with a single candle in its window, but froze as I neared.

"Nym?" Eden asked.

An old cellar hatch on the side of the house caught my eye. In the dimming light, I could just make out a symbol carved into its corner—like a lowercase cursive *Z* with two circles on either side of its unfinished tail.

The same I'd seen in the stolen scriptures. The same I'd seen under the bed in that awful room.

But did it mean good tidings, or bad?

I hesitated, ultimately determining that anything related to Rodsfell and its heinous king was better left alone.

I moved deeper into the village, stopping at a small home still lit from within, with a thin stream of smoke slipping from its chimney. A petite, middle-aged woman opened the door, the sunset dyeing the sky a deep orange. I hoped her eyesight had faded with age, and she couldn't see our haggardness.

"Ma'am," I said in my best Sestan accent, "we're so sorry to bother you. We've gotten lost from our caravan . . . I think we're going in circles." My eyes burned. "I've nothing to pay you with, unless you've someone who is sick. I'm a nurse by trade—"

To my vast relief, the woman stepped back and opened the door. "Come inside, sit by the fire. I'll see to you."

"Thank you," Eden whispered.

The relief doubled as Renn's poured through our connection. Relief that I was relieved, perhaps. Our connection reminded me of what I'd had with Ursa, and I hugged myself, clinging to the sliver of his presence, wishing for his voice.

Tardala's home was small and warm and smelled of herbs; she was a widow with three living children, all moved out of the house, so she insisted she was happy to have guests. She shared with us a potato and rhubarb stew with *pork fat* in it, and truly nothing I had ever eaten in my life tasted as good as it did. It was even better than the pastry Lonnie had filched—

I curled my knees closer at the thought. I didn't even know if Lonnie Swiftmore was alive. Images of Rove, burning, flashed in my mind's eye. I could smell it still, as though the cinders had lodged in my sinuses. I'd healed her in the hallway, but how far could she have gotten before another dragon found her?

Tardala gave us soap to wash, which I thought might have been more for her than for us, for surely our bodies were ripe and my hair a knotted mess. I praised her mercilessly. She was even kind enough to mend a hole in my dress—I'd hidden the blood-stained one—while Eden helped me comb through the growing mats in my curls. We were halfway through the mess of hair when Eden asked, "What have you heard of Cansere?"

My heart leapt into my throat. My fingers turned cold. Eden's Sestan accent was flawless, but her voice was androgynous at best, and even the *mention* of home set my nerves buzzing—

"Depends on who you ask," Tardala replied, never looking up from her stitchwork, perfectly calm. I reminded myself that when a country was at war, it was normal to speak of it, and I forced myself to relax. To focus on my hair so I wouldn't give myself away. "My sister, she heard from a troop marching out that the Phoenix armies are disintegrating, that the king is hiding in the south, licking his wounds, and the fighting will be finished by summer."

I picked at a knot, keeping my eyes down. Listened to Eden's breathing. She didn't react.

"But I talked to a merchant the very next day, and *he* said our armies are far superior, but the Phoenix defense is strong, because even King Nicosia cannot fly."

I stiffened. Even Eden's breath caught.

Now Tardala did look up, reproachful. "I, of course, support our king. I am merely repeating what was said."

"But of course," Eden agreed. "I just . . . did you say *fly*?"

The image of Renn in the basement in Speth, hale and glowing golden . . . Was that halo of light even more than I'd realized?

Angel of fire. Was it true, or merely more propaganda?

The link grew warm within me, even as I shivered. Even as I choked on hope.

"It's just a rumor." Tardala knotted and snipped her thread before passing me the dress, which I accepted with hearty thanks. "They're all rumors. Who knows what the truth will be, if we ever hear it?"

Tardala went to bed shortly after. Eden and I managed to save all but a lock of my hair. We cast the matted offender into the fire.

I dreamed of Ursa and woke with tears clinging to my eyelashes. I felt sawed in two, like I'd become only half of myself. I'd mourned Ursa alongside my parents after their deaths, but I'd never truly let go of my twin sister, just as she had never truly let go of me.

Perhaps the need to run, to hide, and to make it back to Cansere was a blessing of the gods. Surely if I were not so focused on my and Eden's survival, I would drown in heartache.

I hated to leave, but I pushed Eden to rise before dawn so we could flee. The longer we stayed in one place, the more likely we'd be found, and the more likely our host might begin to suspect us or consider reporting us.

I stole radishes from one of Tardala's neighbors before hurrying down the road.

We'd come far enough south that we began to cross paths with other travelers. Every time we did, Eden would move to the far side of the road, keeping me between herself and the strangers. I don't think she did it knowingly, but I didn't mind. I kept my eyes forward and wore Eden's blanket like a pack. With how thin Eden had become, her haircut, and her clothes, she did pass easily for a young man unless one came close to study her. I noted that, despite this, she looked nothing like Renn, and I doubted even more that they shared a parent.

We considered—huddling together in a barn one night, praying we were not discovered—going to the west coast and finding a ship there . . . but we would have to stow away, for we had not a merit to our names, and surely Nicosia would send word to the ports first, for there was no way to reach Cansere except by sea. If Renn *had* rallied troops, the Midly Strait might be a war zone, albeit with Canseren ships along with Sestan. When I started talking about the possible logistics of it, securing passage or stowing away, Eden immediately froze up.

"No. No, I can't."

Her sharp words surprised me; Eden was a kind and mild woman, an easy companion, but those words were knives.

I tried, "Eden, we have to—"

"No." She shook her head, short hair wisping over her forehead. "I will not board one of their ships, legally or illegally. Not with . . ." She swallowed. "Sailors."

I understood her meaning. It had nothing to do with class and everything to do with the fact that most professional sailors were men. I gingerly touched her elbow; she pressed a fist into her mouth, trying to steady herself. After a minute, with red eyes, she croaked, "I would rather die."

I believed her. Eden had suffered tragedy upon tragedy and had not been given the time or resources she desperately needed to heal. So I took her hands in mine and promised her we would find another way. We would go to the Midly Strait, the narrow band of water separating our land from our enemy's, and sort it out then. I had no idea how we could possibly complete that part of our journey—even a strong swimmer could not cross the strait. But we'd done well stealing what we could—what we dared—so far, so perhaps we'd find a fishing vessel to take . . . though neither of us had sailing experience, and I could not fathom how a man-powered boat would handle the currents of the strait.

We still had far to travel. We still had weeks to decide, so I let it be.

On the seventeenth of May, on a bright spring day dampened only by monumental waves of frustration pouring from Renn's side of the bond, Eden and I approached a town called Horgansten. It was about the size of Fount, surrounded by open farmland and divided by cobbled roads. We washed in a brook before entering, ensuring we looked as well as could be managed. We'd yet to run into any soldiers, but the sound of a dog barking—even in a town such as this—put me on edge, so much so that my muscles became constantly sore from tensing them.

Our hope was to find some way of sending a message into Cansere, but while Horgansten had a post cell, we learned all correspondence to the southern country had been cut off since last year. There were no birders in town—no one who might send a pigeon. We were truly an island.

We had to find work.

I assumed crafters were about as rare in the Sestan countryside as they were in Cansere, since those accessing craftlock went to Rodsfell by the age of ten. I learned, through careful inquiring, that crafters *were* dispatched to cities, especially healers, though the closest to Horgansten was in Gaptuawan, eight miles to the east. I was then directed to the village midwife, who saw to immediate medical needs.

I could not boast that I was a healer here. I dared not draw too much attention to myself, and I was not in Sestan uniform—I might be reported for illegal use of craftlock and sent right back to Rodsfell. So Eden and I slipped through the village with our ears and eyes open, looking for anyone who might be sick, who might be willing to pay for my services under the table.

I'd nearly given up when I heard a woman's scream.

Skin pebbling, I followed the sound to a square house near the western edge of the town and stepped up to the door. Lifted my fist, but hesitated.

What if I failed?

Doubt, a dark stranger, wove between my ribs like uncarded wool. I'd become so slow. Out of practice. Haggard.

Was I still enough?

"Nym," Eden pleaded.

Blinking away the disparaging thoughts, I rapped on the door, softly at first, then loudly, until I banged my fist against it.

We had so few options.

A girl of about twelve answered, her hair tied back with a kerchief, a frayed violet cincture tight on her narrow hips, her eyes wide. "What? What is it?"

Death whispered in the room behind her.

I heard moans from deeper in the house and immediately recognized them. "Is your mother in labor?"

Moisture welled in the girl's eyes, and she nodded. "But she's sick."

Eden and I exchanged a glance. "May I come in? I'm here to help."

I didn't wait for an answer. I pushed my way in, leaving Eden in the front room with the girl and following the cool brush of death and the agonizing sounds toward the back of the house. The air was muggy and smelled of sweat; I found the laboring woman in the back room beside an open window, an elderly midwife between her legs, a sister at her head. I knew it was a sister, for they shared a face. Identical twins.

My chest caved in at the sight, the renewed loss stinging like the sword Nicosia had used to pin me to that tree. But I could not think of Ursa. Not yet. Not now.

Bloody rags and towels littered the floor.

"Who are you?" the midwife asked, tendrils of white hair sticking to her sweaty face. She shouted, "We need more hot water!"

"I can help." I couldn't ask for payment, not like this. Not when I might not . . .

Now wasn't the time to dwell on shortcomings.

I, too, had experienced the fear and pains of childbirth. Even without death raveling warning chills around my arms, I would know this woman was dying.

I crossed the small room and knelt beside her bed, taking her hand. Her sister began to say something to me, but I dowsed and fled into the mother's lumis.

She was a puzzle, not unlike me, although her puzzle formed five large rings, each hovering above the next, largest to smallest. The pieces were warping, cracking, tilting, falling. There was no lumis for the baby. Lumie were not shared, and I would not be able to enter the infant's until it came into the world.

Fighting a sore lump in my throat, I hurried to the rings and began soothing them, ushering magic into my hands, trying to be patient with its pace. However weakened I had become, my mind remained sharp. I knew what to do. I pulled magic into paste and reset pieces, turning and shifting until they fit snugly together. Thanks to my hunger, the magic drained me quickly. Still, I pressed on. A few pieces snapped out of their rings, resisting my touch, but I refitted them diligently, until it seemed the circlet would hold.

Moments after I returned to the room, the cries of the baby rang through it.

"Is it well? Is it well?" The mother pushed herself to her elbows.

The midwife looked pleased as she cut the cord. "Well enough, aye."

I did not ask permission; I slipped a hand through the midwife's thin arms and touched the newborn's foot. Her lumis spread before me, three small ponds grouped together with cattails growing along their sides. The image of it was so reminiscent of Ursa's it gave me pause. Shaking myself, I went to the farthest pond, its waters darker, and pressed magic into it, imagining my hand a net to catch dirt and refuse, until the waters cleared.

When I returned to reality, the midwife eyed me knowingly before handing the babe to its mother. "Hale as a harvest," she assured the woman.

The woman cried and clutched the baby to her chest, lying back and staring at the ceiling. Her sister stared at me—not with antagonism, but curiosity. Surely she understood what had transpired.

"You . . ." The midwife crooked a bony finger at me. ". . . Come."

She stepped out of the room and down the hall, to the front area where Eden sat with the trembling twelve-year-old. To the child, the midwife said, "Mother and baby are fine. You might go say hello."

The girl lit up and ran down the hallway. Anger sparked in my heart—not mine, but Renn's. Whatever he dealt with seemed to be coming to a head. I tucked it away, needing to focus on the present.

"Who are you?" the midwife asked Eden.

"He's with me," I answered, not bothering to mask my Canseren accent. I was out of place regardless of whether I came from the south or the north.

"He." The midwife snorted. "Perhaps to a blind fool."

Eden focused her gaze on the floor.

Addressing me, the midwife said, "You're a long way from home."

I nodded. "I am. We're trying desperately to make it back, but the war has barred our travel."

"It's barred most everyone's travel, the war. Only small fishing vessels are making it through."

Eden lifted her head, doing a poor job of hiding her hope. "Has Cansere attacked Sestan soil?"

The midwife shook her head. "Not yet."

My soul shriveled. I had wondered if we might come across a war camp for the Phoenix where we could take refuge. But this had always been Nicosia's war, and he'd decimated Rove. Renn was on the defensive.

"You've a long ways to go," the midwife said. "Hundred fifty miles to the strait."

Breath left me. We'd been traveling so long, so hard. To have so much distance left to cover—*inhabited* distance—I pressed my hand to the wall to steady myself. Eden shielded her face with her hands to hide her weeping.

The woman frowned. "I appreciate what you did in there. Our stationed healer is eight miles away, but he costs too much for most folk to afford. I might have lost both of them." She hesitated. "Maybe just one. I know what I'm doing." She folded her arms as though to protect her pride. "I'll make a deal with you."

I searched her haggard face. "I'm listening."

"I've been meaning to visit my sister in Catalaine."

She waited expectantly, but her statement went over my head. Not Eden's, however. The princess lifted her head. "Catalaine?"

"That's what I said."

Eden looked at me. "It's a city not far from the border."

Hope blossomed in my center, pushing out the wilt and Renn's lingering anger.

"She married a Canseren. He's dead now." The midwife shrugged. "But I could take one of you that far."

The hope cracked. "*One* of us?"

She nodded, mouth pressed into a firm line. Resolute. "My wagon is small. I couldn't possibly hide both of you. And I assume you're hiding, dressed the way you are." She indicated Eden. "So who will it be?"

Eden's eyes watered. "We can't possibly . . . Please, I'll better the disguise—"

"I'm not risking my neck over an ounce of gratitude," the midwife snapped. "One of you to Catalaine. We leave in the morning."

Eden and I exchanged a long glance. Her countenance began to crumble. She wasn't used to this hardship—she'd grown up noble.

I pressed a hand into my heart in an attempt to balm it. Cansere would lose hope if it lost Renn *and* Eden. Technically, since Eden was older and "married," *she* was the heir to the throne, though I did not think she'd fight Renn for it. No Canseren in their right mind would validate that sham of a wedding, nor welcome Adoel Nicosia to the throne. And I . . . I could do this. I had to.

"If I take over your role, as long as I'm able," I bartered, "would you also try to procure my friend a ship? *Safe* passage to Cansere?"

Eden jolted. "No."

The midwife eyed me. Considered for many long seconds. "Yes, I would make that trade."

"Then take her. Please."

Eden rose to her feet. "You don't . . . you don't have to do this."

"You are more important to Cansere than I am." I crossed the room and took her hands in mine. Lowered my voice. "Go, and go quickly. Tell them I'm coming. I'll try to follow your path, through Catalaine. Tell Renn I'm coming."

Her eyes filled with tears. She embraced me, holding me too tight to her slender frame. "I will, I will. I promise."

The fact that she did not protest further spoke volumes of how tired she was, how close she'd come to giving up. Eden needed this. I . . . I could wait a little longer.

Turning to the midwife, I said, "Thank you. You've no idea what this means to us."

She eyed us, a little suspicious, but it passed. "Let me take care of things here, and I'll take you to my home. You've many patients. And I trust you to keep your word. What was your name?"

"Ursa," I answered, throat aching around the word. "My name is Ursa."

Chapter 10

Elantriana—the proclivity for Sestans to have absurdly long names astonished me—ensured all was right with her patient, cleaning up rags and packing up her things, before leading Eden and me to her squat home down the street. It was a two-room affair, even smaller than my home in Fount, with only a half wall separating her sleeping quarters from everything else. For her prickly nature, Elantriana was kind. She saw us fed and washed, and lent me a dress to change into. It should have been tight on me, or so I thought when I measured it with my eyes. But I'd lost so much weight on our journey it fit almost perfectly.

Elantriana's generosity was not free; she put Eden and me to work. I washed the bloodied rags from the birth while Eden struggled to peel potatoes over a basin, a task she'd never done before. When she finished, she swept the rooms and watered the midwife's many plants. Though I wanted to stay indoors to hide my face, when Elantriana bid me to fetch water from the well, I did so without complaint. I would earn her trust, earn my dinner, and earn my place here, until it grew too dangerous to stay. I wasn't sure how I'd know. Perhaps Horgansten would remain under its king's notice, and I'd stay here indefinitely, until the war ended and someone came to retrieve me. I wondered, briefly, if it might be my brother Brien, but such fantasies proved too painful to bear.

Our host showed me everything I would need to know while she was gone. Which stray cats were hers and which I was allowed to feed, when to harvest and hang to dry the herbs in the little garden to the side of her home, how much food she expected to still be in her stores. She told me what to charge the sick and ensured they would come to me, and if anyone asked, I was her granddaughter, and I ought to mask that Canseren tongue of mine.

Eden and I slept on a pallet by the hearth that night, a luxury compared to the cold ground, and before dawn Elantriana roused us, instructing us how to pack her little wagon and feed her mule, which would be pulling it. She made Eden put on a dress far too short for her, so she had to keep her slacks on. "If you pretend you're a man," she insisted, "the patrol will *know* something is rotten."

She gave me a red sash to wear around my upper arm to mark me as her replacement.

They set off south before the sun had fully risen. I stood in the middle of the road, watching them fade into the softening blue, until gooseflesh dotted my skin.

Alone. Well and truly. No Elantriana, no Eden, Ursa.

I clutched my dress over my heart. The road seemed to stretch on forever. Widen under my feet. The shadows of predawn yawned like the onslaught of death in a lumis. The first birds had stirred in their nests, yet the world had grown too quiet.

Please wake up, Renn, I prayed, shivering, though I wasn't cold. *Please wake up.*

Alone. Alone. Alone.

Shutting my eyes, I drew in a deep breath. Let it out and drew in another, trying to feel the ground beneath my feet. I clutched at my bodice until my knuckles ached. *Please wake up.*

I couldn't stand here forever.

I'd only just returned to the house when, thankfully, my first client came knocking on my door, begging for help with his brother's broken leg.

I was eager to fill Elantriana's shoes—an eagerness that warred with my instinct to hide. But I *needed* the work. I needed the people, the voices, the company. Still, I went about my role with care, not completely healing anyone in Horgansten. I could not let on that I used the craft.

I bound wounds and splinted breaks, made harmless teas from the herbs I could identify, used poultices Elantriana had already prepared. I listened when people talked, gleaned little tidbits of information.

"I heard they have no ships," an adolescent boy commented, referring to Cansere.

"Why wouldn't they have ships?" his friend retorted. "They're surrounded by ocean, just like us."

Another time, a woman complained to me, "I haven't had that tea in months! No one can stock it. I don't know why; all the fighting's in the east."

Only to have her sister snap, "Watch your tongue. What if a soldier passes by a window and overhears? He'll cut it out for you, most like."

Or an elderly man whispering, "I'd like to see it. An angel in the sky. See it before I'm gone."

Only to have his son, much like the man I'd passed on the road, insist, "It's propaganda, Pa."

I gave instructions for the medicine and mended lumie just to the point of being whole, then allowed the body to do the rest. Broken bones, rashes, sore throats, a pregnancy check-in. All the while I slept in Elantriana's bed, collected her coin, and ate her food, regaining my strength. Each night, alone in her house, I chafed against the silence around me. I talked to myself constantly to keep it at bay, and when my voice tired, I drowned in answering silence. I'd never realized how quiet the world could become, how silent the fall of night. I was too used to *her* being there.

When I slept, I dreamed of Adoel Nicosia.

I fought against the binding to the tree, bark digging into my back, as I approached, floating as though a ghost. I screamed, and Nicosia shoved a hand down my throat, reaching deep into me.

Ursa screamed.

I'd wake up shrieking, my body doused in sweat, my half-heart galloping and flickering painfully.

The next morning, throat dry, I rasped, "Ursa?"

But she did not respond, and my heart broke for it.

I dowsed and fueled my heart. Checked the locks on the doors. Peered out the windows into the dark town. Then I sobbed into the midwife's pillow, promising myself this would be the last time I cried on Sestan soil, for I was so tired of this place taking things from me. In Cansere, I had been strong. Here, I was weak, fragile, and so desperately alone.

Were it not for the slivers of Renn that came through our shared heart, I might have finally broken. But I held on to him and, in my mind's eye, imagined he held on to me, too.

After that, I spent my nights bolstering my magic-laced puzzle pieces, something I would do for the rest of my life, whether I died tomorrow or in seventy years. Then I would kneel by my golden-threaded merlon and talk to Renn, for I'd grown so used to having someone to talk to, I could not break the habit, even though I knew he couldn't hear me. Each night I felt for signs of him, the shift of feeling through our heart-bond, or an occasional stubbed toe or smacked elbow. I talked and listened until I couldn't keep my eyes open, and slept an hour or two before Rodsfell haunted my nightmares, and I'd wake in bleary panic, or sometimes sleep until dawn, only to wake to my eyelashes heavy with half-dried tears.

My seventh day in Horgansten, after tending a dislocated knee, I felt a jubilation so strong it knocked me off-kilter. I nearly fell into a horse trough. My limbs filled with glee and relief. Renewed, I ran back to Elantriana's home and knelt just inside her door, praying to the gods that it was what I hoped, that Eden had made it across the strait and reunited with Renn. That she was the cause of such happiness in him. I wanted it to be true—I *needed* it to be true—for if Eden had fallen into enemy hands or perished on this journey, I would suffocate beneath the guilt of it all my life. I needed her to be safe. I needed it all to be worth it.

I stayed in Horgansten for eight days. Eight days, until two horsemen wearing black and blue came into town. Scouts, perhaps, or messengers seeking to secure housing for oncoming soldiers. I didn't know.

I'd already packed one of Elantriana's bags, so I was ready to flee the moment I saw them. I did not take the main road but ventured farther west into a forest of white and red spruce. I mourned the loss of the midwife's lodge and the safety it provided, and I let myself mourn it, dry-eyed, hugging myself as I trekked farther south, using the sun and stars to guide me, rationing the food I'd taken from Elantriana's cupboards, foraging as I went.

If I'd thought the town quiet, the forest was mute.

There were birds and insects during the day, but at night the wind lulled life into deep slumber. My every breath echoed in my ears. I slept in thickets or against dense brush, my knees pulled tightly to my chest, and pressed my fingers to my beating heart, imagining every other thump was Renn's. I wondered how much he could sense my solitude, my loneliness, my aching for my sister, for each night, almost as soon as the sun had set, I felt warmth through our connection, like it was not my hand pressed between my breasts but his. I dreamed of the distant music of a string quartet, of Renn's hand on my waist in his salon, asking me to dance with him. Of his lips in my hair whispering, *I love you.*

Four and a half months had passed since I'd last seen him. More than a season. Did he still love me as he'd thrice claimed, or was this warmth I felt his adoration for another, someone who'd come to his side after I'd left it, who helped him with the war while I rotted away in Nicosia's conservatory?

The theory sparked new fears in me. I pushed it away, but time and time again, in the long stretches of loneliness, it reemerged, taunting me. In truth, Renn did not need me anymore. Despite the occasional aches and chills I felt through our bond, his lumis would hold. I knew it held. Knew I'd done it right. The Canseren king had no need for a shadow any longer.

I'd told him, once, that he loved the magic, not me.

I prayed I'd been wrong.

At dusk on the sixth day after I left Horgansten, I came across three wolves. A white one in front, perhaps twenty paces from me, and two with gray coats farther into the forest, peering out from behind trees. I stopped on my path and held the first's stare. Ironically, my first thought was *I have company.*

But fear soon overwhelmed loneliness.

I can endure it, I told myself, even as I trembled. I would go into my lumis and heal it as they tore into my flesh. Heal and fight, heal and fight, until they gave up. Though with the scarcity of food and the exhaustion from travel and magic, surely I would lose my strength before they did.

I thought of Eden, of her promise. *I will die before I go back.*

But if I died, I feared Renn would, too. I couldn't risk it. So I lifted my chin and stared down the white wolf, tense, ready to fight with everything I had.

We stood like that for nearly a quarter hour before the wolf turned away and sprinted back into the trees.

That night I dozed on the heavy bough of a spruce, and in the morning, I left the forest behind.

I found a small road and took it southeast, stopping a band of musicians once to ask for directions to Catalaine. They directed me, and the following day I found a sign for it at a crossroads. My relief was so great

I nearly fainted with it, then smiled to myself, knowing the sensation would be passed along to Renn. Sure enough, moments later, I felt the faintest tendrils of confusion and hope wind through my chest.

I'd made better time than I'd hoped; rations from Elantriana's home greatly reduced my need to forage, and the underbrush of the forest hadn't slowed me too badly. But this sign claimed I had only twelve miles to Catalaine, and that lent me a little more energy.

However, as I spied the city over the hills—the first true city I'd laid eyes on since Rodsfell—my hope died as a moth succumbing to flame.

Soldiers.

There were several of them just outside the city, which likely meant there were more within it. I saw no tents or camp, so Catalaine was either their station or they were boarding there. I shook with hunger and with fear, contemplating my best course of action. Elantriana may have headed back to Horgansten by now, and even if she hadn't, I had no address nor means of finding her here. I uttered a quiet prayer to Hem, the god of kings and justice, that Eden had not been recognized. And to Salm, god of the sea, that she had made it across the strait safely. And to Zia, begging her to look upon me kindly and not take the side of the man who believed himself to be her son. Zia, the goddess of women and womanly things, the youngest of the pantheon and the most overlooked. I sat on the other side of a hill, hiding myself from Catalaine, pleading with her to help me, pleading to be spared. As darkness began creeping over the sky, I offered a similar prayer to Hem: *If you don't care for me, care for Renn. He is one of yours, and if I fall, I fear he will fall as well.*

I assured myself that Renn Reshua Noblewight had borne a completely shattered lumis when I'd met him yet still lived. Perhaps, even if I died, the gods would continue to favor him.

Gods-touched. I hoped it was true.

On that thought, I looked down at my hands, studying them despite knowing I ought to move soon, while there was some light left.

I did not want to be a lone woman in the dark in a strange city full of soldiers.

I would never feel ready, so I tucked my hair into my dress in an attempt to make it look shorter before heading into Catalaine, following one of the roads, trying my best to walk like I belonged there. When I thought I felt a soldier looking my way, I waved to a random man dropping an empty barrel outside an inn and greeted him as though I knew him. Unsure, he waved back, and I hurried along, wondering how I'd possibly make it to the strait. I could not see the ocean from Catalaine, but when the wind blew right, I could smell it.

I had a few coins I'd kept from my work with Elantriana's clients, though not enough to see me easily by. I moved away from the soldiers I'd seen upon entering the city and searched for a place to stay in the rapidly descending night. Stopping at a small public house advertising rooms on a winding street, I opened the door. Only one table was occupied, by an older couple. No soldiers.

A stunning, rotund woman worked the counter, and immediately I knew I could not afford this place, not if she ate and dressed so well on its earnings. But it was dark, and I had to try.

She smiled at me, ignoring the obvious travel wear of my clothing. "How can I help you?"

I put on my best Sestan accent. "I'm trying to find a place to stay; I got in late, and my husband's caravan was delayed. But my allowance has nearly run out. Do you have a small space? I don't need a meal."

My stomach grumbled in protest.

She pursed her mouth in a way that made me think of Renn's mother. "I have two rooms, but they're each three silver merits."

Fear pulsed in my chest. "I see. I don't suppose I could work off what I don't have?"

She shook her head. "I've plenty of staff, miss. But the Green Dragon down the way might have what you're looking for."

I glanced over my shoulder to the window by the door. Black outside. Keeping my voice down, I said, "I can give you five copper merits if you just let me sleep on the kitchen floor. I . . . I really don't want to go out in the city again. Not by myself."

She considered me a moment, and Zia had mercy on me, for she understood my need and agreed to the fee, taking most of my coin in exchange for a wool blanket on the floor by the dying fire in the tight kitchen. I thanked her profusely and laid my head down on the stone, eager to fall asleep and regain my energy.

I woke up easily at dawn, having tossed and turned the night through with discomfiting dreams. The cook, a woman who from behind looked like my deceased mother, didn't speak to me. But as I fixed myself up and headed to leave, she handed me a sleeve of roasted nuts, and I blessed her in the name of all six gods, twice.

I took the busiest roads.

I did this in hopes of blending in, for there were indeed more soldiers in the city, and I did not want them to notice me, should word of my escape have reached this far. I searched faces as I went, hoping to see women who looked like me. Some were close, but their hair was straight, or their eyes were brown. At one point, in the market, a soldier with one silver mark on his collar locked gazes with me. Terrified, I smiled at him and tried to be on my way, but he approached regardless, scanning me head to toe.

"Who are you?" he asked.

I opened my mouth to answer but paused.

Who am I?

I knew the correct answer. That was, the lie I had practiced time and time again. And yet being faced head-on with the question struck something in me. *Who am I?*

I knew who I'd *been*, but I wasn't sure I understood what I had become.

Yet before and now, I'd been a survivor, and those instincts kicked in. "Elantriana," I answered, painting myself a Sestan identity. When the man seemed satisfied, I dipped away as a man with a cart passed through, ensuring he could not ask me any follow-up questions. I followed the cart to the end of the road, then asked the driver—a farmer, guessing by his green cincture—where he was going.

"To Klepton," he answered.

"Klepton," I repeated in my Sestan accent. "Is that far?"

He laughed. "Is the ocean far?" Regarding me, he added, "You've got a dialect on you. Where are you from?"

"Rodsfell." The lie came easily.

He whistled. "No wonder. Happy to give you a ride for a kiss." He winked at me. I could just make out the faded leather cord of his wedding pendant tucked beneath his shirt.

I acted bashful. "On the cheek only, sir. I'm saving myself for my husband, and I doubt your wife would appreciate such a gift."

He laughed again. "That old bag doesn't care a whit what I do, long as I bring home pay." He pointed to the apple of his cheek, above his whiskers. Concerned he'd try to take more, I gave in and pecked him quickly before he could turn his head.

"The rest when we arrive." I winked and slid onto the back of his cart. I hid my disgust at the exchange. To say my options were limited was an overstatement.

I was not tired, but I unfurled the blanket I'd stolen from Eden's room, turning it over so the plain side faced up, and wrapped it around me as though I planned to sleep. It gave me an excuse to hide my face. But, as distance swept by, my fatigue got the better of me, and I did slip away a moment, my head propped up on a crate. I didn't wake until later, one side of my face hot from the sun, to a voice asking, "Who is this?"

I looked up to see three Sestan soldiers inspecting the cart.

Chapter 11

Panic rushed through me, making me lightheaded. "Hello," I tried, remembering at the last moment to adapt my accent. My mind spun through a million stories I might tell them, but I would not give away information they didn't need. The cart was right at the northern entrance of Klepton, and over the driver's shoulder, the city stretched wide, sloping downward before stretching to the sea: the Midly Strait.

"Just asked for a ride." The cart driver shrugged.

The closest of the three soldiers eyed me. He had two silver marks on his collar, no notation as crafter. "Your name?"

"Lissela," I offered, rushing to think of a Sestan surname.

"Your full name," he clarified.

"Lissela Dan." I tried to adopt the unassuming nature of my sister, Lissel. I imagined myself younger and inexperienced, kindhearted and shy. I glanced away and tucked hair loosed from my braid behind my ear.

"What's your purpose?"

"I'm visiting my grandmother," I explained carefully, shaping each vowel with care. "Elantriana. She's a midwife here."

The driver crooked an eyebrow.

The first soldier took my chin in his bare hand and turned my face one way, then another, like I was a fair animal. He glanced to his companions; the second soldier nodded.

Panic rang in my ears. They knew me. I fit a description. I'd traveled too slowly, and word of me had reached Klepton before I did. They were going to take me. I knew it in my half-formed heart: They were going to take me.

Before the soldier announced the verdict, I grabbed his hand and dowsed into his lumis. Barely recognized the shape of it before I tore into pieces marked by death lines. Enough to hurt him. Enough to slow him.

I leapt from the carriage as he cried out, leaving my things behind, sprinting into the city. The second soldier rushed to the aid of the first, but the third took chase, barreling after me. I dove onto a side street, desperate to find and take as many corners as I could to lose him. However, as soon as I veered around one, he seized me by the braid, yanking my head back. His other arm hooked around my waist. I fought as he pulled me back two steps, then forced myself to go limp in his arms. The sudden imbalance of weight sent us both to the slick cobbles, drawing attention from passersby. The man wrestled me down. I kicked my leg, making my skirt ride up, and he made the mistake of grabbing my knee.

I dowsed. I hurt him. Only for a second before he jerked away, sending me slamming back into the city, but it was enough. I kicked my heel into his chest before scrambling to my feet and darting around the corner, west, south, west, south, trying to put as much distance between me and the soldiers as I could. I dove under two men moving a shipment of lumber and dashed between market stalls, the smell of salt and fish growing strong as I went. Someone, a local, grabbed my sleeve, perhaps thinking me a thief, and tore it at the shoulder. I wrenched away. Circled around the next corner, the slope of the city propelling my steps. My lungs burned terribly, and when I took the next corner, I forced myself to slow to a jog, then a quick walk, trying to appear more as a woman in a hurry and not a convict. I could not stop moving to catch my breath or to find a drink of water. I looped onto a main road and took it south until I felt too exposed, then dodged into winding side alleys. Anywhere, as long as it took me closer to the ocean. I would swim to Cansere, if I had to.

At the side of a dress shop, I bent over and threw up. Heard a shrill whistle and darted farther into the alley, hiding behind some garbage. Curled up, wishing myself small. Dowsed, but there was little more to do than strengthen my weak heart. It felt like a bird's—too light, too quick. I urged it to settle.

New fear fountained in me from my connection to Renn. Fear and . . . hope?

I cleaved to it. Formed my hands into fists and imagined that golden thread beneath my grip. I craved an anchor. A compass. Anything to stave off my helplessness.

Trying to keep my desperate breaths quiet, I peeked around the garbage. Didn't see anyone pursuing me, only a family passing by, a young boy complaining about not getting a sweet. I crept down the alley, coming upon a shop for fine porcelain, and peered at my reflection in the window. Gaunt, eyes wide as a doe's and gray as a storm. My hair frizzed around my braid. Spitting into my hands, I smoothed it down. Noted the rip in my sleeve and tore at my other arm to make the sliver of exposed shoulder look intentional. Fisherman's daughter. Surely I could be a fisherman's daughter.

A customer inside the shop met my eye. I turned and hurried, pushing my weary legs forward.

A burst like thunder echoed from the strait.

I didn't know what it was. Collectively, people paused. Stepped out into the street, opened doors and windows to peer out. I moved along with them. Good; they could hide me, though all the while I searched for the black and blue of the Sestan military uniform. A few people pointed, and I heard the words *ship* and *cannon*. I lifted my eyes to see smoke tinting the air gray at the port.

A second *boom* split the air, and this time people gasped. A few turned and began hurrying uphill, north, away from the water. More came out onto the street to find the source of the commotion. I pushed through them, eyeing the strait, spying a ship with a white-and-blue

Sestan sail. Cannon testing? But the murmurs of the throng said this was unusual, unexpected. Whispers of *war* and *Cansere*—

I pushed through faster, ignoring elbows to my side and the feet I stepped on. My eyes locked with the sea, desperately searching over heads and shoulders, shoving back when people tried to move me from their path. Rows of Sestan ships, most with their sails furled, docked. But beyond them I saw two more, one closer and one farther, both without notable colors or markings. Massive ships, not fishing boats.

Boom!

Who would be setting off cannon fire at a far west Sestan port, with ships that size? *Cansere.* It had to be. Eden had told them . . . or Nicosia had moved his armies in attempts to find me, or some other reason I wasn't privy to, but those *had* to be Canseren ships. I begged the gods they were Canseren ships.

I ran. I ran with everything in me, breaking free of the oglers on the main road, feet pounding on cobbled pavement. I ran so wildly I tripped over myself twice. My heart steamed and spat like an overhot tea kettle. *Just a little longer,* I pleaded, gasping for air as stitches formed in my sides. *Just a little farther.*

A second crowd had formed near the docks, city folk more interested in a show than safety. Many Sestan soldiers moved about them, barking orders, hauling supplies onto a ship, or simply marching, searching, watching. As I grew closer, I saw a line of soldiers pushing at the crowd, admonishing them to "Get back!" I squeezed through the masses, bent low to better wind through bodies, earning several curses.

The moment I saw a gap between the soldiers, I dashed.

Body fueled on hope and desperation, I split through the line of soldiers, jumped over a short wall, and sprinted for the docks. Whistles and bellows followed me. I searched frantically for a rowboat to take me out to the nearest unmarked ship, but a soldier had taken off after me, leaving me no time to embark. Nearly twisting my ankle, I bolted east, toward the larger ships.

The soldier grabbed my arm. Jerked me around. I saw his collar before I saw his face. The silver triangle there. Soulbinder.

No!

I could not let him.

So I leapt on him, every bit a deranged animal, kicking and clawing and biting. He stumbled back as I seized his ear and dowsed, unleashing myself on him, wielding magic like the ship cannons against his lumis, enough to make me nauseous. I let go, not lingering to see the damage. More whistles, more men breaking formation to pursue me.

I bolted down the nearest dock. Snatched the rope ladder hanging off the main deck rail of a large ship. It swayed and twisted. My muscles shook as I tried to hold on and climb. Hands grasped at my legs, my ankles. I kicked, I dowsed, I hurt. I scrambled over the lip and toppled onto the deck.

The dragons were right behind me.

I wheezed, pain thumping in my chest, but I could not slow now. Not when I was so, so close. I sprinted across the deck, building up as much speed as I could until I reached the opposite bulwark. I jumped up and *leapt*, just barely clearing the space between that ship and the next. My hips slammed into the bulwark. Hissing through my teeth, I pulled myself over and onto the deck. Spied a rowboat.

I frantically dug my nails into its lashings, tugging rough rope, ignoring the splinters it left in my hands. I'd nearly undone the first knot when a crossbow bolt slammed into the bulwark only inches from my shoulder. Whipping my head around, I spied two more soldiers climbing up a gangplank.

Not enough time. But they would not have me. *I would never let them have me.*

I would drown before I returned to that gods-forsaken tree.

I ran, this time down the length of the ship. An adjacent Sestan vessel, its sails unfurled, was pulling away from the dock. Moving into the strait, closer to the fray. My ticket *out*.

My weak heart guttered as I pushed my legs faster, faster, all the way to the prow. I realized I'd misjudged the distance the moment I sprang from it, reaching forward for the moving vessel as though I might catch its railing with the tips of my fingers. But the gap proved too wide, my body too weak. I jumped and met only air.

Blue sky and blue sea spun around me as I fell, the sick feeling of weightlessness shoving at my stomach. The water struck like an open-handed slap across my entire body.

The blueness faded the deeper I sank. It turned murky and gray, swallowing me as if a great, ghostly maw. The cold shocked my skin and burrowed deep. Bubbles escaped my mouth, my lungs burning for air after such abuse, but momentum sank me deeper, the water pressing in on all sides, clogging my ears and sucking me down, down, down. I reached upward toward a sliver of contorting sunlight, urging my expended legs to kick, to save me, but my calves spasmed. It was as though Salm himself wrapped his fingers around my ankles and pulled.

Light. That sliver of sun brightened as though the great star had shifted in the heavens to beam directly down at me. Brighter, bigger, until it pierced the surface of the water, shooting toward me like a heavenly arrow. It took on the form of an angel, a golden man with wings of gossamer, his hand outstretched toward mine.

My last bit of air escaped my lips. *Renn.*

That I would see a dream of him before dying was a gift.

His hand passed mine. Clamped on to my forearm.

Suddenly we were surging up, up, up, as though the sea had become one great, torrential wave. Salm's hold shattered. Water sluiced away all at once. Cool wind whipped into my lungs as we soared higher, higher, his other arm encircling my waist, steadying me, *holding* me, and as the pressure of rising abated and we banked south, I looked up, looked into his gold-flushed face and his beautiful blue eyes, and knew he was real. This was real.

An angel of fire.

I was home.

I barely registered landing. On a ship, I thought, farther into the strait. I couldn't quite see it, what with my face pressed so tightly against Renn's soaked shirt. Soaked from seawater and soaked from my tears, for I gripped handfuls of cloth and sobbed against him, great, heaving cries unlike any I'd ever had before. His arms bound me completely to him, leaving no space between us. He pressed his face against the side of my dripping hair and whispered, "I'm sorry, I'm sorry, I'm sorry," over and over again.

Another *boom* shouted. I held on to him until my hands went numb, as though he might vanish if I did not, all the while sobbing under the golden glow of wings made of light.

Chapter 12

My wet clothes hit the floor with a sloppy *thump*.

Shivering, I wrung out my hair—again—over them, seawater dripping onto the pile. A round brazier on the floor warmed the ship's small cabin, but gooseflesh speckled my skin anyway. With trembling hands I pulled a wet rag from the basin of fresh water and wiped salt from my skin, then, still damp, grabbed the clean, dry clothes set on the narrow bed for me—a simple shift, a simple dress. I tugged them on and tied up the front laces before again wringing out my hair. It always took forever to dry. I'd worry about the salt later.

Yet even with warm clothes and a lit brazier, I trembled. I stared at my quivering hands as though they were not my own. Forced them to still even as my heart pounded against my chest.

Hope flickered through my heart connection just before a soft rap sounded at the door. Breath catching, anxiety fleeing, I ran to it and flung it open. Renn stood there, changed into a common soldier's uniform, damp hair sticking to his forehead, a small tray of food balanced on one hand.

I burrowed into him right there, chest to chest, absorbing the warmth of him, the realness of him. His free arm circled me and held me tightly. Almost too tightly, but I didn't care. If he crushed me into nothing, it would be a good death.

He felt different. Thicker. Smelled different, like sea and leather and black powder. But I felt that golden cord between us, taut as a lute string. Felt his familiar heart beating hard over mine.

We stood like that for several minutes before he murmured, "You're cold, Nym," and let go, grasping my hand to pull me to the brazier.

"I'm fine," I said.

A soft smile touched his perfect mouth. "I can feel you're cold." He looked at me knowingly as he set the tray aside and guided me to sit on the floor by the hot coals. "And I can feel that you're hungry."

"I don't want to eat," I lied, gripping his hand.

He met my eyes, his own so blue and . . . sad. He looked as though he'd aged ten years in five months. Through our bond, I felt, first, love, and the relief of it warmed me all on its own. But with it, guilt. Intense guilt, growing up as thorns. I'd felt guilt from him throughout our time apart, but it seemed more potent now.

Why? What had he done?

I let him go; he moved the tray to the floor and knelt beside me. I grabbed the apple straight away and sank my teeth into it, the sweetness of it shocking me. How long had it been since I'd eaten an apple? I couldn't remember.

I devoured it, that worm of guilt inching through me. When I finished, I asked, "Eden?"

"She's safe."

I crumpled in on myself, the news releasing a tension I didn't realize I'd been carrying. "I'm so glad," I whispered, picking up a piece of bacon. "She told you? Where I would be?"

He nodded, studying my face like a painting, relearning it. "She came into Toke on a fisherman's boat. My men found her and brought her to Derren."

Gods, it felt so good to hear his voice. I wanted desperately to wrap myself up in him. To fall asleep to that voice. Talking to me, reading to me, anything. "Derren?"

"An old fortress we've retaken. Where we're headed now." He cleared his throat. "I . . . I felt you there, Nym. In Rodsfell. You were so afraid . . ." His voice squeezed, and he swallowed. "I knew you were in Klepton. We'd been holding back, but I knew you were there, *felt* you were there, so I had them fire."

The sound of the cannons echoed in my mind. That glimmer of hope through our bond. Tears pricked my eyes. "Thank you."

He reached forward, cupping the side of my face. I leaned into the touch. Put my hand over his and savored the warmth of his skin. Turned my face and kissed his palm.

His guilt spiked in me. Larger thorns, sharper.

I hesitated, fear clenching my stomach. "What did you do, Renn?"

He searched my face. "What do you mean?"

"It works two ways." Leaning forward, I pressed a hand against his heart. "What did you do?"

My mind twisted through all the possibilities. Maybe he'd razed an entire city, women and children included. Maybe he'd found solace with another woman during these long months. Maybe he intended to take me home to Fount and leave me there, indefinitely. The possibilities were a vise around my ribs, squeezing, *squeezing*—

"What did I do?" he repeated, emotion choking his voice to just above a whisper. "Nym, I did *this*. I handed you right to him. I *left you*, and you . . ." He pulled away, turning his head. The apple of his neck bobbed. Red rimmed his eyes. "And I felt *everything* he did to you." He ran a hand back through his hair. "All this gods-damned power, and I couldn't protect the one person I love most."

My chest gaped like an open hole. Heat prickled my face. "Renn, no. It's not your fault. *None* of this is your doing."

He shook his head, eyes glimmering.

I shoved the tray away and rose to my knees, grabbing his shoulders. "None of this is your fault. Look, see? I'm fine. All in one piece. All—"

My voice cut off as I thought of Ursa. Gone forever. Left with *that man* in the darkness of the dungeon.

He wouldn't be able to keep her like I had. She'd hurt him and then dissipated into the other side, where my parents preceded her. At least there was that. At least she'd have them. Still, I felt the chasmal emptiness she'd left like an open wound.

Renn knit his fingers through mine, stitching up the cut, and I settled down beside him.

"All this power," I repeated, looking him over. He didn't glow, outside his usual, very human radiance. No golden shimmer, no light-woven wings. "You're so . . . healthy."

A dry chuckle escaped him. "Of course I am, Nym. More or less."

My joy faltered. "More or less?"

He shrugged. "I haven't relapsed." He paused, that guilt twisting and shredding between us. "Truly, I'm better than I've ever been, but . . ."

As though to punctuate it, he pressed a fist to his lips and coughed. It clicked and rattled, but no blood passed his lips.

Immediately I put my hands to his jaw, dowsed—

And gasped.

It was the most beautiful thing I'd ever seen in my life. More majestic than Sestan mountains, more glorious than a sunlit sea, more riveting than an autumn sunset. I'd never gotten to step back and see the whole of it, before . . .

Gods-touched. I believed it absolutely, now.

I stood in a brilliantly lit wall-less room, colored orbs of all shapes and sizes orbiting one another, glimmering like starlight and a sheen not unlike the surface of a pearl. They turned and twisted around one great center sphere, about three feet in diameter, which pulsed every color of the rainbow and beyond, colors I'd never experienced before and couldn't possibly describe with any human tongue. All the connections were made of gold and light, not unlike what Renn glowed with when I'd first healed him, or when he'd dove into the Midly Strait after me. Marveling, I walked around the entirety of it, my mind struggling to comprehend this chandelier of globes. Even if I were to cut their likeness from precious stones, I could not re-create the wonder of it. The size of it. The way each orb pulsed with warmth, with *power*. It was enough to make the hardest of men weep. This was prophecy. This was *salvation*.

And all of it, riddled with scars.

Every glassy orb had marks on it. Some like dried glue, others like spiderwebs. Though the spheres were whole, every break Adoel Nicosia had inflicted upon him remained there. I cupped a smaller bauble in my hands and pressed my thumbs into it, expecting the glass to shatter, but to my relief, it held. Pulling magic into my fingertips, I tried to smooth away the scars, but the magic didn't take. There was no effect, no matter how much magic I summoned.

Stepping back, I reveled in the wonder of him a little longer before shifting back into the ship's cabin. The wooden walls looked dingy and decrepit in comparison.

"You have scars," I whispered, searching his face. "It's utterly beautiful, but you have so many scars."

The corner of his mouth tilted up. He clasped my hand in his own. "You have done so much for me, Nym."

"But—"

"But this is who I am." He squeezed. "It will always be part of me."

I swallowed hard, drawn into the blueness of his gaze.

That half smile dropped. "What are you nervous about?"

That's right, he could feel that, couldn't he? There would be no secrets between us. Then again, this relationship had been built on honesty.

But I didn't want to tell him, not yet. It would break this spell between us. I wanted to hold on to this a little longer.

Instead, I said, "The healing held." I touched his shoulder again, his chest, his stomach. He let out a shuddering breath. "You're all here. But I'm confused. I haven't felt your symptoms. Any of them." Because they'd been magically induced? I wasn't sure.

Memory of agonizing pain through our connection came to mind. Pressing my fingertips into his side, I asked, "What happened here?"

He slouched. The thorns reappeared. "Of course you felt that, too."

"Renn." I forced sternness into his name. "What happened?"

"Spear," he answered. "Sestan spear at Molls."

"I don't know it."

"North of Rove," he explained. "I rallied them, after you left. The army, the troops. I sent spies north to find you. They never did. Or, if they did . . . they never made it back." A deep breath punctuated the sentence. "We fought. We haven't reclaimed Rove, but we've driven them out elsewhere. Molls, Speth." He turned fully toward me. "Nym, what did you *do*?"

"In Rodsfell?"

"To *me*," he enunciated. "Like you said, it's held. The sickness . . . it's nothing like it was. But . . . I'm hardly *normal*."

I smiled. "You can fly."

He matched the expression. "I can fly. I can do a lot of things."

Gods-touched. There was so much to say, so much to tell him. So much he needed to tell me. "How?"

"Before we left Speth"—the link grew cold—"I discovered it before I left Speth. But Nym . . ." His voice, his gaze, pleaded for answers.

"When I went back to Fount," I started, "one of our beehives had lost its queen. Without a queen, the bees don't understand their purpose. There's no order, no directive."

He nodded hesitantly, likely wondering why I'd started talking about bees.

"I realized it was a lot like you. Your lumis," I went on. "No order. No matter how much I repaired it, it kept falling apart. I realized you needed a new queen."

His thumb ran over my knuckles. "I'm not following."

I chewed the inside of my lip, debating how to best approach this. "You've noticed we have a special connection."

He nodded. "Definitely. It took me a while to understand what the hell was happening to me."

I laughed. "I imagine it was confusing."

He waited.

"That night in Sten's basement"—Gods, *Sten*. Was he still alive?—"I remade your lumis to look like mine. I told you about Ursa, how she was able to give me part of herself because we were so alike."

Coldness pulsed from him.

"I thought, maybe I could do the same for you, if we were alike, too. So I reshaped you to match me, and I gave you a new queen. Half of my heart."

His hand went limp in mine. Dread, *his* dread, filled me, black and thick as ink.

My mouth went dry. I rushed, "I'd learned how to shape the magic to hold everything together. To fill in the empty gaps. And you don't have two hearts, you just have a guide, something healthy to model the rest . . ."

The way he stared at me set me off-kilter. I forgot what I was going to say. His shoulders sharpened to razors. His eyes shimmered. Fine lines weighed down his brow.

"Renn." I squeezed his hand. "Renn, it's a good thing. You're healed."

He shook his head. New vines, fresh thorns, grew from him and into me. "How much more can I possibly take from you?"

I reeled back. "What?"

"Take from you," he repeated. "All I've done is *take*. I took you from your home. I took you from your family. I took your time, your energy, your *life*. And now I've taken half your heart?"

I frowned. "I *gave* it to you, Renn."

He looked skyward, wilting. Took a beat to level himself. "Why . . . why would you do something like that?"

All of the exhaustion, the pain, the panic . . . everything that transpired in Sesta fell away in that moment. There was only him, only me, alone in this space, as though we were separate from the war and the world. Emotion welled up in me like wine overflowing. Finally, *finally*, after five long, gruesome months, I could tell him. I could right the wrong, undo the silence, bare my soul.

"Because I love you." I didn't whisper or suppress my voice in any way. It was a declaration. It was a promise. It was truth.

He shut his eyes at the confession. A few of the thorns withdrew. Life returned to his hand, and his fingers knit tighter through mine. He set his jaw like he was in pain. So many emotions tumbled through our connection, I couldn't discern them.

When he looked at me, unshed tears magnified the blue of his irises. "Did you know," he whispered, "that no one has ever told me that before?"

My heart cracked. "S-Surely your mother—"

He shook his head. Sucked in an uneven breath. Swallowed, steeling himself. "I was so certain you would hate me, after what happened. After I let them take you. After I let them . . . hurt you."

"Renn, no." I lifted myself again to my knees and embraced him, holding his head to my chest. His arms circled under my arms and over my shoulders. I buried my face in his hair, smelling the sea on him, catching familiar notes of honeysuckle and pinewood. "Please stop saying that," I whispered. "I am safest with you. I only want you. I love you. *I love you.* I will always love you."

Tears filled my vision. I pulled back to look at his face. To wipe an errant tear from the side of his nose.

Hope, desperation, need. They were his, but they were mine, too. So softly, as though he might break all over again, I pressed my lips to his. The warmth of the contact sent tingling waves through my jaw and into my shoulders. His hands came up to cradle my head, to kiss me as though I was a fragile thing, and maybe I was. Maybe we both were. We were scared and hurting, the future unsure, but we were *together* after so long. After so much.

And right now, that was all that mattered.

The cabin was cramped, but we weren't ready to join the rest of the crew yet. To be apart. So I pulled Renn onto the narrow bed and curled into his side, the brazier at my back. Renn wrapped one arm around my waist and used his other to fan out my knotted curls, helping them dry. We lay like that for a while, Renn's warmth far more adequate than the brazier's. Tucked against him, secure in this place where no one else could touch me, I felt the safest I had since January, if not before even that. I didn't mean to doze off, but the weariness of the day dragged at me.

I didn't dream. When my eyelids parted again, Renn had not moved, save for his fingertips patterning circles on my back.

"Renn." His name left my lips like a prayer.

"Hm?"

"What happened that day? In Speth?"

His hand slowed, and guilt seeped through our connection once more.

"Renn." I propped myself up on my elbow. "You were trying to protect me. You didn't know. Neither of us knew."

Letting out a long breath, he traced the line of my jaw. "You are beautiful."

I scoffed. "I highly doubt that. I've been starv—" I caught myself before finishing. *Starving for months,* I didn't say, but he knew. I saw it in the tightness around his eyes, in the flare of guilt between us. However much I wanted to, I could not simply demand his feelings change, so I pressed on. "Tell me about Speth."

Lowering his hand, he looked at the ceiling. "I didn't understand what had happened to me then. After I . . . after I hid you, I went back to fight. Not that I'm much of a fighter, but I knew enough. You saw, before . . . before."

I had. I watched him cut a man in half with a single stroke of a sword.

"It was a company of dragons—Sestan soldiers. Speth was small; they'd come looking for me. I understand why, now. I fought them, Sten fought them. There were a dozen or so soldiers from the palace taking refuge there; they and a few villagers fought, too."

"Brave of them."

He nodded. "It was carnage, Nym. Blood in the snow. More red than white. And I . . ." He lifted his hand, palm down. "I did so much of it. It was like . . ." Trepidation unwound from him.

I remembered strong waves of sorrow pouring into the conservatory in Rodsfell.

"It's war, Renn," I whispered, splaying my hand across his stomach. "I won't judge you."

Dropping his hand, he confessed, "It was like fighting children."

I let that settle over me, prickling across my skin like a limb fallen asleep.

"The others retreated," he went on. "And we went north. Sten and I—"

I sat up, nearly hitting my head on the low ceiling. "Sten is alive?"

The corner of his mouth ticked upward. "He is, thank the gods. Even still." His lip curved a little more. "When you're relieved, it feels like the rain. Cool spring rain."

I clasped his hand in both of mine.

"I looked for you." Hoarseness leaked through his voice. "They retreated, and I searched everywhere for you. Into the night. That's when the wings . . . It was getting dark, and I was panicking, and it just . . . happened. Like they've always been there. Like my arms." He rubbed a hand down his face. "The villagers, those not helping with casualties, they helped me look. I could *feel* you, but I couldn't find you. You were so scared, so desperate. He hurt you . . . I *felt* him hurt you—"

"Stop," I urged. "Stop. It's done. We need not relive it." And yet the need to explain myself pushed at me. "I fought it, Renn. I tried to. But he soulbound me to him. I couldn't leave his side."

His shoulders tensed. "I've heard, since, that he's a soulbinder. Is it true, Nym? That he accesses all of craftlock?"

I nodded. "All of it. Renn, I think he's the Allmaster. The one from prophecy."

He sat up slowly, his hair kinked from where he'd lain on it. "I've heard that theory."

"And *you*, Renn. You might be—"

"The rising blood?" he asked, a mirthless dimple forming on his cheek. "I've heard that, too."

I searched his face. "Do you not believe it? Have you not *seen* yourself?"

"I didn't say that." He sounded tired now. Like this was an old conversation for him. "I . . . I didn't say that."

I swallowed, trying to think how best to present my other theories.

He felt it through the bond. "Say it, Nym."

"I think he's your father, Renn." He didn't react. "I think your mother was Sestan—Eden and Adrinn believed her to be, and her name was Alarna—and that Adoel Nicosia is your father by blood. I think, maybe, she knew more about the prophecy than we realized. I think she took refuge here, and Nicosia found out." I sucked in a deep breath, ready to reveal what had truly made me so nervous before. "Adoel Nicosia is the one who shattered you, Renn," I confessed. "I learned of it in Rodsfell. Whitestone . . . Physician Whitestone told me."

I didn't need the bond to feel the shock that shot through him at the name. His face revealed everything.

I rushed to get the story out, how I'd seen him in the palace, and how the physician had visited me once Nicosia left with his armies. How he'd shared his knowledge, and his part in the breaking, with me in exchange for forgiveness. Forgiveness I hadn't given him.

Renn went very still. "That . . ."

"Is a lot to take in," I finished for him.

We sat with it for several long minutes, emotions flowing between us like waves on sand.

"He thinks only Nicosia can kill you. A scripture in *Prophecies* about blood killing blood."

Half a chuckle died on his tongue. "I know the passage, but I highly doubt that." His hand absently went to his side, where the spear wound was. Still, his brow crinkled with depth of thought. I let him mull it over. A minute passed before he shook his head, dismissing the notion for now.

"How did you escape?" he whispered, breaking the heaviness.

I swallowed against my thickening throat. "It was . . . something like what I did to heal you. He grew frustrated. Took me to the dungeons. I made my lumis look like his . . . so Ursa could pass between us."

He sat up. "Wait. Ursa? Your sister?"

I tried to hold them back, but tears pooled anyway. "It was the only way to get Eden and me out. Ursa hurt him, and I ran."

"Oh, Nym." He bent forward and pressed his lips to my forehead. "Nym, I'm so sorry. I'm so sorry."

I wiped my sleeve across my eyes. "Gods know I am so tired of crying."

"The more you fight it, the more you will."

I nodded, the wisdom sound. I rattled off the rest of it, how Eden and I had jumped—he winced, I thought, at the memory of experiencing that painful moment himself—how we'd picked our way across Sesta. I thought Eden might have told him the story already, but he said, "She hasn't spoken much, since she got back. Only enough to tell us she was unharmed, and that you would come through Catalaine."

I wilted. "Renn . . . Eden is not unharmed."

He stiffened, perhaps ready to receive bad news, perhaps in response to my own rising feelings, the thread of anger knitting them together.

"She may be well physically. I tried my best with that," I continued. "But she has been abused. Even I don't know the half of it, but she has been beaten, and she has been raped. Repeatedly, I'm sure. Nicosia held a parody of a wedding for them. Made her play her role."

Renn paled to nail-tip white.

I clasped his hand, hard. "Do not tell her I told you this, but you need to know. She is hurting, and she will hurt for years to come. Do not leave her alone with men, even those you trust, because *she* will not trust them. She will sit in her fear, brew in it, and not tell a soul for the sake of her dignity. But fear is the antithesis of what she needs."

His gaze broke from me, landing on the brazier for a tense minute. "I will make sure she has an attendant at all times. I will send her away from this."

"Don't send her away," I countered. "Give her something to do. Something *important*. It's the best way for us to heal."

An ember of rage pulsed between our heart-lines. "Nym . . . I know you were . . . hurt, too. I felt it. But I . . ." His free hand made a tight fist around the blanket beneath us. "Did he . . . did anyone . . . ?"

"No," I finished for him, and the ember snuffed into smoke. "No, he didn't."

Renn turned away then and coughed, harder than he had before. I gripped his shoulder, ready to hand him a corner of the blanket if he didn't have a handkerchief, but the cough didn't produce any blood. None I could see. And again, I couldn't feel his sickness through our bond.

Touching the side of his neck, I slipped into his lumis, floored once more by the breadth of it, the beauty. I found myself gawking for a long moment before searching the network of spheres, trying to peer beyond the scars. I found nothing to heal.

Still, as the colors and the light swept from my vision, I touched the side of his face, the beginnings of blond scruff rough against my palm. "It's you, Renn," I whispered. "Gods-touched. It's you."

Grasping that hand, he kissed my first knuckle as coolness spiraled through our connection. "I was afraid you'd say that."

"Do you disagree?"

He shook his head. "No, only . . . hoped. One of my brother's contacts came forward about two months ago. About my mother. Sesta. She . . . knew, I guess." He wiped his palm down his face.

"Renn." I moved atop his lap so I could look him in the face. The bond aside, Renn did not wear his mask, and he started at my forwardness. I took his face in my hands. "Renn, this is a good thing. A hard thing, yes, but a good thing."

He softened. "I know."

"But," I offered for him. He need not explain. *But* it would be hard. *But* he'd been flung into a position of leadership, a position of power, whereas a year ago he'd been bedridden. *But* people would die, following him. *But* he didn't know *how* he would do what scripture claimed he could.

"Tell me what you can do," I pressed. "Tell me exactly who you are." *Give me a truth to hold on to so I can stop falling.*

The little quirk of his mouth felt like a prize. "Besides what you've seen? I'm . . . fast. Very fast. I'm . . . everything I could have been, multiplied. It's hard to explain. I've only just gotten into the habit of not breaking drawers when I shut them."

I twisted a lock of his hair around my finger, but internally, I fractured. "I don't think you need me anymore, Your Majesty."

Who was I, if not the prince's—the king's—healer? Without my sister, my family, my home?

He seized my waist. "I will *always* need you, Nym Tallowax."

I felt the sincerity of the promise through our twined hearts, the warmth of it flooding my chest. But I felt something else, too, lurking beneath it. Desire, want. *Physical* need, though that had not been what he meant.

My pulse quickened. I had never been intimate with a man. Never willingly, at least. It was something I'd closed myself off to years ago. Yet that tendril of want sparked my own, along with a whisper of fear. A whisper of memory of the man who'd once hurt me so badly.

I remembered Renn would feel it, too. The thought of being so exposed to him, so laid bare, brought a flush to my cheeks.

His thumb caressed my hip. "Nym—"

The knock at the door came so suddenly I jumped and hit my head on the overhead locker.

I cursed. Renn winced.

"Sire?" a voice came through the door.

Renn's hands lingered as I extricated myself from him. I started randomly thumbing through cabinets and drawers, trying to look occupied, as he said, "Enter."

The man who came through the door had to duck to do it; he was large and muscled, deeply bronzed, perhaps in his mid-forties. Captain of the ship? Had we crossed the strait already?

Renn stood. "Nym, this is Commander Stonelay. He helped us with this excursion and has been pivotal in our retaliation against Sesta." The large man tipped his head to me. "Commander, this is Nym Tallowax."

He stepped forward and shook my hand, his swallowing mine. His expression, though . . . it looked an odd mix of awe and hesitance. It wasn't until then that I realized how detrimental Nicosia's beatings might have been to the war effort. Surely Renn's officers had witnessed his sudden influxes of pain. Some might attribute it to his illness, but others might know better. Renn would have had to explain to his most trusted some details of our connection. He'd have had to—I was an unknown factor in everything, a vulnerability. "It's good to finally meet you, Miss Tallowax. I would have advised against making the trip out here for only a single soul, but the healer of prophecy deserves the effort."

A shiver coursed down my spine. "There is no healer in any prophecy I've heard of, sir."

He simply released my hand, neither agreeing nor refuting my claim. When he spoke again, he addressed Renn. "Your Majesty, the sooner, the better."

Sooner for what?

I felt the apology through our bond before Renn offered it. "I'm sorry to ask you, Nym. I'm sure you're exhausted. But anything you can tell us about Rodsfell, about what you saw or heard when you were with Nicosia, could be beneficial."

I glanced between the two of them. *"Anything?"* I asked. Like how if Adoel Nicosia *was* Renn's father, that might make him ineligible for the Canseren crown? Unless there was official paperwork from King Grejor. He'd fully disguised and integrated Winvrin—Alarna—into his kingdom. He must have done the same for Renn, not that it mattered now. Not with Rove sacked.

Then again, the ability to glow and fly and bring ancient prophecy to life likely surmounted the logistics of the thing.

Renn straightened. "Before I forget." He reached behind him, to the back of his belt, and pulled out a small, unfamiliar leather sheath. Turned it over and handed it to me.

As my fingers brushed it, I noticed the citrine stone embedded in its handle.

My lips parted. "My mother's knife." I clasped it and pulled it free from its cover. The blade glimmered silver, sharp and polished. I'd dropped it in the snow when Nicosia captured me. Renn must have found it. Kept it, all this time.

Resheathing it, I pressed it to my heart, new moisture coming to my eyes. "Thank you for finding it. For taking care of it."

A soft smile touched his lips. Warmth through the bond nearly overcame the lingering thorns there.

Gesturing to Commander Stonelay, Renn said, "I'll come with you, if you wish," and extended his hand.

I did. Weaving my fingers through his, I let him lead me from the cabin.

We came to a room just below the deck, where a table had been mounted. Commander Stonelay, as well as several other high-ranking officers, attended. Renn took a moment to formally introduce me to all of them, and I wondered what they must have thought of me, about this rescue mission, and about my relationship with Renn, if they understood it at all. If they'd approve, or if they'd loathe it. Were it not a time of war, surely it would be the latter.

I shared everything I could possibly think of, from the partial layout I'd pieced together of the palace, to things Nicosia and Whitestone had said to me, to the king's marriage with Eden, leaving out any additional, personal details on the matter. I told them how we'd escaped. I described the crafter barracks and, while I related a crafter had aided us, I did not give her description, for I had promised. I detailed the canal and the cities, answering questions about potential food supply as best I could. Many things about the workings of the soldiers and military they already knew, but none stopped me when I explained them.

We talked past sundown, with Commander Stonelay asking me to write down anything else that might come to mind. I agreed, and as soon as I left the room, the exhaustion of the day hit me like a falling tree. I stumbled, my half-heart pulsing too quickly. I needed to feed magic into it soon.

Renn subtly took my elbow and bid farewell to his officers before leading me to the main deck, where his cabin lay. "Are you all right?" he asked over the wind. Worry wound from him to me. "More food? Anything, Nym. Just ask."

I gripped his bicep as we walked. "Just rest. I'll be fine tomorrow."

Tomorrow. It was the first time in so long that *tomorrow* held any sort of hope for me. It felt as though a dove perched on my sternum and unfurled its wings.

We paused at the door. "Will it always be this way?" He dipped his head low, close to my ear. "Will I always feel what you're feeling?"

"I don't know. I've never really been in this position before."

He offered me a boyish smile, so sweet I felt it down to my toes. "I don't mind. It . . . it gave me hope, all these months. Knowing that you were still alive, that I still had some piece of you with me, even if I didn't understand it."

"It won't always be rosy."

"It hardly has been," he countered. Sighed. "We should land tomorrow. I want you to take this room, Nym. I'll sleep with the men below deck."

That gave me pause. Images of Sten's mother's house, of that afternoon, flooded my mind. Curled up beside Renn on that cot, my hand pressed to his chest—the last semblance of peace I'd had before Nicosia captured me.

"I don't . . ." He tousled his hair. "I don't want them being untoward with you. The sailors. They can be . . . crude."

Ah. "I suppose even you can't escape that."

He pressed a soft, chaste kiss to my forehead. "Do you need *anything*, Nym?"

Only you, I thought, scared at how true it felt. A fluttering panic started in my gut, and I tamped it down, desperate to keep it from bleeding through the link. I thought of sunshine and aspen forests and Terrence instead. I could not allow myself to become a lunatic because my life was . . . hard. "No, just rest. I'll see you in the morning."

He looked at me a little longer, the night masking half his expression. I felt his unsurety. He waited while I entered the cabin, the brazier still warm, before bidding me good night.

I fell asleep the instant my head hit the pillow.

Nicosia grabbed a fistful of my hair and hauled my head back, hard enough for my neck to pop, and tapped my mother's short, four-inch blade against the underside of my chin, the edge making paper-thin cuts to the tender flesh. "Tell me where you got your power, Nym."

Tears clogged my eyes. "You already took it from me."

He smiled a serpent's grin. "Then tell me what you did. Tell me how you remade him."

I squeezed my eyes shut, yet somehow I could see everything. Exactly how we stood, exactly how he loomed over me like a predator, exactly how the afternoon sun cast a shadow over the Egroran.

My weak heart thrummed too quickly, making the ceiling spin. *Don't tell him, don't tell him, don't—*

He flung me chest-first into the tree, fusing me to it with a soulbinding, and stabbed the knife into the arch of my right shoulder blade. I cried out, pain and the shock of the nerve racing between my crown and heels. I tried to dowse, tried to stop it, but my lumis wouldn't come. My magic had abandoned me.

Nicosia twisted the knife as his hot breath wafted over my ear. "There's a special seal that lives on our northern coast. When it needs a female to cooperate, it sinks its teeth into her neck, uncaring for her cries, for the blood. Usually to have its way with her. Sometimes, she survives long enough to give birth."

The knife dug in to its hilt; my fingernails clawed the ancient tree, the bark unyielding. I couldn't breathe, couldn't think—

"Should we try it, Nym?" he whispered. "Then maybe you'll scream the words I've been so patiently waiting to hear."

I did scream. Mindless, feral screams, clawing at the Egroran, clawing at the soulbinding that pinned me there even as the pain in my shoulder consumed me. Out, out, I had to get out. *I had to get out—*

"NYM!"

The tree and Nicosia snapped into darkness all at once. The smell of coal, of wood, of the sea rushed into my nose. Splinters from the wall had opened the skin beneath my fingernails. Heart too fast. I was breathing, but it wasn't enough, not enough—

Twenty candles came to life. Strong hands gripped my upper arms, forcing me upright. It took me a moment to recognize his face. Maybe because of the light. Maybe because of the tears.

Renn. *Renn.* He was here. I wasn't in Rodsfell. I was on a Canseren ship, sailing home. Home. Safe.

The light emanated from Renn's skin, illuminating the small cabin. His worry became suffocating as it absorbed my ebbing panic.

He touched the side of my face, hand warm where my skin had chilled. The door was ajar, like he'd rushed in. He wore only his undershirt and breeches.

"Are you with me?" he whispered.

I swallowed against a dry throat. Nodded. "I . . . I was there . . ."

Worry creased his brow and the invisible tie between us. He wiped away one errant tear with his knuckle, a second with his lips.

Guilt bloomed like a summer rose inside him, its petals brushing me, its thorned vines reaching, wrapping.

I forced a deep breath into my lungs. "I-I'm sorry. I haven't . . ." *But I'm back, now. I shouldn't have nightmares—*

The guilt formed new buds. "Every time you apologize, it's like you're stabbing me with a knife."

I tensed. *Knife in my back, twisting, digging—*

"Nym." He lowered his hand from my face but still gripped me, supported me. "Do you want . . . to tell me? What it was?"

I shook my head. "No." The last thing I wanted was to relive it. I rubbed my eyes. "No. I'm fine . . . I just need some water, and I'll go back to sleep."

I wondered if he sensed the lie through our bond.

He stepped away, taking his warmth and light with him, and the space between us crushed me, the coolness and the darkness, and for a moment I wasn't sailing for Derren Castle but for Sesta, soulbound to the mastiff in the hold of that ship, starving, aching—

Renn pressed a cup of water into my palm. "Drink."

I did. Too quickly. I coughed.

He left again. I clenched my teeth. *It's fine. You're fine. You're a grown woman, and it's over. Ursa—*

But Ursa wasn't here anymore.

Renn returned and pushed the door shut. Locked it. His glow dimmed to nearly nothing, perceptible only because of the dark of night. He took the cup from my hand, set it on the floor, and then lifted the blanket, one knee on the mattress. Paused. "Is this all right?"

I nodded, overeager, but I didn't care. I scooted back against the wall, making space for him, my nerves calming the instant his leg pressed against mine. I didn't even wait for him to settle before I fell into him, my head on his chest. His arms came around me, holding too tight. His shimmer winked out, leaving the room dark save for the light of the moon through the slats of a tiny porthole. Silent, save for the churning sea and a muffled cough from him.

The rose of his guilt slowly withdrew its vines. I listened to the pulsing of his heart. Our heart. Tethered myself to it.

"I'm so sorry." He breathed the words.

I hugged his torso, inhaling his scent. "No more apologies from either of us."

A full minute passed before he relented. "All right."

For the rest of the night, he kept the nightmares at bay.

Chapter 13

I kept waiting for Renn to be sick. For him to lose his balance on the ship, to cough up blood, to lose his color. The Renn I'd known, the one I'd fallen in love with, was always so sick. But other than a headache and a few stifled coughs, he remained hale for the rest of the trip. Hale as we unloaded the vessel. Hale as we rode toward Derren Castle, me on the saddle before him, and I wondered when he'd learned to sit astride a horse. I imagine he had to pick it up very quickly.

We rode until sunset, then set up camp. Renn whispered he'd share a bed with me again, not mentioning what it might look like to his men. But I turned in before him, as he needed to speak to his commanders around the fire. Almost immediately drifting off, I found myself in the conservatory again, this time with Nicosia's whip tearing lines across my face—

I woke up to Renn over me, shaking me, my name a plea on his mouth. I gasped, shivered. "Don't," I wheezed.

He released me.

"No." I reached for him. "Don't apologize. Please . . ."

He didn't. He shucked his clothes, save for his undershirt and breeches—something that should have been more alluring, or at least scandalizing, but my mind had been beaten so far from lust and propriety, I barely gave his undress a passing thought. Renn held me, his roses and thorns blooming and wilting in a ceaseless cycle, and I fell into a dreamless slumber.

Derren Castle wasn't anything like Rove's.

It boasted only two towers, one of which was partially collapsed. It bore a large moat, also collapsed on one side, full of murky, green-tinted water. Thick stone, crumbled over time, composed its wall, but recent repairs had been made, swathes of rock and mortar that didn't match. One large crack had been half filled with wood as workers continued to labor to fix it. A large ash-stained flag of a red phoenix hung from a front battlement. It didn't have much of a bailey, being a fortress before anything else, built to withstand wars largely lost to history. But it was defendable, it was free, and many Canseren soldiers had made it and its surrounding lands their home—far more than I had imagined Renn able to gather in so short a time, without the benefits of the capital at his disposal. Then again, I suppose word of a prophecy being fulfilled was enough to draw men-at-arms from all walks of life.

And it certainly did.

Word of our arrival preceded us, and even before the drawbridge had been let down, I felt Renn tense behind me. Whispers flooded the men and a few women in attendance, until one shouted, "The gods-touched king has returned!" and a swarm of soldiers and servants cheered. They didn't seem to notice me perched in front of him on the saddle, where I debated whether I should look small to let their king shine or sit up straighter to barricade him from their adoration.

It warmed me, that he was adored.

Yet Renn hated it. I'd know he did, even if our heart-bond didn't reveal it to me. He hated eyes on him, hated the attention. He always had, even the positive kind. Still, he managed to paste on a smile and wave, garnering a second cheer before he entered the castle, where the awing and bowing started anew.

However, as we neared the stables, he drew up short, stalling the others who rode behind us. Surprise flaked through the bond, causing me to follow his gaze to a yellow, white, and blue flag.

"Antsan," he murmured, turning the steed right around as he searched the crowd, calling out to a steward. "Tintier! Are there Antsan emissaries here?"

A gradual sinking feeling pulled on my gut.

The steward signaled something to him, and Renn turned back toward the stables, urging the horse into a trot, squeezing his knees over my legs to keep me secure. He practically jumped off the mount, grasped my hips to help me down, and thanked the stable hands before guards stationed at the castle met us and bid us, as well as Commander Stonelay, into the keep. The castle was obviously built for war and not for comfort, given the low ceilings and tight corridors. I tried my best to tamp down the uneasiness in my belly, focusing instead on the hope flowing from Renn. We desperately needed allies in this war, and King Grejor had been in negotiations with Antsan before his death. I'd heard of them the same night Sesta sacked Rove.

We came into the Great Hall, a third of the size of Rove's. No throne had been erected, nor tapestries; there was only a very old, very heavy carpet laid lengthwise across the worn stone floor. A large delegation of people awaited us there, the majority in gray uniforms with the same yellow, white, and blue flag patched onto their shoulders. A man in the front, who looked to be in his mid-forties, smiled as we approached. He had the deepest shade of red hair, receded halfway across his pate. His friendly face had high, round cheeks and deep-brown eyes. He was short for a man, about my height, and while he wore a gray uniform, it did not look military like those on the men around him, who certainly were soldiers.

I held back with the guard while Renn and Commander Stonelay crossed the space. The redheaded man bowed deeply. "I'm relieved to see you safe from your journey, Your Majesty." He had a melodic accent, crisp, with a rhotic *r*.

"And I yours," Renn offered, extending a hand. "However unexpected."

"I am Jardallen Arquan from Antsan. I'm here with this delegation to continue negotiations with Cansere for allyship between our nations. We had opened them with your late father—my uttermost condolences, of course."

My stomach sank further. I'd begun twisting a bit of my skirt between my fingers.

"Unfortunately, in times of war, there is little time for them," Renn replied. He was such a bundle of emotions, positive and negative, all masked beneath years of practice. I took deep breaths, trying desperately not to distract him with mine. "But thank you. These have been trying times, to say the least."

"The time for strategy is at hand, Your Majesty," Sir Arquan went on. "We have no personal grief with Sesta. King Vitsoph has been rather taken aback by the show of aggression that seems to be motivated"—he turned his hand about, as though searching for a word—"religiously."

My half-heart pulsed hard. I supposed it was not so hard to piece it together—the Heminist prophecies. Yet I wondered if Antsan had spies here.

Renn did not seem—or, rather, *feel*—overly concerned. I studied his features as the two continued to talk, then shifted my gaze to the others in the retinue. A man with a box strapped to his chest took notes. There was a woman in the back—I could see only the crown of her head, from which grew strawberry-blonde locks. To their credit, the Antsan soldiers remained largely neutral.

"—to tell you that the original offer to King Grejor still stands," Sir Arquan was saying. "I understand the dealings had not grown serious enough to involve you personally at the time, but your country is in need of aid now more than ever, and a firmer alliance between Cansere and Antsan is immensely beneficial to all parties. Because of your father's preparation, and because His Majesty King Vitsoph is impressed with your actions these past five months, our troops and ships stand at the ready, should we finalize these dealings."

I was unsure if the lancing from my navel to the back of my neck stemmed from me or Renn.

"I of course am willing to barter for an alliance." Renn glanced at Commander Stonelay. "I've personally written to your liege, though if it made it across the miles of prairie and ocean between us, I know not."

"We received it," the emissary confirmed.

"Adoel Nicosia is breathing down the back of my neck, Sir Arquan. As soon as one bout is finished, another starts. Forgive me if I ask frank brevity over pretty politics."

The emissary smiled, then chuckled to himself. "A relief, really. I get very tired of the dance. I have here"—he turned toward the scribe behind him, who ceased writing long enough to pull a tightly rolled scroll from a bag at his hip—"the exact terms that had been in negotiations with your father. They need to be whittled down and finalized, but both parties had agreed that an alliance of marriage would be the most advantageous."

Another lance, sharper. My breath caught, and I could not release it.

Sir Arquan stepped to the side and motioned for two of the soldiers to part, revealing the woman with the strawberry-blonde hair. She looked no older than Lissel, perhaps sixteen, with sharp hazel eyes, pink-undertoned skin, and a smattering of freckles across her nose. Her layered gown was in Antsan style, but her hip-length hair had been ironed straight in Canseren fashion, so much so it shined as rose gold in the light. She smiled prettily, and though a *whooshing* sound had begun to fill my ears, I still managed to make out what the emissary said next.

"Might I present to you Azra Vitsoph, who selflessly made the journey here herself so she might meet you. She is His Majesty's most esteemed daughter."

Most esteemed daughter. The words echoed back and forth in my head. She was a princess.

I had unknowingly come to Derren Castle to meet Renn's future wife.

Chapter 14

I left.

For all his mask, for all his majesty, Renn surprised me by calling out my name as I did. I glanced back only once, pleading with all I had that he might give me my dignity even as I struggled to keep myself together.

I slipped through the guards and out of the Great Hall, desperate to find somewhere to hide, to be alone, to control myself, because we so desperately needed these negotiations to go well. We *needed* Antsan's aid, or Nicosia might slaughter us all. Even if Renn pulled a miracle and defeated Sesta, the cost would be abysmal if he did it alone.

I sucked in deep breath after deep breath, desperately looking up and down the narrow corridor, utterly lost. I had to keep it together just a little longer. I couldn't distract him. *Just a little longer, Nym.*

I followed the corridor in. Found an armory. Turned when someone from staff came up my way, then again down a narrower hallway. I spied a man with a red band on his sleeve—a physician—leaving a room. He left the door ajar, so I peeked inside. A small infirmary. Empty pallets and half-empty shelves.

I made it inside and shut the door. Desperate for privacy, I dowsed into myself, past the basalt wall, to my gold-limned half-heart. I built up a new black stone dome around it, praying to the gods it would dampen the emotional flow from me to Renn as a sob worked its way up my throat. I blocked out the missing pieces of myself, the shimmering of him. Felt his growing uncertainty, hope, and turmoil fade. Not entirely. Even after finishing the work, Renn's presence lingered. But it was the most I could do.

Back in the present, I pressed a sleeve to my mouth as a sob hard as rock cracked across my tongue. A selfish, horrid sob. In truth, I'd been cheating the universe too long. Had I known that time on the ship and in the traveling camp had been our last together, I might have . . . but I *had* cherished them. I wasn't sure it was possible for me to have appreciated them more than I already did.

Five months apart. A respite, a balm, a gift. And now it was to end. It *had* to end.

Renn needed Antsan. *We* needed Antsan. Every village and town and city needed Antsan. Before my conscription, I'd never considered myself very patriotic. But after Rove, after Sesta, I understood better. Even if just for my brothers and sisters, this alliance would prove crucial.

I retired to the farthest corner of the infirmary and sat on the cold stone floor. Tears soaked my sleeve, so I pressed my other to my face, staunching the tumult, the breaking, the flood. Then, hugging myself, I sent a prayer heavenward, thanking the gods for this turn of events. For the first time, I could imagine an end to this pointless, selfish war.

It was just that I loved him with every fiber that made me. So completely, so entirely. That love pulled me through Rodsfell. It guided me through the forest and across Sesta and into the strait. I would not have survived without that love. I would be forever grateful for it.

I simply didn't know how I could ever let it go.

Perhaps it was the travel, the emotion, the cold, or all three, but I dozed off, head and rump pressed against stone so that when I stirred, both radiated soreness.

Something was tapping my elbow. I sat up and rubbed sore, crusted eyes. The presence of dry tears only reminded me what had transpired, and I felt my chest crack all over again.

When I finally blinked myself into awareness, I realized a person had been tapping me, rousing me. He crouched in front of me, familiar face quirked in the subtlest smile.

The rush of joy at the sight offered some healing. "Sten!" I cried, then threw my arms around his neck. I'd never hugged the man before, but I was so happy to see him again, so happy he'd survived, I couldn't stop myself. "It's so good to see you. So, so good."

"You, too." He relinquished a single dry chuckle before I let him go. My cheeks warmed, and I quickly wiped my eyes once more, embarrassed. "His Majesty is looking for you."

I swallowed, throat already tight again. Tried to smile. "I'm fine, as you can see."

Sten, gods bless him, did not so much as raise an eyebrow at the lie. He knew. He'd been Renn's personal guard throughout the entirety of our relationship—of course he knew about us. He'd been the one to tell me of the potential marriage alliance. And so while I desperately tried to focus on the joy of seeing him again, I began to crumble. "I-I can't, Sten. I can't see him."

"Unfortunately, his authority supersedes yours." The guard seemed the epitome of calm. "Come."

He offered me a hand; I accepted it, wincing as my body uncurled and stood. I took a second to dowse the ache away, but there was nothing I could do for the other hurts. They didn't manifest in my lumis. How easy it would have been to squelch them from the very beginning.

Yet I couldn't regret my choice. I could never regret him.

I kept my head down and hair forward as Sten led me through the castle. Though I'd been here a matter of hours, it felt nostalgic, somehow. As though I'd lived here for months, years. As though I stood in a memory instead of a physical thing. Like I was describing this place to my children, detailing the great adventure I'd once partaken in before coming home.

Absently I touched my stomach, thinking of my lost daughter.

There would be no children to tell the story to.

Nieces and nephews, then.

My eyes watered as Sten led me into the west tower, and I focused on the burn in my legs from climbing the twisting stairs. He opened the door to a room there. It was spacious for the tight design of the castle. A simple bed in the corner, an old circular rug near it. Four slotted windows, each facing a cardinal direction, letting in the cool evening air. The wall jutted inward near the door to make way for the tower's spiraling staircase, and as I came around it, I saw a table and basic toiletries.

No Renn. The room lay empty, but I knew it was his. From the scent, or the make of the bed, or just intuition, I knew it was his.

"I'll be outside the door," Sten offered, but as he stepped away, I asked, "Eden. Is Eden here?"

He nodded. "In the east tower."

Relief cut through the ache. Then confusion. "The east is crumbled."

"Not entirely." Then, again, "I'll be outside," and he shut the door.

I took in a shuddering breath. Folded my arms tightly and crossed the room. Looked out of one window across the castle, then another, with a vantage over the thick wall. A copse of trees huddled out that way, and beyond them, a distant smear of forest, broken by the snake of a river. It must have been the one that filled the moat.

I sat on the bed—there were no chairs—and ran my hand over its blanket, then across one of two pillows. Imagined him sleeping here while I stayed bound to that gods-forsaken tree, thinking of me as I thought of him, wished for him, wanted him.

New tears sprang forth. I cursed and dabbed at them. Needing distraction, I rose and crossed to the table, where I found a few clean handkerchiefs and helped myself to one. Noticed another tucked under the lip of the basin, stained with blood.

I froze, staring at it. But Renn was healed. He had *some* symptoms, but he was mostly . . . It must have come from a bloody nose, or a cut of some sort.

I felt Ursa's absence starkly, again: the absence of her comfort, the absence of her power.

Footsteps coming toward the door hit the stone stairs hard. Despite my resolve, I turned toward them. Moved for the door as it opened. The sight of him struck me as though I hadn't seen him in years. I didn't know if I ran to him or he ran to me, but I embraced him like he'd pulled me from the strait all over again. Embraced him like it would be my last chance, and it might very well be.

I set my jaw until my teeth hurt. Pinched my eyelids shut, but tears still leaked through.

"I'm sorry," he whispered, squeezing me until I might break, then pulled back enough to look at my face, searching it as though I were a book with the answer, coded to not be easily read. "I can't feel you as strongly. I thought something had happened—"

"I put another wall up." The words came out in choked whispers. I'd explained the black basalt I'd built around myself before. "I-I didn't want to be a distraction."

"Gods, Nym—"

"That wall is still there." The realization hit me like a hammer, making me feel even more foolish. "If I were injured, I would jeopardize you. And if you had a healer nearby, he or she wouldn't be able to get to my lumis. I need to take it down." It was the sensible thing to do, but I'd hidden behind that wall for so long, it frightened me to destroy it. To lose that on top of everything else—

"Nothing is signed yet." He smoothed back my hair, eyes still frantic, still reading. "Nothing is set."

"It doesn't matter—"

He cupped either side of my face, forcing me to look at him. He looked so tired. Older. Veins of red in his eyes made the shock of blue so much starker.

More tears, blurring my vision. "I trust you will do what's best for your kingdom."

A flicker of him down the link. "That I will do. But it will not involve marriage to an Antsan princess."

I shook my head. Croaked, "For how clever you are, Renn, you lack wisdom."

"Wisdom is earned by the old and conquered by the young," he stated. It sounded as though he was quoting a book.

Though I wanted nothing more than to sink into him, I forced myself to step back. "Who are you trying to convince, Renn? Me, or yourself?" I pointed to the door. Hated each tear that streaked down my face. "We *need* this. Adoel Nicosia will continue to take and take and *take* until there's nothing left."

"But it doesn't have to be marriage," Renn ground out, set into the floor like one of its stones. "There's time to negotiate."

A chuckle—more like a dry bark—wrenched up my throat. "She is *here*, Renn! We can't *do* anything. We can't *be* anything." I swiped at traitorous, awful tears. "Your future wife is in this castle, and you *need*—"

One stride was all it took to close the distance between us. One stride to block out the room, to take my face and press his lips to mine, to silence, for a moment, every protestation clawing out of me, leaving bloody trails in their wake. But his scents of honeysuckle and pinewood only encouraged more tears. The pulsing of his anguish, even through the basalt wall, mingled with mine and threatened to erode my heart to nothing.

When we broke apart, I blinked my vision clear. "Will you stand here and tell me that marrying her would not be the swiftest way to garner Antsan's support?" I tried to spark a fire so I might hold a single ember, for anger was so much easier than despair.

I found nothing.

"Yes, it would be the path of least resistance," he admitted, "but it isn't the only one. I'll . . . sort it out." His doubt proved strong enough to knock against the basalt wall. "I'm meeting with Sir Arquan in the morning. Politics are not simple. There are ways—"

"You have to marry her, Renn," I interrupted, though my tightening throat choked out my voice. "As soon as possible."

I'd yet to find a spark, but I felt Renn's through the muffled link. Saw it in the way he glowered. "I don't *have* to do anything."

I turned away from him and escaped to the far window, letting the cooling evening air wash over me. Took a moment to steel myself again, to form a rebuttal, but every time I tried, a sob threatened to break my teeth.

He followed me.

"I think," I whispered, unable to look at him, "you are so used to getting what you want that you fail to see the reality set before us."

Oh, his ember burned, and I wondered how hot it would smoke if I didn't have that basalt wall around my heart. "Yes, I'm a king," he said. "Yes, I'm wealthy. I command thousands. I have the mark of the gods and the fear of my citizens." He stepped beside me, his focus hot as the noon sun. "And yet I've never had anything I truly wanted."

The peasant in me wanted to rail against him, but he continued.

"Not the clothes I wanted, not the friends I wanted, not the body or abilities I so *desperately* wanted." His fingertips brushed my elbow. "But I want you. I will sink Cansere into the sea before I let anyone take you away from me."

My lip trembled as I fought not to cry anew. "Am I supposed to be charmed by that?" I countered, looking into the shadowed bailey, too cowardly to gaze upon his face. "Find it romantic that you would let your own people be overrun, enslaved, even drowned for the love of me?"

"If I were saying it for poetry, Nym, then yes. But I am not."

I wiped the handkerchief across my eyes. They'd become raw from all the crying and all the stifling of crying. "There's a bloody handkerchief by the basin. Is that recent?"

"Don't change the subject."

"How sick are you?" I touched his jaw—the sensation of his stubbled skin against my hand both thrilled and scalded me. Dowsed, but again, his breathtaking orbs of color were only scarred, not broken, and my magic had no effect on them.

As I returned to the present, he took my hand and kissed my palm. "All the more reason for my healer to stay close."

I pulled from his grasp. It felt like snapping a finger. "I do believe you. I believe you will *try* to find a way. But this has always been our story, Renn. This was always how it was meant to end."

I might as well have poured cold water on that ember. I couldn't feel it anymore.

My throat tightened more, but I forced the words out. "We can't be together. We can't be seen together. She is *here*, Renn. For the sake of your people, *our* people . . . we can't."

"Nym—"

"I need somewhere else to stay tonight." I dropped my eyes. The glimmer in his, paired with the trembling of our link, threatened to undo me. How would we ever survive with our hearts indefinitely connected?

He turned away from me. I did not look at his face, but tension vibrated from him. His hands formed tight fists at his sides. Anger and sorrow, determination and helplessness, pounded on the wall I'd built. A full minute passed before he said, "The room above mine is empty."

I nodded, even as I shattered. "Thank you."

The room had only a bed with an old mattress in it. Half the size of Renn's, but it would do. Yet I could not simply sit there and wallow in agony and despair. My head ached from thinking and rethinking about the events of the day, as though I might find some balm for the hurt, or some majestic loophole that would let me have him.

There was not, but neither would I allow myself to be a liability to him, so piece by piece, I tore down the basalt wall surrounding my lumis, so if I were to be injured beyond my own ability to repair, another might be able to help me and therefore help Renn.

I wasn't sure if the castle had any other healers. Not ones of the craft. But in the absence of that wall, the gaping emptiness of my lumis echoed back at me. Ursa was not here, and I could not build anything that might squelch the pain of her loss. She was simply gone.

I did, however, keep the smaller wall around the merlon of my heart, afraid to touch it for fear of somehow breaking it, letting the pounding of Renn's misery stoke my own.

I splashed cold water on my face until its swelling eased and sought out Eden.

Somehow the soldiers and staff stationed at Derren Castle knew me, or perhaps simply saw me ride in with their king, for when I asked where I might find the princess, none tried to bar my way. Eden's room was in the partially crumbled east tower, away from most of the ruckus of the castle. And though I had to pick my way by candlelight, I discovered myself desperate to see her.

When I knocked at her door, a young serving girl, perhaps fourteen years of age, answered. "Yes?"

"I apologize for disturbing you, but I'm looking for—"

The door wrenched open, the wild eyes of the princess—far better fed and groomed than last I'd seen her—landed on me. "Nym!"

She pushed back her attendant and flung her arms around me. Began to cry. Nearly three weeks had passed since we separated, without a means of knowing how the other fared.

Oh gods, these tears. Would I ever stop crying? "I'm safe," I whispered, rubbing her back. "You're safe."

The serving girl, whom I later learned was named Piya, stepped out into the stairwell, leaving Eden and me our privacy.

Her room was sparsely furnished, much like Renn's: a low bed, a wicker shelf, an old, splintered table with a few lit candles. The only place to sit was the bed, which Eden led me to, and I perched on the edge of it while she sat in its center, bringing blankets over her lap despite the warm night. Her short hair was uncovered, unadorned, and the circles around her eyes betrayed lack of sleep. I was glad Renn remembered my request to see she had an attendant, and I hoped having another woman in the room with her might ease her stress.

I considered my dark room in the opposite tower. The thought of losing the shield of Renn's body at night, his light in the darkness, the steadiness of his breaths, made my heart twist.

Before she even asked, I told her everything that had happened to me. Talked about Horgansten and Elantriana's clients, my journey into Catalaine and Klepton, my ultimate dive into the strait and how Renn had pulled me from the water, pretending every mention of his name didn't bleed me like barbs pressed to my flesh.

And I realized Eden didn't know—at least, *I* had not told her—that I was in love with her brother, that craftlock bound our hearts together, that he was my daylight and my starlight, or that he had been. No one but Sten knew, though it was likely Commander Stonelay had pieced it together. I had to keep it private. I had no claim on Renn anymore. I would not doom my countrymen, my own family among them, for the selfish sake of my bleeding heart.

So I left off the time I'd spent with him and asked, gently, "Eden . . . are you having nightmares, too?"

At first, my question turned her as hard as the castle walls, but when I said *too*, she instantly softened. "They're terrible, Nym," she whispered, as though not wanting our guards to overhear. "They are relentless. When I take short naps in the day, usually no. Or I'm not asleep long enough for them to become truly horrible. But at night . . ." She shook her head. Blinked rapidly. "At night I'm still there, and *he* is still there, and I can't escape him, no matter how much I fight. I worry what Piya might hear . . ."

Gooseflesh rose on my arms. Surely her dreams were worse than mine. Nicosia had only succeeded in certain forms of abuse with me. Surely Eden had suffered everything that vile man could imagine.

I didn't have the right to feel as broken as I did.

"It gets better," I promised, though the words felt empty. "Eventually, it will get better." I lifted my hands, fingers spread. "Do you want me to dowse on you? Are you in any pain?"

She shook her head. "Nothing your magic can balm." She stifled a yawn.

"Sleep, Eden," I offered. "I'll stay with you. I'll wake you, if I sense any distress."

I knew exhaustion drained her by how quickly she accepted the bargain. She curled up on the bed, seeming only a youth, and burrowed into her blankets as though they might protect her from the world. After she closed her eyes, I lightly ran my fingers through her hair, the way Pren liked me to do when she struggled to sleep.

For two hours, Eden slept peacefully. Piya kindly brought me one of Eden's worn books and some bread and butter to eat, before departing again. But after two hours, Eden's breath hitched. I gripped her shoulder and jostled her. "Eden."

She woke quickly, without fanfare. Stared ahead for a long moment, and I said nothing, letting her regain her senses. It took longer than it should have. She sat up, stretched. "Thank you, Nym."

"You can go back to sleep." I held up the book. "I don't mind." I wasn't sure if I'd sleep tonight, anyway.

Eden shook her head. "No, thank you, but I can't waste the candles, and you need to rest, too."

Yet an irrational fear of that room in the west tower clawed at me, so I sought another distraction. "Do you know if it's possible to send a letter from here? My family—they don't know what happened to me."

Eden frowned but took a beat to consider. "Do I have the supplies to write a letter? Yes. Can we get it to your hometown? Unlikely. Our messenger would have to go so far inland—"

The truth of it hurt, but I was already so battered and bruised, I barely felt it. "I understand, of course."

Reaching over, she touched my wrist. "Write it, though, Nym, just in case. I've found . . . sometimes just the writing helps."

I nodded. "Are you sure you don't want me to stay?"

She straightened, a glimmer of the woman she'd once been shining through. "I am quite all right. I've been writing, and I learned how to knit, see?" She reached under a pillow and pulled out a remarkably straight square of yarn work. "I think I'll work on this." She fingered the stitches. "Go. Rest. We have time yet together."

But we didn't. Renn didn't need me anymore, and my craft was a fraction of what it used to be. That . . . and I didn't know if I could bear watching the love of my life court and marry another woman.

Three for three. The gods had truly cursed my heart. Perhaps revenge for cheating death?

Lesson learned, I thought as I extricated myself from Eden's bed and slipped into the hallway, bidding farewell to Piya with a nod.

A few lanterns hung on the walls, lighting my way. As I neared the west tower, I overheard talking. Spied Sten first, leaning against the wall at the base of the stairs with his arms folded over his big chest, head lowered in that bored way of his, though he looked up as I approached. A few more steps, and I noticed Renn at the start of the stairs, still fully dressed, his presence another reminder, another punch to my gut. But beside him, hair glimmering like fire, stood Princess Azra, all smiles and wide-eyed interest, her pale hands clasped neatly before her.

What time was it?

Renn either heard me or felt me, for he looked up as I approached, and I thought a whisper of guilt slid along that basalt wall. "Nym." My name sounded instinctual.

Princess Azra's gaze bounced between the two of us, unsure, but then she smiled. "You were there in the Great Hall today. And who are you?"

Renn answered for me. "This is Nym Tallowax, my—"

"Healer," I finished for him. "I am, or was, his healer, Your Highness."

Her delicate brows pinched together. "Is Physician Addsmuch not the healer here?" Her accent rang even more melodic than the emissary's.

She must have referred to the man I'd seen leaving the infirmary earlier, with the red tie on his arm. "I am a craftlock healer, Your Highness."

Her eyes widened, but she quickly smoothed her expression. Her attention swung back to Renn. "That's right, your dear mother legalized them, didn't she? And I'm so very glad. A true *angel of fire*."

She reached forward and touched Renn's elbow, and I suddenly felt terribly weary.

Renn pulled away.

"If you'll excuse me." I moved to pass them to the stairs.

But the princess didn't budge. "And where is she off to?" She directed the question to Renn.

Renn's mask schooled his features well, though a tightness limned his eyes. Had he wept? Guilt sucked me toward the floor. He said, "Nym's room is in this tower."

"*This* tower?" Azra repeated, studying me anew. I did not know where the delegation stayed, but it was not the west tower. "Do you think such a thing necessary, Your Majesty? You are obviously well and do not need a *healer* so close."

She enunciated the word like it was vile. I suppose Antsan didn't care for craftlock, either.

Without missing a beat, Renn stated, "It has behooved me in the past to have her close."

A line bloomed between the princess's eyebrows, so I interjected, "I can sleep with the staff." I assumed they were in a barracks, somewhere.

"That will be unnecessary." Renn looked at the princess when he spoke, but then his heated sapphire gaze flicked to me.

The princess twitched, but when she did not retort, I pushed past both of them and took the stairs up quickly, enough to wind myself by the time I got to my room. Enough that I could again focus on the burn of climbing more than my own rawness.

I didn't light a candle. I sat on the old bed and stared out the window into darkness, save for two small fires in the bailey and a smattering of stars. I stared and wept until fatigue finally coaxed me to sleep.

Barren branches grabbed at my dress as I traveled the Sestan forest, the bite of winter night seeping into my limbs. I heard him coming through the trees as a wolf. Eden appeared nearby, sleeping between the roots of a tree, and no matter how hard I shook her, no matter how loudly I shouted to warn her, she would not wake.

"I've been looking for you," the king crooned.

My heart drummed hard against my chest, like it might burst from my flesh. I whirled around, Nicosia's green eyes piercing the darkness, his smile too long, too wide, to be human. I backed away from him, into a tree, only the tree had morphed into a great sculpture of ice towering over me. The forest morphed into Nicosia's lumis, cold and blue, swallowing Eden with it.

Adoel Nicosia laughed, then threw the maimed corpse of Ursa at my feet.

I woke to my own screaming.

Disoriented by the darkness, I clawed for the tree, thinking myself still bound to the Egroran, but my nails hit only stone wall and mattress. Blankets tangled between my legs. The door cracked against the wall behind it. I fell to the floor, my skull hitting stone.

Hands seized me. I screamed again, beating my fists into thick arms—

"NYM!"

Gold light pierced my eyes, driving back the shadows. I came to myself, gasping for air, my hair a noose around my neck. Everything looked wrong, but that's because I lay on the floor, halfway under the bedframe.

Angel of fire. Renn knelt before me, his body glowing gold save where his nightclothes dampened it.

I tried to swallow against a dry throat. "Th-The wall . . . I shouldn't have woken you—"

He cursed and scooped me into his arms. His voice came low and almost callous. "I was awake."

He set me on the bed.

Gods help me, I tired of tears. "I-I'm sorry. I'll build it thicker—"

"*Stop*, Nym, please," he begged, then brushed hair from my face.

I drew in a deep breath, steeling myself as the vision of Nicosia slowly bled away. "You can't be here," I whispered.

"Antsan isn't in this tower."

"You can't *be* here." I reached for his hand, caught myself, and pulled mine back. Felt an ache pulse through the clogged link. "They can't see you in my bedroom at night, no matter the reason. Anyone who knows the *why* can use it to kill you. Anyone else will cry foul."

"They can cry all they want," he bit out. "It's a *political* marriage, Nym."

I sat up. "Renn, *she could say no*."

That gave him pause. His glow dimmed.

"I cannot do this with you every time . . ." My words choked out, and I had to brace myself, swallow, to get more out. "We can't keep having this conversation."

He looked away. Scoffed. "Is it so easy to say goodbye to me?"

An ember, finally. A stoking of something other than despair, even if it would drown as a wick in a pool of wax. Dowsing into myself, I dug ethereal fingers into the basalt wall around my heart and tore it free.

In reality, Renn winced as my hurt flooded him.

"To even question my devotion to you is the greatest slander," I seethed. "You boast of wisdom and strategy, so don't be obtuse, Renn Reshua Noblewight."

Oh, but the *guilt* of him. The vines had grown one hundredfold, their thorns like daggers so sharp the magic itself bled. My heart had begun to fade; I needed to refuel it soon.

He looked . . . defeated. Slouched, he let his light wink out, recasting the room into darkness. "For me, there's only ever been you, Nym."

Salm take the water from me so that the tears might end.

"Women," he went on, a shadow against the slitted window, "they used to treat me like a spectacle. A sideshow. I rarely interacted with them. I wasn't able." He lifted his hand, his first two fingers grazing my collarbone. "Did you know, I had my first kiss at fifteen? It was during the winter ball, and two girls my age snuck away and snooped through the castle, finding my room so they could see the broken prince for themselves." He scoffed, but hurt from the memory panged me. "I was some strange sort of marvel to them. The kiss was a dare, a joke. And I didn't even care, because someone, *anyone*, had bothered to come up to see me." The apple of his throat bobbed. "They only saw the sickness, the misshapenness. Even my mother, that's all she really saw in me." He drew his hand back; my skin pebbled in response. "Nym, you were the first one who saw me. Before you ever fixed me, you saw me. Azra . . ." A dry, hard chuckle passed his lips. "I think she very much sees a prophecy and little more."

"Neither of us chose this," I murmured. "But this is the weight that comes with the title. With the war. I've . . . I've always known it. You've always known it. I owe you my life and more, Renn. You've saved me in so many ways." Another breath, another swallow, to keep a sore lump from my throat. "I can't keep depending on you. I'm broken, Renn. I'm so broken, and I can't let you become the only glue that holds me together." I tilted my head back, trying to withdraw new tears.

Renn touched my hair. "Nym—"

"I think we have to give up what is good now for what is better later." I hated the emotion in my voice, but if I were to wait for it to subside, we'd wait years.

His hand gripped mine, almost enough to be painful. I felt the strength of gods in that grip. His temper rose, breaking through the solemnity. "How can I possibly move on with someone else when I feel you inside of me, every day and every night?"

He might as well have been gripping my heart, crushing it beneath bent knuckles. "I-I'm sorry." I winced. "I can try . . . I'll find a way to break the bond. To fix this—"

"I don't want you to fix it!" He released me and launched off the mattress, toward the window. "Are you listening to a thing I say? I want *you*! Stop fighting me at every gods-damned turn and just let me *love* you!"

I stepped away from him, though the darkness hid my tears. Shut my eyes and rebuilt that basalt wall, because the turmoil was killing me. Truly killing me. Anything to get relief. To give *him* relief. I built it hard and thick and dark, for the little good it did.

After a long minute, I asked, "What will you have me be? A mistress? A rendezvous?"

His silhouette crumpled. Another minute passed.

"I'll find a way," he promised, and strode toward the door. Stopped with his hand on it. "Nym?"

I was too miserable to speak.

"If Antsan weren't part of this . . . if I find another way . . . would you marry me?"

Perhaps I'd been wrong. Perhaps doubting my love for him was not as great a crime as painting a beautiful future we could never have.

He gripped the door, sucking a piece of my soul away with him. He lingered there a moment. Didn't look at me when he said, "Please don't hate me for what I'll have to do to make this work."

I drew my knees to my chest and wept into the blanket, grateful and utterly destroyed when Renn finally departed.

Chapter 15

The next day I found myself . . . lost.

I numbly walked through the castle, learning its quirks and facets and forgetting them just as quickly. I went to the infirmary, but it lay empty even of its physician—no one here needed my magic. I wandered into the sunlit bailey, searching faces, recognizing none save for Beatty—dear Beatty—the cook from Rove Castle, who had made it out and joined the army as chef. She needed no help in the kitchen. The stable hands had no riders going out or coming in. The maids had already hung the laundry.

There was simply no place for me here.

I looped the bailey, my hand tracing the inside of its wall, the only thing tethering me to the present. Staff and soldiers moved about, and yet I felt set apart from them, a ghost in their wake, unseen and unheard. I strained for Ursa's reassurances and found only silence.

My fourth time around the bailey, the yeasty scent of lunch in the air, I saw Renn. It was impossible not to notice him. He had always stood apart, even before . . .

Sten walked faithfully behind him, Princess Azra strolling at his side, tailed by her own guard. The princess laughed at something Renn said, looking up at him like he was a god. I supposed he was, in a way. His hand grazed her midback as he directed her, pointing toward something out of my sight. A tour, perhaps. Exploring a castle that very likely would be hers soon enough.

My eyes lingered on his touch against her tightly laced bodice.

It cracked the numbness, and I mourned the loss of it. Turned and retreated into the keep.

The time had come for me to go home.

None of my siblings knew what had become of me. I'd visited home for a few days, set things in order, and then left again. Word of Rove being sacked would have reached them. Lissel, Dan, Colt, Heath, Pren, Terrence . . . they might very well have believed me dead all this time.

I . . . wouldn't tell them about Rodsfell. I wouldn't burden them with that. But I'd once promised them, after receiving my healer's conscription, that I would return to them as soon as I was able. I needed to uphold that promise. Lissel . . . she couldn't do it all on her own forever. And I no longer had a reason to stay away.

I needed my family. I needed Lissel's humming and Terrence's body curled by mine as I thumbed through a book. I needed my bees and my garden and my parents' roof overhead. I needed Ursa, and perhaps I'd find some trace of her there.

Eden had told me it was too hard to send messengers so far inland to deliver mail; I doubted any soldiers or traveling companions could be spared to escort me. But it didn't matter. I'd crossed the whole of Sesta on my own two feet, the last third alone. I could cross Cansere just as well.

I couldn't stay here. Even if I were to feel Renn in my half-heart for the rest of our lifetimes, I couldn't stay here and watch . . .

Thanks to Nicosia, I had very little to my name, only what had been given to me on the ship. Two dresses, one in terrible repair. My mother's knife, kept safe all these months.

I rubbed my chest. A few coins to see me through would help, but perhaps I could offer my healing services for a copper merit here and there. Beatty would spare me something from the kitchen.

I folded my tattered dress into a tight little square. Set my knife atop it. I'd need a satchel of some sort, to carry it all in—

"Nym! There you are." I'd left my door ajar, and Eden pushed it the rest of the way open. "I had an idea I wanted to run—"

She saw the folded dress and the knife, and somehow she knew. She didn't even ask if I intended to leave, or where I was going or how I would get there. Instead, she rushed at me, grabbing my upper arms with rigid strength.

"No, *no*, Nym," she pleaded, her nose inches from mine. "No, you've only just arrived. You can't leave. You *can't*."

My next breath shuddered down my windpipe. "I have to, Eden. I don't have a place here."

"You do! You do, though. You . . ." She looked around as though the answer might be painted on the wall. "You'll help with the infirmary, or with the delegation—"

I winced.

"—or in the kitchens, or just with me! I don't need Piya. I don't . . ." Her composure collapsed. "Please, *please*. You're the only one who understands. The only thing rooting me to this place. I waited for you and prayed for you, and now you're here! You're here and we're safe now, don't you see?" Her eyes watered even as her grip tightened. "You can't . . . Don't . . . Please, Nym."

Her knees gave out, and I launched to grab her elbows, to steady her. She dropped her forehead to my shoulder, her short hair grazing my collar. "I'm not . . . ready," she whispered. "Please don't leave. Not yet."

I embraced her, holding her tightly. One by one her fingers lifted from my arms, leaving small bruises.

How painfully broken we both were. So broken I wondered if time could ever mend us.

"I'll stay," I promised, absorbing some of her cracks into myself. "A little longer, Eden. I'll stay."

The next morning, I woke groggily from a fitful night to the sound of a trumpet, having dozed upright so I might not sleep too deeply and trigger bad dreams. It worked, in a way. I did not lose myself to the throes of twisted memories, only unpleasant ones. So while I'd overslept, fatigue limned my bones.

It was the first trumpet I'd heard at Derren Castle, so I pulled myself from bed and readied quickly, braiding my mess of hair to keep it presentable. The trumpet bellowed again as I descended the tower, slowing near Renn's room, my fingers brushing his door before I forced myself to continue on.

Soldiers crowded the bailey, one Antsan to every four Canseren. I searched for familiar faces, finally finding one in Beatty. I wound to her side, noting the leather cord of her wedding pendant, my spirit gnawing at the rest of me as I remembered Renn's words two nights previous. Would I have agreed to marry him, if Antsan was not here? If the war allowed it?

My answer pressed hard against my skull, making my sinuses burn. Another trumpet drew my attention, and everyone else's, to the castle wall, where Renn stood.

An awestruck gasp rose from the crowd like steam from a boiling pot as crystalline, ethereal wings spread from Renn's back. They caught the sunlight, flickering like prisms. After the gasps, the people fell silent. Renn did not love attention, but he certainly knew how to command it. His subjects stared at him like they would a god, too mesmerized to look away, though surely talk would come later, and abundantly.

The wings snapped from reality, as though they were never there. Renn needed his people to hear his voice, not gawk at his majesty.

Sten and two other guards lingered near him, as well as Eden. Farther down the wall were grouped part of the Antsan delegation, including Sir Arquan and Princess Azra, whose expressions revealed they were not immune to the magic of the Canseren king.

My heart plummeted as I watched Princess Azra staring at Renn with such adoration. Gods above, was this the marriage announcement? So soon?

I shrunk backward as Renn began to speak, instantly humiliated, searching for some sort of escape, but the press of bodies proved too great. Instead, I dowsed on myself, thickening the wall over my heart despite knowing it would do little good. Magic could only block magic to an extent.

When I came to, Renn's words carried over the hushed throng: "—to bolster our numbers and fight for our kingdom. This will include crafters of *all* disciplines, including mindreaders and soulbinders."

A collective murmuring, punctuated by gasps, filled the bailey. It took me only a moment to realize what I had missed.

Renn was lifting the ban on craftlock. *All* craftlock.

When he spoke my name, my breath caught.

"You see before you the work of Nym Tallowax, the healer who gave me back my legs, who restored what the gods intended." I sensed distantly through the link a discomfort at the words *what the gods intended.* He took a beat before continuing, and a wisp of sorrow danced through the link as well. "Think what more healers in our ranks might accomplish, if one woman can do so much."

He went on to detail how King Nicosia employs all crafters in his armies, giving him a strong upper hand against us. How employing mindreaders would expand our spy networks, and soulbinders—the very same crafters that had breached Rove Castle—would secure our captives. For a man who shied away from attention, he gave a rousing, albeit brief, speech to the men stationed at Derren Castle. Others would learn by missive, as a retinue of messengers were sent out to read the declaration, regardless of whether or not they agreed with it.

Shielding my eyes and squinting at the emissary and princess on the wall, I had a feeling they did not agree with it.

Renn had professed he would find a way to win this war without bringing Antsan onto the throne. Surely this was part of it. But crafters had been illegal for centuries, hated and haunted and even executed. Only healers had been recently tolerated for the sake of healing Renn, and even we still carried a stigma.

This verdict could do so much good. It would help our cause. But Sesta had forcibly employed and trained crafters for far longer. It would not be enough.

Just as importantly, Renn appointed Eden to oversee the collection and training of crafters here at Derren Castle. This was the first time I'd seen Eden in any sort of public setting, and she seemed to stand a little straighter.

It relieved me to see it. *Thank you, Renn.*

The announcement finished, the congregation gradually broke up, talk of the change still rampant among them. A few watched me, perhaps figuring out who I was. Needing to escape their eyes, I pushed through the crowd, picking out a path of least resistance. As folks broke away, I spied Princess Azra again, only this time she had her head bent close to that of a staff member, a young woman around the princess's age, whose name I didn't know, but who had served at Rove Castle. I'd seen her on occasion in the baths. Despite the noise of the throng, the woman spoke quietly, with a hand covering her mouth.

I shouldn't have lingered, but I did, concerned, and so when Princess Azra lifted her gaze, she spotted me easily. She did not look happy.

I knew they'd discussed me, and not merely Renn's mention of me just now atop the wall. I knew Azra was digging. She didn't like that I'd stayed in the west tower. She didn't like the closeness between me and her would-be betrothed. She likely already knew we'd ridden in together.

Beatty headed for the kitchen. Turning away, I followed her and busied myself peeling potatoes.

Not a half hour passed before I felt the kindling of frustration through the link. I might not have noticed it had I not been so numbly focused on stripping potato skins with my mother's knife, its citrine stone leaving a dent in my palm. I wondered at it, but not five minutes later Sten appeared in the kitchen.

I readied an excuse. Renn and I, we *had* to distance ourselves—

"Princess Eden requests you," Sten said, surprising me. I wiped my knife on a borrowed apron, set it aside, and followed the guard into the keep. He took me to a narrow room, a war room, perhaps, above the Great Hall. My eyes first and foremost shot to Renn, who glanced my way and then pointedly avoided my gaze. A square table with a map pinned to it sat before him. Sir Arquan and Princess Azra stood to his left, and an Antsan guard just behind them. He was a thick man, built more like Sten, with tan skin and brown hair cut somewhat similarly to Renn's, if Renn were to grow his out for six months. Princess Eden lingered inside the door. I moved to her side, confused, as Sten took his place to Renn's right.

"—inappropriate. It will not sit well with the king," Sir Arquan was saying, referring to his sovereign, King Vitsoph.

"You fail to recognize that without craftlock, we would not be having this conversation," Renn retorted blandly, and frustration bubbled up softly against the basalt wall.

"Do you mean that Nicosia would not have breached Rove in a single night?" the emissary shot back. "To say magic is *good* because it *can* be is like saying a feral dog is *good* because it takes care of table scraps."

I bristled but held my tongue.

"And yet Nicosia's armies are full of them, Arquan," Renn protested.

Princess Azra said, "You don't fight feral dogs with feral dogs, Your Majesty. You shoot them."

"Our men are mobilized and ready," Sir Arquan reminded him.

"And I thank you for that, again." Renn leaned on his hands on the table, peering over the map. "But Sesta has prepared for this war for years. Neither Cansere nor Antsan have done the same." He turned his head and coughed. I instinctually took a step forward, thinking of the bloodied handkerchief, thinking of his lumis's scars, but the cough was not productive, and I held myself back. "I mean to end the fighting as quickly as possible, not draw it out for the sake of outdated sensibilities."

"Is there a purpose for your attendance, Miss Tallowax?" Princess Azra asked.

All attention moved to me, Renn's slowly, as though it pained him. Sure enough, a faded ache knocked against the basalt wall.

Eden answered, "Miss Tallowax is to be my master-at-arms for the incoming recruits."

My pulse sped. "What?"

She looked at me and offered a small smile. "Not because you are the only crafter here, but because you have shown immense deftness with your skill, as my brother has boldly pointed out. The messengers have already departed to spread the edict; I'll need help organizing and preparing the incoming troops." She touched my shoulder, a whisper of contact, her expression turning pleading. "Please, Nym. I can't do it alone."

"It should not be done at all," Sir Arquan complained.

"And yet as Eden has stated, I've sent out the messengers." Renn pushed off the table, finding a spot on the wall to occupy his focus.

I swallowed. Nodded. "Of course. I would be honored."

I felt out of my depth, and yet I craved something to occupy my time, my thoughts, and my energy. I'd lost much of my "deftness" with Ursa, but I would do my best.

When I turned back to the others, Princess Azra pinned me with a calculating stare. Then she turned to Renn, expression melting to that of pleasantness. "You are, of course, correct, Your Majesty. It isn't our way; our crafters are sent to the south colonies to protect the masses. But this is not Antsan, and this is not yet our war. We will follow your lead."

Sir Arquan frowned but nodded.

Colonies. I tried not to grimace. I wasn't familiar with the geography of Antsan. I imagined me, Ursa, and Dan shipped away from Fount, away from our home, after manifesting powers. Torn from the rest of our family. To do . . . what? Live and farm in a new place where everyone possessed the craft? Would it be violent and anarchist, or some sort of labor camp?

Renn dismissed the meeting; I eagerly left the room, desperate for some distance between us. It felt as though any sort of scab I began to lay over the gaping wound of him tore off the moment I saw him, smelled him, heard him. My chest ached with loss, and my head ached with lack of sleep.

Eden thankfully took me to her chamber so we might discuss plans for the incoming troops, and I blissfully lost myself in the work for hours. When we'd finished and Eden turned to other tasks, I headed to the infirmary. I knew it was wrong to take bliss in others' injuries, but seeing three soldiers in the small space brought me relief.

When you're relieved, it feels like the rain. Cool spring rain, Renn had told me. I wondered how much he could feel now with this wall between us, if he felt it at all.

But I needed to stop thinking of him. Somehow.

I introduced myself to Physician Addsmuch, who was thankfully happy to meet me and not at all perturbed by my abilities. All three soldiers in the infirmary were men. The first had a rolled ankle, which displayed in his waterfall-esque lumis as a small stone breaking the flow of water. I repaired a torn shoulder and bad sunburn in the second. The third possessed a hairline fracture in his forearm that Physician Addsmuch had already splinted, but he allowed me to balm it with the craft.

As the three men left, a new patient entered the infirmary—the Antsan guard who often shadowed Princess Azra. The same as from the war room.

I approached him. "Are you lost or unwell?"

"Is both an answer?" he asked, his Antsan dialect crisp and rhythmic, heavier than that of Sir Arquan's and the princess's. "My, uh, stomach hasn't been feeling well lately. Don't know if it's the weather or the food."

I crooked an eyebrow. "The weather has been pleasant."

He shrugged. "Hell of a lot hotter here than back home. Should I . . . ?" He glanced between me and Physician Addsmuch, which took me right back to the conversation in the war room and the Antsan distaste for craftlock.

"I suppose you have your pick."

He considered for a moment. "I'd pick having it over with sooner."

I gestured at the nearest cot, and the man sat down. I reached for his jaw, but he instinctively pulled backward.

"I'm not going to hurt you," I promised. Sighed and asked, "What's your name?"

"Jonras."

"Jonras, I can take your hand instead, if you'd prefer, but I need to be touching your skin, and I ask you not to break contact until I'm finished."

He nodded and held still. Since he didn't proffer his hand, I gently placed my fingertips on his strong jaw and dowsed.

It took a great deal of self-control not to laugh at what I saw. His lumis was . . . a cake.

It was an enormous cake, colored more like mountains and river bottoms than any actual confection, but it was indeed a cake. A full six layers, unadorned yet masterfully created. I'd wondered if his claim of a stomach ailment was some sort of farce, but sure enough, what I could describe as nothing other than frosting dripped off the third tier. I smoothed and cooled it before checking for any other maladies. Finding none, I released him.

Blinking, he touched his stomach. "Just like that?"

"Just like that."

He sat with it a moment, as though waiting for some ill side effects to settle in. Finding none, he looked up at me. "Thank you, Miss Tallowax."

I don't know what it was, the gratitude or the sliver of mirth he'd given me, but I found myself somewhat contrite, reflecting back on the silly story I'd once woven myself for Renn, imagining him a farmer's son and not a prince, someone I might meet at the bonfire and fall in love with, start a family with, live happily ever after with. On a different turn of time, where I was still young, before the cruelness of men left me scarred and cold.

And I thought to the gods, If I *had* to have opened my heart again, why couldn't it have been to someone like Jonras? Or Sten? Or even Kilg from the Rove kitchens? Why did I have to fall in love with the impossible choice?

Thorns pressed against the basalt wall, dulled but present, and I wondered if Renn sensed my grief, or if something else entirely guilted him.

"Jonras," I said carefully as he stood, "what colonies does Antsan keep for its crafters?"

He touched his chin—Antsan fashion was the same as Canseren in that men shaved their beards. "I've never been to them myself. They're across the channel, a grouping of islands. They ship them there by age twelve and they mostly govern themselves, so long as they fulfill the yearly tax."

I nodded. "And what's to keep them from leaving?"

"Navy, I suppose."

Jonras thanked me again, then departed, leaving the infirmary empty save for myself and Physician Addsmuch, who made a joke about me giving him an early retirement and set to unpacking a small shipment of bandages.

I tried to imagine which land would be the best for a crafter like myself to grow up in—one where I'd be forced into an army, one where I'd be forced into a colony, or one where I'd lose half my heart to a prophesied king.

I intended to keep myself as busy as possible, so I swept out the infirmary and scrubbed the floor, pinching a rag into every crevice between stones until my hands began to chap and my back ached. I was nearly finished when Sten again appeared, wordless when I greeted him. He simply passed me a folded note small enough to fit into the palm of my hand—small enough to be discreet—and left.

The scab pulled the moment I recognized Renn's handwriting.

Please come speak with me tonight. It's important.

He didn't sign his name, but he didn't need to. I debated, but Renn possessed half my heart and claimed the rest of it. I feared I would always give in to him, even to my own detriment.

Yet tonight felt an eternity away, so I headed to the kitchens to help Beatty prepare for the evening meal. I'd missed lunch. Instead, she assigned me to tomorrow morning's bread, so I burned up my energy kneading lump after lump of dough until my wrists ached. I soothed them with the craft and kneaded some more. The kitchen was nearly out of water, so I hooked two buckets to a yoke and set off to collect more.

I might have missed the two of them had I not spied Jonras lingering near the outer wall of the bailey. But spy him I did, and without thinking I scanned for his charge and found her sitting in the shade some twenty yards away on a little bench. Renn knelt in front of her, talking easily with her. I slowed my step long enough to see him reach forward and tuck a lock of her red hair behind her ear.

If he felt the sting that shot through my chest, he didn't show it. Just as I ignored the wall-muted wave of redress punctuated by defensiveness that soon followed. Renn had his fingers in so many pies, how could I ever discern what he felt for what, or who?

I pushed away the hurt as I filled the buckets and found a thread of anger instead, painting it every color I could imagine. Anger at being trapped here, anger at Sesta, anger for Eden, anger for Rove, even anger at my conscription in the first place.

So strange, wondering where I might be now, had the queen's letter never found me. I couldn't bring myself to speculate.

It was well past sunset when I wound my way to the west tower, noting that Sten stayed some distance behind me, perhaps to not draw attention. I kept my eye out for the Antsan delegation, changing my route once to avoid them, then climbed the stairs to Renn's room. I felt very much like a mule on a tether, exhausted and stubborn, yet unable to resist where the rope led.

Not wanting to draw attention with a knock, I simply slipped inside and closed the door softly behind me. Candles and a lantern lit the space. But when I stepped around the little wall that bowed in to accommodate the stairwell, I realized I'd interrupted Renn dressing. I think my surprise through the stifled link alerted him more than the door might have, and when he glanced over at me, my face warmed, even as I tried to grapple with the unseen bond between us, silently pleading to the embarrassment and lust lapping at the basalt wall to not give me away.

He wore soldier's trousers over his breeches, both slung low on his hips, but he'd not yet put on his undershirt—it stretched between his forearms, moments from being donned. Months of activity and good health had added meat to him, though his form was another sign that he was not blood related to King Grejor nor Prince Adrinn; his body was more svelte than theirs. Leaner. But certainly . . . appealing.

The part of my brain registering that sensuality had been in such disuse for so long, I hardly recognized it. As it churned like cogs in an old clock, I caught myself staring at him. Staring and unable to form the thought to *not* stare.

A smile tempted his mouth, but only sadness grazed the bond as he tugged on his shirt. I was about to stammer out an apology when I noticed, at the last moment, the scar on his left side. Only then did my senses order themselves, and I found myself across the room, beside him, lifting his shirt back up to examine it.

The spear wound he got *three months ago*. I touched it, and he flinched.

"Does it still hurt?" I asked.

"No."

Only then did I sense his reciprocation through our bond. Not of embarrassment, but desire. Swallowing, I pulled away. Despite a few nights of sharing Renn's bed, that was all we had done—share a bed. Sleep. In truth, even before the arrival of the delegation, Renn had been surprisingly chaste with me, almost absurdly so.

I thought of his hand on Princess Azra's back. Her hair in his fingers.

It made me mourn anew what we might have had. I withdrew from him, internally chastised. "Do you want me to heal it?" I managed to sound nonchalant.

He shook his head. "No. I . . ." He let out a nervous chuckle. "I want to keep it. A reminder, not to let my guard down. A reminder that . . ." He paused, seeking the right words. "That we all must sacrifice to save what we were, and what we are."

The moment felt too tense, like the west tower's foundation had split and its stones might crumble at any time. "That's quite lovely."

He looked at me like I'd just told him his favorite hound had died. "I've read a lot of poetry books."

"I recall one about a . . . what was it? 'Bullfrog of mine heart'?"

Humor glinted in his eyes at the memory. Things had been so simple then, protected in the keep, his legs returned to him and his lungs mostly so. He'd tried to entertain me by reading from a book of poems and a tome of biology at the same time. It felt like years ago, now. Another lifetime. A dream.

He seemed unsure what to do with himself. Patted empty pockets, turned toward his washbasin. "Do you have everything you need, in your room? A basin, enough blankets?"

"I do."

He inhaled deeply and exhaled slowly. That sore lurch—was that from me, or from him? With the wall . . . I couldn't tell.

I cleared my throat. "You wanted to speak to me?"

He ran a hand down his face. "Gods, this is painfully formal."

"I'm in your bedroom, Your Majesty. I'd hardly call it formal."

"Don't." He pointed right at me, and that painful lurch thumped again. "Don't call me that. Please, Nym. Don't . . . call me that."

My organs felt too heavy to keep up. I looked away.

"How have you been?" he asked.

I snorted. "Such a question to ask."

"You've hidden from me," he retorted softly. "Physically, and . . ." He touched his heart. Sighed. "I don't blame you."

"We can't have this conversation again." My tone was pleading.

"I know. I just . . . I . . ." He put his hands on his hips and tilted his face to the ceiling. "I don't even know what to say to you without having that conversation again. It's not a conversation that can just *end*, Nym."

"I'm sorry." I hugged myself.

"Don't be." He stepped closer to me. Held back. "I could always tell you anything. And now I can't?" A whisper of a smile. "You certainly never had any issue with sharing exactly what was on your mind."

The remark brought me up short. Like I'd been caught in a lie.

He noticed. "What is it?"

I started to shake my head, to dismiss it, but Renn was right—that *had* been me. Anything on my mind. There had only been truth between us from the start. It had been our foundation. And Ursa . . . I could almost hear her urging me to confess.

"Obviously . . . I'm not happy . . . with our situation." I pointedly didn't meet his eyes. "But besides that, I've been . . . lost." The words came out quieter than I'd intended. Like a prayer. I struggled to sort my thoughts and put them in some kind of logical order. "The loneliness . . . I'm getting used to that." Renn opened his mouth to protest—I felt the defensiveness in his bond, the concern. I rushed, "Because of Ursa."

It *would* all be easier were she here.

Worry marred his forehead. The wall I'd put around my heart merlon prevented most of it from echoing in my own chest.

"She's always been there," I admitted, hugging myself tighter. "Even after she died. And then she was just . . . gone."

"Nym—"

"But I'm getting used to it. I am. And I'm so . . . *so* grateful to be home." Home as much as I could be. Derren Castle was another new place, but however much torment it had brought me, it proffered safety. "But then I'm . . . lost again. For so long I was a sister and a mother. Then the castle healer. Then a prisoner." *And a lover,* I didn't say. "And now I'm back, and I don't know who I am anymore."

His glow flickered. "You're still a healer."

"I'm still a healer," I agreed, "but it's . . . not the same as it was. I don't . . . I don't know what to *do* with myself." I turned toward him. "I'm not saying I wish you were sick again. I'm not saying that at all."

"I know."

"And Eden wants me to train these new recruits, but how could I possibly help mindreaders and soulbinders? Healers . . . I'm not what I was. I know it's not right for me to feel this way. You, Eden, you've lost so much more—"

He scoffed. "It isn't a contest. You're *allowed* to struggle, Nym. You're allowed to share it with those who care about you. You don't have to earn our support."

His admonition brought tears to my eyes. I turned my head, blinking quickly. Not that I could hide anything from him with that golden wire connecting us, no matter how much ethereal rock I plastered over it.

Once I regained some composure, I said, "I just . . . I'm a little lost. But I don't think anyone else can find me, if that makes sense?"

He nodded, ever patient. Affection tried to burn through the basalt wall, which only shook my precarious resolve. "No one is going to find your purpose for you. You need to wend your own way," he reiterated on my behalf.

"Yes. Precisely."

"You will, Nym." He reached forward and cupped the side of my face; the warmth of his touch felt new, startling, and I had to pull away from him, I had to remember my country and my family's future in that country, and yet I turned traitor, leaning into his calloused palm.

"Whether you realize it or not, you are extraordinary. You always have been. Nothing will keep you down for long. I truly believe that."

I stared at him, memorizing and missing him, finding comfort in his touch and masculine scent while the internal wound in the shape of him tore and bled. Steeling myself, I stepped back, breaking our contact, as cold and empty as a newly dug grave.

"Do you think they'll accept it so easily?" I pressed, searching for new words. Different words.

He lowered his hand. "Which thing?"

I suppose there were many things that might fit with that question. Including *Do you think the people will accept your partnering with Antsan?* "Craftlock," I specified. "Many are still closed off to healers. Mindreaders and soulbinders have no direct benefit to common folk."

"That's precisely what we've argued over. I think Sesta will make most people more open to it. When a man has to kill the same enemy three times because of healers, he'll want a healer. When his secrets are known, or when his comrade is being cut down because he's soulbound to a tree, he'll want a mindreader and soulbinder for himself." His eyes widened slightly. "Nym, I didn't mean to bring up—"

I pretended the image did nothing to me. "No apologizing. Remember?"

He wilted. I sensed the words on the tip of his tongue, saw the grief warping his expression. Sure enough, that thorny guilt began to grow between us, pressing on the wall, determined to break through it. He averted his eyes. "There . . . is something I wanted to talk to you about."

I held my breath. This was it. He signed the contract. He'd wed Azra Vitsoph and save us all.

It took notable effort to stay upright. "What?"

"Your . . . I don't know what to call it. How you got away from King Nicosia and the others. Would you . . . ? Is it something you can teach the healers, when they come?"

The relief I felt nearly floored me. My wall betrayed me; I could tell by the way Renn straightened. He'd felt it.

"I severely doubt others will have their sisters tied to their lumis." A deep ache coursed through me.

"Not that, precisely." He extended his hands by way of apology. "But healers hurt, too."

I swallowed. Remembered the dragons in Catalaine I'd attacked. Remembered breaking Whitestone's leg. Remembered the soldier in Rove Castle, the one with a mathematical lumis, and how I'd killed him.

Steadying myself to ensure my voice would be even, I answered, "Being able to see death lines helps a great deal with that."

"But you could teach it, if you needed to. Something offensive with lumie."

I took a moment to think it through, Renn waiting patiently near me. Too near me. We needed distance, yet my feet would not move.

How would I instruct other healers? Some may have worked out their abilities as Ursa and I had; some might not have. There were no schools, no teachers, no books on craftlock to guide us. Magic was something crafters had to sort out for themselves.

But in that train of thought I found the seeds of purpose.

"Likely," I answered. "But I think there will be much to teach on either side. Though healing has been legal for two decades, I've never seen apprenticeships for healers. The fact I have any skills at all is sheer luck, and Ursa—" My throat closed with the name of my twice-dead sister. "We discovered a lot of it together. Practiced together. Most people won't have that. They wouldn't be ready to learn . . . hurting. They need to understand the healing first. The healing is more important." *Gods keep this war from getting so desperate.*

"I understand." He pinched his mouth to stifle a yawn.

I managed to take a step back; it felt like whiskey on an open wound. "Go to sleep, Renn. Your days are too long, and your mornings too early."

"There's more, Nym."

Gods, I thought I'd evaded it again. I was already on the brink of crying—

"Not that," he murmured.

I sucked in an unsteady breath and nodded.

He turned from me and began pinching out the candles, his own light replacing theirs. "We're going to strike Serravia."

My lungs tightened. Serravia was a port city in southeastern Sesta. A hub for trade between our two countries, as well as Antsan across Salm's Rest. "When?"

He shifted. "We leave tomorrow."

My lungs squeezed. "So soon."

He nodded. "Little time to relax, in war."

I mulled over the information. "The first time we've attacked Sestan soil, right?"

"Yes. Rove . . . Rove is the ultimate goal, but we need to take out the army's resources. Burn their ships. We strike at the end of the week."

I turned toward him in the dim. "Will . . . will you take me with you?"

A lick of fear from him, and I wondered how strong it might be without the wall. "The other healers won't have arrived in time," he said. "I don't *want* to endanger you, but I should have a healer there. However much I want you to stay, to protect you." He sighed. "However much I want you there just for me."

I nodded, my throat dry. "Of course. But . . . Antsan . . ."

"I'm tying them up with amendments," he answered. "They'll send their present troops with us as a show of good faith."

I chewed the inside of my lip. "But will it be enough?"

"For Serravia, yes. We'll meet with General Cuplend's troops. Nicosia shouldn't be expecting us. I . . ." A hand back through his hair. A finger caught on a snag, and new pain bloomed through the link, so strong it would have floored me without the wall acting as blockade. Not from his hair, but something deeper. "I have some ideas, Nym. If nothing else, Serravia will give me time to sort through them. I'm going to find a way."

His hand on Azra's back, his fingers in her hair. "For me, or for Azra?"

It was unfair of me to say it, but the constant ache had chafed my sensibilities.

He glowered. "I'm doing what is needed. Do you really find me so two-faced?"

My eyes burned. "We can't have this conversation again—"

"I'm going to find a way," he promised, his skin glowing brighter.

I shook my head. "You will be the end of me, Renn." I took a moment to fortify myself. To drag myself away from the addictive aura of him and to the door. Yet as I gripped the handle, determined to retire to my own space, fear sluiced through me. Bone-deep weariness settled in every inch of me . . . even sitting upright, I knew Nicosia would return to me tonight, in whatever grotesque form my creativity might paint him in.

I pulled the door open about an inch before Renn's hand grasped my wrist and pushed it closed. "Stay, Nym," he whispered, breath in my hair.

My throat grew tight. "I can't—"

"Azra isn't here. Nothing is signed." His thumb traced my knuckles. "Stay. Sten won't let anyone in."

"Yet," I weakly protested. Emotion pushed against my skin like too much blood. Like I might burst. "Nothing is signed *yet*."

"Nym—"

"My family is Canseren, Renn," I whispered. "Brien, Lissel, Dan, Colt, Pren, Heath, and Terrence. All of them benefit from Antsan's aid. I would break my heart a hundred times over to save them." I swallowed, my throat tight and sore. "And I would break yours, too."

It was unfair, so wildly unfair, to suffer the ache of those words twofold. To bear my hurt and his as well, even with the wall in place.

But Ursa had been the optimist, not me. She'd been the dreamer, I'd been the doer. And Ursa was gone.

Soon, Renn would be, too.

I left before the tears fell. I could spare him from that, at least.

I slept with my back pressed against the hard wall, gathering wisps of sleep shaped like an ancient, awful tree.

Chapter 16

Renn and Commander Stonelay had the soldiers stationed at Derren Castle packed and in formation to start the trek to Hock, the small port town where we'd be departing to reach Serravia. Even if the noise of preparing soldiers hadn't filtered into my room, I would have woken plenty early. Though I don't know if one can call it waking when one barely slept.

I dowsed away what I could and let a splash of cold water across my face mend the rest.

I peered out the first tower window I crossed. Seeing the soldiers line up now, guilt flooded me. I held back the very thing we needed to save them. I feared my fatigue would hinder Renn, and yet to share his bed for much-needed rest, I drove a wedge between him and our greatest ally.

I had to do better. There had to be a way.

My present life fit into a single knapsack with room to spare. I braided my hair around my crown and down to its tips to keep it from knotting in travel or getting in the way. I packed up bedding for the casualties we'd be sure to have and inventoried resources with Beatty, who would not be coming with us. We'd meet another battalion along the way that would, hopefully, have more food to keep the soldiers going.

While I had ridden into Derren on the king's horse, I would be walking out behind the soldiers, with the other skeleton staff the army required.

A trumpet sounded as I finished my preparations; the first companies were marching. I hurried toward the broken east tower to bid goodbye to Eden, and unfortunately came across Renn and Princess Azra once more, just in time to see him kiss the back of her hand in farewell before heading toward the exit, lightly armored and with two swords hanging at his hip. I thought he faltered, but was it due to his lingering illness, or because he felt the unjust betrayal that wove between my ribs like some sick, shoddy tapestry?

I took another route to the east tower and found Eden in her room, working on additional correspondence to bring in crafters as quickly as possible to the fortress. Setting aside quill and parchment, she embraced me tightly. "Come back, Nym. Bring him back, too. I will not lose another brother, nor another friend."

I promised her and left, winding through the narrow bailey and across the drawbridge, and—

My foot hovered at the end of the drawbridge, where weeds poked up around the wood. Despite the warm morning sun, cold sweat broke out over my skin as I looked at the departing soldiers garbed in black and red, my eyes darting to their collars, seeing silver markings where there were none, and I *knew* there were none, yet my eyes played tricks on me, twice convincing me men with dark hair had four gold bars denoting their rank. That the king of Sesta had infiltrated us. That he'd slaughtered every denizen of the fortress in the night and replaced their souls with dragons.

I froze, as though soulbound to the weeds. *Move,* I pleaded. My heart sped. My mind turned to hot coals. *Move, Nym.*

I did. I stepped back, both feet firmly on the drawbridge. Two soldiers walked around me, carrying something between them. I didn't see what—swirling shadows filled the periphery of my vision.

I needed air. Yet I stood outside, breathing clean air. Surrounded by clean, fresh air. But I couldn't breathe. I heard the gasps filling my lungs and leaving too quickly, yet I couldn't feel them.

I was being ridiculous. I chided myself for being ridiculous. "It's nothing," I murmured, and took a step forward.

Ursa didn't reply.

The darkness at the edge of my vision coiled like spider legs. I felt the soulbond deep in my core, holding me there. The sword run through my middle, leaking the air from my lungs, because I still couldn't breathe. No air. Suffocating—

A *thump* hit the bridge behind me. "Nym." Someone called my name from far away, behind a glass wall. *"Nym."*

A hand dropped onto my shoulder, and I jumped, inhaling sharply enough to choke on saliva. I bent over and coughed, shaking, beads of sweat dripping down the channel of my spine, forming on my temples. A whooshing like a hundred whispers filled my ears—

Light in my eyes. His body blocked the army as he knelt in front of me, one palm to either shoulder. "Breathe, Nym. It helps if you breathe."

The words sounded a little closer now. Familiar. I sucked in a shaky breath. Let it all out at once.

"Slowly," he commanded. The light snuffed out.

I tried again, taking a little longer, the air unable to stick to my lungs. Again, focusing on the air. Just the air. In, out. In, out. In, out. A steadiness sat in my chest—a muted concern, *empathy*—and it wasn't until I felt this pushing against the basalt wall that I recognized Renn. I leaned into him, focusing my thoughts on the movement of air as perspiration dried and my thoughts untangled into a semblance of reason. As I slowly came back to myself.

Dread pooled in my belly as tears burned in my eyes.

"I . . . I can't," I whispered. If this happened on the drawbridge of a remote Canseren fortress . . . how would I ever face a battlefield filled with *real* dragons? Where Adoel Nicosia himself might be leading them?

Renn smoothed hair from my face. "I know. I worried . . . and I felt it. I came as soon as I felt it."

I swallowed. Shook my head. I needed to find a better solution than the basalt wall. I couldn't keep holding him back. "I have to. You need—"

"I need you to survive, Nym." He touched my chin, bringing my eyes to meet his. His forehead pressed to mine. "I need you to survive a little bit longer."

My hands curled into fists. "But there are no other healers—"

"We have healers," he promised. "Not crafters, but we have healers."

No, I had to do this. I had to keep them alive. I needed purpose. And yet as I tried to stand, as I listened to the army's departing footsteps, that stiffness returned to my limbs. Fear dribbled down my ribs like condensation.

Renn scooped me up in his arms like I weighed less than a toddler. His skin glowed—wings of light unfurled—and he leapt once, suddenly at the portcullis of the castle wall. We stepped beneath its shade. Light winking out, he set me down just inside, the hefty stone blocking my sight of the army.

I peeled my tongue off the roof of my mouth. "I-I can do this."

He tapped his index finger on my breastbone. "I feel you, Nym, despite your efforts. I know this feeling well. You can't."

"But—"

He squeezed my knees. "You are not broken. But you . . . are not well. Not at this moment. You're not ready."

Guilt prodded at the wall.

Tears filled my eyes at his truths. As I recognized that, should I try again, panic would overwhelm me once more. I would be a liability, not a help, on the battlefield. Waking nightmares painted me back in Sesta, running from soldiers in blue.

Safe. Safe. You're safe.

"I . . ." He struggled. "I can't stay with you. I have to go with them."

I nodded. *Of course you do,* I tried to say, but I couldn't form the words. This . . . this was a good thing. A hard thing, but a good thing. I couldn't depend on Renn anymore. Even without Antsan . . . I couldn't make the king of Cansere my crutch. No matter how hard it became, or how much it hurt.

"Believe in me," he murmured.

My throat felt like I'd swallowed a stone and it'd lodged just after clearing my tongue. I nodded again, blinking so I would not cry. Renn brushed his lips across my forehead, grounding me a little more. "Stay with Eden."

I swallowed the stone, moving it about an inch. "Come back. You . . . You have to come back."

Only Nicosia can kill him.

But Nicosia might be there.

A sad smile shaped Renn's mouth; I felt its reflection in our bond. "I will. I will always come back to you, Nym Tallowax."

Another trumpet sounded. Just one bleat, not four. Still, I shrunk from it, the noise suddenly too loud. I knew he had to go; his urgency knocked against the wall. But he lingered a moment longer, clutching my hand so tightly in his that I still felt the imprint of his fingers even minutes after he departed. I found no solace in the solitude of his wake.

The stone dropped into my chest, heavy and immovable. I sat on a patch of wild clover and stared at millennium-old rock, breathing in, breathing out. Breathing in, breathing out . . .

"Miss Tallowax."

My name, spoken with that melodic accent, pulled me from my trance. I looked up to see Princess Azra three paces from me, fully dressed, hair ironed to Canseren perfection, a hat with a long train pinned to her crown. The shade blended with her freckles, and she held her hands together over her navel.

I scrambled for an apology for my state, but she spoke again before I could piece together the words.

"I'm aware you're the king's pet," she said, and my stomach sank to the clover, "but the chosen one will not say no to me. He needs my men and my resources too direly."

My tongue dried in my mouth. Had I been so obvious? Had she been watching me, or one of her men? "I-I'm not—"

"I'm not stupid, *healer*." She sniffed. "Just as you are not as quick as you should be. I shouldn't have to explain this to a servant, much less a crafter, but I will be clear: Stay out of my way, and I will stay out of yours. Do not make me repeat myself."

She pulled a fan from her sleeve, unfurled it, and went on her way, back toward the keep. I watched every step she took, trying to retime my breathing, trying to bring myself back down to earth before the princess's tidal wave could knock me over.

And yet I feared I was already drowning.

By the time I peeled myself out of the bailey and headed back into the keep, I spied the princess at the base of the west tower's stairs, and an Antsan maid and Jonras coming down with my few meager things between them, including my pitcher and basin.

Jonras, at least, had the decency to look chagrined.

"I've taken the liberty of moving your quarters," Princess Azra announced factually. "The room above His Majesty's will be mine, and you will join the rest of the staff in the barracks."

My lips pressed into a hard line, but I did not argue with her. Not merely because I *should* not, but because she was right. If Renn were still actively regressing, it would make sense to have a room near his, even if it were more esteemed. But he was not, and I could be nothing to him. By all means, until the new craftlock recruits arrived, I was the lowest servant here. I had no hired place and little demand for my talents.

I held my hand out to the maid for my blanket. The princess stiffened, ready to battle it out with me, but I simply took the blanket and walked toward the barracks where the others slept, Jonras close behind me. He didn't speak until I opened the door.

"It's not my place to discuss with her," he offered.

"I know."

The women had the smallest building, with eight bunk beds close together. With the staff at work, we were the only two there to witness my demotion. The first few beds were entirely full, a top bunk taken on the fourth.

I crossed to the farthest bunk from the door and set my blanket atop it. A community pitcher and basin were near the entrance, so Jonras set mine on the floor at the foot of the bed.

"You need anything else? Is this really all?" he asked.

"Everything else is here." I patted my packed bag, still slung on my shoulder. "Thank you. You should get back."

He nodded, then departed.

I busied myself throughout the day, though with the camped soldiers gone there was far less to do. All the better, I supposed, to help me with my new errands. I borrowed shears from Beatty, which I took back to my new bunk. I used them to cut strips from my ragged Sesta-stained dress, which I then plaited into three braids—two thicker, one thinner. Then I helped with laundry and washing the castle floors until dark. I treated myself to a cold bath and rebraided my damp hair.

I snuck into the barracks well after the others had fallen asleep. Did not light a candle. The floorboards creaked underfoot, but Beatty's snoring helped drown them out. Good. If the others slept through that, hopefully they'd sleep through the rest.

I stripped off my dress and set it aside, lying down in my shift. I arranged my blankets atop myself, then took my thinner braid with a ball of fabric and tied it around my mouth, gagging myself as much as I could without being too uncomfortable. Then I looped the other braided cords around my wrists and awkwardly tied them to the ladder leading to the upper bunk, hoping they'd help keep me from thrashing too wildly.

As I closed my eyes to sleep, I felt for the muffled link. Renn, too, slumbered.

With luck, I wouldn't wake him.

This time I worked in my parents' house, having just pulled laundry off the line and brought it in to fold. None of my siblings were present, leaving the house eerily quiet. Nicosia came up from behind me and grabbed my hair, wrenching me back with an intense feeling of falling. He slammed me into the floor, splinters digging into my shoulders. He wore his military uniform, gold bars gleaming.

"TELL ME WHAT I WANT TO KNOW!" he screamed, spittle raining across my face. I struggled against him, but my wrists and ankles were suddenly tied, and a mastiff lumbered nearby, holding my soulbinding. I tried to speak, but the gag pressed too hard against my teeth.

Nicosia cursed and knelt between my knees. "I ought to break you like I did her." He leaned close, carrying with him the chill of winter, so cold it burned my skin. "If you won't tell me how you did it, I'll discover it for myself."

And he shoved his hand into my chest, tearing through clothing, skin, and bone, until he wrapped his hand around my half-heart and pulled it free from its cavity.

I woke to the blue hour before dawn, breathing hard, slick with sweat. My lips, cheeks, and wrists were rubbed raw. It took me a long moment to recognize where I was, that it was all a dream, and yet I still felt the open wound between my breasts. So much so that when I untied myself, I checked to see if it bled.

Guilt pushed through the bond, pulsing like a second heart. I curled into myself, knees to ribs. "I'm sorry," I whispered, so that if any other servants remained in their beds, they wouldn't hear me. "I'm sorry, I'm sorry. I'll get better. I'll do better."

I had to. If this bond between Renn and I carried from Cansere to Rodsfell, it would easily connect us from Fount to Rove. I'd be a handicap to him all his life.

The pain in my chest persisted. Dowsing, I realized my heart blocks were fading, which meant I had to remove part of the basalt wall to reenergize them.

I did so quickly, my guilt mixing with Renn's until my lumis became nearly toxic to linger in.

Then I sealed everything up and got to work.

After two more nightmarish nights, I finally sought out Eden in the waning hours of the evening, exhausted by the day's labor in addition to my poor sleep. I'd labored hard, avoiding the Antsan princess, which had proven easy, since she didn't mingle much with Renn gone, Sir Arquan with him, and her walks through the bailey were routine, so I knew not to be visible at those times. A young soldier had been stationed outside Eden's room. Inside, I spied Piya knitting in the corner. Her presence surely acted as a balm to the princess; this was the first time since Rove that I'd seen her without deep shadows under her eyes.

She didn't hesitate to remark on mine. "Nym." She set down the ledger she was reading. "You haven't been sleeping."

I nodded, feeling suddenly sheepish. "I . . . came here to speak to you about that."

"Piya, would you give us a moment?"

The attendant quickly stood and set her mending on the chair, offered a curtsy to Eden and a smile to me, then hurried into the hallway.

I wrung my hands together. "I apologize."

Eden shook her head. "She loves any opportunity she gets to speak with Quinn—the guard in the hall. You're doing her a favor."

I let out a slow breath. "I was wondering if . . . if it wouldn't be too much trouble, if I might stay here tonight." Princess Azra and her demeaning relegation of my things sprang to mind. "I know the difference in our stations—"

"Yes." She closed the ledger. "Of course, Nym." She studied my face, then patted her bed. "You're still having nightmares."

I sat near her. "I am. Again."

"One night." She had a number of books and papers on her bed, which she seemed to be using as a desk, and began collecting them together. "I've had *one night* since arriving here when I didn't. Piya . . . her presence helps." Reaching forward, she clasped my hand. "If not for you, Nym, I would be living the nightmares, still. Please, *never* hesitate to ask me for anything. Especially not for help."

Emotion burned the inside of my nose. "Thank you, Eden."

Eden's presence *did* help—I still had nightmares, but they'd simmered down into bad dreams. Dreams I could sleep through and forget by morning. With the basalt wall firmly in place, hopefully that meant Renn's nights would pass uninterrupted. Yet even as I worked through the first of my troubles, I learned quickly to keep to my side of the bed, for touching Eden in the dark of night triggered something in her. She would thrash or cry out when I did, sometimes loud enough to call in her guard.

I'd become so used to being the solution to others' hurts. The cure. It bothered me that we were so broken, and yet I could do so little to fix it. Ursa had died in truth, Eden's work preparing for incoming crafters consumed her, and Renn—

I could not think of Renn.

I threw myself into daily chores, so much so that I simply took the lead on anything that needed to be done without clarifying with the steward first. I lent my hands and talents wherever they could be put to work. As far as I could tell, Renn's feelings stayed relatively even over the next two weeks: eagerness, trepidation, boredom, concern, repeat. I imagined long days of traveling and reflected on my journey through

Sesta, though I supposed it would be different with an army. Different, as a king.

King. My king, and nothing more.

I could not escape him. Not only from our connection; he so often graced the tongues of those remaining at Derren I could hardly go a few hours without catching his name. Any glimpses of the Antsan princess drove home the reminder like unsharpened ice picks. I found myself desperately wanting to go home, and yet every time I seriously started to plan out my route, away from Eden's awareness, I remembered standing on the drawbridge, frozen and useless. A wreck and a mess. For all the gods wanted us apart, I could not bring myself to have that be my last moment with Renn. I didn't want him to remember me so . . . broken.

I promised myself that after the army returned I would depart. After I steeled myself with the time apart and could look him in the eyes, as healed as I could manage and feigning the rest, I would say goodbye properly.

In the quiet hours of the night, when I could not sleep, I sat in my lumis and played with magic, calling it and bending it and shaping it much as I had my months in Rove, desperate to discover a means of severing my connection to Renn without killing us. Feeling keenly the absence of my sister all the while.

Even in that ethereal space, I wept.

Two weeks after Renn and his troops left, the first crafters arrived at the castle. Three healers from two villages. Eden went straight to work, taking down their information and cataloging it, giving them a tour of the keep and their barracks. More crafters trickled in, some as young as thirteen, one as old as seventy. Predominantly men, and all healers. Healers, who had been legal for two decades. Who felt comfortable exposing themselves.

In Princess Azra's walks around the bailey, I noted she brought more guards with her and always had her fan in hand. It was not until she demanded the new recruits be clearly marked as crafters that Eden relented and had them wear sashes like Physician Addsmuch's, in whatever fabric we could spare, for there wasn't much. Which made Eden's gifting me a second dress that much more meaningful.

The healers were a blessed distraction. We shared what we knew with one another, and I instructed them in all the ways I had learned to heal, including that of rebuilding parts of a lumis with pure magic—tying them off and letting them stand on their own, how to feed them to keep them strong, and so forth. I did not speak of offensive strategies, not yet. I explained what to expect with castle life and prepared the infirmary and bailey to receive injured men upon the army's return, as Physician Addsmuch had left with the soldiers. I worked with the recruits from dawn until dusk, letting them practice on one another. Never on me, not with the darkness left from my death, nor with the small basalt dome masking the golden threading thickly woven to one of my merlons. There would be no witnesses. Nothing that could connect me to their king.

Even apart, I was his weakness, and I feared I always would be.

The first nonhealing crafter arrived two weeks after the first healer: a mindreader. She was a woman of about forty, haggard from the journey, asking about payment and requesting promises of amnesty. I worried Eden might shy from her, since our only experience with mindreaders came from Adoel Nicosia, but she dove into the work with as much vigor as I did.

I thought of Dan back home in Fount and wondered how long it would be before the missive reached him, and whether or not he would answer it. He would have finished his apprenticeship while I was in Sesta. He might have started a tannery of his own or was sharing the workload—and pay—with Pern Fursmade. As a young man, he needed to serve his country, but joining the army would hurt his sprouting career and leave Lissel with less money in our coffers and one less helping hand at the house. Perhaps it was selfish of me, but I hoped he did not come, however much his presence would balm my aching soul.

I missed my family.

I thought of my siblings as I lay awake in Eden's bed four weeks after the army left, painting their faces in my mind's eye, drafting letters to them with my thoughts, wishing I could send the two I'd physically penned without taxing the war effort. Should I forgo my final farewell to Renn and promise to Eden and return home sooner? Had the gifts Renn provided them in January been enough to keep everyone afloat? Did Lissel worry over what had happened to me after the sacking of Rove? With healers coming to Derren Castle, my skill set was no longer unique or necessary, and Lissel had been running things so long on her own.

I truly did not want to travel by myself. I managed it in Sesta, focused on one solemn goal, pushed ever forward by the need to survive. And though I'd made the journey from Fount to Rove on my own, I feared I'd crumble from the isolation. And I did not trust . . . I did not trust the strangers I'd surely meet along the way.

Simply put, I was afraid.

Forgive me, Lissel, for thrusting onto you what was thrust onto me. For making you a mother too soon.

As for Brien . . . I had not seen my brother Brien, my sibling closest to me in age, in over a year. I brought up pointed memories of him, detailing his features, ensuring I painted them with exactness for fear I might forget. To forget felt like the greatest crime I could commit against him.

I wondered if I would have forgotten Ursa's face if I did not see it in my reflection. I thought of my dear twin, of the vision of her dead at Adoel Nicosia's feet, and I feared another Sestan dragon might have done the same to my brother. That night, I wept anew.

It seemed the gods would never run out of reasons for me to mourn.

The following day I instructed a few healers in what I considered to be the basics of our craft. It went well; as far as healing went, I felt much of the magic intuitive. I excused myself to the privy. Exiting, I'd barely gotten outside the reach of its smell when Princess Azra came from my left and seized my arm, forcing me to turn toward her. I only just pulled back the instinct to physically defend myself. Jonras, ever loyal, hovered some distance away.

"When you are called, you answer, Miss Tallowax," she commanded hotly, melodic dialect discordant.

Had she called me? The woman didn't give me a chance to ask.

"I know about you, and I mean to make myself clear as to my and the king's expectations."

I narrowed my eyes at her but held my tongue. A feat I had to thank Queen Winvrin for, I supposed.

"Your being His Majesty's second hand so long has made you act above your station," she ground out quietly, like a pot just starting to boil. "I will remind you that his healing was your duty, nothing more, and certainly not a task to be perpetually rewarded."

I held up a hand to stall her, to speak, but she barreled over me.

"You will *not* interrupt me." Her pale skin reddened. "I know about you, Nym Tallowax. I've heard every rumor—"

"You've dug for every rumor," I offered, but it went unheard.

"—and I know *everything*. I know the queen loathed you and you were a frequent bar-licker."

That one must have been an Antsan idiom. I missed part of what she said trying to figure it out, and determined it must refer to the bars in the castle dungeon. My stomach tightened.

"—heard not using his title, and your own soldiers confirm you have shared his tent, which is wholly unnecessary for a *crafter*"—she spat the word like an insult—"whose services are no longer required. Unless, of course, you're offering a new set of *services*."

That rankled me. "Your assumptions make you look daft, Your Highness."

She raised a hand, I thought to strike me, but lowered it again. I almost offered an explanation . . . but what good would that do but to confirm her anxieties?

I was already losing him. I didn't need this woman to pour salt onto my bleeding heart.

Through gritted teeth, I asked, "May I be excused?"

She sniffed and lifted her chin. "Do not humiliate yourself further, and you will *not* humiliate me, is that understood? Abandon your ideas of grandeur and remember your place." She looked me up and down. "You may still play sycophant to Eden—for whatever reason, she seems to tolerate you. I will not, and do not."

Ursa save me. Anger rolled in my shoulders and singed my fingertips, but I managed a simple nod. It did not appease her, but she didn't batter me further with her obtuse sentiments. She nodded toward Jonras, who approached and did not make eye contact with me. They left together.

I very badly wanted a rug to beat. Instead, I went to the kitchen and kneaded dough, seeking exhaustion as medicine for my anger and everything that was tied to it.

I said nothing to Eden of the exchange and went to bed early, but it took hours to finally fall asleep.

At the first light of dawn, a surge of energy poured through my basalt armor, Renn's emotions high and quick. I woke with my heart racing, fear stoking it, while excitement laced the edges of my awareness. I dared to crack open the wall. Hugging myself, I forced my breathing to stay even as courage and patriotism steamed into my throat and nose. And beneath all of it, hot coals of anger.

I knew then, without a doubt, that the army had reached Serravia.

The battle had started.

That morning, I experimented with different patterns for buttressing the basalt wall. Techniques I'd used against Nicosia, reinforcing it with magicked blocks or ethereal inventions of granite, ice, and steel. None seemed to hinder my connection to Re—*the king* better than before, so I refueled my heart and sealed it in basalt. I kissed the magic-glistening stones and whispered down the connection everything I wished I could say to him. Things I could no longer say to him. Things no one but me would ever hear.

I noted Jonras near the east tower when I descended and asked Quinn, Eden's guard, how long the Antsan man had been there. Apparently on and off, since shortly before dawn.

Frowning, I ignored Princess Azra's spy and got to work.

More crafters came. Eden and I learned their skill sets, their training, ages, occupations, and fighting abilities, if relevant. We checked their citizenship records, turning away only one, who did not have his papers, for we could not risk admitting potential spies into our fold. The majority remained healers, predominantly men, and fell under my jurisdiction.

Princess Azra complained to the steward about the increasing traffic and demanded they be camped outside in tents. However, as all our tents had gone with the army, her solution was moot, so she took to taking her walks both earlier and later in the day, often atop the bailey wall instead of within it. More than once I thought I felt eyes watching me. Sometimes, when I searched, I saw her glaring at me from the rampart, unabashed. Other times, it was Jonras doing it for her. I felt certain that was his mission; he was a loyal soldier who did as his mistress bade, even if he disagreed with it. Yet I didn't know what Princess Azra expected to find. Renn—the king—was not here. I could do nothing to foil her.

When the first soulbinder reported, I flinched when she told me her craft. Flinched, and in that fraction of a second my eyes were closed, I saw the Egroran behind my eyelids, the beautiful, ancient tree that had been my prison, and I felt Nicosia's leash around my spirit, pinning me to its rough bark.

Her name was Phin. She was twenty-five years old—equal in age to me, her hair as dark as the Sestan king's.

Eden, to her credit, showed no emotion when she recorded Phin's ability; she welcomed her and gave her directions to the women's barracks. Eden had rarely been soulbound in Sesta. Phin later confirmed that a soulbinder could only form one binding at a time, just as a mindreader could only delve into one mind, and a healer could only heal one body. Since I'd been perpetually bound to that tree, I had occupied the entirety of Nicosia's binding magic. Unless the Allmaster of legend did not possess the same limitations as the rest of us, but I'd experienced his magic firsthand. I did not think that to be true.

He'd been so enraged, to know I had power he didn't.

I miss you, Ursa, I thought, then comforted myself with a vision of her with my parents, running through rolling hills of white flowers and white aspens. A place of peace, so unlike the mortal world.

That night, as we scrambled together enough food for our craftlock troops in the bailey, the Antsan princess watching from the wall, Eden stood on an overturned crate and announced, "We are grateful for the miles you have traveled to come here and serve your country, and your king. We admire your bravery, both in coming forward as the ban against craftlock is lifted, and to defend your families and your homes. Here is an army unlike any Cansere has ever boasted, an army blessed by the gods. An army with true power.

"But I will make one thing clear." Her voice took on a hard edge. "Though our enemy has taken Rove, the law still stands. Though Sesta beats down our door, the law still stands. Though you wield magic, the law still stands. Our king, Renn Reshua Noblewight, has embraced craftlock for the good of his people, but crafters are not immune to the law. There will be *no* use of craftlock against one another or others without express permission from commanding officers, myself, and your mentor, Nym Tallowax. Power does not equal immunity, and the misuse of it will be dealt with swiftly and harshly."

Several of the men and women exchanged stiff glances. They were still so new to this—to magic, and to war. I feared Eden's words would frighten them, and yet I was exceptionally glad she had shared them.

"I believe I am understood." She nodded with the regality of a princess, of a woman used to getting what she wanted. Of a person doing an impeccable job of hiding how broken she was, and how terrified she must have been of the mindreaders and soulbinders around her.

I did notice her exchanging a glance with her future sister-in-law and wondered if Azra Vitsoph had met with Eden personally. If she'd disparaged me to Eden the way she'd disparaged me to my face. If she had, Eden had said nothing of it, and her behavior toward me hadn't changed.

There were some things only Eden would ever understand about me, and some things only I could understand about her. That bond was unbreakable. If given the chance, I would erase all of Rodsfell from our lives. But I was grateful for her.

Most of the craftlock troops nodded back, not that Eden lingered to ensure their consent. She did not ask it, she demanded it.

But I watched, and I knew not every head had yielded to the princess's warning.

Chapter 17

The room was dark save for the light of the moon; we tried not to use candles unless strictly necessary, spreading our resources as thin as possible, for we didn't know how long we would need them. Eden combed her short hair in the dark; I dowsed into myself, cracked the black stone around my heart merlon, and poured magic into my magic-made implants until they glimmered, bright and healthy. Coaxing the stone back more, I touched the gold threads there. He was at peace. Sleeping, likely. I crouched beside the netting of gold. "Come back," I whispered. "Be wise, be careful.

"I've been thinking about the library. How you let me in when your mother forbade it. How you pressed books into my hands so casually, not realizing how precious they were to me. I miss that library. I miss sitting there with you, even if I was only dowsing, occasionally glancing over your shoulder at the words in your hands. They weren't easy times, but they were simpler. Safer. I want to go back there with you, Renn. I want to share stories with you. I want to beat you at danerin."

I smiled to myself. They were memories I would cherish, always. Memories I should write down, when I had the time and the resources, before they frayed in my mind. Memories that would hurt less to revisit, years from now. Decades, perhaps, if time soothed them at all.

I rose from my lumis, returning to Eden's dark room. She still had not lain down for the night, but sat upright, staring ahead at shadowed stone.

"Are you well?" I asked.

She nodded.

A few seconds passed. "Does she bother you, the soulbinder? The mindreader? Their magic is . . . different than healing."

"No. No, I thought I would hate them," she confessed, "but each name I take, I imagine how they might hurt Adoel. I imagine what horrible things they might do to him, magic or otherwise."

She said it so serenely. My skin pebbled beneath my shift.

"I understand her. Princess Azra," she added. "The ban on healers lifted when I was so young, and so many came to the castle, I never thought to fear them. But after Sesta . . . I understand why one would. I will kiss the feet of every crafter who crosses my path if it means revenge," she went on, absently touching her short hair. "I want to make sure he can never take anything away from another person again." She glanced at me. "I think you're the only person I could say that to, Nym. Adrinn I could have, once. If he were still with us. His heart would burn with hatred, too, though he was always too brash with his anger." She inhaled deeply. "What Nicosia has—" Her throat constricted around the words.

My heart felt like a stone in my chest. I sat up, understanding where she meant to lead the conversation. "Cansere won't recognize your marriage, Eden. Renn certainly won't."

She shook her head. "It isn't just the marriage. It's everything. Nicosia doesn't want a political claim to the land, but a religious one. He wants worshippers. He wants victory. This is all a game to him. If he wants to win, he can deal with Antsan himself."

The remark shouldn't have hurt me, yet I flinched at the reminder anyway.

I proceeded cautiously. "Do you think he'll try to leverage the marriage?"

"Renn would refute it, as you said." She pulled blankets over her legs. "From what I've seen, especially with the sacking of Rove, what we *need* is more troops. I don't understand why Renn putters around with this alliance. He needs to sign it and be done."

My next heartbeat felt more like a full-knuckled punch to my chest. I remembered the night before Sesta attacked. I'd just returned from Fount to find Renn sick. I'd healed him and gotten him into bed. It was the first time I thought the possibility of us might work.

Sten had warned me, even then, that it would not. I'd known about the talking between Kings Grejor and Vitsoph. It had been an easy thing to forget, bound to that tree. Focusing on surviving the next hour, the next day, and the next, and the next . . .

In that moment, it was as though the golden thread linking Renn and I pulled tight enough to cut into me, slicing my flesh deeper than any blade. I felt Eden's eyes on me, and despite the darkness, I schooled my face.

"He never expected to rule," I whispered into the darkness. "Between being the third born and so ill . . . it's very new to him."

Eden made a noise of agreement before lying down, so I did, too, clutching fistfuls of blanket to me, staring at the low stone ceiling. Praying silently that that pain wouldn't writhe its way through my barrier and wake Renn.

"Nym."

"Hm?"

She rolled to face me. "What is he to you? My brother."

Shock like a heralding trumpet shook my core. I swallowed. "He is my king, as he is to all of us."

"You might be subtle," she murmured, "but he is not."

I stared at the ceiling, sure my pulse shook the mattress we shared.

"Before," she continued, "I admit, it would have bothered me. Back in Rove, when the war was just a rumor from the border. If I'd known then, I would have found it disgraceful. I might even have confronted you. I certainly would have confronted him."

Oh, that this bed would open its mouth and swallow me whole.

"We need this alliance with Antsan. You know that as much as I do. And yet I can't bring myself to care about any of it. That world, it was never real. Court and nobles and parties . . . All of it was a façade, wasn't it? Foolish, self-centered people weaving foolish, self-centered stories for themselves, blind to the world as it truly is. Did you see it that way, Nym, when you first came to us? When you answered the draft and my stepmother pinned you to my recluse of a brother? Did you see it then, before it came crumbling down all around us?"

I released my grip on the blankets. "Yes," I murmured. "Yes, I did."

She joined me in watching the ceiling. "I thought so."

Seconds ticked by. A minute, two, before I found the courage to speak again. "I love him, Eden. I'm so . . . so very sorry, but I love him."

Either she'd fallen asleep or had determined the declaration did not require a response.

I helped Beatty with breakfast, peeling potatoes and watering down porridge to make it stretch. We had two dozen crafters at Derren Castle, another dozen staff members, and a retinue of soldiers left behind to guard the fortress in the king's absence. The small kitchen was packed with women, sweating and working, but we'd learned to move around each other with efficiency, and soon I carried the first load of porridge and bread out in a thickly woven basket, for we had no trays at our disposal.

The hall boasted a few tables, but most of the men took their meals in the bailey, sitting on rocks, blankets, jackets, or the bare ground. I went to the farthest of them first, the earliest risers, and passed out their meals before quickly heading back to the kitchen to get more. However, as I swept by the portcullis, I heard something that made the hairs on the back of my neck rise on end. I wasn't sure if the speaker meant for me to hear or if he'd thought I'd left the reach of his voice. But in the early-morning hour, the castle not yet fully roused, I heard him well enough. Only two words, but it only took two, and the timing and situation was such that they could reference none but me. He was an Antsan soldier, a man about Brien's age, usually manning the walls or guarding the west tower, where Princess Azra now resided. He spoke to the castle pantler.

"King's whore," he'd jeered, husky and low.

My pace slowed for three steps before I pushed energy into my legs and hurried on my way. Indignance thickened my skin to iron, and I told myself the sinking in my stomach was hunger. I loaded up bowls and porringers and distributed them fast enough to make my face flush. When I gave meals to the small group of female crafters, one asked me, "Is it really safe for us here, Miss Tallowax?"

The tremble in her voice softened my hide. "It is," I promised. "I know the king well. He does not fear us. Where there is no fear, there is safety."

I pulled from her a small smile, which I did my best to return, but my mind was spinning from the earlier slander.

And I had a cold, heavy feeling I knew who had initiated it.

Merchants arrived in the late morning, bringing with them much-needed supplies. I directed the lead merchants to Eden, as I knew nothing about means of payment, and then directed available staff, including some soldiers, to help me unload the wagons. There was not much in the way of medical supplies, but with the number of healers now at our disposal, I did not think it necessary. But there was food—dried beans, cheese, and wheat berries, namely, as well as linens, oil, whetstones, and leather. I thanked each merchant personally, even their hired help, not only for the supplies themselves, but for the unity of it all. It gave me hope that Sesta had not torn us apart completely. Not yet.

However, as I hefted bags of beans into a storage room, that sense of unity quickly came unraveled as the noise of a small crowd wafted through the keep's halls like the stench of bad meat. Knowing Eden was dealing with paying the merchants, I left the supplies and hurried out into the bailey, toward the barracks.

"—was personal," growled a man as I approached, a young healer named Geth. His hands were balled into fists, his hackles raised like a dog's at a thicker, younger man named Tal, if I remembered correctly. *Man* was stretching it; he was no older than Dan, surely. A few others, including regular soldiers, crowded around, talking amongst themselves, but otherwise didn't interrupt the spectacle.

"Then don't think it *so loudly*." Tal laughed. "Really, Geth, you'd think your mother would have taught you better."

I knew, instantly, what this was about. Tal was a mindreader. Using his magic where it was unwanted.

Deliberately disobeying Eden.

Geth's face darkened. "My mother is dead."

Tal shrugged. "Pity."

Every muscle in Geth's body pulled as tight as a lute string. "You filthy piece of—"

"Stop!" I shouted, my eldest-sister timbre edging the words. *"Now."*

A few in the crowd stepped back, less to let me through than simply to gawk at me. Geth stood down, quivering with anger, but Tal remained unaffected. Phin, the soulbinder, immediately dropped her head and took the hand of a healer named Seln, pulling her away from the scene.

Turning to me, Tal started, "Do you really—?"

"Are you dumb?" I spoke over him, unwilling to let him bully his way with me. "Do you have a brain in that thick skull of yours, or must you borrow bits of everyone else's to compensate for the cobwebs?"

Tal's mouth went slack. A few soldiers snickered. I whirled on them. "Get. Out. If you are not assigned to the walls or the field, then drag your sorry asses to the merchants who have traveled here in time of war to see we are fed. *Go*."

In actuality, I had little authority over these men, but they were loyal folk, and the reminder of their duty was enough to turn them away, for now. I could only hope that, in the absence of Renn, his general, and his commanders, the castle did not gradually fall into anarchy.

I readdressed Tal, though I spoke loud enough for the rest to hear. "Did your princess not speak of this? You are not to use your magic unless strictly necessary. Unless ordered by your commanders."

Tal snorted. "You are not—"

"Finish that sentence," I snapped at him, "and see how true it proves when your gods-touched king returns and learns of it."

It was not fair of me to drag Renn into this, even though I knew he would defend me. He had left me here because I lacked the strength to follow him, not because he had trusted me to lead his craftlock troops. Still, my goal was to bring order *now*. I could worry about the rest later.

Mention of Renn, or at least the gods, finally gave Tal pause.

I let my eyes drag over the others. "You are not immune to the law. If you are not helping your country, you are hurting it. If you do not help us defeat Sesta, you are submitting to Sesta. You think it's been a hard life for you?" I pointedly looked at Tal and the other mindreaders. "So hard living a normal life with a secret easily hidden within your own minds? I have been to Rodsfell. Adoel Nicosia takes crafters as children and pens them like animals. They are used for their magic and their magic alone: no dreams, no aspirations, no families, unless their king bids it. He has fitted each one a dragon, garbed in black and blue, trained to annihilate *us*. And if he succeeds, if he doesn't slaughter us like the pigs he thinks we are, then we will be penned, too, to do his will, however dark or macabre it might be."

I stormed forward until I stood a pace away from Tal. "Do you think I lie, little boy? Read my mind. Go ahead."

I held out my hand. I did not want him anywhere near my thoughts, but I had done this once with Nicosia, and I readied myself to do it again with Tal, to feed him exactly what I wanted him to see before breaking our connection. Tal, however, didn't take the bait. He sneered, then turned his back to me, heading toward the barracks. One by one, the rest of the crowd dispersed. A few unintelligible whispers followed, a couple muttered "Sorry" in my direction.

"Be careful around crafters," a young, melodic voice chimed behind me. I turned as Princess Azra approached, fan in hand, Jonras trailing her. "They're a foul and conniving sort."

I gritted my teeth, understanding her entirely, but it was not my place to correct her, and what would be the point? She didn't care. So I merely tipped my head in a weak semblance of deference.

I noticed a white cincture slung on her hips, something not in fashion in Antsan. I looked again and recognized the weave. It was one of Renn's. Renn's cincture.

I highly doubted she'd stolen it. He must have given it to her.

A headache had begun to form behind my forehead, and I rubbed it, sure it was not the kind of ache dowsing could cure. Turned and went the way Phin and Seln had. I had been feeling better today. A little more myself, more the woman from Fount who'd yet to be bruised by love, torture, and politics. I desperately swam back for that comfort, trying to step into the shadow of myself. I couldn't let Nicosia, Princess Azra, or even Renn break me. Somehow, I had to remain whole.

Surely if I could piece together the shattered king, I could rebuild myself as well.

That night, I was reminded that stubborn, prideful boys like Tal were not so easily swayed.

Piya came into Eden's room to wake me. "Sorry, miss, but someone's said Cook's gotten real sick. Cramping badly."

Groggy, I nodded, glancing at Eden. She had woken as well but fell back asleep as I rose and pulled a dress over my shift. Sleep had mussed my curly hair into halos of knots. I did not bother to put on my shoes, though the July night did little to warm cold castle stone. I nodded briefly to Quinn, who watched our room. Piya looked half dead on her feet, so I told her to go back to bed. She bowed her head graciously as if I were her mistress and not Eden, and went on her way.

I had only just stepped foot out of the east tower when a hand grabbed a fistful of my hair and pulled me into moon-cast shadows; a flash of Nicosia in that conservatory passed through my thoughts, sending my heart into my throat. But my mind planted me in Cansere, in Derren Castle, and the scent of unwashed adolescent filled my nostrils. I reached for my mother's knife, but Tal pressed his thick palm over my mouth and pinned me to the castle wall.

"You cur," he spat. "You think you can—"

I did not let him interrupt me before, and I sure as hell would not let him interrupt me now. I flashed into his lumis, an unremarkable stack of crates with tricolored wood, and ripped apart a plank dangerously close to a death line.

Distantly, I felt him release me, but I brought my heel down hard on his instep and grabbed his hand, blinking back to his lumis and hitting him with raw, unshaped magic, albeit away from anything that might kill him. I was no honeybee with a quick sting; I was a hornet plunging in my venom again and again and again, and I wanted him to know it. I wanted him to *feel* it.

How dare he come upon me alone like this. How dare he strike in the night like a coward. How dare he lie to Piya to intimidate me. Were he my brother, I'd switch his bare hide until he cried for our dead mother. But this would do just as well.

I released him. Shifted back to reality to find him on his knees in the dirt, shaking and wheezing, face as pale as the stars.

Staying out of arm's reach, I crouched in front of him. "You are pathetic." I didn't bother lowering my voice. "Go home and tell your family, your friends, that you were so selfish and *useless* with your gift that you couldn't even march a single step past these castle walls. You will leave at dawn. Your right to craftlock is revoked."

He snarled, glaring at me with the eyes of an injured badger. "You can't do that."

I tilted my head to the side. "Princess Eden trusts my judgment, and I have the king's ear. So yes, I very much think I can."

He laughed, though it was more a sound of pain than mirth. "You have more than his ear, so I've heard."

Now I did lean in and lower my voice, meeting his eyes, burying my own fears, my own pain, so he saw only the she-wolf I wanted him to see. "All the more reason for you to fear me."

Any trace of smugness lingering on his face vanished.

Standing, I picked up my skirts and marched back into the keep, up the steps of the ruined tower, and into the room I shared with Eden, stopping only long enough to inform Quinn that Tal wasn't allowed anywhere near Eden's room. Once inside, shivers overtook me. I leaned against the closed door and sank to the floor, hugging myself, pushing down nausea and revulsion. Not at Tal, but at myself.

I had never done something like that before. Hurt someone to get my point across. To win an argument. To prove I was better.

He would have hurt you, I imagined Ursa saying, but she would have said it to make me feel better about myself, not because she agreed with it. Ursa had been kindhearted, like Lissel. She would have been appalled at my actions. Perhaps it was a mercy she was not here to witness them.

I sat there on the floor, staring at the lump of Eden, picking through the day's events in my head until I could distance myself from them. Understand them.

It had made me feel better, I realized, putting Tal in his place. Verbally, earlier, and magically, moments ago. I had been so absolutely powerless with Nicosia. Even in my magic, having lost Ursa's extra strength, I felt weak. But here in Derren . . . here I was not powerless. Not anymore. And that felt good. That felt *safe*.

The faintest press from the basalt wall. Reaching into myself, I cracked it open. Cool concern and the warmth of affection spread through my center like dandelion seeds. *Renn.* I mouthed his name, not daring to whisper it aloud. *Did I wake you? I'm sorry. I'm fine, now. I'm fine.*

I hugged myself, hugged that warmth, until it dissipated. Then I replaced the basalt, picked myself up, and softly climbed into Eden's bed, pulling the blankets up to my chin.

Tal had departed by the time I served breakfast that morning.

Shortly after breakfast, I took Seln, one of our female healers, to one of two shallow culverts in the bailey that directed water from the natural stream through a junction in the wall. It was a safe means of providing water for those in the fortress, and an easy way to fill barrels in case of future siege. We carried the laundry of the craftlock troops. I'd established a rotation for daily chores among the soldiers, and today was ours. When we arrived at the washing spot, Piya and Phin—the soulbinder—were working there as well. We filled a second basin and sorted out the uniforms from the undergarments and got to work.

It was nostalgic for me, scrubbing through a massive pile of clothing that wasn't mine. It reminded me of Fount, of my seven living siblings' clothes heaped up for washing or mending, often both. If I closed my eyes, I could almost hear Terrence working through his letters while Pren and Heath played and argued in turns.

I was scraping a pair of trousers down a washboard when I caught sight of Princess Azra on one of her daily walks, Jonras escorting her. The nostalgia soured—at first, I thought, because of the arrival of the princess. However, the melancholy notes deepened to such an extreme my breath caught in my throat. I dropped the trousers into the basin and peeled away from the washboard, breathing hard against the sorrowful ache devouring me.

Not mine, his. Despite the basalt wall.

"Nym?" Seln shifted toward me.

I shut my eyes. *Renn.* So much grief, so much heartbreak.

Seln abandoned her laundry. Touched my shoulder. "Here, let me—"

Instinctively, I swatted her away like a bee. Stumbled to my feet. "I—no, no thank you. I need a moment."

Seln and Piya both stood. The former said, "I can heal you—"

"Please don't touch me," I whispered. Were I not so drawn into the anguish flooding me, I would have felt guilty at her confused expression. I teetered back, trying to hold myself together—

"One of these things is not like the other." Princess Azra continued to approach, and only then, between pained breaths, did I realize the others had bowed down their heads to her. Distracted, I quickly nodded and began to limp away, holding my chest.

"Miss Tallowax," the princess pressed, and admittedly I did not hear the rest of her words. I needed to be somewhere else. Anywhere else. My knees threatened to buckle beneath me.

I didn't get far, just around the next curve of the castle wall. Leaning into its shade, I dowsed into myself and peeled back the basalt wall around the gold-threaded merlon.

The pain waterfalled in. I fell to my knees, hugging myself, trying to hold the both of us together. Tears stung my eyes and burned my throat. Fear and worry pushed my head down, down, down, weighing down my neck brick by brick by brick.

Are you hurt? I winced, nose starting to run. *Did you lose? How badly, Renn? What are the casualties . . . ?*

The pain came in unrelenting waves, the next starting before the previous settled. Regret and unhappiness, suffering. I tried to push back against it, tried to swim against the current even as it drowned me. *I'm here,* I cried out, even as he knocked me down. *I'm here, Renn. I'm always here. I'm so sorry. Please, help me help you. What should I do? What do you need?*

I sank into the earth, sorrow like thick vines wrapping around my limbs, sucking the energy from them. He was alive. He was safe. I felt no physical injury from him—if there was, the anguish overpowered it. So I held myself, held *him*, and whispered, "I love you, I love you, I love you," over and over again like a mantra. His ache throbbed in my heart. His tears fell from my eyes. His shudders shook my shoulders.

"What are you doing?"

That sickly lilt followed me. I couldn't even look up at her. I was drowning.

"I asked you a question," the princess pressed.

Quieter, Jonras tried, "I think she—" And the princess must have made some gesture that cut him off.

I could not get away, and neither did I rebuild the basalt wall. Praying Princess Azra would lose her interest, I stayed with Renn, endured with him, held him. I allowed the pain to ravage me, to tear me apart even as I accepted it, until my knuckles grew white and stiff and my breathing ragged. Until my bones ached and I pressed my forehead to trampled grass.

The passing of time became moot. The world outside, nothing. By the time the sadness ebbed, the sun had drifted, taking away most of my shade. I opened my eyes, realizing the only reason my exposed skin had not burned phoenix red was because Jonras had taken station near me, his body blocking the sun. The princess had left.

I wiped my eyes and nose, body creaking as I pushed myself into sitting. An orb of warmth, muted by the wall, formed in my core, and I knew Renn felt me, too, and that little piece of recognition, of togetherness, filled me with hope.

I tried to speak, but my throat squeezed around the words.

"Are you . . . hurt?" he asked.

Leaning against the wall, I got my feet under me, utterly famished. "Not physically," I croaked. "But I think . . . I have a terrible feeling we lost Serravia. I think we lost very badly."

I pushed off the wall and stumbled; Jonras grasped my elbow to steady me. Sorting myself, I stated, "I don't think she'll like you helping me."

He frowned. "She told me to watch you."

I shook my head. "I pose no threat to her."

Softly, so much so that I could barely discern it, he said, "She *will* win, Nym. In the end, she gets what she wants."

Ignoring the jab in my heart, I coolly replied, "I don't need reassurances. Again, I pose no threat to her."

He studied me for several seconds. "Even so, I'm happy to keep you company."

I did not think he meant it in a friendly manner. I could only imagine what sort of rumors and filth Azra had relayed to him.

I did not reply, and Jonras did not solicit me further, but he did help me back to Eden's room, where I rested until the bulk of the feelings passed, until I could rebuild the wall and make my apologies to Seln and the others, worry imprinting my every step.

More troops arrived at Derren Castle, crafters and nonmagic folk alike, including the same healers I'd once met with in Rove—Sarra, Fil, Denwick, and Brekk, who had personally healed me twice, once after the rat plague, and again after Whitestone's assassin ran a knife through me. Between assisting them with living arrangements and their assignments, I also spent days and nights healing fatigue and minor injuries among them, as well as a rash that broke out in one of the barracks and spread faster than madness among bees before a bad storm. But the other healers and I stayed on top of it, and no one became too ill.

It was during the bustle of the lunch hour, a week after Renn's anguish-ridden collapse, that another newcomer rode to the castle. He wore the red and black uniform of a soldier, badly travel worn. His horse frothed at the mouth and fell to its knees as he arrived. He limped ahead, waving an arm to the castle guard to let him in, but before the drawbridge lowered, he shouted above the din, "The gods-touched king has led us to victory! Serravia has been sacked!"

And then he, too, succumbed to exhaustion.

Chapter 18

The messenger lived, and the castle celebrated.

The news confused me, for I had not felt victory through my bond with Renn. Or, perhaps, I had not interpreted it as such. Perhaps the dragons had been conquered while I slept, my wall had blocked it, or I simply did not understand the emotions of war.

The war was not over. No—as long as both Renn Noblewight and Adoel Nicosia both lived, the battles would continue. But this was the first major victory for Cansere, and so while there was no extra food for a feast, there was dancing, singing, and games throughout the bailey, barracks, and camp. Princess Azra led the celebration, taking on the role as though she had already become a leader of our nation. She pushed for as much of a feast as our meager supplies could manage and lit a bonfire that first night. She danced with her guards and the few remaining soldiers, never with castle staff. But she was lively, weaving around the flames like a fire sprite, and I could see a world where Renn might fall in love with her. He would not be the fantasized farm boy dancing around a Fount bonfire, but a king joining the princess at hers.

He had so much more opportunity with her. With the war, yes, but with future politics. Better trade options, more international connections. That, and Azra was nine years my junior. Therefore, more opportunity for children as well.

Eden did not participate in the festivities, but watched with a small, hopeful smile on her face.

I, too, did not celebrate, but stood atop the rampart, gazing toward the northeastern horizon, seeing that golden thread in my mind's eye stretching endlessly between me and it.

The messenger had traveled hard to get word to us. He was not the only one; others had set out to the rest of the country to spread the news and garner more troops, as a broken and displaced government could not uphold the draft. Armies could not travel as quickly as single men on horseback. And while I knew Renn could cut through the air more swiftly than any of them, he would not. A good king did not leave his men.

Despite the glow of victory, I worried. I felt Renn's agony from a week ago as though it had left physical scars, still healing. Feared what he had sacrificed for the win. I worried, and I wondered if he felt that worry, or if my emotions just blended in with his everyday sensations the way his so often did with mine. All I knew was this: Renn had been hurt gravely, and a victory today did not promise victory for tomorrow.

It came to me then, standing alone on the rampart with summer wind tousling my hair. The weight of loneliness I had endured for months now, that I still worked to combat.

Was I inflicting the same on him?

By putting up this wall, by cutting myself off from him to protect myself, was I leaving him to bear the burdens of war, of leadership and death, alone? Renn was surrounded by people—generals, commanders, soldiers. But I also knew how easily he shielded himself from others. Knew his defaults of hiding his own pain to please people, and to be accepted by them.

A deep shame bubbled in my breast. *I'm so sorry, Renn. I've been selfish.* Even if my future was not at Renn's side, he would always be dear to me, and I to him. We would always have my shared heart, until we shared death.

I tore the basalt wall down.

Emotions and physicality flooded my being—my regret, repentance, worry, and hope, alongside his exhaustion, relief, concern, sorrow. Then, after a moment, surprise, and then relief again.

I pressed my apology through the link as best I could, my half-heart flickering with the effort. I needed to refuel it soon.

Come back to us, I pleaded, invoking each god by name. *Let him come home.*

Yet, in truth, Renn's true home was still far from our grasp, the heads of his family likely still decaying on its walls.

I settled myself, until the sun sank too low to see the horizon the army would pass over to return to Derren Castle. Renn Reshua Noblewight would return soon. Eden had the craftlock troops well underway, which meant the only thing tethering me here was the proper farewell I desperately needed.

I considered my words as I retreated into the keep, lighting a tallow candle and making my way to the small war room, where a map of the dyadic continents still rested on the table, with no markers to indicate future war plans. Holding the candle close, I leaned over the map and studied the roads. Found the one many of the merchants used; I could take it halfway to Fount, and then a smaller road to Grot. I knew my way from Grot. If I met up with a caravan, I could make the journey safely, and swiftly enough.

Which meant all I had left to do was say goodbye.

I knew when Renn's company had returned. Knew before the bugles blew and the soldiers hollered, before Beatty went into a frenzy to prepare enough meals for the arrival.

It was just past noon, eight days after the messenger had arrived with news of victory. My end of our bond lit up like a freshly kindled fire, sputtering with hope, urgency, and the undercurrents of relief. The sensations of a man nearly home after a long time away.

I abandoned my chores and rushed up through the west tower, feet so quick on the stairs my calves cramped by the time I reached the rampart. Breathless, I threw myself against a merlon and gazed northeast, sun streaking my vision. Wind tousled my hair, making it wilder than it already was. I waited, watching, nails clawing the keep's ancient stone.

Half an hour passed before I saw the first flag bearing the phoenix, the first horses, the first glimpses of red on the long meadows in the distance. I bounced on my feet, feeling fifteen again. Tears moistened my vision as the first trumpeter rang out a triumphant note, and soon the grounds filled with shouts that the king had returned, and to make way for the officers, and that Hem himself looked down on us with blazing approval.

There were so many of them—far more men than had left Derren Castle: other regiments and soldiers who had joined us at Serravia, returning here until the next battle began. A single Antsan flag waved among them. In the back of my thoughts I worried about sleeping arrangements, about provisions, about integrating the craftlock troops with the rest, but at the front, all I could think of was him. I searched the growing army for his golden hair, though many wore caps, making the men blend into a red-highlighted black mass. I leaned between merlons for a closer look, my fingers trembling, my breath still caught somewhere in the tower's winding stairwell.

Then I saw him, a beacon of fire among the troops, just off-center in the army, and relief snowed across my limbs. His body lit up with that unearthly light, prismatic wings extending from his back. The trumpeter bugled again, his call met with two more from the army, and people on both sides cheered. It felt sacred. It felt historic.

Eden had told me Adoel Nicosia believed himself a god in the making, a child of Zia. Yet he was nothing—absolutely *nothing*—in comparison to Renn Noblewight.

He's safe. My eyes finally confirmed the magic threading between us. *He's safe, and he's back.*

A second Antsan flag caught the wind as the snaking army neared the castle. Princess Azra rode from the bailey with her small entourage; Jonras held aloft the blue, white, and yellow flag.

She rode the white mare from the stables, a beautiful purebred horse with braided mane and tail. I was close enough to spot something else.

The princess, who had straightened her hair in Canseren noblewoman fashion every day since I'd met her, had instead meticulously curled every strawberry lock. She wore them loose, the perfect, uniform curls bouncing against her back as she rode out to meet the army.

I touched my hair, the curls frizzy and wind-tossed, wild and uneven, and wondered.

It reminded me of my upcoming farewell. The jubilation of the army's return dimmed.

Then again, I'd never expected it not to destroy me.

It took hours for the soldiers to come in, find their places, and stake their tents. I busied myself in the kitchen, unsuccessfully working through my nerves.

Water was heated for baths, though most of the men washed cold in the stream that ran by the castle and through the bailey, caring little for their modesty. I knew Renn stayed and washed with them. After I greeted Sten in the bailey, the faithful guard revealed as much.

So much work over hot coals and ovens had me sweating, my knotted wreck of hair tugged into a merciless plait. I worked hard, trying to stay ahead of my own turbulent emotions, trying to mask the way my hands shook.

When the work was done, I stepped into the back and washed my face and hands. Scrubbed my apron and left it to dry. Tried to finger-comb my hair, but it refused to give in to my administrations.

I had not fully crossed to the keep when I saw Renn near the portcullis, Sir Arquan and another general, whom I presumed to be Cuplend, at his side, along with Princess Azra and two of her guards, neither one Jonras. She had her mare with her, and she held the horse's lead and gently petted its nose while speaking to Renn, full of smiles and pleasantry, looking hale and lovely in her layered Antsan-style gown. The setting sun highlighted her fair skin and the red in her hair like she was woven from the sunset itself.

I couldn't hear their conversation, but she laughed, and Renn smiled, and she propped herself up on her toes to kiss his cheek.

Such a simple thing, but it added weight to my already tipping scale. *His hand on her back, his fingers in her hair, his lips on her knuckles, hers on his cheek.* And she still wore his white cincture, as though she were Canseren. As though he'd already made her his queen.

It was not a surprise. I'd had long enough to understand it, even if it would take the rest of my life to come to terms with it. Yet understanding could not stop my heart from tearing at the sight.

He felt it. Stiffening, Renn searched the bailey, looking for *me*—

I slipped inside the keep, sucking in deep breaths, willing the sensations away without raising the wall again. I'd have to get used to it sooner or later, and who was I to cheat grief? I certainly was no stranger to it.

I've survived worse. An old mantra I used to tell myself often. It felt oddly hollow, now. Or, perhaps, simply false.

I didn't know where to put myself. I no longer had my own space, and so many arrivals at the castle crowded the walls, bailey, and keep. So I wended my way to Eden's room, relieved to find it empty. I shut the door, poured the last of the water pitcher into the basin, and washed my face one more time, meaning to focus on the coldness of the water to shock myself to rights, but at the end of a hot summer day, the water had gone lukewarm.

If I made my goodbyes tonight, I could leave just before dawn, as soon as Rolys gave me enough light. I never slept well . . . it wouldn't be hard to hit that blue hour.

Gods, I was crumbling again. A brick wall built with too much sand in its mortar. I'd taken three steps forward during his time away, and now I fell four steps back.

Just for a moment, I told myself as I dowsed, ready to build up the wall. *Just until I get my wits about me—*

The banging open of the door startled me from my lumis. I expected a flustered Eden; what I got was a very intent king.

The way my heart zinged in his presence left me lightheaded.

"Why are you not in the west tower?" he asked. Our link sparked like kindling.

My mind pulled in too many directions. "Welcome back," I managed.

He shut the door and crossed to me, seeming larger. Light flared in his blue eyes. "I went to find you. You weren't there. None of your things were there." He looked around the space. "Why are you staying with my sister?"

I cleared my throat. "She helps me sleep." Truth. I fought to ground myself. "You can't just barge into a woman's room."

He snorted. "It's my castle and my country. I can do what I want."

"I see the war hasn't dampened your arrogance," I muttered.

He didn't seem to hear me and pointed back toward the door. Westward. "Did she do something?"

I knew he meant Azra, but my own embers began to smoke. "You'll have to be more specific."

His pale brows knit together. "And you'll have to be less obtuse."

I looked away. Steeled myself. "I did need to talk to you. I . . . I'm glad you're back. So glad." I cursed inwardly as my eyes began to water. I had tried to prepare myself so I might be straightforward and stoic. "We've many crafters here, now, and Seln, one of the healers, is very adept. Eden has things underway."

"Stop," he demanded.

"And with the commanders returned, I think most of the crafters can integrate with the other companies." I didn't quite meet his gaze, though I felt it on my face like two fire pokers. "I-I think it's time that I—"

"*Stop*, Nym!" Fire blazed through our link and into his voice.

I finally looked at him, meeting fire with fire. "I am not one of your soldiers. You insist I do not address you as my king, and yet you seek to strip away my autonomy—"

He moved so quickly. A gods-touched speed, surely.

Renn seized me, one arm looping behind my back as he bent my body to his, claiming my mouth with his own. I startled for only a beat before my traitorous, awful half-heart surged, desperate for him, all of him. I grasped his face like I was to dowse on him, kissing him like my lips were a sword, like this were a battle of our own, and I refused to lose. Anger and want and sorrow coiled between us, lashing as whips, burning and razing. He pushed and nipped and begged. I opened my mouth to him, letting his heat fill me, melt me. I grabbed fistfuls of his hair, guiding him all the closer, tasting rain and spearmint and something spicy and devouring the lot of it. I poured myself into him: all the waiting, all the hoping, all my brokenness and fear. He took every bit of it, drinking and giving in uneven cycles, our heartbeats thundering offbeat one another, too loud to hear anything else. Outside of us, nothing else mattered. Nothing else existed.

His palm came to the back of my head just before we hit the stone wall, cushioning the blow. I hadn't even realized we'd moved. There was nothing but him. Everywhere, him. Desire kindled in my belly, feeding into our bond, only to echo back white-hot from him. Back and forth, back and forth, until my body felt too tight and too warm. Like all of me had become pure sensation, every touch echoing into eternity. Yet it was a heat I would happily embrace. I would willingly burn alive on the pyre of Renn Noblewight.

His other hand caressed my stomach. Came around to the dip of my waist, descended to my hip. I pulled back from him only long enough for a breath before reclaiming his mouth and running my tongue along the inside of his lip. The white fire flashed bright as lightning. An unearthly sound escaped me, and he devoured it, pressing me harder into the wall. I nearly ripped his hair from his scalp as I demanded more, more, *more*. His fingertips dug into my hip, his arousal against my stomach.

In the depths of the hunger and the hazy lust of it all, however, something cool flickered. Not from the woes of our present, but from a tattered memory five years old, of Ford's hands holding me down, of *his* pressure atop me, of Terrence crying my name from the doorway—

Renn sensed it. Even in the throes of want, he sensed it. His mouth slowed against mine, his touch gentling. He pulled away slowly; I followed the motions, eager for one last taste of him. My fervor had pinkened his lips, and I could only imagine what mine must look like. He pressed a lingering kiss to my jaw, beneath my ear, my neck. I shuddered with each touch, forcing myself to reel in my appetite for him until I again found myself in a four-walled room. Present, as though I'd just slipped from a lumis.

We stood there, breathing heavily, trapped in the gravity of one another. Just a moment longer, before reality returned—

"I know how to do it," he murmured, smoothing an errant curl from my face. "I know how to get them without marriage."

The proclamation was a stone hitting still water. "Wh-What?"

He cradled my face. Caressed my cheek with his thumb. Took a step back, yet left not even a full pace between us. "It . . . won't be easy. Any documentation that might exist would be in Rove, which is out of our hands, assuming it hasn't been destroyed. And with my mother dead, I can't ask her. I have no testimony or further proof."

I shook my head. "Renn, what are you talking about?"

"Sesta," he clarified, caressing my cheek again. "If I can prove I'm Nicosia's son, then I'm the heir to his kingdom. Sesta's kingdom for Antsan's army."

My pulse began to pick up again. Though I ached to stay near him, I pulled myself away, needing space to think.

"The Sestan throne?" I asked. "Would you lose claim to Cansere, if you proved Sestan parentage?"

"If I had a younger brother, or if Eden claimed her marriage and fought me for it, perhaps. Beyond her, there are no other heirs. But Grejor was my father. Winvrin was legally queen of Cansere, and she is my mother by blood." He took a deep breath. Let it out. "I already have spies in that country. Many placed to search for you. I'm sending them into Rodsfell. To retrieve Wald Whitestone."

Strength fled my legs. I dropped to the edge of the bed I shared with Eden. "Whitestone knew your mother, before." The very idea sat across my shoulders like a yoke, and each spoken word was another weight added. "You think Whitestone will have proof?"

"He'll know where I can find it. Perhaps know where my mother lived before I was conceived." He lowered himself to the corner of the bed, leaving a few feet between us. "She figured out the prophecy before any of us. If there's anything, it will be there."

"If not?"

He didn't answer, but the link scalded.

Hope, raw and painful, rose in my breast. I tried to tamp it down. "Even so . . . even if you succeed, to forfeit an entire *kingdom*—"

"I never wanted Sesta," Renn said.

"You never wanted to be king, either, but none of this is about what we *want*." I rubbed my eyes, balancing the information. "If you don't find proof . . . would you give Antsan Sesta anyway?"

He frowned. "This war has been about defending what is rightfully ours. To turn it into one of conquering, to push onto Sestan soil until it falls . . . it would take too many years and too many lives, even if Nicosia were out of the picture. I don't think Antsan would agree to that. I couldn't ask my people to sacrifice so much."

I nodded slowly. "And Whitestone?"

"Nicosia was at Serravia. Far from Rodsfell. I intend to get Whitestone to talk and then get him across the strait."

I hated Physician Whitestone. I hated him in Rove and I hated him in Rodsfell. The thought of seeing him again turned my stomach. But if he'd been sincere in his regrets . . . if he could help Renn, help *us* . . .

I swallowed. "It seems so far-fetched." It hurt to hope.

He pulled off his leather bracers. Set them aside. Flexed his hands. "It will work. It *has* to work."

That familiar lump began to re-form in my throat. "And if it doesn't?"

He stayed carefully masked, but he bristled through the link. Bristled, and bled.

I sifted through what we'd exchanged. "What if I believe you?" I asked, the words cracking as they dribbled over my lips. "What if I let myself believe you, let myself hope all will be well, that I can have all of you, and then I can't?" I blinked away tears. "I'm . . . I'm barely holding on as it is, Renn. I can't survive that. Can't . . . I can't come back from that."

He opened his mouth to argue, then tensed to hold back a cough, but the scars on his lumis won out, and he turned away, coughing hard. Took a moment to compose himself as frustration trickled from his heart to mine. "It *has* to work, Nym."

I shook my head, confusion rising like dark smoke. "I don't understand. You and Azra, I've *seen* you two together. You're paving the way for her—"

He rolled his eyes. Gods help me, but it made him look like the aloof, arrogant prince I'd met when I first came to Rove, and the cavalier manner of it bothered me. "I told you, it's strategy. To appease the emissary. To garner information."

My brow drew low. "You told me no such thing."

Chagrin through the bond. Hesitation. "Didn't I?"

I combed back through our time together since arriving at the castle. Hinged on one moment in particular: *Please don't hate me for what I'll have to do to make this work.*

I took a deep breath to still my trembling.

He ran a hand down his face. "It's . . . helped," he offered by way of a bandage. "Antsan has a strong navy, but they're not the type to invoke war. They have no quarrel with Sesta. What they do have is raze mites."

I tilted my head. "Raze mites?" An infestation?

He nodded. "They've created a famine, a food shortage in Antsan, especially with their wheat. They have to burn whole fields to be rid of them, but the pests spread quickly. Cansere has fertile farming land. A lot of it."

I frowned. "But to offer Sesta—"

"Sesta has good farming. Not as good, not with their tundra, but enough. And Cansere yields enough crop to make up for any deficit. But that can be negotiated through trade, rather than marriage."

I mulled this over. "You've gleaned this from their princess?"

He nodded. "And more. And I intend to use every last syllable to my advantage." His countenance softened. "It will be enough. It has to. Nym, I hope—"

"Hope isn't enough." The confusion choked me, and the possibilities burned without mercy. "This is reality. You're not only a king, you're a *prophecy*." My chest constricted. "And even if it was . . . even if all your efforts paid off . . . how do you know *I'll* always be enough for *you*?"

His expression shattered like glass beneath a hammer. "Nym, no."

"You haven't had opportunity to . . . get out there." My nose stung and my palms sweat. The bed became a bottomless pool I struggled to tread water in. I thought of him and Azra, backlit by the sunlight, the vision of perfection. "There are . . . phenomenal women out there. Women like Azra—"

"Was I enough for you?" he countered. "Before?" He moved closer to me, so that our knees touched. Traced the curve of my shoulder. "If you'd never succeeded in healing me, if I was a burden the rest of our days, would you still love me?"

It was more of a rhetorical question than anything else; Renn knew the answer. We both did. I had hunted him down and kissed him before I ever unraveled the enigma of his shattered lumis.

"Asking me isn't the same, and you know it," I whispered.

"How is it not—"

"Because you have power," I interrupted. "You have responsibilities and a duty to your people, and I do not. To pretend otherwise is obtuse."

"A characteristic I'm fine adding to my repertoire."

"Renn—"

Hand to the back of my neck, he kissed me roughly, challenging me, tracing the seam of my lips with his tongue. As though staking his claim could resolve the issues between us, and admittedly, for the present, it did. I wanted him, however wrong it was. I lacked the courage to stand strong. After so long apart, *again*, I couldn't find my resolve. I softened against him like honey in the sun, as malleable and compliant as an adolescent who'd yet to suffer the weight of the world. When he pulled back, it was only with enough space to look into my eyes. Our noses brushed; our breaths mingled.

"I will claim both kingdoms," he murmured. "Antsan will take the boon. I will remake Cansere the way you remade me, and our people will love you, because who on this gods-given planet wouldn't love you?"

Breaking me. He was breaking me, and I couldn't tell if it was for the better or for the worse.

"You say I'm a prophecy," he continued, "but you are part of that prophecy. The scripture is only true because of you."

I rolled my lips together. "It was true without me. If Nicosia hadn't broken you—"

"Do you really think the gods did not take that into account?" he asked. A nostalgic sadness passed from him to me. "I loved my brother, but can you imagine if *he* had been given this kind of power?"

A dry, sore chuckle tore up my throat and died on my tongue.

Pulling his hand from my neck, he combed fingers through my hair, working out a snag as he did. "I'd hoped the prophecy would be enough, but Antsans are humanists. They don't believe in our gods, yet even they are impressed with what they've made me." He studied his palms. "But they're greedy bastards, just like every other sovereignty. If I can end that bastard Nicosia and prove my right to his throne, we'll have their armies. We'll have each other. All of it . . . it will all be worth it, Nym."

He dropped his hands and sighed. "I had a lot of time to think on the road. About the war, about the treaty, and about us. And in truth, Nym, the only thing I've ever been certain about is you."

Now I reached for him, tracing his chin, jaw, and nose with a knuckle. "Fifteen days ago, something terrible happened to you." He knew what I meant, because his mask went up immediately, and a tangle of emotions traversed our connection—sadness, embarrassment, shame. "Will you tell me what hurt you so badly?"

Moisture shimmered in his eyes. He looked away. "I didn't want you to feel that," he whispered.

I touched his thigh, trying to be reassuring. "I . . . understand the sentiment. If you don't want to talk about it, I won't hold it against you." Truth, all of it, however curious I was. I had not detailed to Renn exactly how Nicosia had hurt me, again and again, while I hung staked to that tree. I didn't need to; he would have felt every blow. If I could have spared Renn from that hardship, I would have. It was only right that I give him the opportunity to do the same.

I didn't think he would answer. He stared at the floor, silent, for minutes. I massaged the back of his neck. Traced shapes on his back. Leaned against his shoulder. I was about to suggest he retire for some rest when he spoke.

"It comes down to me, every time," he said, and I felt the physical ache of it as though it were my own. "Every skirmish, every battle, it ends with me. I kill so many of them, Nym." He hunched over, setting his elbows on his knees. "Men just doing as their king commands, just like mine. And I slaughter them like rats in a cellar. Soon I'll have killed more people than I've lived days. Adrinn . . . he could have done it. He had the spine for it. I . . . I don't."

"Renn." I slid from the bed so I could kneel in front of him. "Renn, do not ever think that mourning the dead is a weakness, even if they are your enemy. *Never* think that." I gripped his knees, hard enough to make him look at me. "This is war. It is not *your* war, but if you don't answer it, more people than those will suffer. What you have, what you are, is a gift from the gods, and you are a gift to us. That pain, that sorrow, it means you're human. It means you are *good*, Renn. And I will bear it with you time and time again. Even if this link between us faded, even if you must swear yourself to Azra to spare your people, I would bear it with you." My eyes watered. "You will be the best king this country has ever known. I think . . . I think you already are."

He slid off the bed so that he kneeled, too. A million emotions braided between us. I kissed his lips and a single errant tear.

"Don't lock me out, Nym," he whispered, dropping his forehead to my shoulder. "Let me feel you. Let me know that you believe in me."

I shuddered, throat sore. "My hope of you will destroy me."

His lips grazed my neck. "I would battle the gods themselves for you. Give me a little longer. I'll make this work. Just give me a little longer."

I wanted to believe him. I wanted to protect that hope he'd built for us. Between us was a complex game of chance, both our hearts on the table. All in.

There was no way to know if Renn would succeed. But through our link, I knew he meant every word.

So I believed him. One day in the near future, I might regret doing so. I might rail against my past self, hate her, and curse her for doing so. But hope was all I had left, however much it hurt.

So I believed him.

And yet, until the thing was done, I could not claim him. Renn and I parted ways, his physical absence like the loss of a limb. The magic linking us was both a boon and a curse, but that night it was a comfort, for I knew Renn went to bed thinking of me, and his warmth lulled me into a dreamless rest not even memory of Nicosia managed to puncture.

I woke to the noises of drills just past dawn. Eden had vacated the room. I took a moment to myself in the bed, arms sprawled, mentally tracing the lines of the stone ceiling. Settling into my quiet solitude, absorbing it carefully like the tip of a cloth set into the edge of a spill, I sorted through my thoughts, simple and complex alike. Took stock of myself. When I rose, I felt refreshed. *Aren't you impressed, Ursa?*

Piya had refilled the pitcher—bless her—so I stripped and washed. Plaited the front of my hair around my crown and left the rest loose to dry. I had no appointments with the other healers this early, so I headed to the kitchen, which already bustled with activity. I helped build a stone stove in the bailey, one of many attempts to expand the kitchen to better accommodate the influx of soldiers. Rove Castle would have managed the numbers well, but while Derren was formidable, it was not built to be roomy or comfortable by any means.

Younger soldiers came to help distribute breakfast, so I took to hauling water from that little culvert stream and washing dishes. My hands were pale and wrinkled, the midsummer sun above the castle wall, by the time a trumpet sounded.

I finished my load and dumped out the water. Beatty returned, thumbing the leather band of her wedding pendant, and I asked, "What's the bugle for?"

"Next wave of them has returned." She released the necklace and lifted the corner of her apron, dabbing perspiration from her face. "More mouths to feed. At this rate we'll have to take care of only the officers and let the rest do what they can over cookfires."

More soldiers at Derren. The barracks were flooded, and there was no way to allow the women one to themselves. Soldiers would have to camp tight and close, which also meant we healers needed to be on our toes, watching for disease.

"That's no shortcoming of yours," I offered. "Times of war, and all that."

She nodded before hurrying to a bowl of rising bread dough. Beatty was a busy and frantic woman, but she got things done. Still,

I wondered if there was a way to bring in more staff. I'd just begun stacking porringers when Beatty jumped, dropping a spoon. "Your Majesty!" She curtsied low enough to kiss the floor.

I turned around to see Renn entering the kitchen. I thought he was glowing at first, but it was only the late-morning sunlight at his back. I began to smile, then quickly schooled my features and bowed low. It was a good thing, for once he stepped out of the sun, I noticed he had Princess Azra hooked on his arm. Her presence didn't carry the same sting as before, but I could not bring myself to like it.

He addressed our cook first. "You've done remarkably well for all we've thrown at you, Beatty. I wanted to thank you personally."

Beatty flushed darkly and curtsied again. "Doing my duty, Your Majesty."

To me, Renn crooked a finger. Confused, I set the porringers aside and followed him out into the bailey.

I bowed again to both him and the princess. "Your Majesty, Your Highness. Has something happened?" I asked, markedly putting a pace's distance between us. I wasn't sure if the burst of displeasure through the bond was from that or from my use of *Your Majesty*, but Princess Azra seemed pleased by it.

"I have a surprise for you."

Entirely focused on Renn, Princess Azra said, "You are too charitable for your own good."

He acknowledged the princess with a tight smile and curt nod before leading me toward the portcullis, located on the northern side of the castle, her ever at his side. His stride was so long and swift, Princess Azra struggled to keep up. To think only a year ago he'd been walking with a cane.

I eyed him, turning over in my mind the nature of this "surprise," and what might be so important he wouldn't send Sten or someone else to take care of it for him. Renn wasn't really a woo-with-gifts kind of person.

Sir Arquan loitered near the portcullis; here, Renn gently pulled his elbow from Princess Azra's grasp. "A war camp is no place for a noblewoman. I'll need the healer's abilities for a few grisly casualties. I will return swiftly. Sir Arquan?"

Princess Azra didn't show any disdain for their separation and joined the emissary with nary a wrinkle to her nose or brow. "I'll be waiting."

This confused me even more. What was he up to? And did Princess Azra really buy that my surprise was gruesome injuries?

. . . Was it?

I determined then that I did not care for surprises.

"Nym." Renn beckoned me to follow. I pointedly did not meet any Antsan eyes as I did.

I trailed him to the drawbridge. With no Sestan army awaiting me, I had no issue crossing the moat.

"It might sound better if you called me Tallowax," I commented, trying to stay a step behind him, but Renn kept adjusting his pace so we walked side by side.

"I'd prefer to call you Noblewight," he countered.

My face flushed hot. "Renn!"

He grinned, delighted with himself.

"And," I pressed, "you lied to her. You should be careful."

"I did not. There is surely an injured soldier among this lot"—he gestured to tents upon tents, group upon group of soldiers—"and I've no idea how grisly they might be."

"Is that to be my 'surprise,' then? Someone with a kettle burn, or perhaps a broken leg? I haven't seen a good, splintered femur in a while."

His face twisted. "That's rather macabre. But no, something I found just before we marched on Serravia. I think you'll like it."

Something he could not give me at the castle?

I tried not to worry what the appearance of us together in camp might incite, though in truth, walking out in the open with him, bantering with him, healed something in my soul. I could spend hours like this, enjoying his company. I craved it like a drug.

And yet his claim of a surprise niggled at me. I couldn't think of anything of Sestan make that could possibly gratify me. There were hundreds of soldiers about, some setting up tents, others talking. Any who spied Renn immediately turned and bowed or became awestruck in their expressions. Renn pointedly looked forward, though he still waved or nodded when he made eye contact or was directly addressed. His discomfort was enough that it whittled down our connection. Even now, he did not like the stares or the attention, and especially not the worship. I wondered how much of that was from a life in seclusion versus his natural personality. A little bit of both, perhaps.

He appeared to rub a headache from his temple, and since I couldn't feel it through the bond, I knew it hailed from his lumis scars. He didn't comment on it. He both looked and felt too excited, too pleased with himself, to linger on it.

He led me east, past a few tents. I asked, "Is it so overlarge that you couldn't bring it with you?"

He smiled. "I thought you could do with a bodyguard."

I slowed, but when he didn't, I quickened my pace to keep up. Certainly not the sort of surprise I'd expected. "Is this about Tal?"

His step faltered. "Tal? Who's Tal?"

"Nothing of import. A . . . misunderstanding. He's no longer at Derren." I nearly told him I already had a bodyguard, since I knew Jonras watched me, playing eyes and ears to Azra. But Jonras would never harm me, and I didn't want to further stress Renn or . . . however much I hated it, add discontent between him and the woman who might still be the mother of his future children. If fate would bind him to Azra Vitsoph, the least I could grant him was as tolerable a marriage as possible.

She was so young. Quick as a fox, yet untried. I attempted to mask the all-too-familiar ache the thought of them produced.

"Sten will do," I remarked.

"I agree. But he'll need to take shifts with someone."

I rolled my eyes. "I'm a healer. Basic staff. I don't need a—"

"Ah, here we go." Renn touched the small of my back—the illicit contact sent shivers up my spine—and led me around a doused campfire. A soldier seated on the ground rose and approached us. His uniform was more dust than fabric; he was one of the newcomers returning from the Battle of Serravia. A good three weeks' worth of chestnut beard covered the lower half of his face. He was taller and a little broader than Renn, though looked to be about the same age.

He removed his cap. More chestnut hair plastered to the top of his head with sweat, and his eyes—

Gray, just like mine.

Chills like snowfall on bare skin coursed head to toe. I shrieked loud enough to draw the attention of nearby soldiers. Sprinted across the space between us; the soldier grinned just before I launched at him, nearly knocking us both to the earth. But he maintained his balance and spun me around, laughing. Laughing while I sobbed, for I had not seen my brother in over a year. I had not even known if he'd lived.

But Brien was alive, he was healthy, and he was *here*, and that was all that mattered.

Renn had other matters to attend to—matters I did not wish to dwell on—so he left me and my brother to catch up. I didn't so much as let Brien take a bath before dragging him away from the other soldiers and sitting us in the shade of an overgrown dogwood, demanding his story from the moment he left Fount, for not a single letter had been exchanged between us. Even when I had the ability to write, I had no address to which to send mail.

"I reported to Garton, then to Toke," he explained. "The training . . . the training was hard. Commander Stonelay was merciless."

"Stonelay? The same here?" The man had seemed rather . . . paternal, in my experience.

Brien nodded. "But once that was done, things went smoothly enough. Not any worse than harvest in an early winter."

As though that could ever be described as smooth.

He lowered his voice. "It was weird, Nym. Not just the skirmishes—those weren't anything like Serravia. Like Sesta was a cat batting at mice, trying to figure out which one to eat. Strike and retreat, strike and retreat, often not even at major ports. And then . . . like I was in another country altogether. My superiors would send word to Rove, information and requests for supplies, and it was like no one heard. This all before the sacking."

I thought of the nobles and the winter ball and felt a shiver. "They didn't take it seriously." Though I thought Prince Adrinn had. Despite his obvious shortcomings, from what Eden shared with me, it seemed Prince Adrinn *had* cared. He'd been investigating his mother. On his way to uncovering Adoel's secrets, and Renn's. If the eldest Noblewight, original heir to the throne, had survived the sacking, how differently would this year have gone? Would Cansere have struck sooner, and harder? Would that have hurt us or helped us? Then again, Prince Adrinn had taken much of his advice from Renn. Perhaps it would all be the same, but with a different figurehead. And *Adrinn* would be the one negotiating peace with Antsan. He'd be the center of Azra's focus.

Though I wouldn't put it past Prince Adrinn to use his younger brother as a pawn for political gain, leaving me in the same tormented situation.

Yet how would Prince Adrinn have handled his younger brother's awakening power? Would he have celebrated it, or hated it? On one hand, I could picture Cansere a more unified force under Prince Adrinn. Deadlier, swifter, merciless. On the other hand, I could envision a civil war tearing the nation apart, half for the heir and half for the gods' chosen, while Adoel sipped wine, waiting for us to destroy ourselves.

Only the heavens would ever know.

"And then Rove was sacked, and we marched there. It was awful." Brien winced. "Cold. Not a lot of food. We took out a small company of Sestan soldiers, then found His Majesty." He let out a long breath that whistled past his teeth. "Let me tell you, Nym. Seeing a god among men after that march was an answer to prayer. He actually *cared* what happened to us. Sesta killed all the rest."

"Don't," I said, before I could stop myself. Brien hesitated, an eyebrow slightly raised. "I mean . . ." I sorted through my thoughts. "They were imperfect people, but I lived with them, Brien. They were still people. There were good people, there." I thought of Lonnie Swiftmore again, the kitchen maid who had extended kindness to me when all of Rove seemed to hate me. I still didn't know if she'd lived or died. I had to assume the latter. But King Grejor had been a good man. Even Queen Winvrin, for all her anxious unkindness, had meant well. Had loved her son and fought for him for twenty years. None of them deserved death. "Renn loved his family."

Brien nodded slowly. "How long have you called him by his first name?"

My cheeks warmed. "I've spent a lot of time with him."

Brien leaned back on his palms, taking in the horizon. "He told me, at Serravia. Soon as someone called me 'Tallowax,' he asked if I was your brother." He grinned. Brien had marched in that day with the new wave of soldiers; Renn had wanted to ensure Brien's safe arrival before enlightening me about his well-being. "I had *no idea*, Nym. I didn't even know you'd been drafted! We knew it might happen eventually, but . . . damn." He glowed with pride, which made my cheeks warm all the more. "The royal healer for our king. My sister. I bet you did it just so people would stop complaining about it."

I snorted. "I did very little. I had every intention of failing and hurrying back home. But fate did not agree with my plan." I told him my story, the overview of it, at least, for it would take too long to get into the delicate nuances of it all. His eyes rounded with every sentence. It was the most still I'd ever seen him.

"I figured it out in Speth." I did not detail the *how* of healing Renn; that truth was still safest not shared, even with Brien. "And then Sesta attacked and captured me."

"I know." His face went slack. "I knew that as soon as we met with the king's forces. That is, I knew the royal healer and the princess had been taken hostage. I didn't know one of them was you until . . ." He clamped a hand on my shoulder. "Are you . . . all right?" His expression soured. "What a stupid question to ask, but what else am I supposed to say? You were always better with words."

"Ursa was always better with words," I countered. "And Papa. But it's over now, and I'm here. All ten fingers." I held them up to demonstrate.

He nodded, accepting the simple answer. Lowered his hand. "What does she think of all this?"

I felt myself pale. Brien pushed himself upright. Got a knee under him. "What, Nym?"

The vision of him warped in my sight as healing cuts opened. "She's gone, Brien," I whispered. "She finally moved on, in Sesta. Our sister is well and truly dead."

I talked to Brien for a good two hours before we grew sore on the ground and the lunch hour neared. Since he'd been appointed my new guard, his commanding officer gave him leave, and I saw the ingenious move by Renn in the appointment. *Thank you,* I thought, pushing gratitude through our link. I led Brien across camp and into the bailey, sharing stories and reminiscences of home. As luck would have it, Sten lingered just inside the portcullis.

"Sten, this is Brien," I offered. "My brother. His company went to Serravia."

Sten proffered a hand, and the two men gripped each other by the wrist. "We've met."

I gave Brien a tour of Derren Castle, though the fortress was relatively straightforward. Fatigue and satisfaction wove through the connection from Renn, and I wondered what had occupied him. Training, perhaps, or more battling-of-contract with Sir Arquan. I introduced Brien to those I knew when we saw them, such as Seln, Phin, and Geth. He knew Commander Stonelay, of course, and was familiar with Physician Addsmuch, who had found himself with more and more free time as the castle collected healers. Unlike Physician Whitestone, however, he appeared to be at peace with it.

Whitestone. I tried to picture the traitor within these walls, but my imagination couldn't stretch far enough. How odd, that the man who'd once tried to murder me might be the key to my happiness, to my future.

The rest was a rather wondrous thing. Perhaps it was the proof that I belonged at the castle, knowing its people, nooks, and crannies, or perhaps it was the presence of my closest sibling in age, but I felt very much *myself* as I led Brien around, as we chatted about all we had missed.

We headed for the keep, approaching the east tower just as Quinn, Eden's guard, exited it, with Eden and Piya close behind.

Upon seeing a large, travel-worn, and disheveled man at my heel, Eden stiffened.

"This is my brother Brien," I quickly assured her, grasping him by the crook of his elbow. "The one conscripted." We'd spoken at length of our families during our long journey from Rodsfell to Horgansten.

"Brien Tallowax, yes, I recall." She relaxed and tipped her head toward him. "Thank you for your sacrifices for our country."

He nodded back.

"This is Princess Eden," I added.

Brien suddenly stood straighter, then bowed at the waist. "My apologies, Your Highness. I didn't recognize you."

"I take that as a compliment. Please, rise. Nym is a dear friend of mine, as are any kin of hers."

My chest warmed at the endearment.

"Are you a crafter as well?" she asked.

That made Brien start. "No, Your Majesty. That was only Nym and Ursa."

Someday, hearing her name wouldn't hurt.

She nodded. I patted Brien's arm in reassurance as Eden and her small retinue passed by, then led him into the keep.

"Why does she stay at Derren, instead of taking sanctuary farther south?" he asked after climbing the first story. I'd given him a basic overview of my time in Sesta. Sparing the unpleasant details made the story rather short.

"She leads the craftlock soldiers." My step slowed as we neared the top.

"Tired already?" Brien jested.

I turned to him in the stairwell. "I didn't tell you about Dan."

His brow lowered. "Dan?"

Pressing my lips together, I climbed a few more stairs before unlatching and pushing open the door to the room there. Once Brien followed me inside, I explained, "Dan is a crafter. A mindreader."

A chuckle escaped his throat. The second died on his tongue. "Dan? *Our* Dan?"

"I learned it when I returned to Fount." I placed my mother's knife on the bedside table. "I made him swear to me to keep it a secret, but I suppose that doesn't matter anymore." I met his eyes. "You had no inkling?"

"Honestly, for the last couple years, when I was home, he was at the tanner's." He scanned the room, taking it in.

Brien hadn't been home often; he was always picking up work around town. Farmwork, labor, paving, whatever was hiring.

I softened and touched his elbow. "It's a wonder you're not an officer yet, Brien. If you put half the effort into soldiering that you put into taking care of us, you ought to be a general."

He scoffed. "Maybe if I were noble."

But his uniform had more black than red on it. He'd been promoted at least once during his time in the army. Yet Brien wouldn't be one to make a fuss of it.

He crossed the room. Touched an ink vial and a ream of paper on a table. "Is this all yours?"

"I share with Eden."

He snatched his hand back like the table had turned to an oven. "With the princess?"

"She wasn't lying when she said we were friends."

He whistled, turned, absorbing the space. "I guess so much time in Rove, and then Sesta . . . Never would have thought, people like us, and people like them." He crossed to my side of the room. Touched our mother's knife. Bent down and picked up two leather bracers.

"But these?" he questioned. They were obviously a man's bracers, and obviously of fine make. More than that, Brien seemed to recognize them. "Guess it makes sense for the king to visit his sister, and his healer. But he seems cured. Guess not, if he still keeps you so close."

My face warmed at the thought. "He *is* healed, more or less," I answered softly, flushing deeper under his scrutiny. "He is whole."

He turned the bracers over in his hands. "You don't heal him in here, do you?"

"I don't think I have."

He set his jaw. Studied the bracers before dropping them on the table beside the knife. "Nym. I . . . There have been some rumors. One rumor that I caught. And I thought it was just men being men, speculating, but . . ." He eyed the bracers, and I knew what he was going to ask. Even if he didn't, he'd sort it out eventually. But he fumbled, awkward, practically begging me to rescue him.

So I played along. "What rumor might that be?"

He sighed. "That you and the king share . . . affections."

I let the words sit in the air a moment, artless and tight, before giving in and quietly confessing, "We do."

My brother's eyes widened to saucers. "Are you out of your gods-damned mind?"

Chapter 19

I couldn't really be surprised by the outburst. Yet still it pierced me, enough that I felt a subtle responding question through the bond from Renn.

"I might be," I answered honestly, feeling my energy drain through my heels. I sat on the edge of the bed. "I *am* aware. I'm . . . aware."

My brother shook his head, shifting back and forth as though confused about what to do with himself. "N-Nym, he's a *king*. He's *the* king."

"In my defense, that's a more recent development."

He barked a mirthless laugh. Grabbed his hair and let it go, leaving it poking out at an odd angle. "So his being a prince was acceptable?"

"Brien—"

"You know what else is recent? *Antsan*, Nym."

My posture sagged. "Yes, it is. I've . . . kept my distance, since their arrival."

He relaxed a hair. "So it's stopped."

My thoughts twisted back to yesterday, in this very room, pressed against the wall just behind my brother, my fingers knotted in Renn's hair, his hands splayed over my hips.

The guilt must have been apparent on my face. Brien looked ready to split apart. "What are you *thinking*?"

My temper rose, and Ursa was not there to balm it. "Do you assume it hasn't plagued me constantly? I am nothing and he is everything."

He ran a palm down his face. Paced. "Is it . . . the magic?"

For a moment I thought he meant the link, and it terrified me that he knew, yet I realized he merely asked the same question I'd presented Renn the first time he'd told me he loved me. Did he love *me*, or just the magic that healed him?

"No," I answered.

Brien tried to lean against the wall but found himself too restless to stay there. "Nym—" Emotion creaked in his voice. "After Vin and Ford—"

I winced at their names.

"—do you really think this is *wise*?"

"If you want to get philosophical with it," I countered, "I'm sure I could find something in my defense. Perhaps we should ask Renn. He likely has the words of every ancient scholar memorized and could recite something applicable."

He let out a long exhale. "*Renn.* Again. How long have you . . . ?"

I couldn't quite remember.

Brien began pacing again. I let him get a few good strides in before demanding, "Sit down."

"I can't *sit down*, Nym. My commoner sister is sleeping with the king—"

"I'm not sleeping with him," I retorted, even as my cheeks warmed. I recognized the fallacy of my statement—I had *slept* with him, in the same bed, but not in the way Brien assumed. "That is . . ." He'd flustered me. I stood, my energy suddenly renewed. "I'm not having sexual relations with him."

An unbidden thought, of Renn in his room in the west tower, rising in the morning, Princess Azra's red hair splayed out on the pillow beside him—

Brien crossed to me and grabbed me by my shoulders. Not harshly, but firmly. "I don't know him well, Nym." He'd lowered his voice. "I don't know what he and the Antsan king have decided. But even so, nobles . . . I don't need to remind you of Lord Fell—"

"He is nothing like Lord Fell." The nobleman who had caused the carriage crash that killed our mother, father, and sister. The one who had paid five silver merits for each of their heads as recompense and never looked back.

"Is he using you?" he asked, concern moistening his eyes. "If he's healed, why does he need to keep you around?"

My throat thickened. "He loves me, Brien."

He didn't seem to hear. "You already have a reputation in Fount—"

I wrenched from his grip. "What reputation?"

Renn stirred, concerned. I was tempted to build up the wall, to hide my pain, to protect him . . . but he'd asked me not to. So sincerely, he'd asked me not to—

Regret limned Brien's features, but he pressed on. "Sure, people don't talk about it anymore, but they know. They can't *not* know, Nym."

Two failed engagements, a pregnancy. They were hard things to hide. Harder things to live through. Venom leaked into my voice when I answered, "Anyone who judges me for those has a soul blacker than Adoel Nicosia's."

"So you're on a first-name basis with him, too?"

I reeled back from him. He winced. "Too far," I spat.

"Too far," he agreed, and finally sat on the bed, the strength gone from his legs.

I stood there, and he sat there, in silence for a long minute while I wrestled with my anger. While I imagined Ursa telling me, *He cares about you, as he should,* or *You would behave the exact same way if the roles were reversed.* Though her voice no longer echoed in my mind, thinking of the sentiments helped calm me, and I lowered myself to the mattress beside him.

After Ursa, Brien was my closest sibling. My dearest friend.

I rested a hand on his knee. "I know. *I know.* I promise you, I won't stand in the way of the treaty. I'm not at the warfront, but I understand our limitations. I know what Antsan brings. I've already spoken to

Re—*His Majesty* about it. I've tried . . . to keep my distance. I even tried to leave, but Eden has asked me to stay—"

"Has he?"

I didn't answer, but Brien easily equated the silence with an unspoken *yes*.

I squeezed his knee. "You know I never learn."

He chuckled. Genuinely, this time. "Gods know you never learn. You're the most stubborn person I know, and I've been in the military for fourteen months."

I steadied myself with a deep breath. "Listen. There's water in the pitcher. Do you have a change of clothes?"

He patted his bag. "Clean enough."

"Wash up. Leave your uniform outside the door. I'll wash it. Eden won't be in until evening."

"I'm not going to strip down in the princess's room, and I can wash my own clothes—"

"You will, and I'll wash them, and you can have a moment to not be surrounded by men. A moment of peace."

He grappled with the idea, then nodded, so I left him to his thoughts, waiting outside the door for his uniform.

I ran my hands ragged dragging it across the washboard. Hung it out to dry. Saw the too-few cooking staff struggling with setting up dinner for so many new arrivals, so I hurried into the tower to see to Brien, then excused myself to help with the evening meal. With luck Brien and I could eat together afterward.

I helped drag cauldrons full of stew across the bailey, so those assigned to a kitchen meal today could form multiple lines and get their dinners faster. Seln helped me haul mine closer to the east tower. Even with her help I found the task surprisingly tiring. Soldiers lingered nearby, pups waiting for a scrap to drop, but Princess Azra stood apart from them, like a wine stain on white linen. I wondered how she kept her gowns so clean, especially with the grounds constantly turned up by passing soldiers. That easy smile of hers was nowhere to be seen. Instead, she scowled so deeply even Seln remarked, "Is she very hungry?"

I wished again that the link allowed words to pass through. *Did you say something to her?* I'd ask Renn. Yet perhaps he hadn't. Perhaps Azra had dug into her growing network for more rumors about me. Perhaps a maid or soldier had mentioned I hadn't healed anyone in camp, or that Renn had come to my room after his return to Derren.

Did I pray to Hem or to Zia for patience? Gods knew I needed it. And an extra morsel of energy. The day's work had left me lightheaded.

Beatty whistled. Soldiers came at the ready with bowls from their personal kits. Pushing back my sleeves, I greeted them and ladled out soup as swiftly as I could, making sure I kept my enormous plait of hair out of the cookpot.

I spooned a ladleful into a younger man's bowl and began reaching to the soldier in line behind him, but the younger stopped me. "We've had hard training today." He tried to influence me with a lopsided grin. "A little extra?"

"You'll have to get back in line if you're hoping for seconds," I offered.

The soldier comically mourned, earning a chuckle from his compatriot. They were well trained and efficient, and soon I was scraping the bottom of the pot and directing lingering soldiers to the next cauldron.

As I wiped my hands on my apron, Princess Azra strolled up to me in a very carefree manner, twisting the stem of a wildflower between her pale fingers.

"Did you wash before serving?" she asked.

I bit back a sigh, dropped the ladle into the cauldron, and leaned on the pot's giant lip. "Your Highness, I assure you, your ire is better placed elsewhere."

She stepped closer and lowered her voice. "I can *assure* you that you've only had a taste of it."

Patience failed me, as it so often did. I glowered. I glowered at her smug expression, at the curls her maid surely spent hours winding into her hair to mimic mine, at her expensive clothing. She was just like the nobles at the winter ball, overly concerned with herself and completely ignorant of the suffering outside the castle walls. She stood on the edge of war yet seemed blind to everything but her own ambition.

"Stew?" I ground out, hefting the ladle.

Wrinkling her nose, Azra stepped back from me. "Whore," she spat, and started toward the—

"What did you just call her?"

My heart jumped, struck my clavicle, and dropped into my gut. Turning, I spied Renn coming from the east tower, only a few paces away, a bowl in his hand as though he'd been waiting for me to finish serving before he ate.

Princess Azra had enough modesty to blanch. "Y-Your Majesty." She plastered on that smile, but it quivered in place. "You misheard me."

Renn strode right up to us, the faintest glow emanating from his skin. I don't think he noticed it. "I can hear a hawk take flight from half a mile away."

"But you asked—"

"Redundantly." He stopped in front of her, the toes of his boots touching her slippers, his cobalt gaze blazing. "I asked you a question."

Renn's anger seared my insides. My heart pulsed too rapidly, reminding me that I hadn't yet nourished it with magic today. I stepped around the pot. "Re—Your Majesty, perhaps here is not—"

Jonras, nearby, started forward, ready to help but unsure of protocol.

Princess Azra's hands formed fists. "Do not patronize me. I am your *betrothed*."

"Not yet you aren't," Renn countered darkly, "and you forget you have eligible sisters."

The absolute vehemence in his voice, let alone the words, floored me. My shock and his enmity clashed and brewed through the link, building a deep, visceral ache in my chest.

The princess turned porcelain, lips parted and breath still.

Others had noticed. Others were listening.

Eden's voice rang in my ears. *You might try to be subtle, but he is not.*

"She means more to me than the gods themselves," he hissed. "That makes your words blasphemy."

"Renn," I pressed. I wavered and grabbed the lip of the cauldron.

Tears welled in the princess's eyes, making her look especially young. She whipped around and darted for the keep, pushing Jonras out of her way. Lingering bystanders quickly averted their eyes and continued on their way.

My left arm began to tingle. Renn's sickness . . . but he appeared so hale. And I couldn't feel his symptoms through the link. I couldn't bring myself to be embarrassed by the exchange. I felt . . . ill. The vision of him wavered.

"Renn," I whispered.

He finally turned toward me, and the anger in his countenance receded instantly. He rushed to me, gripping my upper arm.

I dowsed into myself. The magicked blocks of my heart's merlon flickered. Shrunken, like ice in the sun. Had I missed refueling them? Yesterday, too? I'd been so busy with Brien, the infirmary . . .

How very stupid of me.

I started to pull magic in to feed them, but using craftlock fatigued me, and I was already so tired—

Renn called my name from far away. An ocean away.

I fell, and I fell, and I fell, swallowed in darkness. Sounds of people—calling over, worrying, moving, grew weaker even as Renn shouted for a healer.

A weak pulse of a half-formed heart. A second, a third. In between each pulse, a glimmer of consciousness, a stick of pain in my chest. A quick realization of coldness before it flickered out.

"Nym."

Then nothing. Not even darkness. Nothing to see, nothing to feel.

"Nym, how do we help you?"

Ursa?

But Ursa was dead.

"Nym, tell me what you need."

My heart, I tried to say, but I had no mouth. *I need magic.*

The next beat hurt. Someone was shouting. Renn?

"Hold on. She's coming."

The pain withdrew. The nothing shifted into darkness, into distant sounds. Into the sensation of grass beneath me, the wisps of setting sun on my skin. A strong heartbeat in my chest.

I opened my eyes to the bailey. Renn leaned over me, clutching my hand. He shrunk back in relief. Beside him knelt Seln, her eyes unfocused, dowsing on me. *Seeing* my lumis.

I jerked upright, pulling from her grasp. "D-Don't—" I started.

But then someone behind me said, "Sorry, Nym. She had to. I told her how to."

Twisting, I looked behind me to a familiar face. My father's brown eyes. Dark-blond hair. A face that had shed its youth since the last time I saw him.

Tears pooled in my eyes. It couldn't be. "Dan?"

"Broke my promise," he confessed with an easy, relieved smile.

It took me a beat to understand what he meant. His promise. Not to tell a soul he was a mindreader . . .

He'd arrived for the conscription. He'd been here. He'd read my mind.

He knew exactly what I'd done to save Renn.

And now it seemed Seln did, too.

In the infirmary, away from prying eyes, I took a moment to absorb the situation. Renn, Dan, and Seln had followed me, along with Sten, who had been nearby. Seln reached for me, but I put my hands up, walling her off. "I'm fine now. I can do the rest myself."

Turning away, I did. Seln had strengthened the faulty pieces of my heart, and I fed them a little more, enough to make me feel more myself again, though I could not keep the apprehension from pulsing through my veins.

Two people, *fallible* people, knew the secret I had given my heart and body to protect. The weight of failure pressed into me on all sides, and it took great fortitude not to let it crush me right there in the infirmary.

When I came back to myself, Seln said, "You don't need to be ashamed of it, Nym. Your lumis *is* a bit strange. I thought you were far worse off at first, because of the color. And I've never seen one so eccentric, either, but that's kind of special, isn't it?" She set an assuring hand on my forearm. "Mine's just a painting. Feels like every other person here has a lumis like a painting."

I swallowed, nodded. *Eccentric.* Of course she couldn't possibly piece together what the gold threading meant.

"You're on another level, really," she went on, by way of comforting. "Pure magic for your heart—that's what the mindreader claimed, I mean. That level of craft is beyond me. How did you hurt it so?"

I swallowed. "Accident as an adolescent." I ignored the way Dan's eyes narrowed at me.

Renn's concern made our link heavy in my chest. Resting my hands on Seln's shoulders, I said, "Thank you so much for your help. But I am . . . self-conscious . . . about it. Would you promise me not to mention it to anyone else?"

She was about to consent, but for good measure, Renn cut in: "Swear it."

Seln startled and turned toward her king. Bowed. "Of course, Your Majesty. I'll keep it to myself." She passed a curious glance toward me.

Renn nodded. "You may go."

Silence followed Seln's footsteps until she cleared not only the infirmary, but the hall outside. Shutting the door, Renn said, "I would prefer this information does not leave this room."

"I'm aware my sister is eccentric," Dan offered. Then, as an afterthought, "Your Majesty."

Sten knew that Renn and I had a supernatural connection, but I didn't think he understood the finer details of it. He simply nodded.

Renn's concern darkened. I glanced over to see his eyes narrow on me, but before I could address it, Dan approached, and my attention turned fully toward him.

I embraced him, first. Stepped back and looked him over. He wore his usual clothing, peasant's clothes, and they were travel-stained. "When did you get in?"

"Literally a quarter hour before you passed out in the bailey." He grinned. "Good timing, eh?"

I touched his face. "You've grown."

"Been eating better." He turned toward Renn. "Thank you, for the packages. They helped."

Renn nodded, his countenance like a wolf's. It made me think of his brother.

"Packages?" I asked.

Dan offered only a crooked half smile in response. Had Renn been even more generous to my family, and during such a hard time? Surely before I'd returned from Sesta—I couldn't fathom where he'd find the time and a willing messenger after. "And Art brings in a lot."

"Art Millstone?"

Dan snapped his fingers. "Yeah. We . . . we didn't have anywhere to write, Nym. But Lissel married him this past spring."

The news hit me as though I'd opened the door to a hot oven. "M-Married? She got married?" My stomach sank at the thought that I hadn't been there. I hadn't given her a blessing nor my counsel. I hadn't weaved a crown of flowers for her hair or helped sew a wedding gown. I blinked rapidly to keep my eyes dry.

A few thorns of guilt prodded through the link.

Dan nodded. "She likes him, you know? He's a good man, Nym. Real good. Stepped up a lot after you left. And his family is kind. He lives with us, or he will until he's drafted. Says he'll build his own place, but we didn't know when you were coming home . . . *if* you were coming home . . ."

He cleared his throat.

I hugged him again. "It's all right. I'm happy for her. I am. I'll visit as soon as I can." I released him. "But your work—"

"I'll take it up again when I'm back."

I searched his face. "You came here alone?"

"I met up with a few healers in Grot and traveled with them." He shrugged. "I'm here, ready to serve. Ready to be somewhere else, you know?"

I wanted to snap that war wasn't a vacation, but who was I to tell Dan to go home when we needed crafters so desperately? How could we ever stand against Sesta if we didn't have magic on our side?

I perked up. "Dan, Brien is here."

He jolted. Hesitated. "What?"

"Brien. Brien is here." I grabbed his hand. Glanced toward Renn and Sten. "If it's all right—"

"Go." Renn waved his hand, though that wolfishness still haunted his countenance, and dark concern rippled from him. "We'll talk later."

I nodded my thanks and pulled Dan from the infirmary. "He was in another line to get food—"

Our hands linked, Dan was able to speak directly into my mind. *"I didn't go too deep, Nym. You were thinking about your heart when you fell; it was right there at the top. Didn't have to flip very far."*

My steps slowed. "Flip very far?"

"People . . . I see them in weird ways. Maybe like a lumis? Most of them are like books. And I have to turn pages to find the information I'm looking for. The deeper the thought, the longer it takes. But yours was right under the cover. I didn't see anything . . . embarrassing."

I pressed my lips together as we entered the bailey. *But you saw why.*

He heard me. *"I saw enough to hazard a guess. But even without the king swearing me, I wouldn't share it. It's not mine to share."*

He tilted his head like he was listening. *"I don't hear Ursa. I was hoping . . . maybe I'd hear her."*

Tears stung my eyes. I breathed deeply and banished them. "We'll talk about that later," I managed. Released his hand, so he wouldn't hear of our sister's demise before I was ready to tell him. Happy things, first. "He's here, somewhere." I searched for him among the soldiers, noting Sir Arquan entering the keep, likely to speak with Renn . . . and tried not to think too hard on what they might discuss. Family, first. The rest . . . after.

I spied him sitting beside two others of similar rank near the wall. Picking up my skirts, I hurried over, Dan on my heels until he, too, spotted his brother.

A muffled sob caught in his throat.

Brien turned at my arrival, then noticed Dan behind me, and his face went slack. He stood, nearly dropping his bowl. "Gods be, *Dan*?"

He laughed and hugged his younger brother, beating a hand on his back as men do. "I barely recognize you! What are . . . ?"

You doing here, he was going to say, but as he looked over Dan's shoulder to me, I knew he remembered. Dan was a crafter.

And like Brien, Dan would be going to war.

I stayed out late with Brien and Dan, after dark, until Sten came to fetch me. Even then, I made sure Dan got situated with the other new recruits, that the officers knew his name, and that he'd have a decent place to sleep. Only then did I return to the keep, Sten gesturing I was to go to the west tower and not the east. I took the stairs a little too slowly, twisting the end of my braid clockwise, then counterclockwise, around my index finger.

His bedroom was perhaps not the best place to meet, but I hadn't seen any of the Antsan delegation since entering the keep. Then again,

Renn had utterly spoiled any good feeling he'd crafted with Princess Azra already.

Renn had retired for the night, still dressed, sitting on the edge of his bed, reading over what looked to be a report of some sort. He didn't look up as I entered, yet the moment I shut the door, leaving Sten in the hallway, he said, "You realize how hypocritical it is to constantly worry over my health when you take such poor care of your own, yes?"

Biting the inside of my cheek, I crossed the small space and sat beside him. Defensive anger prickled beneath my skin, but cool logic won out. He was right.

"Yes," I admitted. It'd been easy to look after myself in Sesta. I'd so little else to do but play in my lumis as a child would a sandbox. But here I became busy. Distracted. Seeking out anything and everything that *didn't* involve my heart.

"Is this a once-a-year thing?" He set the report aside and fixed those vivid blue eyes on me. They rivaled the candles. I was surprised he'd lit candles when he could ignite the gods' light so easily. "Should I mark in my calendar when you intend to pass out next?"

I frowned. "If this is an attempt at a jest, it's poorly done."

"Is it? I find myself hilarious."

Anger bristled, and I was sure he felt it. "I apologize for the oversight, but you made it a spectacle long before I did."

He glowered.

"I don't like Azra," I confessed. "I don't trust her. But we need her."

"*May* need her."

"You humiliated her. Publicly."

He scoffed. "She humiliated *you* publicly." His eyes narrowed.

"She is a princess. An ally."

"A figurehead and physical pressure to sign the deal *they* want, only."

I threw up my hands. "And how will the negotiations fare now? I know Sir Arquan spoke with you—"

"He is aware of Azra's miscreance. He apologized."

My blood simmered. "And did you? To either of us?"

He flinched, chagrined. "I forget how toilsome it is to argue with you."

"Did—"

"I did not"—he stood and faced me fully—"and I will not. She is showing a pattern of perniciousness." Thorns prodded the bond. "Is she the only one?"

I recalled the Antsan soldier speaking with the pantler near the portcullis, weeks ago, calling me a whore. Brien, too, had heard rumors. How many thought such a thing of me? Had the rumors spread naturally, or had they been intentionally planted by a naïve and jealous woman?

Scalding anger and twisting guilt bloomed through the link. "I . . . didn't think of it," Renn confessed. "On the ship . . . my men are loyal. Private. I didn't think what my indiscretion might do to you." He wiped a hand down his face. Looked away. Blond hair fell into his eyes, but he did nothing to push it away. "I'm sorry, Nym."

I clutched the edge of the mattress. Peered out the east window, but it was too dark to see much. "Thank you, for looking after my family while I was . . . away."

I received a subtle grunt in response.

"Will he be safe, Renn?"

Wilting, he dropped back onto the mattress. "I presume you mean Dan."

"He's only sixteen."

"I will do my best. I swear it." Another thorn of guilt. "The crafters under drafting age will be looked after. I *am* glad he reported. We need all the help we can get." He glanced at me. "Did you know? About his craftlock?"

I nodded. "I found out when I went to Fount last winter."

He considered this.

"I'd wondered if he would answer the draft. I'm glad he did, and yet I wished he'd stayed home."

We sat in silence for a few beats, before cold fire began licking at the bond.

"Who else?" he murmured. "Who else has that harpy poisoned?"

"I hardly know any by name, and it will gain you nothing to make an example out of them. Even boorish men can hold a sword and defend their country. Even harpies make useful allies."

Renn dropped his head into his hands, elbows on his knees. "I'm the source of all your suffering, Nym. I'm the one who took you from your family. I'm the reason Nicosia—" Emotion choked his voice, and he took a moment to bridle it. "Antsan and Azra, and your . . ."

Had the events of the day happened differently, the deprecation would have confused me. As it was, I knew what he meant.

My heart. Half my heart.

"I gave it to you, Renn," I insisted.

His eyes shimmered fiercely, but in the bond the roses grew, and aged, and died, their thorns hardening and digging.

Renn cursed again, because he knew I felt it.

Cautiously, like he was a spooked horse, I touched his arm. He gradually relaxed under my touch, almost like a lumis would. I embraced him from the side, pressing my cheekbone to his shoulder.

"You have given me hope," I whispered, carefully unwinding the thorns. "You have fed my family. You've protected my honor. Made me laugh. Navigated this new . . . maze . . . of myself and guided me through my brokenness. Held me, even when we were continents apart."

The thorns softened, new and green.

"You gave me freedom, purpose. Healing. And you gave me a very nice necklace."

A chuckle caught in his throat. "You broke it," he murmured.

I chastely kissed his cheek, released him, and turned him so he faced me. "This is all . . . trying . . . but it only breaks my heart because you gave me a heart to break. So why should I not give part of it back to you?" I ran a knuckle along the stubble on his jaw. "I'll do better, caring for it. I promise."

He let out a long breath.

"And you must do your part."

He snorted. "I'll marry King Vitsoph before I bind myself to that viper."

"Renn—"

A knock on the door, firm, not soft.

Renn cursed. "I should have met you in Eden's room. This isn't going to look good." He rose and crossed to the door, pulling it open hard enough that his gods-touched strength nearly ripped it off the hinges.

But it was only Sten. Sten, with a grave expression.

Fire and thorns receded entirely. I stood as Renn asked, "What? What's happened?"

"Whitestone." The guard spoke just above a whisper. "He's here."

Chapter 20

Physician Wald Whitestone was a shadow of his former self.

He'd lost weight since I'd last seen him, which added a hollow gauntness to his every feature, magnified all the more by the uneven shadows cast by lamps, sconces, and Renn himself.

When Renn entered the storage room where his men had brought the Sestan, softly glowing to drive back the dark, Whitestone visibly winced. When I followed, his cracked lips formed around the words "So you did make it."

No thanks to you, I did not say, but I lingered back by the door in a patch of shadow between lights.

Renn didn't address the physician first but rather one of the travel-stained spies who had brought him in, a tall blond man with peachy skin, his hair shorn close to his skull. "Does he know why he's here?"

"Yes, Your Majesty. We pulled information from him before moving him physically, as you requested. He hasn't resisted us at any point."

Renn's emotions were at a low simmer, like he'd grown so skilled at his mask it could hide the unseen as well. "How did you get into Rodsfell?"

"He wasn't in Rodsfell, Your Majesty."

That gave me pause. When had Whitestone left?

Renn didn't ask for specifics; he'd likely be debriefed later. His cool gaze swept to the prisoner. "Whitestone."

The physician's head drooped, his eyes on Renn's feet. "I had nothing to do with the attack on Rove. I never would—"

"That isn't what I need to know."

Gooseflesh rose in long streaks up my arms at the coldness in Renn's voice.

Whitestone swallowed. "Your mother's order was called Unfallen of Zia, headquartered in western Sesta."

The spy added, "Potsburn and Liftwell set for it while the others and I brought him here. The information appeared sound. We'd crossed near the location in February when hunting for Tallowax."

The man had never met me; he likely didn't realize I was in the room.

"If the sisterhood kept any records, they will be there, but I don't know the exact location. Only that it was west." Whitestone shifted on the overturned crate he sat upon. "She might have brought something to Rove, to prove to King Grejor whatever she needed to prove."

"If she was smart, she wouldn't have left them there." Renn rubbed the bridge of his nose. "How do you know it's west?"

"Because I knew of the order before I left. They came to Rodsfell often. And because once, your mother slipped in her Canseren dialect. Her Sestan tongue had a western accent." He ran a hand down his face. "I never knew her . . . before. But every order has a symbol. The Unfallen of Zia . . . it looks like the number three."

My spine stiffened as if cooling glass. "Wait."

All eyes turned to me.

"With two circles?" I patted my pockets, turned, searching for something to write with, then noticed the grime on the walls and traced directly into that. I drew the unfinished cursive *Z* with its two circles—the symbol I'd seen in Rodsfell. "Like this?"

Whitestone's brows drew together. "Yes. That's it."

Wiping my finger on my skirt, I turned to Renn. "I saw this symbol when Eden and I traveled through Sesta. *Western* Sesta. I don't know the name of the village, but it's a small one north of Horgansten. This symbol was on the cellar hatch of a small home on its outskirts."

Renn's expression lightened only a hair, but through our connection I felt the inflating warmth of his admiration. "Then we will search north of Horgansten." He looked toward another spy, a dark-haired, dark-skinned woman in the back corner. "Any luck with Adrinn's network?"

I perked up at this.

"The lead for Wendway dried up. He's either dead or left the country," she answered. "But the last report seemed promising. Harplay is suspected to be in Molls. If we haven't made contact yet, we will soon."

I remembered Adrinn barging into my room and pinning me against the wall, a knife to my neck, as though it were yesterday. Asking me directly if I was a spy. He'd been following my movements. Suspect of my closeness to his brother and the letter I'd had Lonnie post for me. He'd been suspicious of Winvrin as well, suspecting her Sestan heritage.

If he had his own spy network, if Renn could use it, that would be incredibly helpful to us. I wondered if any of them had reached out to Renn personally. Then again, I knew nothing of the work, nor the dangers that came with it.

"I know Horgansten." Whitestone sounded like pouring gravel. "For what use it is to you, I know it."

He slid off the crate onto his knees, the movement causing the spies in the room to lunge forward and draw their weapons. Renn didn't budge. Whitestone made no effort to attack; he simply knelt on the floor, shriveled and weak. I noted he favored his left leg.

"Forgive me," he whispered. "I didn't realize . . . I was a fool, Your Majesty. A hundred times over a fool."

Renn simmered through the bond, a collection of emotions I couldn't quite parse out.

"Put him in the dungeon for now, until we have need of him. Make sure he's fed," Renn commanded, and the spies immediately went to work. Renn's light snuffed as he opened the door—Sten lingering outside—and guided me out with a hand to my mid-back.

In the hallway, I whispered, "What if I'm wrong? What if your mother's order didn't keep documentation?"

Renn stood close to me, his lips brushing my hair. "Have faith in me. Adrinn always used me for strategy; I had very little else to do. Azra's misstep may play into our favor. We need Antsan, but Antsan wants us."

I looked into his eyes, midnight blue in the dim corridor. "I do have faith in you, Renn. Surely you feel that I do. But if this marriage is the only way . . . I *understand* that. I would never hold it against you."

The link turned heavy, cold. He had no reply. But the spies were pulling Whitestone from the room, so he touched my hip, moving us from his reach, despite the fact that the physician's wrists were tied behind his back and he made no effort to fight.

"But if it is . . ." My throat thickened and my navel pinned itself to my spine. ". . . I can't stay here. You can't ask me to do that."

The link became a sinkhole, drawing me down, ensnaring me. Renn opened his mouth to repeat, but Whitestone's voice broke the melancholy.

"He's coming for Derren, Your Majesty." The physician finally lifted his eyes. "I heard it before I left. He'll come to Derren Castle soon. A fortnight at most."

My breath hitched. The Sestan army, here? *Nicosia*, here?

Renn merely nodded. Sensed my growing trepidation, for he put his hand on my shoulder, rooting me. The spies dragged Whitestone down the hall, toward the dungeon. I hadn't even known Derren Castle possessed one.

"Your forgiveness, please," Whitestone croaked, trying to turn in the grip of his captors to behold the king of Cansere. "Forgive me, please, Your Majesty!"

Renn's lips pressed into a hard line. Once Whitestone cleared the hallway, he whispered, "I will give you anything you need for your journey, if you go. Food and money for travel, a wagon, even my best men to escort you." He lifted his eyes to Sten, who lingered a few paces away. "But." His eyes leveled to mine, his lips close enough to kiss. "If I succeed, I ask for your hand, Nym. There is no priest here, but as soon as we find one, I ask for your hand."

Tears burned my eyes. I nodded. He kissed my forehead.

"You have very little time," I said.

He looked at me, tracing my features in the dark. "Sten, make sure she gets to her room." He stepped back, giving me and his guard space to pass. My legs felt too heavy to walk, my half-heart thrumming to keep up with the turmoil spinning through my chest.

At the junction, I glanced back, but if Renn lingered, it was too dark to see him.

I didn't see Renn for two days.

I looked for him. I felt him. But never once, to my knowledge, did he step outside of that war room, holed up with Sir Jardallen Arquan, discussing the nature of the alliance they would have, because Renn would make sure they had it, one way or another. There was no time left to dally or play games. Not with the dragons approaching.

I would never be glad for war, but I welcomed the distraction of preparing for a siege. Distraction from my heart and from my stirring anxiety of facing Sesta. I helped staff stockpile water, in case Nicosia had his men poison our supply, and put up food for the siege. I divided healers by experience and worked with Eden, under the direction of Commander Stonelay, to designate where we would be posted when the army attacked, and how we would best be able to help the injured. While men reinforced the gate and castle walls, Brien and I prepped the infirmary. With luck, it would merely serve as a holding place for casualties, not a hospice. While men sharpened swords and fletched arrows, I aided Beatty in stacking firewood. After General Cuplend gave speeches to improve soldier morale, I spoke quietly with Brien and Dan, more so to lend support to the latter, who had never before faced war. As a mindreader, Dan was designated to be a spy. While that meant he would not be at the front lines, it did not excuse him from battle. We needed every man—and boy—we could get, and Dan had been training with the rest of them; every evening after dinner, I healed his blisters, just enough that they wouldn't bother him—not enough to prevent calluses from forming. He'd need those, in the long run.

Another commander, Hawksend, took a battalion of soldiers away from Derren Castle. Leading them to another skirmish, or perhaps to come around and flank the Sestan army. Perhaps they would go clear to Rove—I was not privy to the information. Neither Brien nor Dan went with them, but a handful of the craftlock soldiers did.

In Renn's second day behind closed doors, I finished outfitting the newest craftlock recruits with uniforms. They were a little piecemeal—things in Cansere didn't run as smoothly since Rove fell—but they would work well enough. I handed out my last set to a soulbinder before marking it in a ledger and coming back to the table set outside the east tower, where Eden oversaw everything. She sat at the table over a ledger, a pencil gripped tightly in her white-knuckled fist, her eyes unfocused. Her face held a chilling sort of serenity, like one who had accepted death, or perhaps one who had already died.

Flashes of Rove Castle zipped behind my eyes. Bodies in the corridors, the Lords' Hall—

"We will be ready." Eden's voice rang, free of intonation. Of any emotion at all. "We've been preparing all this time. Derren Castle is well fortified."

The impending siege, she meant.

Rove Castle had also been well fortified, or so I thought. I swallowed the thought. "We have soulbinders now, too," I pointed out.

Neither of us shared what haunted us—that the enemy's craftlock soldiers were far more numerous and better trained than our own. That Rove, a far larger fortress, had fallen in a single night to those soldiers.

"We have Renn," I added, even if only to myself.

She nodded. Drew in a deep breath.

We stayed like that for a full minute, lost in our thoughts, our scars.

"If you want to go farther inland," I tried, "you can." Commander Stonelay had made the same offer to me. *I think His Majesty would prefer it,* he'd said.

Eden shook her head. "I will stay. I will fight. I . . ." Her lip trembled, and she bit it until it stilled. "I will not run from that man. I will kill him myself."

I, too, had determined not to run. Not from the war. I wouldn't leave Renn, Brien, Dan. I couldn't. To run would be to tell them I didn't believe in them. That I wanted to save my own skin while they flayed theirs upon the blades of Sesta.

I shut my eyes against the harsh metaphor, tasting darkness in the back of my throat, the cool touch of—

My eyelids shot open. Pushing off the castle wall, I looked around the bailey.

The cool caress of death fluttered across my collarbone.

"I'll be right back."

Eden didn't complain as I moved eastward, sniffing out death. It had been some time since the old sense had visited me; I'd nearly forgotten our unsightly bond.

I neared Beatty and a soldier she spoke to, but death didn't hover around them. Passing by, I found an older soldier whittling near the portcullis. Death choked out my lungs like I'd put my face into the bowl end of a pipe.

"I'm a healer." I approached and kneeled, since he sat in a mangled bed of clover. I might not have been as strong or fast as I once was, but I was a healer, and I couldn't do nothing.

His knife stilled. "I know. But I've no need of you."

I extended my hands. "Please."

Sighing, the man set aside his work—I thought he was carving a hound, but the work was too new for fine details—and allowed me to touch the underside of his jaw.

His lumis mimicked chain mail, albeit in a more equine shape. Off-center, a cluster of the chains had darkened, some disintegrated entirely. The darkness stretched outward like veins of infection, nearly touching the outer edges of his lumis. Death lines spiraled out in all directions.

If I interpreted it correctly, his heart was about to fail.

I pressed my palms into the rotting gap and pulled magic through me, urging ashy links to re-form themselves . . . noting the slowness with which they did. Ursa's powers were no longer with me, and working in haste, I felt it keenly. Still, I summoned the magic and twisted my hands, encouraging it to mimic the shape of the links, to reseal the hole, then to act as a balm and polish to the other blackened links, refortifying them one at a time. The magic held; the black did not encroach to the edges of the lumis. The chill of death across my skin abated entirely.

Sighing in relief, I slipped from the soldier's lumis and pulled back.

"Huh." He rubbed his chest. "I . . ." He hesitated. Studied me. "How did you know?"

I wondered what symptoms he had felt before my intervention. If he'd thought them normal conditions of warfare, of drills and late nights, much in the same way I'd ignored the early signs of the rat plague in myself last year. Offering an assuring smile, I answered, "You looked pale."

He accepted this, thanked me, and returned to his whittling.

As I walked away, in my mind's eye I found myself in another's lumis, not of chain links or even broken glass, but of floating numbers of endless math equations. They swirled around me in a lazy dance, and distantly, against my skin, the cool air of Rove Castle raised gooseflesh on my arms, and the tangy scent of spilled blood stung my nostrils.

I formed my hands into fists, my fingernails carving ravines into my palms. Yet I felt something tangible there, much like the number three

I'd wrenched from that dragon's lumis, the one the death lines pointed to. The weakness.

I'd snapped that piece and dropped the Sestan there in the hall. It was the first and only time I'd used my ability to kill someone. And yet, in that instance, it had been him or me.

I no longer had Ursa, but I had been touched by death, and death directed me to the spaces that would hurt bodies the most. It mattered not who it was—a peasant, a soldier, a king. Death would have all of them, eventually.

With my help, it could have them sooner.

I paused then, in the shadow of the bailey wall, the sounds of training echoing nearby, scents of sun-hot grass wafting on the breeze. I turned northward, though the stone prevented me from seeing the horizon. Still, I know I faced it. My prison, my fears.

Sesta.

I am not afraid. I heard it through my thoughts as though Ursa recited it along with me. *I am to be feared.*

I swallowed. Pressed my open hands to the wall. *I am not afraid. I am to be feared.*

I'd died once already. Death was *my* companion, not theirs.

"I am not afraid," I whispered, digging my nails into the mortar between stones. "I am to be feared."

Even the self-proclaimed son of the goddess Zia, Adoel Nicosia, hadn't wanted me in his lumis.

"I wield death as a sword," I finished, and pushed back from the wall, looking upward to the sky above it. I pressed my lips together. Tightened my fingers into fists. Squared my shoulders.

Adoel Nicosia could bring his armies. I would not balk.

He would fear me.

He *has* feared me.

And I would show no mercy.

By evening I'd grown antsy. Renn's presence rolled through me like the sea, undulating and churning, crests and troughs. Little pricks of worry here, caresses of victory there. He proved increasingly difficult to read. For all the confidence he'd had, the amount of time it was taking to finalize this treaty had me worried.

I was not beyond eavesdropping, so I asked Beatty if I might take the king his tray for the night. She'd sent one up a couple of hours before but prepared a tray of treats for Renn and Sir Arquan. I carried it carefully to the top of the keep where the meeting was held, relieved to see Sten standing outside the narrow door to the room.

Setting the tray on the floor, I approached the door and pulled my hair back, pressed my ear to the old wood. Sten did not stop me, merely shook his head and folded his burly arms.

"—out of time to debate." Sir Arquan's accent made him easy to pinpoint. "I will say it again, Your Majesty. You *need* Antsan. You are looming dangerously close to default."

Renn was far harder to make out; he spoke in low, dulcet tones, unbothered, measured. "That is an Antsan law, not Canseren. You've told me time and time again that your troops—forgive me, King Vitsoph's troops—are at the ready. To be so eager, I believe you need this deal just as much as I do."

Silence, for a moment, before Renn continued, "You've shown your hand in—" Then he spoke so low I could not make out the words, but I felt an inkling of his boldness through the link. "—not doing me a favor."

"You make many assumptions—"

"Are your people starving yet, Sir Arquan?"

I held my breath, listening for the response. Something—a chair, maybe—creaked.

"Let's take the focus off the Vitsophs for a moment and speak of that," Renn pressed, and I hoped by the emissary's lack of response that Renn had hit true. "Perhaps we need not waste food on a wedding when it could be feeding your people."

I remembered, so long ago, when I'd first heard of these talks, that King Grejor had not wanted an Antsan woman on the Canseren throne. It was the reason he wasn't willing to barter with Prince Adrinn. Was that something Renn had brought up, or was it too insulting a play? I knew little of politics and less of strategy. Surely Renn had already brought up his connection to Nicosia . . . or was he trying to tire Sir Arquan first? Perhaps lose as little as possible before getting what he wanted?

I'd missed something. The voices came through as mumbles.

Sten put his hand on my shoulder; I brushed him off. They were talking about Princess Azra again, Sir Arquan relating her many talents.

Renn interrupted him. "She has made claims and comments I might consider acts of subversion. I'm not interested. One of her sisters, perhaps."

My heart squeezed. One of her sisters? What? Yet I knew he didn't mean it. *Strategy, Nym. It's all strategy.*

Renn's voice, in memory, sprung to mind. *Please don't hate me for what I'll have to do to make this work.*

Perhaps I shouldn't be listening in after all.

"A sister would be amenable, but not the eldest." Sir Arquan spoke with measured grace. "She is already promised, and that cannot be broken. But an Antsan daughter beside your throne would guarantee our people fed."

"And what if I were to tell you I had twice the land you perceive? Endless acres for farming."

A long pause. "You would divide your country?"

"But there is the fallacy in your question." I could see in my mind Renn leaning forward, folding his hands beneath his chin. "Would I divide my *countries*."

"I don't follow."

"I have men in Sesta as we speak. Men searching for documentation Adoel Nicosia would very much like to see destroyed—"

I stepped back. Met Sten's eyes. He raised an eyebrow as if to ask, *Satisfied?* But he had the decency not to voice it. If I could hear the men in the room, they would hear us as well.

Instead I picked up the tray and handed it to Sten. Murmured, "Make sure you're eating," before departing back the way I'd come, praying to find something—anything—to take my mind off the negotiations that would fundamentally decide the course of my life.

Chapter 21

"I don't want her to do it."

I didn't hide my displeasure at the soldier's words but folded my arms and looked at him like he was a petulant child. Let him suffer with his traditional way of thinking, then.

I stood in the infirmary with Physician Addsmuch; we were trying to inspect the health of as many soldiers as we could before the attack, which had been confirmed by Renn's spy network. Dragons were massing in Klepton. Whitestone had spoken the truth. Brien lingered in the doorway, on guard duty, and Dan spoke with him, having had a break from his own training, which was far more physical than magical. His loose shirt bore long sweat stains, but he didn't complain. He never complained, ever since our parents passed. Like he couldn't bear the thought of being a burden.

This soldier, however, didn't have the same grace. He suffered from a rash across his torso, likely from an allergic reaction of some sort, but while I could heal it with a touch, he shied away from me, preferring the physician treat it instead.

Addsmuch shrugged. "Your choice, lad. Let me mix up a salve for it. See if you can change out the soap you're using for your laundry. That might be the culprit." The physician turned toward his now heavily stocked shelves and selected a few things. "Nym, would you grab—"

"I've got it." I took a mortar and pestle off another shelf and passed it to him. The soldier flinched as I reached over his cot. "I'm not contagious, you lackwit. And better for you if I were."

Brien snorted. "Play nice, Nym. He's in my platoon."

I turned back to the shelves. "I'll see if we can't track down some new soap—"

The link exploded.

I gasped, hand flying to my breast. My heart began racing as *brightness* poured in, filling my lungs, my throat, my stomach. Bubbles pressed against my ribs, and a sweet sensation, like golden honey, ribboned throughout me, warm and cool in waves: joy and relief, joy and relief.

Tears sprung to my eyes. *Renn.* Two things came to my mind that might ignite such exuberance. The first, the end of the war. Unlikely. The second—

"Nym?" Brien's fingers brushed my arm. "Are you all right?"

Physician Addsmuch said, "Perhaps sit down a moment."

I fled from the infirmary and darted down the hallway. Brien called after me, but I hardly heard him. My blood ran circles through my limbs and rushed in my ears. Warmth enveloped my core like I'd swallowed the sun. Burning, aching hope tugged a laugh free as I wiped tears from my eyes. I felt half crazed as I took a turn down a corridor, but upon seeing it crowded, retraced my path to take the servants' stairs that hugged the perimeter of the keep.

The door to the war room was ajar when I arrived. I grabbed its handle and swung it open, but the space within was dark, empty of bodies. Delirious with elation, I turned full circle in the hallway before rushing to the nearest slitted window. The setting sun burned brightly at the corner of my eye. Squinting against it, I searched the bailey for him, searched for—

Pressing a hand over my half-heart lest the thing beat its way free from my chest, I returned to the narrow servants' stairs and took them up, thighs burning, stumbling a little, for the steps were steep and uneven. I came out on one of the ramparts, the full marigold sun greeting me. Shielding my eyes, I searched the bailey again. The portcullis had been lifted, the drawbridge lowered. The delegation could not be here for the attack; it was too dangerous for them, and should they perish, no word would make it back to their king. No news yet that a deal was struck. And surely a deal had been struck.

I nearly called out his name. It popped and crackled at the back of my tongue, but there were so many bodies, I'd only call attention to myself, and I was *barely containing* myself. My quickening faith, my erupting hope, mixed with the flooding of his revelry and respite felt like some kind of drug. Like something wild pumped through my veins. Like the gods had touched me, too, and I might fly off this keep and dive into the sky.

I ran the length of the rampart, overenergized, sweat forming on my temples as I searched, gaze shifting from soldier to soldier to staff to soldier. I came around the east side of the keep and followed the battlement all the way down to the southeast corner, practically throwing myself across the merlons for a better view, tears flowing from the piercing sunlight and uncontained jubilance.

A breeze and the soft *tap tap* of boots touching down. I spun around and saw him, two paces from me, just as his light-woven wings dissipated into the sunset. The brilliance of the sky made him look crafted of fire, and when he grinned, I beheld heaven.

I don't know who stepped forward first. Maybe it was simultaneous. But one breath we stood apart on the rampart and the next I was in his arms, clutching him as I had after he'd pulled me from the sea. I wept and he laughed, lifting me off my feet and swinging me around. Then he kissed me, bending me back over his forearm, pouring into me the rest of his victory, as though it hadn't already engraved itself onto my very soul.

"You did it," I whispered when we broke apart.

"I did it," he sang against my mouth.

I grasped his ears and kissed him again. A freeing kiss, without the fear of watching eyes, without the fear of devastating consequences or partings. I made promises with my lips, my breath, my tongue, drawing out each one, savoring every moment of him.

"You are mine, Renn Noblewight," I murmured.

"I have always been yours." He kissed the juncture of my jaw. Unwound my hands so he might clasp them in his. Kissed each of my knuckles and then held them like something precious. His eyes glowed like sapphires, like blue moons and deep summer skies.

"We had a deal," he said.

I smiled so widely it hurt. Laughed so genuinely it sounded like a dream. It was not a flight of fancy, where I was young again and he a farm boy, but neither was it a hope chained and desiccated, where I was a woman too broken by men to ever trust another.

He was my everything.

"Yes," I whispered, and that heavenly smile returned. "I will marry you."

I realized then that we were not entirely alone on the rampart; I spied my brothers in my peripheral vision, having tracked me down here, concerned over my welfare. I only glimpsed them before Renn kissed me again; Dan, looking all-knowing and satisfied, and Brien, looking shaken and awkward.

But the winding joy, the trading of victory, overwhelmed anything else I might feel. I knew the moment would be fleeting. The war lingered, ever-present, and soon would come to our very doorstep. The future, however long or short it may be, would be littered with turmoil and trial.

I wanted all of it. Every tear and every smile, every angry word and gentle touch. He was worth it.

We were worth it.

No success of the heart would stop Sesta's dragons, and so before the sun crested the eastern horizon the next morning, the Antsan delegation gathered in the bailey, preparing for their long journey back home, a trek across Canseren soil, and then sailing across Salm's Rest. I'd heard Antsan ships were the fastest in the world, but the march on land would be hard on them. We didn't know exactly when Nicosia would strike, but the princess and her retinue ought to be as far from here as possible when he did.

I left the kitchen and approached the soldiers; we'd tied up travel rations in spare burlap from onion bags. I passed my last to Jonras, who nodded at me kindly before affixing it to a mule. Just beside him was Princess Azra's white mare, fully saddled, mane and tail braided, but I did not spy her telltale red hair among the group. Renn lingered by the portcullis, speaking with Sir Arquan. Over what, I'd have to ask later.

I was about to step back into the kitchen when Princess Azra emerged, two freshly baked loaves of bread in her arms. She scowled at me straightaway.

"I pray for safety on your journey," I said, and I meant it. Even surrounded by guards, trekking across a foreign country at war was dangerous. I knew it personally.

Her delicate brows pinched together. "I don't need your prayers, *healer*. Nor your well-wishes. I imagine you wish to gloat, your conniving maneuvers superior. But you are not. And you never will be."

Perhaps a year ago, her words would have rankled me. But in truth, Princess Azra merely made me tired. It seemed exhausting, pouring so much energy into a fight no one else wanted to join. Wringing oneself into a bucket no one else would carry.

She did not break away, which I took as invitation. Softly, I asked, "Do you really believe that?"

She leaned back. "Pardon?"

I clarified, "That the random circumstance of your birth truly makes you better than others."

She scoffed. "The fact that you think it random speaks volumes about you."

I studied her face. Her days at Derren Castle had brought out more freckles across her nose and forehead. She was still so young—only Dan's age. "I don't believe you."

She opened her mouth to retort, but I pushed on.

"I think you are far deeper than you let others believe. And in that depth there are pains you try to hide. Errant motivations that drive you to act as you do. We all have them." I took a deep breath. "A princess is no different, to that end. I hope you are able to overcome them. I hope you find true happiness, Your Highness."

If my sentiments had any effect on her, she masked it well. "You are a liar and a fiend," she growled through clenched teeth. "A liar, a fiend, and a *whore*, and you will not manipulate me into thinking otherwise."

I clasped my hands before me. Yes, I was tired, but the Antsan princess burrowed under my skin so easily. She got the better of me. "How much more the pity, knowing you lost to that."

It was a catty thing to say. I knew it the moment the words left my lips, and I regretted them. But Princess Azra had no retort save for the flushing of her cheeks. She pushed bodily past me, and I let her go, returning to the kitchens to scrub dishes for the next meal.

By the time I exited again, the Antsan delegation had gone.

Chapter 22

Eleven days later, the vile stirrings of death whispered over Derren Castle.

I knew it before the trumpets called. Recognized the shiver of death over my skin, so similar to that on my return to Rove Castle the day Nicosia's forces flew over its walls and slaughtered so many.

There's a strange formalness to war, I discovered. Almost like the start of a ball. The dancers line up, eyeing each other, searching for a suitable partner and stepping onto the floor just as the musicians begin playing.

The Sestan army lined up much like that, taking their time to instate order, as though they were going to ask Derren Castle for its hand in marriage as opposed to utter surrender. I wanted to search their ranks, try to find Nicosia among them, or any of the others I'd met in Rodsfell. Instead, I stayed in the infirmary with the other healers, passing out helmets for when we'd have to crawl onto the ramparts to reach our injured.

If Sesta tried to fly over on its soulbound warbirds, our archers would be ready.

When a distant horn sounded—richer and lower than the brass at Derren—I winced. I felt the army coming upon us like a wave upon a ship, growing as it swept off the horizon, silent, then muffled, then buffeting as a great storm right before it fell onto the crew and smothered them all.

I am not afraid. I am to be feared, I told myself.

Drawing on a fraying string of courage, I reminded the others, "Our role is to keep the soldiers going. We are not spectators; do not let the battle distract you from healing. If we become overwhelmed, prioritize fatal wounds first. You've all been assigned a district; don't go outside that district. We cannot afford to let any side of the castle weaken."

My gaze flitted from face to face, seeing terror, determination, anger. Brekk, one of the healers from Rove, stood over the rest in the back, remaining darkly calm. He nodded when our gazes met.

Seln asked, "Where will you be, miss?"

I lifted my head against the weight of the question. "I will focus on the king." For I knew his lumis unlike any other. Should Renn fall, I would be the swiftest in healing him. If Seln ever saw the golden threading in his lumis, I feared she'd make the connection between us she'd so far failed to piece together.

Fear cut through my gut, and I was glad Renn would not feel it too sharply. I'd rebuilt the basalt wall—Renn's idea, initially. He feared hurting me, and I feared distracting him. If Renn fell, all of Cansere would go with him. I'd merely be the first.

I continued, "If you're hurt, heal yourself first. You're not good to anyone slow, dead, or dying. You six"—I gestured to a group of healers standing together, including an elderly man named Hord and Sarra, from Rove—"will wait here. If any soldiers come on their own or bring injured, those will be your charges. Otherwise, you will need to replace the present shift when they grow too weary to continue."

Quiet nods.

I hated this next part, but it had to be said. "Officers take priority over the enlisted." Visions of my brothers passed behind my eyelids; I blinked them away. "Do you all have rations on your persons?" It was imperative we keep up our strength.

I took my time looking over our crew, ensuring a confirmation from every soul.

I clenched my hands into fists so they would not tremble.

"Prepare yourselves," I whispered.

And the wave crashed down.

I slipped in a puddle of blood.

My heel skidded out from beneath me, one knee dropping to the hard stone. The soldier in question had already bled out, an arrow to his eye. There was no saving him. His gore added to the dozens of other stains permanently etched into my dress.

Righting myself, I hurried past, keeping my head below the battlement, where another soldier writhed, holding the burned side of his face.

Nicosia's dragons breathed fire. They hurled it over the wall in delicate glass vials.

I grabbed the soldier's ear—his armor covered the rest of him—and dowsed. A simple pegboard for a lumis, thank goodness. It took little effort to return fallen pegs to their holes.

He ripped from my grasp the moment I finished, disorienting me; I could not blame him for it. He picked up his bow and shot into the fray below.

I took a few seconds, letting dizziness wash over me. I'd been at it for hours. Wisps of hair freed from my braid stuck to perspiration on my forehead and temples. A man cried out—one of ours, I was sure—farther down the wall, but Fil was down that way. He would tend him.

Turning, I peered through a sliver between merlons, spying two suns in the sky.

One dove into the army on wings of light.

The way he fought was mesmerizingly gruesome.

Renn moved as though his armor were made of feathers, swifter than any man on horseback, cutting through the sky like a ship through the sea. The way he unfurled his wings and charged into the fray, knocking down entire squads at a time before rising back up toward the heavens . . . he looked like the phoenix of Cansere. But instead of a beak and claws, he wielded an enormous glaive, bloodied blade reflecting the sky.

I heard a thump behind me and drew away from the wall, an archer filling in my space almost immediately. A man lay unconscious down a set of two steps. Checking his lumis proved quicker than checking a pulse.

His death lines were erratic, but he lived. The unbalanced scales of his lumis made me think of Lonnie, gods help her wherever she was now. Merciful, that it wasn't here.

I rebalanced them. In the present, he blinked, confused.

"Hurry back," I commanded, even with my tongue heavy in my mouth. I needed to head back to the infirmary. I would be a fool not to take my own advice. An hour of rest, and I could return.

Only for every hour I slept, Renn's risk increased that much more.

Crawling past a low part of the battlement, I hurried as best I could toward the keep. A limping soldier nearly knocked me over.

I recognized him at the same time I heard Death cackle in my ear. Our heads were higher than the battlement.

"Brien!" I cried, grabbing his elbow and hauling him down. An arrow soared over us just after I did so. I dowsed into his familiar lumis of grapevines, pressing magic into twisting stems that had wilted, healing a twisted knee. When I came to, I could barely keep my head up. My heart fluttered, overtaxed.

Brien grimaced. "Go back, Nym!"

I nodded. Or I tried to. "I am."

Cursing, he took me by the elbow and tugged me into the bailey. "Ursa is gone. Your strength won't be what it was."

As if I didn't know. I twisted from his grip. "I may not be able to run as fast, but I can still run." A headache pulsed behind my eyes. I clasped Brien's armored wrist. "Stay alive."

He nodded and hurried back onto the rampart.

I dragged myself to the infirmary.

"Sarra," I called. To my relief, that was all she needed. She secured an apron and headed out to the wall, taking my place.

I looked hard at Hord. "If I sleep more than two hours, wake me."

He looked like he might argue, but the man nodded.

And I slept.

Renn cleaved a horse and rider in two with a single strike.

I looked away reflexively, then back to ensure he hadn't been hurt. I could barely tell dragon from phoenix on the battlefield, but I could always spot Renn.

And so could everyone else.

I watched through a slit in the stone as an arrow embedded near his groin; I felt a dull bruise in my own leg, the pain partially blocked by the basalt wall. The foolish man didn't retreat to the castle, but flew out of sight, returning moments later with an enormous shield, plowing through his assailants like a wedge through snow. Then, pushing off corpses, he launched into the air and volleyed himself into the bailey.

I sprinted from my perch to his side, as did a few other soldiers. Limping, Renn waved them off.

"It's not that bad," he hissed.

I grabbed his sweat-soaked face and dowsed into his lumis, swallowed by light and rotating baubles of color. Lit up in all his godliness, his lumis was almost too painful to look at. Like falling into a sunset. I found the break in a large red globe and mended it, the glass giving way to me easily like it were a purring cat.

I knew the moment Renn yanked the arrow out, because the orb cracked again. I smoothed the breaks away, leaving only the residual scars from his breaking. The pain in my thigh abated.

There was no time for well-wishes or promises; as soon as I released him, Renn soared into the air again to carry Cansere on his back.

Another thing I had not expected in dealing with craftlock-edged war was the battle continuing in the darkness. With healers aiding soldiers, the men could come back, back, and back again, pushing their advantage, driving us to weariness.

If the dragons had not realized Cansere had crafters, they soon would.

Once night fell, Sesta sent its birds.

Men soulbound themselves to great birds to fly over our wall, just as they had in Rove. But Derren Castle had prepared itself. Volleys of arrows shot through the air, hitting bird and dragon alike.

And then Hawksend's battalion charged from the shadows.

Canseren soulbinders dove into the fray, linking enemy soldiers to one another, to horses, roots, or anything soul-filled to make them easier targets for swords and spears. Cavalry stormed in, riders soulbound to their steeds. Nicosia's men attacked on one front and defended on the other.

I was glad the darkness hid the violence, though even within the walls of the infirmary, I could hear it, and on the blood-slick walls, I healed it.

By the end of the night, I had to pull Sarra and Denwick from our small healers' brigade. Their hearts could not endure the war, and I feared their minds would break for it.

They came for the gate in the morning.

The portcullis was well fortified, its teeth sinking deep into the earth, with a heavy barbican gate behind it.

The dragons launched for it, heaving an enormous iron-tipped battering ram.

We could not allow Sesta to break through the castle walls. Even with Renn, we'd lose the battle if they did.

And so the brutality continued on the edges of the moat, Hawksend's men falling to northern swords while Stonelay's sent volleys into armor and shields. Heavy cauldrons of boiling water were upended onto those who got too close. I crawled the ramparts, trying to prioritize injuries, closing the eyes of those whom I couldn't reach in time.

I shivered with death. Its breath knit into my skin.

Yet the gods watched over us, for we had Renn.

When he slaughtered the men carrying the battering ram, when he gutted the warbirds, when he cut through bodies like a scythe through grass, I made myself watch.

I adhered to his wish. I kept the basalt wall up.

But I watched. I felt deeply I needed to witness what this nation cost us. I wanted to understand the agony of war. I refused to be ignorant of Renn's purpose, or his pain.

I still felt Serravia echoing through him.

After another forced rest, I discovered something that chilled me to my core.

The dragons had built bridges.

Makeshift things, temporary crossings for the castle's moat. They came from all sides, ready with hooks and ropes, with ladders—some long enough to form bridges on their own.

Commanders and generals bellowed orders to their men.

We could not allow them to breach the wall.

I healed a soldier with an arrow wedged between the plates of his shoulder and breast. As I returned to the carnage, a grappling hook swung up, nearly striking me in the head, and latched on to a crenel's stones.

Shrieking, I grabbed the metal teeth but could not pull it free. I desperately pushed my hands into my pockets until I found my mother's knife, then sawed at the rope until the weight of its climber overwhelmed the threads, and he fell.

I took an arrow to the side of my face in retribution. It streaked across my cheekbone, tearing scalp and ear.

I dropped, cradling the wound. The shock of it might have stalled me, but Nicosia had given me so much practice in healing amidst panic, I acted by rote. Worked my way into my lumis to my crenellated wall, mortaring up cracked and falling stones.

When I lifted my head back in reality, my hands slick with my own blood, I glimpsed between merlons something that made my weak heart stutter.

Dan.

Dan.

Had he worn a helmet, I wouldn't have recognized him. But mindreaders hadn't been assigned armor; they weren't supposed to be at the front, unless we'd grown more desperate than I'd believed. He hugged the castle wall, sidestepping the inner scarp of the moat, sword in hand. Coming toward a battle of phoenix and dragon on one of the larger temporary bridges.

I gasped when he leapt into the fray, barely armored, barely armed, barely trained.

"No!" I screamed from the wall, but the symphony of war swallowed up the cry. I clung to the merlons, putting up my forearm to protect my face should another archer target me, feverishly searching the clash for my brother—

A large dragon swung out, arcing his sword, Dan caught on the end of it. The blow had him sailing over the bridge and into the murky waters of the moat.

"NO!" I rushed to my feet. A nearby soldier grabbed my arm, trying to force me down, but I twisted from his reach. Narrowly missed another arrow in doing so.

The keening emptiness Ursa left behind groaned and stretched.

I would not lose more family.

I would not lose more family!

Before I knew my own mind, I'd leapt. Off the wall, down into the moat below.

The water slapped, shockingly warm. My knee touched a body, and I grabbed it, then recoiled as I recognized the corpse of a dragon.

Breaking the surface, I swallowed air and dove. *Ursa, help me!*

A headless phoenix pressed by me. I swam deeper. He'd fallen just—

There.

The lack of armor made him easier to find. The last bubbles of air escaped from his nostrils.

I seized Dan's hand and dowsed.

His lumis, a great clay sculpture resembling something of sea waves and stalagmites, was drowning, water rushing in from the space's ethereal walls. I could not work as swiftly without Ursa, but I'd healed Dan his whole life. I found the deep cut to his torso immediately and remolded the great clay spike exactly as it should be.

My lungs burned for air.

I blinked back into the depths of the moat. Kicked my legs, dragging us upright, breaking into sunlight—

Dowsed and forced water back, back—

Dan gasped, air flooding into him. Not from healing, but from an arrow.

Another wave of volleys fell. My physical hand pulled free an arrow from beneath Dan's clavicle as my sorcerous ones mended the skin, the bone having prevented it from burrowing too far—

We submerged. I forced myself wholly into the present and kicked. Dan grabbed my upper arm and pulled us back to the surface and toward the scarp; he'd always been the stronger swimmer.

An arrow struck so close to me, it lodged in my hair.

We'd drifted toward another makeshift bridge holding two dragons. One saw us and pulled his sword—

A great ball of light struck them from behind, sending them flying overhead and into the moat.

A new hand seized my arm, bruising down to the bone. My vision burned with light as Renn hauled both Dan and me out of the water and over the wall, dropping us into the bailey. He'd lost some of his armor; blood seeped from a shallow wound on his arm.

I reached for him to heal it, but his blazing blue-fire eyes met mine as he seethed, *"Do not,"* and took off into the air again.

War spared no time for pleasantries, even of the unkind variety.

I should not have diverted him from the attack, yet I could not regret diving in after Dan.

My brother lay supine in the bailey, breathing hard. I dowsed into him first, clearing away whispers of disease and infection from the foul moat water before doing the same for myself. I had to pull down part of the basalt wall to infuse my flickering heart-stones—

Renn overwhelmed me. Battle lust, worry, anger, sorrow. I pushed magic into my heart, whispering apologies, before resealing the wall, slipping from the lumis, and turning toward Dan.

I slapped him.

He touched his cheek but didn't recoil or gawk. Merely said, "I deserve that."

I ran to the infirmary, leaving him behind.

Brekk took my place, allowing me a moment to change.

The assault lasted four days.

We lost a number of men off our ramparts and in Hawksend's battalion, men who died too swiftly, or too far away, for me and my healers to reach. On the third day, Renn assaulted Sesta's rear echelon. If Adoel Nicosia was present, if he perished, we had no word. But Renn targeted the healers.

I understood the reason why. A siege could last forever with both sides regenerating their soldiers, but the dragons had far more healers than we did, and we could not leave the confines of the castle walls. We were at a disadvantage. And so the Sestan healers had to fall.

They were soldiers, too. I reminded myself of this when the news first wound its way to me. All crafters in Sesta were military trained. Still, I couldn't help but picture the face of the woman who had helped Eden and me escape and found myself hoping she was not among the dead. Even if she were, I'd keep my promise. I'd tell no one of her.

In the mess of Sesta's hasty retreat, I ached anew for Ursa. Wished for her reassurances in my thoughts, her words of comfort. Shaken, I wondered if I should seek out Eden, that we might reflect and mourn together, but however close the princess and I had become, we lacked the depth of relationship I'd shared with my sister, and I feared unburdening myself would burden her further. For however long my own road of healing, Eden's was just as long, if not longer.

I felt the basalt wall within my lumis like a physical thing I carried, and it had begun to chafe. I needed Renn. It felt so selfish, wanting him for comfort when the battle had barely settled, but I craved him like a woman starved.

Yet I could not find him.

The healers, including Sarra and Hord, worked endlessly to help residual casualties, many of which were soldiers who'd sustained non-life-threatening injuries, Brien among them. I stayed to heal bruises, rolled joints, and torn tendons. Did my part to bear the fatigue that came with use of the craft.

Still, I did not see Renn.

I passed through the bailey, searching for his head of golden hair, and found myself lost among soldiers and staff. I pulled Beatty aside and asked after the king, but she did not know. Sten had not seen him, nor had Dan. I asked a random officer, who shook his head. I might have feared him dead if I could not sense the simmering of his presence through our link.

After walking through the keep once and the bailey twice, I spotted Commander Stonelay and jogged to meet him.

"Have you seen His Majesty?" I asked, weary and out of breath.

He nodded to a passing soldier before his eyes fell upon me, softening in a paternal manner. "He is well, Miss Tallowax."

"But where is he?"

The commander let out a long breath and rubbed his eyes. He looked ready to fall asleep on his feet. "He often vanishes after a victory. It's . . . hard on him."

My heart beat harder against my ribs. I thought of that harrowing pain through our connection when I'd been imprisoned in Rodsfell, and again after Serravia. My bones seemed to hollow out of their own accord.

The basalt wall grew heavier. Ached deeply.

"Where is he?" I asked, softer.

Commander Stonelay hesitated. It was good of him to hesitate. To not offer up such personal information on his liege so easily. But Commander Stonelay had been on that ship. He'd seen Renn and I together. I imagined he'd also sorted out the eccentricities of our connection. And so, when it became clear I would only press again, he gave in. "I saw him fly south," he admitted, tipping his head in that direction. "Toward the woodland."

Swallowing hard, I nodded. "Thank you."

He offered the faintest smile before heading for the keep. Turning back, I retraced my steps, angling first toward the infirmary for a healer's satchel, then toward the kitchen. Multiple cookfires had started as Beatty desperately tried to get warm food into soldiers' bellies.

I found Sten and Brien near the cold smithy, chatting quietly. Their conversation was cut short when they saw me approach.

"I'm going to the south woodlands," I announced. "You can come with me or stay behind, I have no preference. But if you will insist on guarding me, as I'm sure you will, then guard me now, because I will not wait."

Brien opened his mouth as though he were about to protest, but Sten straightened and so easily slipped into my shadow that my brother took note. When I left the castle wall, which was surrounded by lounging soldiers and half-built tents, they followed.

I tried not to look at the bodies, still awaiting either burial or pyre.

Derren Castle occupied what I would best describe as a meadow; the woodland was farther out than I'd anticipated, but I walked swiftly, energized by purpose. I occasionally scanned our surroundings for signs of blue—a dragon lingering behind—but I saw none, and while my guards kept their hands on their sword hilts, neither ever drew.

Oak and beech trees, I noticed, sentineled green and bright with summer; we were nearly halfway into August already. Soon enough the leaves would turn and the air would cool, and I wondered how it would affect the war efforts. Strange to think not even a year had passed since Sesta first launched itself on Rove. It seemed an eternity ago.

The trees were not thick, and even with the basalt wall I sensed him and followed unmarked trails until, far ahead, I spied a silver gauntlet settled beside a tree root. Staying Brien and Sten with my hand, I continued onward by myself, crushing wild grass underfoot. A stream babbled to my right, and along it came other pieces of bloodied armor—another gauntlet, a helmet, a gorget—and finally him, crouched like a hawk at the edge of the stream, staring into the rippling water. In another time and place, I might not have recognized him for all the blood. It tinged his hair auburn, caked around his ears and neck. Marked the lines of his hands, which sat open in front of him.

Slipping my satchel from my shoulders, I crouched beside him. He still wore his cuirass; I gently unhooked its buckles, one at a time. It was surprisingly heavy; I had to stand to tug it free from him.

Even beneath the breastplate, blood soaked his clothes.

Grateful for the stream, I unpacked my satchel. Grabbed one of many rags and dipped it in the shaded water. Wrung it out and started at his forehead, wiping red grime from his brow.

"I can't stop," he whispered, eyes still locked on the water. "I can never stop. I'm the reason we win." He coughed, hard, the rattle in his chest shooting alarm through my heart. Grimacing, he swallowed.

I pressed my lips together to withhold rising emotion, cleaned his temples and the bridge of his nose, his lips. "I know," I answered, and rewet the cloth. Returning to him, I got the blood off one ear and the surrounding skin and hair. It completely soiled the cloth.

Renn's eyes shifted to it, and even through the wall, I felt a pulse of anguish.

"Close your eyes," I said. "You don't have to see it."

He set his jaw. "I can bear it, Nym."

Kneeling in front of him, I clasped one of his red-inked hands in my own. "But you don't have to. Not alone."

He swallowed, his throat's apple bobbing. Clenched his teeth. After a few seconds of steeling himself, he said, "You don't—"

"Just let me love you," I whispered, repeating words he'd once given me. I rinsed out the cloth and returned. His eyes shimmered like the sunlit sea.

Then he closed them, and I continued my administrations. They felt so personal, so reverent, I couldn't bring myself to be offended by the gore. With every swipe of the cloth, I found a little more of myself. *Healer.* It was what I wanted: a healer in all things, physical and elsewise. However special I was, or wasn't, didn't matter. I would heal him again and again. And in doing so, I would heal myself.

I cleaned his neck, his hands, then clasped the hem of his shirt and pulled it off him, setting it aside. Pointless to scrub it, I thought, but he'd need it for his return to the castle. I washed his hair and his feet, until gooseflesh from the chill rose on his skin. Until I couldn't see any more blood to remove.

Then, sitting beside him, linking his fingers with my own, I tore down the basalt wall.

I held my breath, my best show of stoicism, as the emotions overwhelmed me. As though I'd been buried in a shallow grave and the entire Sestan army marched over. The heaviness of agony, the sharpness of melancholy, the drowning of despair and regret. They flowed into me, coursing over each other and knotting in their misery. My throat thickened and eyes watered, but I leaned into him, sharing in it.

He was not alone.

And neither are you, came the memory of Ursa's voice, and new tears traced down my cheeks, falling onto his shoulders.

Squeezing his hand, I focused on the warmth beneath the waves, on the softness of trust and the glow of love, the cool rain of relief. And, gradually, as the sun purpled the sky, I found their echoes through the torrent. I held on to them, holding them in my hands as though they existed in a lumis, and I felt him holding them, too, a cluster of light at the end of a long and dark tunnel.

Twilight fell, and Renn murmured, "Thank you."

And when stars pocked the sky, the four of us walked back to Derren Castle.

Chapter 23

My dream-stupored mind only distantly recognized the sound of someone knocking on the door.

Renn's stretching roused me; my head was perched quite comfortably on his chest. I couldn't tell if the disquiet and curiosity flitting behind my skull was mine or his. Perhaps both. Dawn light licked the window ledges. In protest of the interruption, I dug my nose into his collarbone.

"That's something I still haven't gotten used to," he grumbled, voice low with sleep.

I hummed into his shirt.

"Answering my own door."

A flicker of humor through the bond.

The knock sounded again, strong and persistent. Groaning deep in his chest, Renn kissed my hair before sitting up. I curled into the warmth he left behind as he pulled a pair of slacks over his drawers, and almost immediately delicate twists of sorrow and despair flooded into me as the king remembered what had transpired the last four days.

I let them flow through me, trying to accept them as one might a cool breeze.

Renn opened the door. I sat up and smoothed my hair down, glimpsing first General Cuplend, and then, to my surprise, Dan. The general's gaze locked on to Renn, but my brother's passed directly to me.

I was almost too groggy to be embarrassed, but I couldn't help the chagrin. Perhaps because he sensed it, Renn closed the door against him, limiting visibility into the room. Still, Dan had spied me, yet I saw no shock or judgment in his features. I wondered if Brien had already spoken to him of the situation, or if he merely wasn't surprised because he'd read my mind previously . . . which made me wonder exactly how much he'd seen each time.

I stayed where I was, not wanting to draw attention to myself. We had done nothing but sleep, and I had nothing to be ashamed of, other than being seen in only my shift. I could just pick up what the general was saying: "—good insight into what's to come."

Renn turned to Dan. "Is that why I had to fish you out of the moat?"

My interest was piqued, and I slid to the edge of the bed to better hear.

Dan nodded, incredibly sober. "I read it from one of the men trying to scale the wall, Your Majesty. A directive from his commanding officer before they marched. This was only the first assault; King Nicosia has two more to follow if the first didn't wipe us out, which it didn't. He sounded doubtful—the soldier I touched, I mean. Like he thought this would be an easier claim than it was."

My lips parted. *That* was why Dan snuck outside the walls? To read the dragons' minds?

Anger bristled in my core. *Stupid boy!* Surely there were more mindreaders employed elsewhere in the field to do what he'd nearly died doing.

And yet, if his information weren't unique, the general wouldn't have taken such an interest in him. Woken his weary king early to pass the message on.

But the coils of misery spreading from Renn had died down as concern took over. "Do we know when to expect the next army?"

Dan shook his head. "I'm afraid I couldn't get that far, Your Majesty."

Renn nodded. "Thank you." Then, to General Cuplend, "Can you have the officers together in half an hour?"

"Yes, Sire."

"Do it." And Renn closed the door.

I curled my legs beneath me. "It's not over, then."

Renn grabbed a fistful of hair. "It's never over." He steeled himself with a breath. "I have some ideas. Mind if I run them by you?"

I blinked. "I'm not a strategist, Renn."

"Still."

I nodded. "Please. I'll advise you the best that I can."

I thought it was genius.

So, too, did General Cuplend.

Others—Renn did not say who—were less enthusiastic, but surely Sesta would attack again soon, before we could fully refortify ourselves, so a decision had to be made quickly.

We would lose Derren Castle for something better.

The idea took me back to my conversation with Renn when the Antsan delegation arrived, how I'd believed we would have to give up the good thing we had now for something better in the future. And so we would make Derren Castle as appetizing as possible. Make it seem bristling with soldiers and citizens, housing the gods-touched king. We would draw Nicosia's army to the north, while we marched south.

To retake Rove.

A skeleton company would be left to man the battlements. Tents would be erected around the walls to boast of a larger army. The company would regularly light cookfires. We would take uniforms from the fallen and stuff them with whatever we could find—grasses, leaves, potato skins—to station dummies on towers.

In two days' time, we made Derren Castle look well and truly occupied.

Then we packed up everything we could carry and marched south, leaving Whitestone to be discovered by his countrymen.

The method of the march fascinated me.

The army broke up into six parts, which also divided up the crafters, leaving me and Seln the only healers to reside with Renn, Commander Stonelay, and our company. Each part took a different route toward Rove, which lay an astounding 230 miles away—not quite the distance from Fount to Rove, but we would not be able to shorten the journey by ship. One company went by way of the main road; another set out east before venturing southwest, adding time to their journey. Their march would be the hardest, as it would need to be the swiftest. Renn's company crossed through the woodland—our designated path, as seen on a map, mimicked a staircase. Once we were well away from Derren Castle, the tracks of "retreat" masked, we, too, would use the roads.

Multiple messengers had been sent to the east coast, toward Antsan, some on horseback, two soulbound to captured warbirds—the feathered animals' only loyalty was to whoever fed them, apparently. If our ally's armies and vessels were as prepared as Arquan had claimed, then we would be able to fall on Rove before Nicosia could get reinforcements there.

The marching was hard, but I found myself appreciating it. Physical exertion felt better than being stagnant.

Brien had been sent with the fourth company, with General Cuplend. Dan, however, was the first company's mindreader. On the third day, when we could talk and travel a bit more freely, I sought him out and walked beside him.

"I would ask you not to do anything so reckless again in the future," I said by way of hello. I had not spoken to Dan since he reported his gleaned information to Renn. Renn who, while appearing to lead the company with ease, still fought against the crush of the bloody assault.

Dan scoffed. "It's war, Nym. Recklessness is assumed."

"Is assumed?" I repeated. Laughed. "Gods, you sound like Father."

He glanced over at me, brown eyes searching. "Do I really?"

I nodded. Stepped away from him to let a sapling pass between us. We'd exited the woodlands, but copses of trees littered the entire expanse ahead of us. I thought I spied a few pale trunks—aspens. I did love the beauty of an aspen forest.

"He had a matter-of-fact, passive way of talking when he jested."

We walked a few paces in silence. "I think I remember that." Dan had only been seven when our father passed away, in the same incident that had taken our mother's and Ursa's lives and nearly my own.

"But," I retorted, "I think you're misled. War is a time for careful planning and strategy. The chances of failure are too high otherwise."

"Perhaps," he countered.

I rolled my eyes. "Perhaps you should admit I am right."

"You always think you're right."

"Because I always am."

He shoved me lightly, only enough for one step to falter. "I'm a soldier now, Nym. Best you treat me like one."

"You're still a boy."

"Hardly."

"Barely." I pulled at the hems of my sleeves. "I will accept 'barely.'"

Commander Stonelay rode by on his mount, checking over the marching company before trotting ahead. I imagined Renn would use the high sun to scout on wing, but perhaps we were still too close to Derren Castle for it to be safe. Through the link, he seemed . . . focused. Determined. Hopeful.

"I see you made your choice," my brother said softly.

"Hm?"

He adjusted the pack on his back so it rode a little higher. "With His Majesty."

My cheeks warmed. "It isn't what it seems—"

"I don't care, Nym." He reached for my hand, and before I could remember his craft, I took it. He held it for only a few seconds before releasing me. He frowned.

I focused my eyes straight ahead. "I'm not sure what you can see, Dan, but—"

"I see that you're happy, with him," he answered. "Don't worry, I didn't dig."

"Thank you." I kneaded my hands together. Stepped over a tree root. "Brien was not pleased with me."

"With the king?"

"With *me* and the king."

Dan snorted. "He's one to talk."

The remark pricked my curiosity. "What do you mean?"

He side-eyed me in a very serpentine manner. "I am a man of many secrets."

"Barely," I emphasized. "As your eldest sister, I demand recompense for such a remark."

Dan merely shrugged. But after another few paces, he added, "Watch his face the next time he's around the princess."

We took a country road that traced the edge of a beautiful aspen forest and came upon a sizable village, about twice the size of Fount, on the seventh day of our march. It was a sight to behold after a week of endless walking and camping on hard ground. Commander Stonelay and a handful of soldiers rode ahead; by order of the king, accommodations would be made for the soldiers. The village, called Trest, lay about forty miles north of the Canseren Sea and roughly a hundred miles from Rove. Had the entire Derren army come, the houses would not have been enough to host us. But in this company, everyone managed to find space, even if it was in a barn.

Dan and I separated. Unable to locate Renn, I ended up walking through town with Seln, deciding instead to offer our services to better compensate the unexpecting villagers. We healed a few colds, a broken foot, and an earache before I noticed Renn crossing the small town square, wearing a military uniform and nothing else that might denote his rank. Still, I spied an older woman who appeared to recognize him and bowed from far off.

Renn was headed toward me. Nervous excitement spun from our link.

"Go on without me. I'll try to catch up," I told Seln, who nodded and hurried on her way, weaving between wandering soldiers and villagers. When Renn approached, he grasped my hand. "I've found a place for us."

He guided me across the square, heading northwest.

"Are you so eager to sleep on an actual bed, or is it something else?" I asked. The sun had passed its zenith; it would be the dinner hour soon. "Or perhaps a meal not half burned over a cookfire."

He smiled. "Something far better, if you're still up for it."

I watched him, a dimple in his cheek as we took stone stairs up a short hill and wound past a modest barn and gazebo shrine to a simple house brimming with carefully cultivated flowers. They lined the path and filled boxes hanging from windows, shutters pinned open. An older man and woman stood waiting for us, thin and darker-skinned, she with a thick mane of silver hair, he with a half-bald pate and a multicolored cincture braided around his waist.

My step slowed. "A priest."

Renn paused. Shifted to look at me, face-to-face. "We agreed that if I found a priest . . ."

My heart grew light and rapid in my chest. *That we would get married.* The words danced across my tongue.

This . . . Was this really happening? Was he sincere? But of course he was—I could feel it between us. Hope, sincerity, affection.

"You're nervous," he whispered, uncaring that the couple had their eyes on us.

I swallowed. "Of course I'm nervous. I . . ."

I didn't need to explain again my terrible deficiencies regarding matrimony.

His gloved fingertips caressed the side of my face. "We don't have to do it now. Nym . . . you deserve a real wedding, a proper affair. A dinner and a honeymoon. After we take Rove—"

"Tonight, then?" The words came out breathy. Hope blossomed in my center, and I focused on it, trying to ignore old fears. Trying not to imagine a life where history repeated itself and Renn never bound his hand with mine.

The corner of his lips ticked up. I couldn't help but reciprocate the bright joy pouring from him. Still clasping my hand, he brought me up to meet the priest and his wife.

"Mr. and Mrs. Swiftmore," he explained, gesturing to them in turn. "They've agreed to house us and perform the—"

"Wait." I squeezed Renn's hand. "Swiftmore? Are you—?"

A clamoring of falling firewood sounded from the side of the house. The young woman carrying it went wide eyed and wide mouthed at the sight of us.

Tears filled my vision. "Lonnie?"

"Nym Tallowax!" She shrieked and bolted toward me, completely heedless of her king standing there. She threw her arms around me and squeezed until I couldn't breathe. I squeezed her back.

"You're alive!" I cried.

"You're alive," she sobbed in return.

I knew Renn washed up with freezing cold water, because even while submerged in a tub of warm, my skin pebbled.

The nerves wrapping songs around my heart came from both of us.

"I never would have guessed." Lonnie plunked down on her narrow bed in her narrow room, evening colors of mauve and salmon dancing across her latticework window. "I mean, I suppose you *did* spend a lot of time with him—"

I scrubbed dirt out from beneath my nails, half-soaked curls of hair floating on top of the water. "Believe me, it had not been my intention." Sitting up, I looked at her, past the half-finished plate of dinner her mother had so kindly brought me. Half a plate was all my nerve-riddled stomach could handle. "Do you think it's . . . odd?"

"Odd?"

I lowered my eyes. "Me being what I am, he being what he is."

"I think it's wonderful." She laughed, picked herself off the mattress, and came to kneel by the bathtub, reminding me of the late nights we used to spend washing and talking at Rove Castle. "I think everything is changing, Nym. First the edict legalizing craftlock, now one of the people on the throne."

Throne. I sank into the water and stared through the ceiling. "I . . . try not to think too hard on that part."

"It's the same as managing a house full of children. The house is just a lot bigger, and there are a lot more children." She grinned. "And now my father will marry you! It's a fairy tale, really."

"In a time of war," I whispered.

"Even better," she countered. "Heaven forbid we have something to celebrate."

She moved to stand, but I reached out of the tub and grasped her hand, my index finger brushing the violet braided bracelet on her wrist. "You haven't told me about you, yet. I saw you in the castle . . . How did you escape?"

She lowered herself back down, somberness schooling her features. "I remember you, Nym. I know what you did for me."

I withdrew my hand, chest tightening.

"After you healed me, I hid. They were everywhere. *Everywhere.*" She shuddered. "I hid with the linens. Buried myself under them.

Almost three days I just lay there, listening for them. I knew I'd die of thirst if I didn't move. I thought, *I'll sneak down the hallway to somewhere with water. Surely one of the bedrooms still has water in it.* But when I snuck out, the way to the servants' stairs was clear, so I ran for it." She chewed on the inside of her lip, remembering. "There were a few dragons around. I swear one saw me, but they didn't seem interested in me. They were looking for someone. His Majesty, I assume. I ran and met up with another refugee family and traveled with them to Trest. Or near enough. I covered the rest on my own. I've been here ever since."

Flashes of the attack on Rove wriggled into my mind. "It was a terrifying night," I relented.

"It was. And you? You left with the king?"

My skin pebbled again, this time with the memory of Speth, of crouching in the snow before Adoel Nicosia seized me by the hair and dragged me to Sesta, stealing away five months of my life. The hollowness Ursa left behind yawned. "I caught up with him," I answered truthfully. "I've marched with him."

"Healed him, too. I didn't think it was possible." Reaching behind the tub, she grabbed a jar of soap for my hair. "Like I said, a fairy tale."

Memories of Vin and Ford, the past men in my life, shivered down my neck. "I hope so."

Lonnie helped me wash. When she revealed a small vial of hair oil, I tried to stop her. "You'll use up the entire thing on this mane. Save it."

But she had none of it. "Consider it a wedding gift."

I dried off, pulled on a clean shift, and together Lonnie and I carefully worked the oil through my mountain of curls, twisting each one, carefully splaying them to dry. She dabbed some rosewater on my neck and décolleté, then stole away to another room, coming back with an armful of bluish-silver satin.

Walking over, beaming, she held the dress up in front of her. "Would you wear this? I know you haven't been able to plan much for tonight."

Standing, I ran my hand over the gown. It was an unassuming affair, something likely to be mocked at a palace function, but for a common woman it was elegant, simply cut and sewn, with a crimped waist panel, wide neck, and billowing sleeves gathered at the wrists.

"This is lovely," I murmured. "Did you make this?"

"It was my sister-in-law's." She smiled again, but sadness dipped her brow. "She married my brother in it but died in childbirth less than a year later."

I whipped my hand back like I'd been burned. "Lonnie, you never told me. I'm so sorry."

She quirked an eyebrow. "Just like you never told me about His Majesty?"

The responding flush started in my chest and licked heat up the sides of my neck.

Yet she forgave me instantly. "Try it on. I think it will fit."

"But, Lonnie, your sister—"

"Truly, Nym." Dropping the gown over one arm, she embraced me with the other. "My mother and I both would be so honored for you to wear it. I can't think of a more deserving soul."

Blinking tears from my eyes, I nodded, and Lonnie helped me step into it. It was the finest thing I'd worn since Rove fell. Lonnie did up the laces in the back; it fit well enough, though hugged me a bit too tightly in the bust.

I touched my chest as Lonnie surveyed her work. "I don't think there's enough seam allowance to let it out."

She snorted. "I think it looks better that way." She grabbed the top of the waist panel and tugged it down. "A pleasant emphasis."

I couldn't help but laugh. "I suppose it is." As I adjusted the fabric as well as I could, a sudden horror struck me, so much so that Renn's echoing concern pushed through the link. "Lonnie, I don't have a pendant for him." The necklaces were given during the marriage ceremony, measured and clipped so the pendant hung right over the heart.

"That's fine," she assured me. "My father's a priest, remember? He has a few."

I wrung my fingers together. "The pendant is supposed to be meaningful." Vin's I'd made out of an ivory key of his grandmother's broken piano. Ford's had been rose quartz I'd found shortly after Ursa died, cut and polished until it shined. I'd sold both years ago.

"It will be meaningful." She retwisted one of my curls. "It will be coming from you."

I slouched, feeling at a loss. "I suppose. But Renn . . . he is the love of my life. For me to give him something not—"

My eyes passed over my travel bag, and my heart surged.

"Nym?" she asked.

I hurried to my bag, kneeling and dumping its contents onto the floor. Clattering out last was my mother's knife, its four-inch blade set in a damask handle, embedded with a round citrine.

I ran my thumb over the stone as I stood.

Lonnie peered over my shoulder. "That's lovely."

I nodded. "Do you think we could refit this?"

"Let me ask my mother . . ." She held out her hands, and I gently laid the knife across her palms. ". . . But I definitely think we can."

Night had long fallen by the time Lonnie guided me into her modest front room, where a shrine to the gods—featuring Hem—had been set up on the mantel. Renn, dressed in a clean and pressed military uniform, a cincture of white low on his hips, spoke softly to the priest, and turned when I arrived.

Adoration overwhelmed our bond and made my eyes water. I smiled, even as I masked a tremble in my hands. Even as I feared that, at any moment, something would go awry. The dragons would find us, or Renn would realize the political disadvantages tying himself to me would create.

He clasped both my hands in front of the shrine.

Already it was farther than any man had ever taken me.

Mr. Swiftmore began singing the song of matrimony, a lilting tune that came from deep in his throat. Using a cincture of all colors similar to the one he wore, he bound our hands together, starting at Renn's elbow and ending at mine. Then, placing one hand on my forearm, his other on Renn's, the priest spoke the ritual words.

"By Hem, I deem this union just. By Salm, I bless you to be nurtured. By Rolys, I gift you light and joy. By Evat, I wish you wealth and surplus. By Alm, I give you health. By Zia, I grant you children. By Hem, I seal these promises."

I blinked away a tear, my gaze never leaving Renn's face. His never left mine. Heat pinged between the two of us, back and forth. If I looked down, I was sure I'd see a flying ember.

Mr. Swiftmore unwrapped our hands. Took the cincture and laid it over his neck. Nodded to Renn.

Releasing me, Renn pulled a long chain from his pocket, gold, the links nearly microscopic, with a circular gold disk at its end. Set into the disk was the largest pearl I'd ever seen. White, but in the candlelight it shined opalescent.

My lips parted. I knew a humble village priest did not keep necklaces like this in storage. "Where did you get that?" I whispered.

He pressed his lips against a smile, stepped closer to me, and set the pearl beneath my collar. "I commissioned it when you were in Sesta," he murmured.

I blinked back new tears. Even then, without any promise we'd ever see each other again . . . he'd wanted this?

The priest took the ends of the necklace; Renn pressed the pendant over my heart so that Lonnie's father could cut the chain at the appropriate length. I found myself mesmerized by Renn, lost in the sapphire of his eyes.

The clasp set. Renn stepped back, and my wedding pendant hovered exactly where it ought to. Right where the agate necklace he'd gifted me once lay. As if the gods had known, even then.

Throat thick with emotion, I turned to Lonnie, who approached with a folded cloth in her hands. Pulling the soft cotton aside, I retrieved the necklace hastily constructed. It had only a pewter chain—it was the finest option available to me—but my mother's citrine stone, a rich honey color with the faintest glimmer of chartreuse, had been set into a large square mount. Perhaps not a necklace for a king, but certainly one to make my own father proud.

Renn recognized it immediately. "Your mother's." Astonishment pinched his forehead and glided across our link.

I met his eyes, warmth blooming from my stomach down to my toes at the marvel I saw there. "She would have wanted you to have it. *I* want you to have it."

He nodded nearly imperceptibly. As he had, I closed the space between us and draped the pendant before giving the ends to the priest. Pressed the citrine stone over Renn's heart. I felt his pulse beneath it, heart hammering as hard as mine did.

The pendant set, I stepped back, and Mr. Swiftmore took up our other hands, binding them as he had the first, repeating the vows under each god's name, starting and ending with Hem.

No cries went out through the village.

No arrows flew through the window.

No messengers arrived to bellow a threat.

No storm raged, no monster struck, and no doubt filled our linked hearts.

The priest stepped back, the cincture still binding my hand to Renn's. I gazed at him, wondrous, sure this was a dream—

Clearing his throat, Lonnie's father said, "You seal it with a kiss, here."

Renn laughed. I cried. Tugging me to him, Renn pressed his lips to mine, sealing the priest's administrations.

Marrying us.

Renn. My husband.

When he pulled back, I embraced him, a hug made awkward by our still-joined hands. Lonnie and her mother chuckled; Mr. Swiftmore graciously unbound us. Mrs. Swiftmore handed us each a flower and kissed my cheek.

"A blessing on this household." She spoke through falling tears. "I am so grateful to you. To the both of you."

"And we to you," Renn replied. "Truly."

"You will take our room," she continued. "We've gotten it ready for you."

I started. "We couldn't possibly put you out—"

"I'll share with my daughter, and there's an extra bedroom for this old fool." She weakly gestured to her husband. "I insist."

"But—"

Pulling me close, Renn pressed his mouth to my hair near my ear. "It would be rude not to accept, Nym Noblewight."

The name dropped my organs into my shoes. *Noblewight.*

Gods above, I was a Noblewight.

We spent another quarter hour in thank-yous, accepting a toast of mead to our union, before retiring to the largest room of the house, which was about the same size as my parents' room in Fount. The one I'd shared, until a little over a year ago, with Lissel. It was modestly decorated, with a bed just wide enough for two, a wreath of juniper branches on the wall, a simple table with a single drawer, upon which rested a clay pitcher of water, two lit candles, and a well-worn copy of scriptures. A woven maroon rug covered the center of the wooden floor.

It felt . . . strange . . . being ushered into this unknown place as husband and wife. Expectant. Awkwardness dripped down the bond.

Renn rubbed the back of his head. "I admit I didn't plan this far in advance."

I played with the sleeves of my dress. "We march tomorrow, yes?"

He nodded, solemn. "We have to stay ahead of them."

Through the wall, I heard the Swiftmores in conversation. Not clearly enough to make out their words, just their voices. They sounded jovial.

I barked a laugh. "Goodness, they'll hear everything, won't they?"

Chagrin down the link. The lightest dusting of pink crossed Renn's nose as he chuckled.

The gods-touched king of Cansere and heir to Sesta, bashful over a consummation jest. I ignored the way my heart started pounding, blood running quick enough to make me lightheaded. My skin felt too tight. I told myself it was the dress and recognized the lie straightaway.

An idea came to mind, and the more I turned it over, the better I liked it.

"We don't—" Renn began.

Ignoring him, I grabbed the neatly made blanket off the top of the bed and pulled it free.

Confusion tickled the bond. "What are you doing?"

"Fold this." I chucked the blanket at him. He hesitated, then obeyed as I stripped off the next blanket, a scratchier gray wool, and rolled it up. Then, going to my bag, I retrieved one of the simple dresses I'd been given after my return to Cansere, set it on the mattress, moved my hair aside, and presented my back to Renn. "Would you untie these?"

He did so without comment, but that perpetual link whispered something heady. Something that warmed the pit of my stomach.

I swallowed. "I'm not going to tear Lonnie's sister's dress." With the laces loose, I carefully tugged it off. Renn had seen me in my shift dozens of times, and yet now it felt different. His gaze was a physical thing, forming prickles against my skin.

I pulled my simple dress over my head, buttoning it in the front, then went to the window.

I felt Renn's amusement before I turned to see his half smile. "You are a creature, Nym."

I sat on the sill and swung my legs over. "Bring the blankets."

I winked, then dropped down, wild grass and a few flowers breaking my fall. I winced at the latter and hoped Mrs. Swiftmore would forgive me.

Two blankets under one arm, Renn followed after me, his landing graceful as a cat's. Yet he paused a moment, appearing dizzy. I supported his elbow, but the vertigo passed quickly. So instead, I took his hand.

"Our last walk through aspen woods was cut short," I whispered.

"Happy to make it up to you," he replied.

A grin splitting my face, I pulled him away from the house, away from the village, to where the beautiful, white-barked trees grew thickest, ensuring I didn't follow any previously cut trails. Deeper and deeper into the wood, away from roads and people, until I found a quaint little grove dotted with mushrooms and ringed with green-crowned trees, the moonlight overhead half hidden by lazy clouds.

I took it in, inhaling sweet-scented air, absently touching the pearl of my wedding pendant. I turned back to Renn, the moonlight making his hair white, his eyes pale. Closing the space between us, I stood on my toes and kissed him.

The press of his lips flared that deep warmth within me, eviscerating all my hesitations. Peasant and noble, unmarried, too broken . . . all of them ceased to exist. I wore his pendant over my breastbone, mine over his, our lumie and hearts fitted together like pieces of some divine puzzle. It was bliss. It was light. It was fire.

Dropping the blankets, Renn's hands came firmly around my waist, pulling me tightly against him. He nipped my lips apart and ravished my mouth, tugging, sucking, caressing. I melted into him until his strength held me up more than my own did. My heat mirrored his, stoked like a bellows had been set to it. Heat that surged lower, brighter.

I grabbed fistfuls of his uniform's shirt and untucked it from his slacks.

He hummed against my lips before dipping down, winding an arm under my backside and lifting me like I weighed nothing at all. His skin began to glow as he carried me closer to a tree.

"You can't do that," I whispered, pressing my lips just under his ear. "You'll get us caught."

"No one is out here," he protested.

"Stop glowing."

He did, sucking the light in, but the moment he pinned me against an aspen and began placing hungry kisses down the column of my neck, he lit up again.

I laughed. *"Renn."*

He growled and put me down, then stepped back and snatched one of the blankets off the ground. Unfurled it and threw it over a low branch, forming a makeshift tent. Grabbed the other one and unrolled it at our feet—

But I was on him like a wolf to prey, frenzied by freedom, by delight, by passion. I kissed his mouth and his clavicle. Deftly unhooked the closures of his shirt. He tugged it over his head before kissing me again, his hands tracing up and down my back, then lower to my hips, fingers digging in. Glowing again, but the blanket masked it.

The burning made me dizzy, the way it bounced back and forth through that golden thread, the invisible link. Back and forth, back and forth. The want felt illegal, like a drug.

He cradled my face, his kisses growing softer. One knuckle glided down my throat, my clavicle, my breast. Seeking permission.

I unbuttoned the bodice myself and yanked off the dress. Pushed against him until his knee buckled. He went down with a laugh, the half-folded blanket breaking his fall. The angle of the moon sent a band of light into our improvised tent, falling between us.

Reaching up, he trailed his fingers up my jaw, into my hair. "You are beautiful. Every part of you is beautiful."

I bent down and chastely kissed his mouth. "You are everything," I countered.

We looked at each other a long moment, much as we had during the ceremony. Studying each other: nose, cheekbones, brow. I fell into his eyes over and over, absorbed by their endlessness. Our hearts seemed to pulse as one throbbing entity.

Slowly, deliberately, we removed the rest of our clothes. There was a reverence to it, a deference. Passion became worship as I traced the lines of his chest and stomach, his hips and thighs. As he savored every inch of me, whispering again, "Beautiful."

He kissed my shoulders, my neck, my mouth, and turned me under him. Yet however perfect this moment was, however free and aching I'd become, my body did not forget its past hurts. Through the heat and the desire, a cool tremor shivered—memory of another's hands on me. Violent hands. Hateful hands.

Renn felt it, too. Immediately, he stopped. Began to pull away.

"Wait," I murmured, grasping his shoulder, keeping his body against mine. I closed my eyes. Breathed through it. Let the warmth of him spread over and through me until, one by one, tight muscles relaxed, nerves settled, and the chill dissipated.

When I opened my eyes, he hovered a breath away, watching me. In a voice as soft as goose down, he whispered, "I don't want to hurt you, Nym."

A single tear pooled in the corner of my eye. "You're not hurting me. You're healing me."

Radiance, through the bond. Radiance lighting his body over mine.

As he kissed my forehead, his glow flickered. "You've only half a heart because of me."

I pressed my lips to his jaw. "You have all of it, Renn. Now and forever."

Lowering his head beside mine, he held me tightly. If my own skin could glow, I knew it would. And maybe it did. Maybe it wasn't moon- and starlight falling across us, but a new magic igniting beneath my skin. A new, wondrous form of craftlock I'd always believed to be just out of reach.

But now I held it in my arms, and *forever* did not seem enough.

The revelations, naked honesty, and tenderness could not keep that carnal heat at bay long. I craved him like a bee does the first spring flower. That fervency roiled between us, bare and unfiltered. His touch became magnetic, searing through flesh and bone, and I demanded all of him, sure I would burst for the want of him. He gave in readily.

Desire and love filled the bond, but so did pleasure, so that mine was his and his was mine. I wept for the perfection of it all. He breathed *I love you* into my ear, and I felt it down to my very soul. I erupted in his hands, completely undone, yet wholly remade.

Sickness, war, death, and crowns . . . everything that tied Renn Reshua Noblewight to this world, I would take just to keep him.

And I would keep him, always.

Chapter 24

I was not so adventurous as to choose sleeping on the ground over a generously gifted bed, so when dawn cracked and the company mobilized for its ongoing march, I groggily stirred within the Swiftmore home. Not for the light or the noise, but because Renn's hand traced long ovals on my thigh.

"I hate to wake you," he whispered, "but I can't have the men losing time because I vowed to be a lovesick servant."

I turned to face him. "Lovesick servant?"

"Wen Straymoth. Opal-age poet. *And oft my soul settles o'er her grave, for I vowed to be a lovesick servant.*"

I stretched, my body protesting its lack of sleep. "Straymoth, of course. How could I forget?"

His glee—and lustier sensations—trickled through the bond. I was pure contentment; a perfect day would be staying right here from sunup to sundown. I curled into him, breathing in his scent of honeysuckle and pinewood, mixed with the cool green of a woodland night. He surrounded me in a circle of warmth. Kissing the underside of his jaw, I slid my thumb just beneath the waistband of his breeches.

He groaned, "Don't tempt me," rolled over, and pinned me to the mattress. Kissed me chastely and sighed. "If only."

I smiled at him. "I request you retake your home swiftly so we might amend our present schedule."

He chuckled. "As swiftly as I can, I promise."

Regret limned our link.

Wiggling free from his grip, I cupped his face in my hands. "We have all our lives ahead of us."

He nodded, a flash of sadness crossing his features. He was completely unmasked. "Gods make it so."

Propping myself up on my elbows, I kissed him. "I love you, Renn."

"You are my always, Nym."

He kissed me one last time and rose, true to his duty. However much I wished to sleep away the morning and practice the art of the marriage bed, I, too, didn't want to delay the others. I'd reserve that selfishness for another time.

I dug a comb from my bag and tugged it through my curls, further roughing up Lonnie's careful administrations to them the night before, then tamed the bramble with a tight plait. Renn distracted me with his mouth when I attempted to get dressed, but duty called, and regretfully he pulled away and went to be the leader the gods had forced him to become. I washed my face and brushed my teeth, then slipped outside to the privy. The bane of being a woman—I could not simply relieve myself in the trees as a number of soldiers were doing that morning.

I started back for the house, still unfamiliar with the weight of the pendant between my breasts. I freed it, tilting the pearl in the growing light, watching it play off its smooth surface. Feeling . . . full. Content. Wanted.

Lonnie came from the house, a small linen satchel in her hands. I slipped the pendant beneath my bodice and smiled at her.

She presented the satchel. "Breakfast for the road. I was hoping we could eat together, but that doesn't seem a possibility today."

I accepted the gift. "Thank you. For everything. I'll send for you, if you're willing. If we end this war. If we win back Rove and settle there again. I'll send for you."

"Please do." She kissed my cheek. "Take care of yourself, Nym. And take care of His Majesty."

I cherished the advice and the farewell, and carried them with me to the main road, which wrapped around Trest rather than cut through it. About two-thirds of the company appeared ready to march, with Commander Stonelay atop a white steed at the front. Renn's black was saddled and ready, but he wasn't there.

My *husband's* black.

Pleasant nerves bubbled through my middle as I scanned for him. Not finding him, I searched for my brother—

A hand to the dip of my waist startled me. I glanced back to see Renn.

I noticed his nerves now. "Because we're closing in on Rove, or because of something else?" I asked.

He sighed as we walked toward the line. "I don't even know, Nym. I've stopped trying to understand it."

Just before we'd need to part so he could head toward the front of the column, he bent over and kissed my hair, which sent a shock through me, since he'd never done anything of the like in public before, and being king, eyes followed him everywhere. Even now I saw eyes on us. We were surrounded by his men.

But then he looped his pinky under the collar of my dress and pulled out my wedding pendant, releasing it so it settled right over my heart, in plain sight.

I did not think his nerves were for that. On the contrary, I dare say smug victory trickled through the bond.

The king of Cansere headed toward his mount, but the eyes of dozens of soldiers remained fixed on me. More precisely, fixed on the pearl I wore.

Ignoring the heat growing in my ears, I continued onward, spying Dan near the wagons in the back.

When he saw the necklace, he laughed, and once I took my place beside him, all he commented was "Of course you did."

The first time someone referred to me as *Your Majesty*, I turned around, thinking Renn had approached.

He had not.

Exhausted from the march, I shakily informed Renn of this new, unsettling title after we'd erected the tent we'd be staying in that night. The insufferable man merely whispered, "It suits you," and made love to me as though I were Zia herself.

No one commented on my commonness, at least not where I could hear. I mentioned this in passing to Dan, who pointed out, "We're all common, Nym. Even Stonelay's father is a merchant."

The simple fact settled on me like a light shawl.

The next day's march was so grueling, without a stop until past nightfall, that we had no energy to set up shelter. Renn fell asleep in my arms under the stars, made all the clearer in our shared darkness, for none in our company lit a fire.

It took thirteen days—breaking into the month of September—to march from Derren Castle to a rendezvous point where we joined companies two and four. We met in a dense forest of aspens, cottonwoods, and the occasional fir. Renn sent scouts out immediately, to survey both the surrounding area and ahead to Rove, which lay only a day's travel away.

My heart tremored at the thought of it. All this time, the thought of recapturing Rove, my second home, seemed only a dream. A philosophical idea from Renn's books, forgotten with the turn of a page. Yet it was very close, and very real. I feared the battle at Derren Castle would be nothing compared to one at the capital city. How many people still resided within its walls? How many dragons?

Adoel Nicosia surely had sorted out our ruse by now.

I'd taken to worrying my hands after seeing to the blisters and bruises of our company, when General Cuplend approached me. He crossed a hand over his chest and bowed before addressing me, which I found startling. I might have corrected him, but he spoke first. "Your Majesty, your presence is requested in council."

My lips parted. Questions flooded my tongue—were they sure they wanted *me* present for a war council? Did they realize my background, my unimportance? And yet I had lived with these soldiers, fought beside them, marched among them. I had been behind the walls at Derren, and behind enemy lines. I had lived in Rove Castle and mingled with the royal family. I had married the king, the last of the Noblewight sons.

So I swallowed down my protests, my insecurities, and squared my shoulders. "Lead the way."

We wove between trees, over the bumpy forest floor, to a larger tent erected so tightly between firs the trunks pushed in on its sides, making it an oblong shape.

Renn, Commander Stonelay, Commander Hawksend, and a woman I didn't recognize stood inside. No chairs or rugs, only a barrel used as a table, a map pinned to its top. Only Renn glanced over at my entrance, and while his face remained neutral, warmth floated up our link.

The woman, who looked to be about forty years of age, dressed as a middle-class shop owner, was saying, "—more than that."

Commander Hawksend frowned. "But there's no whispers of our approach? Nothing from Derren?"

She shook her head. "None that I've heard." She raised her hands, revealing leather gloves that trailed under her long sleeves. She likewise gestured to her high collar. "I've stayed covered at all times, in case a mindreader decides to get curious. I haven't been questioned—completely overlooked, really. I'm good at blending in—that's why His Highness utilized me." It took me a beat to realize she referred to Prince Adrinn; Renn's officers must have been successful in accessing what was left of his network. "I wasn't followed here, either." She noticed me then, her eyes dropping to my collar, where a sliver of gold chain was exposed. It wasn't uncommon for newlyweds to openly sport their wedding pendants, but it felt . . . unsafe, letting something so valuable, so meaningful, dangle from my neck in what could be enemy-occupied territory. Even

Renn wore his beneath his shirt, and the close collar of his uniform hid the entirety of it.

Yet she knew; weighty rumors traveled fast. "Your Majesty." She bowed.

"You're a spy," I guessed.

She nodded.

"The tunnel?" Commander Hawksend pressed.

"Still clear, from what I saw two days ago," she answered. "It doesn't look to be in use."

"Surely it's been discovered." Renn's gaze drifted to the map, which depicted Rove and its surrounding territories.

"But not in use means not well known," Commander Stonelay offered. "It might still be viable."

"But I haven't shared the most critical thing," the spy said. "You won't like it."

General Cuplend snapped, "Out with it, woman."

She frowned at him but spoke directly to me. "I'm fairly certain Adoel Nicosia is in residence at Rove Castle."

A chill coursed through me. I thought I saw Renn shiver, but perhaps that was my own trembling. Soft but firm, Renn said, "I thought he was across the strait."

The spy shook her head. "The increase in soldiers, the regular watches, the food being brought in . . . I think he's in Rove. He's not stupid enough to parade through the streets. He isn't accepted by the people, not yet."

"Not ever," I muttered, and General Cuplend harrumphed his approval.

Commander Stonelay turned to Renn. "Derren?"

Folding his arms, Renn answered, "I never saw him. I looked, but I never saw him."

"We didn't, either," Commander Hawksend added.

"It changes nothing." Commander Stonelay planted his hands on the map and leaned into the barrel.

"It changes everything," General Cuplend retorted, moving away from the tent's entrance. "Rove Castle is heavily fortified. He may be waiting for us."

"Or he intends to move on with his plans regardless of who tries to prevent them," I inserted softly, wringing my hands. "Adoel Nicosia is a prideful man. Powerful, but prideful. He believes this is his divine right. He believes himself the son of Zia."

The spy snorted. "That cur's mother was a whore in Rodsfell, from what we've found. He'd be nowhere if his uncle hadn't died on the throne. Poisoned. Terribly curious, isn't it?"

I closed my eyes and drew in a deep breath. "Regardless, we're to be his worshippers. Perhaps he believes he'll transcend with enough collective faith. I don't know. But . . ." I looked at Renn and tried to dampen the fear taking root behind my navel. "Renn is the greatest threat to that legacy. And Nicosia is the greatest threat to Renn."

We all considered this. The tent grew quiet enough for us to hear the sounds of the wood around us and of the resting soldiers nearby.

"I agree with both of you." Renn gestured to Commander Stonelay and General Cuplend in turn. "It changes nothing, and everything. It doesn't change our plans to infiltrate. It does change the course of this war. If Nicosia falls, so will the rest of them."

"So might you," General Cuplend protested.

"I don't intend to." Renn lifted his eyes to me at the statement, as though to reassure me.

The plan was straightforward and would need to be enacted as soon as we received word from the other companies. The element of surprise was to be guaranteed at all costs. Companies two, three, and six would attack the wall two hours before dawn to use the darkness and take advantage of the oncoming light. They'd then make a western assault on the castle, with the other companies following suit to refresh the troops. Meanwhile, a platoon led by Renn would use the distraction to get into the castle via the very tunnel we'd used to escape it. While yes, Renn could easily just fly over the wall, the sooner we got men inside the keep, the sooner it would fall. And if King Nicosia was inside the keep, we'd take every possible advantage against him.

Renn turned from the group and coughed, the effort strangled as he tried to hide it from the others. He pulled a handkerchief from his pocket, but if any blood passed his lips, I did not see it; he disposed of the cloth as easily as a magician.

The moment he turned back, General Cuplend said, "The queen will go with you."

I nearly retorted, *The queen is dead*, before I realized he referred to me.

My heart skipped a beat.

"Absolutely not." Renn's expression remained collected, but fire blazed between us.

In a softer tone, Commander Stonelay added, "Your Majesty, you are necessary for Cansere to survive. You must take a healer with you. She understands your lumis. She is the obvious choice."

"I don't have time to train someone else," I offered, my nerves dancing like bees in a brood box. There was so much to take in—Rove, Nicosia, battles, war. And yet the need to *protect Renn* surpassed all the rest. However new this was to me, however dangerous, if I had the opportunity to keep Renn's heart beating, I would take it.

Renn rubbed his forehead and sighed. "I remember what happened the last time I left you behind." Lowering his hand, his deep-sky eyes met mine. His fear braided through our bond. "I won't do that again."

Heat bloomed behind my eyes.

"However"—hardness leaked through his mask—"she will be armed and armored, and remain in the rear."

Commander Hawksend rolled his eyes. "She can't carry plate nor a sword—"

But General Cuplend retorted, "We'll find something to suit her."

I swallowed. Tried to keep my own mask in place. Tried to be strong for the others. "Whatever it takes. I'll do it."

For all the sorrow flowing from Renn through our connected hearts, he did a remarkable job of keeping it from his face.

Commander Hawksend looked ready to say something, but the sound of heavy boots running toward the tent caught his attention, mine, and the rest of the group's. General Cuplend bent his knees and put his hand on his sword; the spy pulled a dagger from her belt.

The flap to the tent whipped open, a boy in military uniform spilling inside, red-faced and sweating. A messenger. I feared the worst; apprehension from Renn flooded the link, and his skin started to glow.

"Your Majesty!" he announced. "Riders coming from the north!"

My gut sank.

But then the messenger smiled. "It's Potsburn and Liftwell, Sire!"

Before I could place the names, Renn's hope burned through me. "How far out?"

"You'll see them if you come. Come! I mean, if it suits you, Your Majesty."

Renn practically dove over the barrel to follow the messenger. It was then that I connected the names.

A dimly lit storage room. Whitestone crumpled before us. I'd drawn an unfinished cursive *Z* in the muck on the wall, two dots on either side of its tail. Potsburn and Liftwell were the spies sent to Sesta to track down Winvrin's sisterhood, the Unfallen of Zia. If they had returned, then they'd either hit a dead end or uncovered something useful. I prayed for the latter.

I chased after Renn and the messenger, but Renn was so fast, he was already out of sight. Didn't fly; he wouldn't risk drawing attention that way. But by the exuberance that overwhelmed our connection not half an hour later, I knew the spies had been successful. Renn had promised Antsan the Sestan throne and foodstuff from Cansere; now, should we win, he could secure both.

Sure enough, the men brought proof that Renn was the rightful heir to the Sestan throne.

All that was left was the perilous task of claiming it.

The other companies moved into place with little trouble. Not wanting to lose our advantage, we marched toward Rove, as close as we dared without being seen. Renn's platoon—roughly twenty-five soldiers—split off early on, and as the companies moved forward to launch their attack, I found myself in a cold camp nestled in a dark glade of trees, Renn lacing up hard leather armor over my shift. It didn't fit perfectly; there was no time to cut and shape armor to fit a woman, let alone fit to my measurements. The brigandine laced up in the back and crushed my breasts, not quite to the point of pain. It had a flat metal plate over my heart and two overlapping metal strips across my gut. Beneath my shift we'd already strapped matching greaves to my shins and mismatching cuisses to my thighs.

Renn's concern simmered in our bond. He sought distraction in detailing everything ahead of us, what we might and might not face, sometimes more than once. I distracted myself by holding on to his every syllable.

"Do not let the soldiers out of your sight. You need to have one within line of sight at all times. Hug the inside wall when we turn in corridors. Keep your chin close; your neck is more delicate than your skull. There may be times of waiting—long times. Try to utilize your knees when you crouch so the blood doesn't pool in your legs. If we need to move quickly, you'll get dizzy when you stand."

He stepped away and coughed into the darkness, muffling it with his elbow. I saw the scars in his lumis behind my eyelids. However much they were a part of him, however much he accepted them, I couldn't help but feel their marks were a failing of my own.

Without Ursa, I'd never mend them, if such a thing were even possible.

He returned to me, tugging the strings of the brigandine like it were a corset before tying them over my tailbone. "You might want to put the basalt wall up again."

I shook my head. "There's no point to it. If we're infiltrating together, marching together, fighting *together*, wouldn't it be better to know what you're feeling, what you're doing?"

He picked up my dress, grimacing, and helped me get it over my head. "Not when you're distracted by my . . . feelings."

I shoved my arms through my sleeves before grabbing his forearms. "I already know you hate it. I hate it, too."

Fear flicked within him. Sorrow. His movements remained entirely stoic. "Put up the wall, Nym."

"That mask won't work with me, Renn."

His brow twitched. He sighed. "This is foolish. If we both die, who will lead Cansere? You shouldn't come."

"Foolish!" I exclaimed, but kept my voice low. "What does it matter, Renn? I feel everything you feel. You suffer what I suffer. We both die if only one of us dies. Better we do it together than apart."

Guilt dug in its thorns between us. I held on to frustration like it was a life raft.

"None of that." I shoved my finger into his breastplate. "We have all made sacrifices in this war. Accept mine."

"I do."

"Then. Stop. It." I poked his breastplate with each word.

My irritation reflected in him. "I can't just turn it off."

"Try." My eyes watered suddenly, and I blinked rapidly to dry them. Touched the straps of his breastplate as though they needed adjusting, which they didn't.

"Nym." My name sounded like a plea.

"If the gods want you to be victorious, you'll be victorious. Isn't that how it works?" I sniffed, cleared my throat, and squared my shoulders. *Unless Nicosia has been right all along and they're on his side,* but I stuffed the worry away.

I met his eyes, challenging him for . . . I wasn't even sure. Challenging myself, perhaps. A desperate grasp for proof that I was strong enough to do this. That on top of a sister, mother, healer, and wife, I could be a soldier, too. That I could succeed and not be a regret for him.

He stared at me, eyes midnight blue in the dark, reading me like a book. Touched his gloved hand to the side of my face.

Hands against his breastplate, I stood on my toes to reach him. To press my mouth to his, to absorb the lightning and embers of his touch. I learned him like this was our first time, carefully measuring his lips, tracing their seam, tasting his heat. He pulled me as close as our combating armor would allow, kissing me like it would be our last. As though we might both die in the upcoming hours, because we could.

I dowsed as he tilted his mouth over mine, devouring me. Peered through the beauty of his lumis, the colorful globes in a dozen sizes strung together like some fairy chandelier, searching for breaks, cracks, and scratches, soothing even the smallest of them. I ran my hands over the scars of the largest bauble, willing magic into them, begging them to smooth, but they resisted my administrations. *We are healed,* it seemed to say. *Your efforts are futile.*

If Renn detected my clandestine craftlock, he said nothing of it when we finally parted.

Two hours before dawn, the army attacked Rove's wall, battering down its gates.

We lay in wait until they broke through, and snuck through the city to the castle's tunnel.

Chapter 25

One thing rang clear through our platoon as we cleared brush and hefted the first of two heavy gates barring our path into the bowels of the keep: Adoel Nicosia could not escape.

If we found him, if we stopped him, this would be the turning point of the war. This could be the beginning of the end.

The archers had been told to watch for him. Being a soulbinder, Nicosia could escape on a warbird or even a starling—the weight of souls overrode the weight of flesh. I feared that the spy was wrong, that Nicosia wasn't in Rove, or that he'd left before we could attack. I feared, perhaps more, that he *was* here, and he lay in wait for us, slinking through the shadows of the bailey like those diseased rats, ready to destroy us all.

I could still feel that unnatural tug on my soul, as though I were still bound to the Egroran. Trapped with invisible chains, as he took out his frustrations, his jealousies, and his rage on me.

I shivered, and not for the coolness of the tunnel. This was my third time below the castle, but the pathway felt longer this time. Darker, despite the three torches spread between soldiers. As the stairs made my calves and thighs ache, as we neared that nondescript door that led into the keep, I dared whisper a reminder into the darkness: "Do not let him touch you."

The quiet thickened around us. I knew the soldiers felt my words as much as they heard them. One touch, and Nicosia would have it all—soul, mind, and body. One touch was all he needed.

The Allmaster of legend.

I could not see Renn in the narrow stairwell; he led at the front of the platoon, while I took up the rear. Yet I felt I watched him. Saw the shimmering outline of his body behind my eyelids. Gods-touched. And yet I could not understand why the gods had created an Allmaster. Why Nicosia existed in a world where Renn had been chosen. Balance, perhaps? Or was it some phenomenon of breeding?

Perhaps, were craftlock not banned in these lands for so long, we'd have enough knowledge to pinpoint the answer. But we did not, so we'd do the best we could.

We waited on the stairs. I thought, at first, that those at the front heard footsteps in the connecting corridor and waited for them to pass. Then I heard the subtlest clearing of a throat, a trickle of embarrassment, and I knew the scars on Renn's lumis bothered him. He waited for the symptoms to pass before acting.

The door opened with the faintest creak, like the complaint of a mouse.

We were in.

The nostalgia, the strangeness, of being in Rove Castle again might have overwhelmed me if not for my own fear and alertness shrieking like a blue jay in the back of my mind, my own need to keep every sense open for possible enemies. Renn's presence—for I had not erected the basalt wall, in case I were to be injured in or near my heart and needed quick healing—further kept me focused. This narrow hall appeared unoccupied. The platoon split, half the soldiers following previous direction to head to the donjon—the inner keep—to see if Nicosia hid there while our army assailed the castle walls. The other half—including me and Renn—would make our way to the war room.

They were the two places we'd most likely find the Sestan king. And if we didn't, we'd keep searching until we did.

We'd burrowed too deeply into the keep to hear much of the assault outside, though an occasional distant scream or bludgeoning sound pricked my ears. Before moving on, Renn approached me. "Do not follow until the way is clear." His blue gaze radiated stoic focus, while the link pulsed with fear and apology. "For both our sakes."

I nodded, and he again took the lead.

I glanced over my shoulder constantly as our group of ten pushed through the corridors, trailing behind the last soldier by several paces. I waited at every corner, hugging the inside wall as instructed, ready to spring to action if I felt injury to Renn's person. It seemed Rove Castle had grown dozens of new corners in my absence—a veritable maze that made my body antsy and my fingertips numb.

Death curled around my neck.

Before I turned the third corner, slaughter broke out.

Wincing, I pressed back into the wall, pulling out a short sword Renn had strapped to my hip, my grip slick on the hilt. The battle went far quieter than I expected. Not like the wails and shouts of the assault at Derren. This was quick breaths and grunts, curses and gurgling.

The cool touch of death dried out my nostrils and made my eyes water. I realized, uselessly squeezing that hilt, that I didn't know who prevailed. If the slump of bodies and wheezing of last breaths were from dragons or phoenixes. All I felt was the sharp alert and frenzy of Renn through the bond. *Stay alive, stay alive, stay alive.*

The softest, sharpest whistle from another soldier's lips darted through the now eerily silent hall. Swallowing, I peered around the corner to our platoon and the handful of dragons bleeding on the floor. One of our men had a gash in his thigh; I hurried to him and healed him, sword still in hand.

We moved on without conversation. One of the dragons, an older man who looked a little like my father, still breathed. It would take only a moment for me to heal him. To right him. And yet I knew I could not, for he would only come at us again. He might feel mercy toward me for the kindness. Or he could run a blade through my heart, ending the war all on his own.

So I gritted my teeth and moved on, following the soldiers, every sense attuned to the spaces between stones.

We didn't get far before another surge of enemy soldiers came upon us. Again, I held back, but hearing thundering footsteps coming down the opposite end of the corridor, I panicked. Grabbed the closest door and wrenched it open. There was little space within, but I pushed through and pulled the door shut behind me just before the runners passed—

It took me a moment to recognize the scratch of linens. Stacks and stacks on shelves. This wasn't a room, but a closet.

Was this where Lonnie had hidden for three days when Sesta first fell upon Rove?

The panic of war, the fierce determination of a leader, pounded into my heart. I focused on it, letting Renn's focus become my own. Faced the door and readied my short sword, the tip of its blade pointed at the handle—

A slice on my elbow. Renn's elbow. Shallow, but it stung.

Fear rose, but I held on to that link. Held on to Renn. *Focus.*

It ended so quickly. I knew more from Renn's reactions and emotions than from my own senses. Hugging the sword to myself, I pushed open the closet door and stepped around the corner. We'd lost three men. Some of the dragons had been slaughtered so gruesomely I had to look away.

Cool relief trickled when Renn's gaze found me. I lifted a hand, gesturing to heal him, but he shook his head. Instead I healed two of our soldiers with larger wounds, and we started down the corridor. I let them get several paces ahead of me before following—

Death sang in my ears before a dragon seized me by my braid. He yanked me back without fanfare—

My half-heart arrested as he drew a dagger across my throat.

The way he'd grabbed my hair, the angle of my head, and Renn's earlier admonition to keep my chin down made the slice uneven, half of it on and under my chin. But the blade bit deep into my neck, spilling warm blood over my flesh.

He released me and surged ahead as I dropped. Ahead, someone cried out, "The king!"

Stay calm, I imagined Ursa admonishing me.

Coppery bubbles filled my breath as I dowsed, shock keeping the pain at bay.

Deeper shadows ringed my lumis as death neared. I had moments. Hurriedly I replaced and repaired stones, so focused I barely noticed the lack of my sister's power. The shadows lightened, pulled away, and then disappeared entirely.

Back in the corridor, I sucked a great, tangy breath into my lungs and sat upright, spitting blood onto the stones. Wiped the back of my hand over my throat, smearing blood onto my knuckles.

Grabbing my sword, I hurried ahead. The platoon hadn't gotten far, and the dragon who'd attacked me lay dead across an old rug, run through the middle. Renn was assuring the others he was fine, but mortification spiked. He looked at me, gaze dipping to the blood on my skin. Blood seeped into my dress.

I nodded to him, promising I was hale, but the worry lingered there, his fear glimmering in his eyes.

There was no time to waste. No opportunity for either of us to change our minds.

Jaw clenched, he nodded to one of the soldiers before tilting his head toward me. When we moved deeper into the castle, that soldier did not move on without sight of me.

A loud fracturing like thunder echoed deep in the castle, somewhere below my feet. My heart surged into my throat—I was sure the floor would crumble beneath me. A catapult from the assault, perhaps? A great door busting in? But the stone here held, and I had no time for conjecture. The army outside had drawn away many of Nicosia's dragons to the outer walls, but we were hardly alone.

As we surged up a narrow set of stairs, we came across two more dragons. To my surprise, they immediately surrendered, one knee to the floor, hands up.

"Highness," one of the soldiers warned, and in that moment I saw it—the flash of silver on their necks. Pips denoting not the ranking of normal soldiers, but of crafters.

I knew instantly they could not be permitted to live. Not with power that could hurt us if we spared their lives. These weren't like the warbirds, who bowed to whichever hand fed them. These would be loyal to the Sestan king.

I turned away, unwilling to witness their easy demise. When I passed the bodies, I took the coward's way and did not look down.

And then as swift as autumn surrendering to winter, we were there.

The war room.

A flash of light—Renn moved so swiftly I could scarcely track him. The guards fell. With one heavy kick, Renn sent the locked door off its hinges.

One of our soldiers cried, "Go, go, *go*!" and they flooded the space—a place I had never before seen, and did not see now.

Pushing my tongue hard to the roof of my mouth, I pressed back into the cold stone outside the room, forcing air in and out of my chest. My cold hand again grew slick against the hilt of my sword. I became painfully aware of the empty corridor, tuned into every sound and draft, terrified that more Sestan men would find us.

Death slid, slick, over my mouth. Plunged into me like a lover. I cringed at the sounds of ringing steel and thumping flesh, of gurgled cries and severed screams.

A blow to the hip on Renn; it echoed in my own. Dull and hard, not piercing the flesh. *Gods protect him. Help us. Help him.*

Something like furniture breaking near the ruined door made me cringe and duck instinctively. I held my sword ready, scanning the corridor—

Gasped as the mimicry of a cold knife slid between my ribs, carving me from just under my armpit to my breast. Shock pebbled, but pain took over quickly, sharp and hot.

Renn!

I rushed to the door, taking in everything at once. The war room was larger than I'd pictured. Longer than it was wide, with great triangular windows cut into the stone of the far wall, large enough to let in light, high enough to be difficult to breach. A giant table, meant to take up the center of the room, had been cast onto its side and knocked askew. Blood-spattered papers and maps littered the stone. No carpeting. And bodies. Red uniform, blue uniform, all of them fallen, all but Renn and—

Nicosia.

The sight of the Allmaster slammed into me like a battering ram. Memories of him had begun to feel more like a nightmare than anything substantial, and yet here he was, flesh and bone, terror and horror. For half a breath, I found myself again in Rodsfell, unable to move from the soul-lashing to that tree, this viper walking circles around me, playing with his food before devouring it whole.

Renn bled from his side, breathing hard, a sword—one of Sestan make—in each hand.

Nicosia, appearing uninjured, crouched, ready for an oncoming attack. But the blood on his clothes—not all of that was from attacking soldiers. Renn had hurt him. The bastard had merely healed himself.

Great wings of light sprouted from Renn's back; he soared up toward the high ceiling before diving—

A wet cough to my right.

I spun. A man in red reached weakly toward me—the same Renn had appointed to keep an eye on me.

Dropping to my knees, I clutched his face and dowsed into a realm riddled with death's shadows, his lumis a cabin with a dirt floor. In the center, a single bed with a badly cracked frame. The mattress was torn, hay spilling out, and blankets and pillows littered the floor.

I went first for the frame, reconnecting its splinters, pouring in magic to glue it into place. I imagined the craft as a breeze and sent it to gather hay and tuck it away, then circled my finger to mimic stitches to reseal the mattress.

The shadows lightened. I grabbed the blankets and threw them on the bed, imagining great ethereal hands smoothing them for me. Then the pillows.

I returned to the war room as glass shattered behind me, hard enough that little shards of it lodged in my hair.

"Go to the donjon," I urged, pulling him up. "Get help."

He nodded and launched to his feet, racing for the door—

A dagger flew into his back, and the phoenix dropped before breaking the threshold.

I gaped, frozen for a second before whirring around to see *his* hateful face, *his* venomous green eyes shifting to me. The subtlest hint of surprised recognition flashed there before my husband slammed Nicosia into the wall.

Several things *crunched* with the impact.

And yet as Renn moved to strike again, he couldn't. His body had become plastered to Nicosia's, keeping the king inside Renn's reach. Renn growled and tried to beat at him, sliced open the Sestan king's calf with the tip of his sword, but the close quarters made it impossible to do serious damage.

Soulbound. All the while, Nicosia healed himself.

Healed. Pain blazing across my ribs, my hip—

Jumping the table, I bolted toward Renn, feeling his alarm before he turned to look at me. "No—"

I grabbed his neck and fell into the realm of baubles. General Cuplend was right—I knew it better than any. Found the broken baubles immediately and eased them back together, re-forming them like a puzzle I'd done a thousand times—

Renn shoved me, breaking our connection just as Nicosia withdrew the soulbinding and barreled into him, knocking them both to the floor.

I felt the impact of stone on Renn's shoulder blades, felt the tip of a knife piercing near my navel, dragging upward, as Renn pushed it away.

Renn kicked out, dislocating Nicosia's leg. Nicosia took it with a grunt, his hands hooked in Renn's hair—

He was going for Renn's lumis.

Again.

The image of an ethereal room filled with nothing but shards whipped across my memory. A broken man on a couch, one who wept the first time he walked outside by his own strength.

On my feet, I launched myself at Nicosia, latching on to his back, anchoring myself with one hand around his neck, the other clawing onto his ear.

I dowsed, too.

The basalt wall, similar to mine, still guarded his lumis. I tore at it, wringing magic from myself and into it. It didn't disintegrate so easily, now. Each blow took out a little less without Ursa's strength—

"Why is it so smooth?" I asked my mother as I crouched at the edge of the stream, cool spring water licking the toes of my boots. "The rocks in the garden aren't smooth and pretty like this."

"The water brings out the colors." She picked out a stone and traced its edges with her finger. "These ones have been in the water a long time. Hundreds, maybe thousands of years. The water washes over them constantly, again and again, taking off their edges and corners. That's what makes them so lovely."

I stepped back from Nicosia's wall and summoned a storm.

I molded magic as whipping rains, as ice-laden winds. Imagined overflowing riverbeds and waterfalls beating across the wall from all sides and angles. Basalt chipped and cracked, its edges growing soft until it seemed I might fit my fingers in and pull the shell away—

Nicosia swung his elbow, striking me in the mouth. His lumis ripped away from my hands as I flew back, copper pooling around my tongue, stone bruising my tailbone. I'd been so utterly focused on his lumis I hadn't noticed the way my bones—Renn's bones—had begun to crack, or the sharp pains bursting in my gut—

Grabbing Nicosia's other arm, Renn flung him bodily across the room, but not before Nicosia's eyes locked on the great pearl hanging from my wedding pendant—a gem loosed from my collar.

Nicosia crashed into the far wall, something that could have killed a normal man. He hit sideways, his shoulder taking the impact instead of his head. He fell, but so well-practiced with craftlock was he that his shoulder mended almost instantly, the blindness caused by healing brief.

"Nym." Renn dropped to one knee, pain radiating through the bond in the same places it radiated in me. Nicosia had broken things in his lumis—things I couldn't heal on myself. Standing poured pure agony into my legs. I limped toward him and collapsed, but close enough to grab his hand. Golden-bound orbs burst to life before my eyes. I demanded magic sweep over them like the wind, picking up shards and fitting them into place—

My body moved, breaking my focus. Renn hauled me behind him as Nicosia approached us, perfectly healthy, his lithe body moving like a predator's, making me think of the wolves in the wood.

The Allmaster smiled.

"I think I understand now." A dampened delight edged the words and flared in his eyes. In this lighting, they looked so much like Renn's. "Why you wouldn't accept all I could offer you. Why you're limping so badly when I broke *his* leg." A slight chuckle, and his countenance darkened. "But I want to see *exactly* how the magic works."

He lunged, but not for Renn.

For me.

He snatched my hair and wrenched me away from Renn, popping my neck; I gasped as a dagger slid easily into my side, my skin, my intestines. Flinched when Renn, charging for me, faltered with the same wound.

"Found your little secret," Nicosia whispered into my ear, just before he twisted my hand and broke my wrist.

I screamed; Renn echoed the sound, not just from the injury but from watching me break. The thorns pierced through our bond so thickly I thought they'd shatter my merlons.

"Let her go!" he bellowed, and never had I heard such hatred in his voice. "She's not part of this!"

Nicosia dragged me away, out of reach. I dug my heels into the stone, but the effort proved wasted. "Oh, but she very much is, my boy."

Renn pushed to his feet. Nicosia ripped the dagger out of my side and plunged it into my thigh. My body shuddered at the damage. Renn tripped, feeling every torn fiber.

His weakness. The only balm I had at being his demise was that I wouldn't have to live through the guilt of it.

"But"—Nicosia ripped the blade out, causing me to whimper—"one thing I want to know before the knowledge is forever destroyed." I realized only distantly that he addressed *me*. "What unhallowed trick did you use on me in that dungeon?"

The answer flitted through my mind through the white haze of pain. *Ursa.*

The moment I thought her name—the moment Nicosia repeated it on his lips, for he had delved into my thoughts—I realized something. My connection to my sister had been so very similar to my connection to Renn.

So *very* similar.

I acted before the thought truly formed. Before Nicosia might find some way to stop me.

I grabbed his fist, the one closed around the dagger, shoving my nails between his fingers so he could not pull away. Reached through the blind agony of my wounds and grabbed his ear for a second hold.

Dowsed.

And this time, I pulled from *Renn.*

I demanded strength from the golden threads vining through my heart. I tugged and jerked, wrenched and pulled from his strength, from the gods themselves, and the magic in my ethereal hands burned as golden fire. I thrust it into Nicosia's wall, melting it away like the wax of a candle. He tried to twist away, but I dug in with nails and teeth, breaking skin as his three icelike pillars rose before me, just as I had seen them before. Just as I had once re-created in my own lumis.

Beneath the brilliant gleam of gods-touched magic, the Sestan king's death lines snapped sharply into place.

I struck those first.

I shaped craftlock into a massive hammer and slammed it into the first where a thin, black hair whispered the Allmaster's weakness. I made it a hefty spear and threw it upward where the three sculptures met, just off-center near a mark of green, to another thread of death. In the war room, my ankle gave out as Nicosia attacked me in return, but I didn't let go. Couldn't let go. I pulled every ounce of strength I had, fueled by the gods-touched savior of Cansere. I swept it out in spinning rings of power, rippling from the ghost of me as a boulder cast into a pond. With the first, the lumis shook. With the second, the sculptures cracked and darkness welled. With the third, I shattered him, breaking him as he had broken a babe in his cradle twenty-one years ago.

My half-heart shuddered. Though I did not release my grip, my vision faded to that of the war room. I hit the stone floor, my head barely protected by Nicosia's bicep as he fell with me. The ceiling filled my senses—it was the only thing I understood. Dark stone. Cold. Distant.

Exhaustion crept into my limbs as death cooed in my ears. The beat in my chest grew too weak, too erratic. It *hurt*, hollow and echoing. My side pulsed, my leg burned. My bones ached and flared. I shifted to move the anvil off my chest, but there was nothing there but a failing half-heart. So hard to breathe . . . I couldn't breathe . . .

Nicosia lay unmoving beside me.

Renn.

A chore to move my eyes, like they'd become clay marbles in dry sockets. He lay only six feet from me on his side, arm outstretched as though reaching toward me . . . his chest barely rising. His eyes closed. His body broken in all the same places mine was.

I didn't need to see my lumis to understand we were dying. I couldn't fix it—I'd used up everything we had. There was nothing left to give.

My eyelids fluttered—dark, light. Dark, light. Dark, light.

Two of Nicosia's fingers curled around mine, sending a weak jolt of panic through my core. Alive? No, he couldn't be. I'd seen the shadow of death. It pushed me out of his lumis—

The first hard beat of my heart was like an arrow to my breastbone. I gasped.

The second sent warm blood rising through my neck, down my abdomen, and into my limbs. With the third the pains faded. With the fourth, my thoughts cleared.

But this was . . . this was craftlock. *Healing.* Why would Adoel Nicosia heal me?

How could he know to start with my heart?

Nicosia's fingers went lax and lifeless.

I shot upright, hissing at the pain in my head, bruises in my hips, a broken rib still unmended. I looked first to Nicosia—to his pale skin, blue lips, half-lidded eyes. A corpse.

Then a whisper, almost like a spring breeze, drew my attention to the window.

I saw her. I swear I saw the outline of her against the sun, her curling hair and innocent smile, her delicate hand as she waved. Her voice gracing my ears one last time as she murmured, *I'll always be with you, Nym.*

Tears pooled in my eyes, enhancing the prismatic vision even as it faded.

"Ursa," I croaked.

But she was gone.

All this time . . . had she been with *him* all this time . . . ?

Green among the sculptures. I'd seen green—

The softest groan from Renn had me blinking, tears running down my face. I scrambled to him, injured but healed enough, *healed enough,* and I grasped his calloused hand and dowsed into his lumis, soothing the worst of the breaks, lifting two orbs back into their golden orbits before saving my dwindling strength and shifting back into the war room.

He lifted a bloodied hand to my face and wiped away a tear. "Nym, what—" Then, pushing up, he saw Nicosia.

The king of Sesta, dead.

"Ursa," I whispered, new tears following the paths of their predecessors. "Ursa was here. She saved us, Renn."

Surprise, shock, warmth through the bond. A glimmer of light kissing his skin, disappearing into his hair. "Nym, in the sunlight. I thought I saw—"

Footsteps thundered outside. Renn launched to his feet and grabbed me, ushering me to where I could hide—

But it was the soldiers sent to the donjon, minus one. A phoenix cried out, "Your Majesty!" as they poured into the wrecked war room. "What ha—?"

They froze at the sight of Nicosia.

Renn pressed a quick kiss to my forehead. *Later,* it whispered. *Everything for us, later.*

Another soldier blurted out, "Antsan is here!"

My core sparked. Fingers tingled. "Wh-What?"

The soldier rushed, "We saw their flag over the wall. An army of them, heading this way!"

The utter relief, like lapping sea-foam, that spread from the bond nearly liquefied my knees. I grabbed Renn's elbow to stay afoot. Already? They'd come already?

The emissary had been honest in his promises.

"Then we've no time to waste." Golden light surged from Renn's skin. He stood tall, though I knew his fifth rib on the left pained him as it did me, as did his hip and tailbone, the throbbing beneath the back of his skull. Knew he was healed enough to function but would soon fatigue. Yet such was the cost of war.

"Let's finish this," he announced.

And within three days' time, Rove was ours.

Broken, but ours.

Epilogue

One Year Later

I heard the faintest testing of the door's lock before careful footsteps moved away. Groaning, I rolled over in the bed toward Renn, overlapping half his body with mine.

"They've come to wake us," I murmured into his neck.

He didn't move. "They know not to when the door is locked."

"It's always locked."

A feline grin tempted his lips. "Exactly."

Alas. While staying in a too soft and overlarge bed with my beloved husband *was* one of my favorite pastimes, today was not the day to put off responsibility. I felt the liveliness of the castle through the stone. Knew the kitchens cooked in a frenzy, the maids rushed to serve the overabundance of guests, and the steward ran half out of his mind with arrangements. So I stretched and sat up, my hair a wild thicket tumbling past my ribs. Grumbling, Renn rolled and slung an arm over my bare hips.

"You can be late for your coronation"—I moved to push his arm away—"but I won't be late for mine."

Unfortunately, Renn's arm was immobile, and when I pushed against it a second time, it snaked under my backside, heaving me up and then down onto my back, where the king of Cansere pinned me bodily.

"I've been king for two years already," he mumbled as he nipped at my ear.

"Eighteen months." I bit down on a laugh as shivers ran down the side of my neck.

"I'm rounding up."

Grabbing the sides of his face, I kissed him, then retorted, "How many complaints do you want to hear from your staff today, let alone the Antsan delegation? Are you going to tell Beatty dinner will be late, or shall I?"

He growled.

"Perhaps I should take the other suite," I offered. "Then this wouldn't be such an issue—"

"Stop arguing with me."

"I fear I'm the only one who does"—I poked his shoulder—"and therefore I must be consistent."

He kissed my mouth, my nose, and my brow, then pushed himself up and dramatically threw the covers off both of us. The castle chill rarely bothered Renn, but my skin instantly pebbled. I shot him a look of exaggerated distaste, at which he only laughed before wordlessly excusing himself to the bathing chamber.

I threw on a silk shift and got a comb halfway through my hair when I caught a familiar scratching sound at the door of the attached salon. Crossing over to it, I let Lonnie in. She took one look at my hair and frowned. "Really?"

I shrugged. "I didn't bother braiding it last night."

She hummed under her breath. I led her into the dressing room, sparing her from any risk of seeing her king and sovereign naked. As she helped me work through the curls, she said, "You can't wear this."

She meant my shift. "It's the nicest one I have."

"Did you forget *the dress*?" She pointed to the open armoire, where my coronation gown hung, designed by Verdanian Truline, the renowned Sestan tailor. It had been cut with the purpose of presenting my wedding pendant for all to see, which meant a broad and plunging neckline.

It was a beautiful gown, albeit far more revealing than my normal fare.

"So you want me to go into court without underwear?" I countered.

She rolled her eyes. "There are drawers under the dress. I pinned drawers under the dress." She poured water into a basin and wet her hands to smooth my curls.

"Your father?" I asked.

She smiled. "Both my parents got in last night. He'll be ready."

We carefully twisted and set my curls, and then Lonnie pulled sections away from my face and pinned them with an elegant rhinestone barrette, one that took the shape of a phoenix feather. She touched my nose with a bit of powder before stripping me down and helping me into the Truline gown. Silver satin from neck to toe, with impressive glass beadwork over the bodice—what there was of it—and waist. Even choosing satin over silk and glass over gems, it felt too luxurious for me. We'd been frugal in our management of the capital since it started properly running again, with so much of the country still recovering from war. The Antsan regent in Sesta saw resources went to Cansere to bandage what Adoel Nicosia had wrought, but they were regulated and carefully paced, to be divvied out over ten years, just as our food allotment to them would be. I feared some would have to wait as long for true relief, but such was the cost of war.

My initiatives with the noblemen added a little extra to our coffers, which I'm sure made me unpopular with them, but not only did we need the funds, we only received them from policing the upper class. Rich men had become overly comfortable doing whatever they pleased, especially with war as an excuse. Now if they broke the law, they were heavily fined, and those fines went toward rebuilding their country . . . and funding my other project, which was establishing schools for crafters. The education would not only help crafters, and others, understand their magic, but would make the new registration program roll out a little more smoothly.

Familiar stress built up in my shoulders, but I shrugged it off. Today was a day of celebration. The kingdom would be right where I left it tomorrow.

I looked at myself in the mirror. This was the finest gown I owned. Something out of a fairy story. It was beautiful, and it made me feel beautiful. Lonnie had styled my hair expertly, as always, but it looked particularly regal today. The gold setting of my wedding pendant contrasted starkly against the silver fabric, but I'm sure Verdanian had done such on purpose. Even after the changes war brought to us, not everyone liked the idea of a common woman on Cansere's throne. This pendant was to remind them who I was. Their eyes were meant to go to it first.

As a final touch, Lonnie tied a plaited white cincture around my hips.

I kissed Lonnie's cheek and let her go to enjoy the day and her family. Renn had already left to see to his own duties, leaving Sten and Gill, another of Renn's guards from before the war, lounging in the salon to watch over me. I found myself suddenly nervous, and so I picked up a book of poetry to try to distract myself, though it failed to do so. Instead I began to pace, and then, feeling foolish, decided to leave the rooms altogether.

The guards shadowed me as I went, but I'd grown used to their tailing by now. Gill, at least, had a sense of humor. Sten remained a man of few words.

In the corridor, a maid carrying freshly pressed linens awkwardly bowed to me; I nodded in return, and two passing noblewomen from nearby provinces gossiping together did the same. The housekeeper spied me and approached, asking about table placement in the Great Hall after the coronation, fretting we would not be able to fit the academic guests Renn had invited last minute, but we had it sorted quickly, and I soon found myself walking down the gallery, where portraits of past kings hung—at least, those that had survived. Many had been stripped from the walls during Sesta's occupation, burned, broken, or disfigured. Any that retained some likeness had been reframed and returned to their walls. The others I wanted to have repainted, once the budget allowed. It felt wrong to lose so much history.

I paused by one portrait, an oval about the size of my head, framed with gilded hickory. Someone had put out a cigar repeatedly on it, but even that someone had borne enough respect not to disfigure the woman's face.

Lifting a hand, I gently traced Queen Winvrin's forehead, as though smoothing back her hair. Though the woman had caused me endless grief, I found myself smiling at her.

"Thank you for protecting him," I murmured. "I promise to keep him safe in your stead."

The portrait did not answer, and yet I felt it was pleased.

More people crowded the Great Hall than I'd ever before seen, and that included Queen Winvrin's final winter ball. I understood now the housekeeper's concern for seating them all. So numerous were they that we forewent the ceremonial walk down the center of the room to the three thrones set on the dais at its head. Instead, we came through the door behind them.

The hush that settled over the space struck me with its reverence.

I exited second, feeling the familiar weight of eyes on me. Noblemen and noblewomen, lords and ladies, from Cansere, many of whom I'd yet to meet. Jardallen Arquan, the emissary from Antsan, and his entourage. Even Pallin Vitsoph, the Antsan king's nephew and regent over Sesta, had a place near the dais. He nodded to me as I passed, and I returned the favor. I noted a great deal of women had forgone straightening their hair and had curled it instead.

Eden already awaited me and rose from her appointed throne. She wore an elegant but overly simple dress, yet it still caught my eye—Eden had not worn finery of any sort since her return from Sesta. She hated all of it. She'd continued to keep her hair short, cropped straight and even at her chin, unadorned. Since we had retaken Rove, she'd used her position of power to get the city running again, to invite back refugees and boost the economy. Yet she had no interest in leading, in any coronation of her own. Cansere law mandated a royal woman marry before taking the crown, but Renn could have waived it, if Eden truly wanted it.

It had taken days of convincing to get her on the dais at all.

I clasped her hand and nodded; she bowed. Over her shoulder, I saw Brien, garbed as a royal guard, sword hanging at his hip, eyes watching the two of us carefully. He smiled at me, though his gaze never strayed far from Eden.

As practiced, I turned to face the congregation. This time I bowed, and they followed suit, the rustling of fabrics as bodies bent rippling through the space. I spied my family among them, near the front; all my siblings had been brought to live in Rove, minus Lissel and her husband, Art, who had taken over the house and the apiary. Yet they, too, had made the long journey to be here for the coronation, despite Lissel's pregnancy—she being much further along in hers than I in mine. I intended to ensure her back safely in Fount for the birth.

Lissel, Dan, Colt, Pren, Heath, Terrence. All here. All safe, all happy.

And, if I peered directly into the sunlight spilling from the far windows of the hall, over the tapestries of the gods, I felt I could make out Ursa's profile. She was smiling, her hair caught in the breeze. *I told you it would work out,* I imagined her to say.

I'd promised myself I wouldn't cry, yet found myself blinking to keep my vision clear.

Dan wore a uniform almost like that of a soldier, but it had a gold ring around his left bicep, marking him as a licensed crafter. Renn hadn't returned the ban on craftlock after the war; rather, he'd enacted laws for education and licensing, as well as harsh punishment should the magic be misused. The same had been placed on the denizens of Sesta as well: Nicosia's program disbanded, but the schools maintained.

A trumpet in the arcade played five ascending notes, and Renn appeared on the dais. I beamed at him, though I'd been told it looked more regal not to smile. Eden approached him first, greeting him as she had me, and then I repeated the exchange, trying not to snort at the amusement pouring from him through our bond—the link between my heart and his lumis we would share until our dying day.

Renn turned and bowed to his people, who bowed back. He hated being the center of attention, but today I didn't feel it. Not from his presence, and not through the link. He didn't even wear his mask; his reserved, genuine countenance shined with contentment.

Mr. Swiftmore approached the dais, and beside him were two other priests, each carrying a candelabra. From the stems hung hooks, and from them dangled crowns: a simple silver one for me, and a thicker gold one for Renn—the same his father had worn at formal events.

Taking the silver crown, Mr. Swiftmore approached me and bowed. Held the crown over my head. "Swear thee, Nym Tallowax Noblewight, before the eyes of Hem and the gods, to oversee and protect the kingdom. By Hem, to be just. By Salm, to let goodness flow to the far reaches of the country. By Rolys, to be a beacon of light to those who look up to you. By Evat, to see your people fed. By Alm, to heal the hurt, sick, and afflicted." He paused here and then, quietly, added, "Not you personally, Your Majesty." He winked.

I bit the inside of my cheek to keep from barking a laugh and nodded.

"And by Zia, that you may birth heirs to fulfill these promises."

Looking him in the eye, I answered, "I do."

It was so much like my wedding vows that nostalgia bubbled up in me, threatening tears again. Renn reached over and grabbed my hand, squeezing it. I bowed my head, and Mr. Swiftmore placed the crown atop it. He bowed again, and I sat in my throne.

All eyes turned to Renn.

When the priest took his crown and approached, the choir in the arcade began singing softly Cansere's country song, stunning harmonies that raised gooseflesh on my arms. Mr. Swiftmore repeated the same vows, adding on, "As your father before you, and as the gods have chosen you."

Heat flooded the bond. Renn's eyes sharpened when he said yes, and the priest placed the crown on his head.

The moment Renn sat in his throne, the crowd erupted into applause and cheers. Colt pulled a white cloth from his pocket and spun it over his head, hitting Art in the face with it. Someone made the call of a crow from the back, which made me laugh.

Renn opened his hand on his armrest, and I placed mine into it, my content half-heart beating merrily in my chest. The way before us seemed set, now. A road paved with tears, blood, and glass. It would not always be easy, but it would be ours.

Looking back toward the light, my gaze fell upon the six tapestries of the gods.

And I could swear I saw them smile.

Acknowledgments

Well. Another book done! And what a whirlwind it has been.

I want to thank, as always, my delicious husband for all his support. For helping me with writing time, brainstorming, troubleshooting, and the works. And to my children, for being patient when Mom is in book-land.

Thank you to Emily Schwarzmann, for not only her continued support, but for being vulnerable with me to help me make this book as real and heartfelt as possible.

Thank you to Caitlyn McFarland, for helping me yet again to iron out the kinks in the story and fix a sagging middle. And to Leah O'Neill and Brekke Felt for reading early versions and giving me helpful feedback.

Thank you to my editors Elizabeth Agyemang and Sasha Knight, for beating weaknesses and discrepancies out of this manuscript like it were a dirty rug. Y'all know how to make a girl shine. And to all the staff at 47North and the contractors who polished this novel to shining.

And again, thank you to the Big Eternal Kahuna for my mind, my time, and whatever talents I can scrape together to get stories on paper. I owe you one (er, I guess I owe you twenty-seven, at this point . . .)

About the Author

Charlie N. Holmberg is a *Wall Street Journal* and Amazon Charts bestselling author of fantasy and romance fiction, including the *Paper Magician* series, the *Spellbreaker* series, and the Whimbrel House series, and writes contemporary romance under C. N. Holmberg. She is published in over twenty languages and is a Goodreads Choice Awards, ALA, and RITA finalist. Born in Salt Lake City, Charlie was raised a Trekkie alongside three sisters who also have boy names. A BYU alumna, she discovered in her thirties that she's actually a cat person. She lives with her family in Utah. Visit her at www.charlienholmberg.com.